# Shaped
*by the*
# Waves

## Books by Christina Suzann Nelson

*More Than We Remember*
*The Way It Should Be*
*Shaped by the Waves*

# Shaped
## *by the*
# Waves

A NOVEL

CHRISTINA SUZANN NELSON

BETHANYHOUSE
*a division of Baker Publishing Group*
Minneapolis, Minnesota

© 2022 by Christina Suzann Nelson

Published by Bethany House Publishers
11400 Hampshire Avenue South
Minneapolis, Minnesota 55438
www.bethanyhouse.com

Bethany House Publishers is a division of
Baker Publishing Group, Grand Rapids, Michigan

Printed in the United States of America

Library of Congress Cataloging-in-Publication Data
Names: Nelson, Christina Suzann, author.
Title: Shaped by the waves / Christina Suzann Nelson.
Description: Minneapolis, Minnesota : Bethany House Publishers, [2022] |
Identifiers: LCCN 2021040486 | ISBN 9780764235405 (trade paperback) | ISBN 9780764239854 (casebound) | ISBN 9781493436064 (ebook)
Subjects: LCGFT: Christian fiction. | Novels.
Classification: LCC PS3614.E44536 S53 2022 | DDC 813/.6—dc23
LC record available at https://lccn.loc.gov/2021040486

Scripture quotations are from THE HOLY BIBLE, NEW INTERNATIONAL VERSION®, NIV® Copyright © 1973, 1978, 1984, 2011 by Biblica, Inc.® Used by permission. All rights reserved worldwide.

This is a work of fiction. Names, characters, incidents, and dialogues are products of the author's imagination and are not to be construed as real. Any resemblance to actual events or persons, living or dead, is entirely coincidental.

Cover design by Andrea Gjeldum
Cover image of seagulls by Dawn Hanna / Trevillion Images

Author is represented by the Books & Such Literary Agency.

Baker Publishing Group publications use paper produced from sustainable forestry practices and post-consumer waste whenever possible.

22  23  24  25  26  27  28      7  6  5  4  3  2  1

This book is dedicated to the memory of my granny,

*Frances Bogart.*

She changed my life by choosing to love me,
spending untold hours reading to me, and showing me,
through her actions, that every single person is important.

# 1

The Pacific Ocean licked the heat from her feet. Cassie shouldn't have been there, shouldn't have been indulging herself when there was a paper to revise and a four-year-old left in the care of her overly generous roommate. Lark was her daughter, her responsibility. But once again, Cassie had accepted Terri's offer to take Lark to church and keep her for the rest of the day. She needed a moment to breathe, a moment to figure out what she was doing with her life—why she was continuing her education in an area in which she'd exhausted her possibilities.

She wiped sweat from her forehead. At eighty-five degrees, the day was hot, even for mid-March in Southern California. Her Pacific Northwest self hadn't acclimated to the dry heat in the three years since making the move. Instead, her body cried out for the dampness of the Oregon coast. At that moment, even the sting of cold rain pelting her skin would have been as welcome as a hug.

Kneeling forward, she let the foam curl over her hands, felt the sand wash away beneath her palms. The tug of home pulled at her like the receding tide. She was no longer the awkwardly shy girl who had left for college with the support and encouragement of her eclectic community. Only her aunt, the woman who had raised Cassie on her own, was a true relation, but Gull's Bay had provided a ragtag family circle. There was Mr. Watkins, the old man who drank his coffee at Aunt Shasta's shop every morning; Mrs. Collins, the baker whose tasty treats were a calling card for the little town; and Ms. Aubrey, her aunt's best friend and helping hand to everyone. She even found herself missing Mrs. McPherson, who worked in the church office and knew everyone's business. They'd been all Cassie needed without having to share the subtleties of familial features. They'd been hers until she'd let them all down and run away.

Behind Cassie, the laughter and shouts of the beach crowd drowned out the calls of the marine birds she loved so much. Days like this one made her wonder why she'd ever left Oregon. She could have done her graduate work there or skipped it altogether, finding a job she loved rather than turning into a coward and running south with only mounting student loans as a reward.

Cassie pulled her cell from the pocket of her shorts to check the time. She'd missed three calls. Prickles ran across her skin as fears for Lark pulsed through her bloodstream. She swiped the phone to life and checked. Every single one had come from her aunt, yet it wasn't Saturday. Shasta's calls came in religiously at the end of the week, arriving with updates on everyone in Gull's Bay and a solid reprimand for Cassie to get herself back to church and to Jesus. Yet when Cassie really thought about it, this hadn't been altogether true for a couple of months. Shasta had missed a call here and there, and the conversations had grown short, as if her aunt were letting her go.

Turning toward the parking lot, Cassie slipped her feet back into flip-flops and swiped the screen to return Shasta's call. After only one ring, the call was picked up, but the voice on the other end wasn't the one she'd expected.

"Cassie, it's Aubrey. I have your aunt's phone."

Her heart crashed. She gripped the rail along the three steps off the beach. "What's going on?"

"Shasta is okay." Her aunt's best friend had a voice that could soothe a hungry sea lion, but still Cassie's skin grew clammy as the seconds of not knowing ticked by. "She took a fall right after church, and you know Shasta, she was in a hurry to get the shop open for the lunch crowd."

Without Aubrey's having to say the words, Cassie could picture the set look on Shasta's face and the exact location of her fall. "On the steep stairs that overlook the ocean?"

"Those are the ones. I tried to get ahead of her, but she took off while I was saying good-bye to Lillian McPherson. I'm so sorry."

"It's not your fault. Shasta has a mind of her own, stubborn and hardheaded. Luckily, she seems to be physically tough too. So, what's the damage?" Cassie couldn't help but smile as one of Shasta's pet phrases fell from her own lips. "Why are you making the call if she's fine?"

"I said she was okay. In my mind, that's a whole lot different than being fine. The doctor said she's remarkably unscathed by the fall, only a few bumps and bruises. Rest and physical therapy will help with those things. But she's been struggling for a while. I promised I wouldn't say anything to you until she could no longer walk along the shore. Well, she hasn't been on the sand in months. She just didn't want you worrying. She loves you so much."

Silence expanded for a moment, making the space around Cassie fill with increasing pressure. The signs of something serious, some kind of trouble with Shasta's health, had been there. She'd known it. Why hadn't she taken the trip home for Christmas? Cassie had used a series of excuses, but Shasta hadn't fought to change her mind. "What is it?"

"They say she suffered a mild stroke. But that's not the biggest issue." Time ticked away as three seagulls landed on the pillars in front of Cassie's car. "I'm sorry. It's Parkinson's."

It was a thirty-minute drive from the beach to the tiny, worn-down two-bedroom cottage that took most of the money Cassie brought in from her meager graduate teaching income and student loans. Even with Terri to share expenses and rent, Cassie dove deeper into the hole each month. Fortunately, Lark didn't eat or require much . . . yet. Life had better turn around before they came to the point where her daughter would need things like braces, team fees, and clothes that didn't come from a thrift shop.

Cassie threw the car into park, hopped out, and checked the locks.

This wasn't how life was supposed to play out, but maybe she should have known all along.

Being raised without a mom and having a father she'd never met should have made her future as clear as sparkling salt water. Even though she'd started college with a generous scholarship, every dream she'd dared to imagine had been crushed under the pounding of her own bad decisions.

The front door squawked open before she could locate her house key.

"What in the world?" Terri had her hip cocked, Lark on her side. The four-year-old was stuffing a banana in her mouth like a competitive eater. "You look horrible."

"Thanks. That's helpful."

"You know what I mean. Is everything okay?" She set Lark on the floor by the card table they used for meals.

"Hi, Mama." The words were formed around yellow goop, but still, they provided the salve only Lark could offer.

"Hi, sweetie. Slow down, please." Cassie flung her bag onto the couch, then turned her attention back to Terri. "Has everything ever been okay with me?"

"Oh. One of *those* days. What can I do to help?"

That was Terri. They'd been close since undergrad, when they were assigned the same room, the exception to the random first-year roommate horror stories. She'd become the closest friend Cassie had ever had. When the need for a man's attention had rocked Cassie's world, Terri hadn't tossed her aside. And when Cassie had come home from the student health center sobbing, a very unplanned baby on the way, Terri stood by her. She'd been as steady and unchanging as Aunt Shasta.

It was Terri who first suggested California for graduate school, but Cassie had jumped on the plan without hesitation. Cassie had finished her master's here and was just beginning a doctorate, giving her a few more years before she had to figure out the rest of her life.

"Tell me not to go home." Cassie plopped down on the floor, her spirits too low for the comfort of the sofa.

Terri lunged for Lark, swooping her into the air a millisecond before her banana-smeared hands came into contact with the threadbare blankie she still dragged around. "Sounds like a Daniel Tiger conversation." She wiped Lark's hands clean with a kitchen towel.

A smile snuck up on Cassie. They'd been using that phrase anytime they wanted to talk without interruption.

At the mention of Daniel Tiger, Lark hopped onto the beanbag, pulled her blankie to her chest, and started sucking on the frayed hem, a babyish habit Cassie should probably do something about before kindergarten.

With Lark lost in her show, Terri slid onto the floor at her side. "Okay. Spill."

Just like that, tears flooded her eyes. Cassie tried to put words to the situation, but they wouldn't come. Instead, a storm raged, weighing her down with choices, mistakes, and consequences. The loss of all she'd been raised to accomplish collided with who she'd become.

Terri's arm came across her back, pulling Cassie close.

The kindness broke Cassie, who dropped her head to Terri's shoulder while the silent tears washed over, soaking into her shirt.

Whatever it took, Lark and Cassie had to go home, at least long enough to assess the situation. She owed Shasta that much.

The road in front of Cassie glowed as the darkness faded with the rising sun. Lark pounded a happy beat on the box at her side. Another box filled the passenger seat beside Cassie. It was better to be prepared for a longer stay, especially after all she'd read about Parkinson's. Google was a nightmare factory. After years plagued by an irrational fear of open water, Cassie had a new demon. Parkinson's made drowning seem peaceful.

After an hour on the road, Lark grew tired of her confinement. "I need out."

"I'm afraid that's not an option, sweet girl. Do you remember when we went to visit Aunt Shasta? Remember how long it took to get there?" Of course she wouldn't. Lark hadn't even had her third birthday the last time they'd made the trip.

"What about Teacher Trish? She'll miss me."

Cassie took in the image of her daughter in the rearview mirror. Dark curls framed her face. The once-chubby baby cheeks were beginning to narrow, transforming Lark into a little girl who was growing up too quickly. "I left her a message. She knows you're on a trip."

"I need to go potty."

It hadn't taken long for Lark to remember the golden ticket. Cassie could keep driving through hunger, boredom, or restlessness, but potty stops were nonnegotiable. She did a quick calculation. There could easily be eight restroom breaks added to the fourteen-hour drive. If each took ten minutes, that would add another hour and a half to the trip, and that didn't include stopping for food.

At two o'clock in the morning, having been beaten by her poor estimation of toilet stops, meals, snacks, and Lark's need to stretch her legs, Cassie breathed a sigh as she spotted the sign announcing they'd arrived in her home county. The hospital was no more than a mile away, but Gull's Bay was another twelve at least, and Cassie's last tank of coffee was losing its ability to keep her awake. She pulled into the hospital parking lot.

In the dim glow of a streetlamp, Cassie took in Lark's pouty lips and the perfect crescent moons of her closed eyes. How could a mistake have turned into such a precious gift? It didn't make sense, but there she was.

It seemed like only moments had passed when Cassie was brutally woken by something tapping the window, followed by Lark's panicked cries.

Cassie swung around, her mind fumbling to make sense of the figure staring at her in the early dawn.

The man tapped again, then indicated for her to open the window.

Warnings from one of Cassie's favorite true-crime podcasts flashed in her mind. Without taking her gaze away from the stranger, she reached back to Lark, then lowered the window less than an inch. "Can I help you?"

"Ma'am, I'm with security here." He indicated something on his shirt she couldn't read through the fogged glass. "This is not a campground. I cannot allow you to sleep here. I can give you directions to a shelter where they can help you out."

Cassie's face tingled. She slid the window down another inch. "We're here to see my aunt. We drove all night, and I was exhausted."

"So then, this won't become a regular thing?" His expression remained vacant.

"No, it won't happen again." Cassie maintained control of her eyes, not letting them swirl around in the roll they wanted so badly to make.

As he turned back to his vehicle, she took a deep breath. "Lark, what do you say we get out of this car?"

Lark nodded, her blanket hanging from her mouth. Chalk up another mommy failure. Lark would have plenty to tell her future therapist.

As she twisted to unbuckle her daughter, Cassie used the box beside her in the passenger seat as leverage, freeing a smaller box that dropped, corner first, onto her cheek. "Ouch." She rubbed the spot that rose in an immediate welt.

"Mommy, do you have an ouchy? Do you have Band-Aids?"

Cassie forced a smile. At least this had gotten Lark's mind away from waking up in a car to a strange man at the window. "I'm fine." She needed out of the car as much, if not more, than her daughter.

~

Hospitals wore an atmosphere of death like the mandatory open-backed gowns donned by their patients. It couldn't be helped. People died here and would continue to do so long after today. Cassie walked past the nurses' station, all decorated for spring with paper flowers and pastel streamers on the walls, but what was the point? It didn't calm her nervous energy in the least, and it certainly didn't soften the institutional scent that made her queasy.

Lark's reaction didn't match her mother's in the least. She tugged at Cassie's arm, reaching out for the adornments.

Butterflies bigger than any of those in the bright exhibit bounced around Cassie's stomach as they reached the right room. She knocked gently on the door. "Aunt Shasta? It's Cassie and Lark."

Shasta looked up from the tray of food stationed on a bed table in front of her. It might have been Cassie's imagination, but it seemed as though Shasta's head jolted toward her in a clicking motion rather than a smooth turn. "Of course it's you. Who else would call me Aunt Shasta?" Her face was expressionless, but the dim light that shone in her eyes let Cassie know this was still the same woman who had taken her in and raised her as Shasta's own daughter, not the child of a much younger cousin.

She settled a hand on her aunt's shoulder. It was awkward, like she was trying to say something but didn't know how to express it. They'd never been super touchy-feely.

Stillness placed a blanket over the room, creating a tension they'd never shared before.

"Aubrey told you, huh? The woman never can keep her jaw closed." Shasta's words were rounded off at the points. She looked away, her face turned toward the blind-covered window.

Even as a teen, Cassie had never raised her voice to her aunt. She'd managed to maneuver through the curves of puberty with the books Shasta left on her bed and a large dose of Google searches. It didn't have to be said that neither of them wanted to broach the topics of changing bodies and attractions, so they hadn't. It might have been odd, but the two of them had also avoided the reverberating fights other teens had with their mothers.

For the first time, their carefully manicured relationship felt fragile, as if it were about to crack open and be glued back together in a completely different shape. Silent tremors below the surface began to do their work. "Yes, of course she told me. You should have been the one to do that, but at least I know."

"There's no reason for you to be burdened by a thing like this. I told her that too. This is my problem. I'll figure it out."

"Wow. That sounds an awful lot like you're dismissing me. Did you forget we're a family?"

Shasta shifted under the sheets, then crossed one arm over the other. "It's not that simple. You have a life, a child. You have your studies."

Fear beat on the door to Cassie's insecurities. "Maybe so, but you're the only family Lark and I have. I think I should be told when you have a health crisis."

"This is hardly a crisis." Yet the slight slur in Shasta's words told another version of the story.

Cassie's shoulders lifted and fell.

Lark climbed up on the heating unit by the window and threaded herself between the blinds and the glass.

Instinct had Cassie about to snap back with words she'd regret, but it was only the three of them, a small but steady team, and there was no telling how Parkinson's was going to affect Shasta's future. Cassie didn't have the luxury of angry words she could take back later. Each day from here forward was shrouded in a fog of ignorance, something she planned to cure ASAP.

The words Cassie wanted to say got lost in the beeping of the hospital, the uncertainty of her daughter, and the vulnerability of her aunt. They were replaced with feelings she could only identify as nerves, like the way she'd felt at her thesis defense with all those eyes on her, judging the product of her research and holding her future, along with Lark's, in their hands.

Cassie leaned on the side of Shasta's mattress. "I just want to be sure you're okay. Can you tell me what the doctor says?"

"It's nothing really. I have a couple . . ." Her forehead furrowed into a series of rivulets, and she touched a black and blue splotch on her arm. "What's that word?"

"Bruises?"

"Yes. That's it. I'll be better soon. Back to myself."

Lacing her fingers around Shasta's hand, Cassie was all too aware of the changes taking place, the shifting of roles. They hadn't practiced for this. There wasn't time or warning. Yet here they were anyway, bracing for the tsunami that roared toward them, and Cassie was the one in charge of their survival.

# 2

Nora Milford sat in the examination room, tapping an agitated rhythm with the toe of her shoe. She looked down at her growing belly, oddly bigger than it had been with her first two daughters. Number three, yet another girl, was making her presence known not only in size but in the constant rolls and turns that looked like ocean waves under Nora's shirt. She rubbed her palms over the bulge, hoping to calm the cheerleader within. Why did God feel it necessary to give her another girl? The mother-daughter relationship wasn't one she had much experience with. That fact was already becoming evident with her four-year-old. Gwendolyn was nothing like her mother, but why would she be? Nora had been raised by her father, alone. A girl in a man's world, and she'd loved every minute of it. Well, mostly.

A rap on the door; then Dr. Wheeler stepped in, bringing with him the wave of guilt Nora carried for rescheduling this appointment and having her glucose test at thirty weeks, two weeks past the clinic's normal time. "Nora, thanks for coming in today." He sat on the rolling stool and bent forward, his elbows pressing into his thighs. "I don't want to alarm you, but I am concerned about some of your test results."

Nora's hands stopped moving. Could there be a more concerning phrase than *"I don't want to alarm you"*?

"Your glucose tolerance test leads me to believe you have developed gestational diabetes. This is something we can manage, but it's not a condition I take lightly."

Nora's pulse throbbed behind her eardrums. "How did this happen? I didn't have any problem with my other pregnancies."

He nodded as if he understood, but how could he? "It's just one of those things that doesn't occur every time, but then it does. Did your mother have any issues like this?"

A familiar curtain dropped over Nora, bringing the shame experienced only by the kind of people unloved by their very own mothers. "I wouldn't know. She's been gone since I was a baby." She used the word *gone* to leave a bit of mystery in the response. Had she died or left? No one besides Nora needed to know that her mother had walked away from her tiny newborn because the bundle she'd given birth to wasn't a good enough reason to stay.

"How about sisters . . . a grandmother?"

"My dad's mom died when I was little. And I don't have any siblings." Her husband, Ferris, had gifted her with a DNA test for Christmas, but Nora was hesitant to see the results. She shouldn't have sent in the saliva sample. Some doors were better off closed.

Nora's thoughts swirled around worry for her unborn baby, questions about what other time bombs were waiting to ignite in her bloodstream, and wonders about what Tammy had done in the years after she'd departed Gull's Bay without ever looking back.

She shifted in her seat, suddenly feeling every movement and jab within her womb, like punches from a child she would never fully understand.

The doctor clicked away on the keyboard. "I'm putting in a referral to the dietician. She's going to give you more details on the changes we'll need you to make to what you eat. I've also got you set up with a diabetic specialist who will instruct you about regular testing." He paused, swiveling the stool her way. "This isn't going to be easy, but it's important for both you and the baby that you follow our directions to the letter."

Nora rubbed at the tense muscles in her neck. Her mouth had gone as dry as her father-in-law's sense of humor, all sarcasm and condescension. "I will." She flipped open her letter-sized planner and made a few notes, prepping herself for the research she'd pour herself into at home.

By the time she stepped out of the clinic doors, Nora could barely swallow with her need for a beverage, preferably caffeinated and sugared. But even without having met with the nutrition specialist, she knew this was not to be, not if she was going to take the diagnosis seriously, and that was another no-brainer. Her child's safety was at risk. Nora wasn't her own mother.

Outside, it was a typical gray, the color of most mid-March days on the Oregon coast. Seagulls called overhead, but she could still hear the crash of the waves from her location on the top of the hill.

She left her car in the parking lot and walked toward the main part of town. The doctor had told her to increase her exercise, which meant even this short walk would accomplish a check mark for that task. When had she become so lazy? Most of the residents of Gull's Bay walked around town rather than using their cars. Her house was only about a mile from the clinic. She'd made the hike up that hill for every appointment up to the births of her first two babies.

Her father had always told her that laziness was the luxury of fools. In the six months since his massive heart attack, she'd become one of those fools, wasting her time on television shows, staring out at the ocean, sleeping in until the girls woke her. He would be embarrassed by her now. Even if no one in town saw the changes that had happened within her, Nora still felt their eyes watching, as if they knew she wasn't made of the tough stuff her father had been.

Sugar seemed to lace the damp air as she passed by the bakery. A rumble in her stomach pleaded with her to get just one more treat, one more of Beverly Collins's cupcakes with the two inches of fluffy chocolate frosting towered on top. She covered her mouth and nose with the end of her scarf and crossed to the other side of the street.

Inside the coffee shop, dishes clanked from the kitchen, where someone must have been washing up the lunch plates. The guy who lived with Merv Watkins stood behind the counter, wiping up the surfaces as if there'd been some kind of spill only moments before she'd stepped in. If she remembered correctly, he was in a master's program for either school administration or counseling.

"Good afternoon." He dropped the bar towel somewhere out of view. "How are you doing today?"

Nora had to bite her tongue before an entire outline of her appointment spilled out where it was no one's business. "I'm great. How are you?"

He grinned. "As good as ever. What can I get you?"

Her gaze strayed to the display of cookies.

"Those are fresh. Just got them in an hour ago. They might still be warm." He rubbed a hand in circles over his flat stomach.

"No. Thank you, though. I will have an iced tea, and . . . that's it. Just the iced tea."

"You want a couple of sugar packets with that?"

She paused to take a deep breath before depriving herself of another desire. "No, thank you. Unsweetened will be just fine. And I'll take that to go."

Once she had the tea in hand, Nora stepped back onto the sidewalk and stared up the hill to where she'd left the car. If laziness was for fools, why did she feel so foolish for having walked down here?

Nora gave herself a pep talk as she stepped out of her SUV. Her mother-in-law would be waiting inside Nora's house with an open laptop and a fully pinned Pinterest board of baby-shower ideas ready to scroll through.

Helen wasn't a horrible woman. In fact, she was quite nice, but she and Nora had virtually nothing in common. Helen was one of five sisters, all nearly identical in looks. Though she'd raised four boys, her close relationship with her siblings and nieces had kept her as girlie as any woman Nora had ever met.

"Well, there you are." Helen sat on the couch, Gwendolyn beside her, her hair in a freshly woven French braid. "How was the appointment?"

"No big deal." Nora shrugged. "How did things go with the girls?"

Helen tied a bright pink ribbon around the hairband at the base of Gwendolyn's braid. "Perfect as usual. Peyton is sound asleep." She stood from the sofa with more grace than Nora had had before her first pregnancy. "I wanted to go over a few details about the baby shower."

Nora gave herself a mental high five for calling that one. "I really don't think we need to do one. It's our third baby, and another girl. We don't need anything."

"My thoughts exactly."

A layer of tension melted off Nora's shoulders.

"I think a ladies' tea would be a better way to celebrate."

It took only a fraction of a second for her muscles to shrink back up tighter than before. "That sounds like a lot of work."

"Nonsense. It's my privilege. You're the only daughter-in-law I have living close enough to spoil." Helen looked back over her shoulder. "This is what I live for."

Nora picked up Gwendolyn and placed her on her lap. "Are

you sure?" There would be no arguing about this without hurting Helen's feelings. This Nora knew from experience.

"Absolutely." Helen lifted her purse off the table. "You look wiped out. How about I take Gwennie with me for a treat, and you take a rest?"

Nora cringed at the nickname, but her daughter vaulted off her lap and threaded her hand into her grandmother's. Memories from her childhood, when Nora had thought being an adult would give her the power to make her own choices, came rushing back. She'd been wrong about that and so many things. "Okay. Have a great time, and you listen to Grandma." She motioned for her daughter to come close and kissed her head.

As the door clicked shut behind them, Nora tried to remind herself how fortunate she was. Helen was a devoted grandmother. The woman actually drove around with two car seats in her van just in case she had the opportunity to spend time with her granddaughters. And Nora really was tired. More than tired. Her body ached for rest.

She stared across the room at the laptop. Maybe it was time to look at the DNA results, but her eyes were heavy, and her body felt like she'd run up that hill rather than walked at the pace of a slug. A look into the past was like opening a deeply buried coffin. It wasn't something to take lightly. Once the lid was removed, Nora would never be able to unsee the contents.

She could do it later. Or never.

# 3

By the time Lark and Cassie drove into the town limits of Gull's Bay, Lark was no longer willing to have her meal put off by granola bars. Her frustrated and exhausted tears were coming in a rage now, feet kicking the seat beside Cassie.

Cassie's old home was in the middle of what was considered downtown Gull's Bay. She pulled into a packed-dirt parking area alongside Coastal Coffee, their shop designed into the bottom of a towering Victorian house. Cassie's gaze lifted to the windows on the top floor, the apartment where she'd lived since her toddler years, the only home she could recall having until college. "Larkie-bird, look. We're here. Time to get out and have something to eat." Cassie's voice couldn't get any higher without breaking glass.

The thumping stopped and the sobs softened. "I need out, please." The words were followed by full-body shudders.

Outside the car, Lark struggled to be let down, the stress of the last two days regressing her. Cassie pointed out the familiar storefronts that lined the street paved with fitted stones, telling Lark about the friendly people who ran each business. Coming home to Gull's Bay was like stepping back in time to a place where people mattered and big chains were not yet commonplace.

She set Lark's feet onto the soft ground. "You have to hold my hand, okay?"

Lark nodded, but five steps closer to the entrance, she slipped Cassie's hold, lunging forward.

The door swung open, with an exiting customer nearly colliding with Lark.

"I'm so sorry."

The woman glanced down at her coffee cup. "No spills, no problem," she said, walking off.

Easy for her to say.

Inside, the scents of freshly baked goods and coffee made Cassie's stomach growl and her skin warm. This was the place she felt at home, surrounded by locals and tourists, and always coffee.

Lark's eye caught on the small corner with children's books and toys. Without missing a step, she was there, diving into the box of goodies.

A familiar laugh behind the counter soothed Cassie's nerves. "Aubrey."

This woman never seemed to age, always looking much like Cassie pictured her in childhood memories. The dark hair she kept swirled into a twist at the back of her head had highlights of silver that only seemed to call attention to her shining dark eyes. "How are you doing, sweetie?"

The words made Cassie want to crawl into Aubrey's arms and be a child again, if only for a moment, long enough to catch her breath. "I'm good."

Aubrey slid her teal reading glasses down the bridge of her nose. "I could be wrong, but it looks to me like *good* is probably an exaggeration. How about a great cup of coffee?"

Much like Shasta, Aubrey believed a warm mug of java had actual healing powers, but Cassie wouldn't turn down the offer even if caffeine wouldn't cure her hurts. "Absolutely."

Before the word was out of her mouth, Aubrey turned toward

the elaborate espresso machine. It sizzled and hummed as she thumped the portafilter, then crammed it full of freshly ground coffee beans. As it dripped into the tiny cups, bringing another wave of the earthy coffee scent, the milk steamed up into a thick froth.

By the time Aubrey turned around to offer Cassie the drink, she was salivating. Cassie wrapped her hands around the warm porcelain, letting the sensation soothe her, then inhaled. The first sip reminded her of who she'd been once upon a time. But the memory wasn't bitter. It touched her tongue with a gentle sweetness, the reminiscence of being loved and cared for and always safe.

"Have a seat. You look like you could use a break." Aubrey indicated the couch along one wall, its overstuffed burgundy fabric so tempting, Cassie might never make it up the stairs.

She settled in, allowing her back to fully relax for the first time since Aubrey's call. For a moment, she closed her eyes and let her mind believe the only responsibility she had in the entire world was to keep the coffee from spilling onto her lap.

Cassie's eyes popped open as a scream brought her back to reality. In the corner, Lark stood holding her finger, her face bright red and tears streaking down her cheeks.

Depositing the cup on the stout coffee table, Cassie moved toward her daughter, scooping Lark into her arms and holding her close. "What's wrong?" Exhaustion edged Cassie's voice, even as she did her best to sound sympathetic.

Lark leaned back, holding up her pointer finger. The tip had a line running across the pad.

"Did you pinch it?"

Lark nodded, still unable to speak.

Cassie took the tiny hand and kissed her finger. "Any better?"

Again, Lark nodded. Her face had already begun to soften, and the tears were no longer pouring out.

Aubrey came up beside them with a plastic plate topped with

one of Mrs. Collins's giant cinnamon rolls, cream cheese frosting oozing over the sides. The scent was enough to draw both of them away from their worries.

The growl from Cassie's stomach brought an amused smile to Aubrey's face.

Lark squirmed from her arms. "That's for me."

It wasn't a question.

"How about we share?" Cassie took the plate and set it next to her cooling coffee. "Aubrey, you know me well."

Aubrey pulled her into a hug befitting a woman who had always been like an aunt to her. "It's going to be okay."

But would it really?

Cassie's body ached with complete exhaustion. Something about the task of driving always sapped her energy. With Lark finally asleep in the portable crib she'd long ago outgrown, there were things that had to be done, issues to manage before Shasta could come home and be safe.

Stacks of items were piled around the space, things Cassie didn't even recognize in a place that was still her home. All around her, scatterings of this or that created clutter, as if someone had been looking for something, but with a chaotic and unusual kind of order. None of this was like Shasta. She'd never been one to hoard or leave a mess out, but here it all was, evidence to the contrary.

Even Shasta's studio was in disarray, paint tubes left without their lids, brushes unwashed. Canvases, unfinished creations, leaned up against the walls.

The first thing Cassie did was remove the area rugs and stash them in the linen closet, out of sight. They'd been a concession made for her years ago, when they'd ripped out the carpet and Cassie had continued her habit of walking around the house barefoot. Now they posed a tripping hazard for both Shasta and Lark, and Cassie didn't have time for falls. Shasta had always wondered what it would take to get Cassie into a pair of slippers. Neither of them would have guessed Parkinson's was the answer.

Somewhere beneath the chaos, there was the simple and homey apartment Cassie had always loved. The kitchen was open to the living room, and down the hall were two bedrooms, a bathroom, and Aunt Shasta's studio. With the height of the building, they had a beautiful view of the ocean through the oversized windows that took up much of the wall space in the front room.

Cassie stepped close to the glass and looked out on the moonlit waves. They rolled in like glistening sheets of silk blowing in a breeze. After she slid the window open, her muscles eased as the crashing of the water became the music of the evening. That sound and the scent of fresh salt air was like safety. Even though she wasn't much of an active Christian, they made her feel that God was bigger than anything else, and He was in control.

A chill ran across her skin, but she didn't close out the ocean. Instead, Cassie pulled a plush blanket from the back of the sofa and wrapped it around her shoulders. When her body couldn't stand for another minute, she curled up on the cushions and scrolled through the notifications on her phone.

Cassie's advisor had responded to her email with understanding about the sudden absence, for which she was very grateful—a tiny worry chipped off the top of the mountain of concerns. Before she knew it, she'd sunk into the endlessness of Facebook posts, memes, and quizzes. It was an indulgence she allowed herself until her eyes grew weary and she could fall asleep without letting the unknowns of Shasta's future keep her mind spinning away from dreamland.

She must have dozed off right there on the couch, because

Cassie was woken by the clanking of dishes downstairs and the light streaming through the windows. The chill in the air was more than the blanket could hold back even through the jeans she'd failed to change out of the night before.

She checked on Lark. Without Shasta, Cassie would surely need to adjust the schedule and manage the shop the way her aunt always had. If only Cassie had been clearheaded enough to start a list the night before.

Just as she stretched her legs, Lark bellowed, probably feeling the panic of waking in a new location. The insistent calls took away the last of Cassie's heavy drowsiness.

"Good morning, sweet birdie." She lifted her daughter from the crib, smelling the top of her head the way she had since Lark was a fresh little newborn.

"I'm not a baby." Lark wrapped her blankie around her shoulders as Cassie set her on the floor.

"I know. But I thought you'd be more comfortable in the"— Cassie struggled to find a word other than *crib*—"in the playpen than on the floor."

Lark pointed to the bed. "I can sleep in there."

An odd defensiveness rose up. That was Cassie's bed, even if she hadn't used it last night. It was the bed she'd grown up with. What kind of mother wasn't willing to give her best for her child? Parenting was seriously a never-ending exercise in learning to sacrifice. "We'll talk about it."

Cassie yanked on clean clothes and brushed her teeth while helping Lark to do the same. At four, her daughter still needed help with everything if Cassie wanted it done in a timely manner and with any order, but Lark insisted she could do it all on her own.

They headed downstairs, where coffee and fresh scones scented the air. Years back, Shasta had had the brilliant plan to sell Mrs. Collins's baked goods in the shop. By marking them up a little and giving the customers' praises back to Mrs. Collins, along with a point in her direction, everyone came out on top.

A new guy stood behind the counter. He was tall with dark hair. His skin was the same color Cassie considered the perfect marriage of cream and coffee, caramelly and rich. As she and Lark came closer, he greeted them with a very bright smile. "Good morning. What can I get started for you two?"

Lark gave them each a look, then went for the toys.

Cassie's eyebrows tightened, a habit she'd been trying to break, as Terri said it made her look intimidating. "No worries. I'll get it myself." She slipped behind the counter and pulled the milk from the refrigerator, starting to prepare her double shot of espresso like she'd done a thousand other times.

Before Cassie could press the button, he had his hand on the machine. "What do you think you're doing?"

She raised and lowered her shoulders. "Making a latte. Isn't this how you do it?"

His index finger tapped at the *Marshall* name tag attached above his shirt pocket. "It is, but I work here, so I get that privilege." He stood at least six inches above her, and if she was one to let that bother her, he would be the guy to pull it off.

"And I *live* here, so I think that supersedes your claim to the espresso machine."

They seemed stuck there, neither ready to give over the coffee duties to the other.

"Shasta is the only one who lives here." He said this as though she were lying.

Who would make this stuff up?

In turn, Cassie pointed to the painting near the register of herself in a cap and gown, the ocean in the background, her graduation tassel waving in the wind. Shasta's work was like a photograph, but deeper feelings were transmitted through her brush and into the eye of the observer. "And me . . . when I'm not at school."

A tapping at the walk-up window drew their attention. Cassie expected a customer but could see now, by the way the counter beneath was stacked with supplies, that it hadn't been used for the purpose of walk-up service in a while. On the other side of the pane, a male western gull in prime adulthood knocked his beak on the glass.

Marshall popped the top off a can, reached inside, then slid the window open and dropped pastry crumbles onto the stretch of shelving attached to the outside of the house. Without a word, he closed the window again and looked back at Cassie.

"What was that about?"

"Him?" Marshall pointed a thumb over his shoulder. "We've been calling him Bogart. He comes by every morning, just wanting a breakfast treat."

"You realize he'll keep coming back as long as you feed him, and sooner or later, he'll bring friends." She crossed her arms, hoping she conveyed a tough look.

Marshall rolled his eyes. "So, you're one of those 'seagulls are just pests' kind of people. You know this is their home too. And they aren't rodents. They clean up the messes left by tourists and everybody else. Did you know seagulls can even drink salt water? It's because of these things above their eyes . . ." He pointed to his right eyebrow.

"Glands." Now she was the one rolling her eyes. Middle-school Cassie was about to make an appearance if adult Cassie didn't stuff her back down quick. "I doubt there is anything about gulls or any other marine bird you can tell me that I don't already know."

"Hmm. Are you challenging me?"

She tried to stop it, but her mouth twitched up into an awkward smile. "Know your competition before you make any bets." Cassie held her hand out. "I'm Cassie George."

"Marshall Baylor."

Before they could get any further into this uncomfortable

introduction, Aubrey burst through the door, two reusable grocery bags hanging from one arm and a satchel on the other. "I'm so sorry I'm late. Marshall, is everything under control?"

"Aside from a coffee snatcher who apparently thinks seagulls should use the front door, all's well." He took the bags from Aubrey's arms and set them on the counter.

"Oh my goodness. In all the craziness, I totally forgot to tell you about Cassie coming home. Did you get the note I left about Shasta?"

Marshall's eyes darkened. "No. Is everything all right?"

Cassie dumped espresso into her cup through the milk she'd steamed, taking advantage of Marshall's distraction.

Aubrey entered the kitchen and came back with a damp sheet of paper. "This must have fallen in the sink. She took a pretty bad fall. The doctor says it was due to a stroke." Aubrey dumped the paper into a recycling bin. "They're keeping her at the hospital and working on some new medications to help with the instability and mood issues."

"I've been afraid of this. Do you think she'd mind if I stopped by to visit after my shift?"

Aubrey laid her hand lightly on his upper arm, much like a mother would do. "I think she'd love that."

Had Cassie really been gone so long that a perfect stranger was now a close friend? It sat wrong with her, all lopsided. Aunt Shasta was vulnerable, a trait Cassie had never before assigned to her aunt. But after seeing her in the hospital yesterday, the way she worked the sheets in her hands as if trying to wring them of undetectable water, Cassie would never be able to miss her frailties again. The truth covered her like a curse. It occurred to Cassie then that growing older wasn't about the changes she would go through physically, but instead, aging was about watching the people she loved transition from mighty to dependent.

She palmed her coffee, collected her daughter, and pulled a couple of baked goods from the display case. Waving at Aubrey and Marshall, she headed out the door with Lark. There were plans to make, and Cassie needed to smell the ocean and stand on the beach to be able to see the big picture.

# 4

A virtual appointment had sounded like a brilliant idea to Nora when the nutritionist's office offered it as an option. She wouldn't have to beg childcare from her mother-in-law, forcing her to answer questions about the additional appointment, and she could keep her feet comfortably tucked into slippers. But reality played out far differently than the plan.

Ten minutes into the meeting, Gwendolyn spilled orange juice across the dining room table, where Nora sat with the computer. She'd snatched up the laptop and moved to the kitchen counter without calling too much attention to the chaos around her.

Five minutes later, Peyton smacked herself in the head with a wooden toy, and the screaming began. Nora thought she might have been in the clear when her toddler moved past the trauma, quickly finding the juice still dripping through the gaps in the table to be more interesting than her own injury.

That's when Ferris stepped into the house through the door that led in from the garage. He wasn't two steps in when the doctor brought up that word again. *Diabetes.*

Nora cringed. It wasn't that she was afraid to tell her husband;

she just didn't want to. There was something embarrassing about the diagnosis, though she knew in her brain she couldn't fully be at fault. Still, that knowledge didn't dilute the shame she carried along with the extra weight from the donuts she'd indulged in all through her first trimester, and really, her second too. The thought of them made her mouth water. Donuts alone might not have caused this problem, but they were off-limits from now on.

She held a finger to her lips, indicating that she couldn't talk, then slipped the connector for the earbuds into the laptop's port, cutting off his access to the other side of the conversation.

The woman went into a long explanation about the importance of milk, then explained that it should be consumed in small amounts.

Nora caught her hand going to her forehead, her image reflected in the screen. When had she become so crabby and impatient? She'd made it to thirty weeks, and the Milford girls were known to show up according to the schedule. Only ten weeks to go.

"I know this must be a hard adjustment, and many women find their diagnosis to be scary, but this is manageable. How are you doing with the blood-sugar monitor?"

"Works like a charm." Nora forced a smile, correcting its flaws as if she were looking in a mirror.

"Good. Now, be sure to contact the office if you have any questions. I'll check back with you in two weeks."

When the meeting disconnected, Nora breathed as deeply as her unborn daughter would allow, then closed the laptop, readjusting her smile again as she turned to her husband. "What brings you home this early?"

Ferris set Peyton on the counter near the sink and ran water over his hands. "I thought I'd pop by for a late lunch. I'll miss dinner tonight."

"That's the third time this week. Doesn't Porter know you

have a family?" She threw the question out to guide the conversation away from the chaos he'd walked into.

He ran Peyton's hands under the water now, then splashed some on her legs.

Nora would need to scrub the carpet on her hands and knees to get the orange juice puddle to fade away.

"So, what's this about diabetes?"

She handed him a kitchen towel that he used to dry their daughter. "It's nothing."

Scooping Peyton into his arms, Ferris gave her the kind of look she imagined him giving criminals in the midst of investigations.

"Look, I'm not a perp. I'm your wife. If you need to know something, I'll make sure and tell you."

He raised his eyebrows but said nothing. It was no mystery why he was so good at his job as detective for the local police department.

"My blood sugar was high. The doctor put me on a diet, and the baby will be fine." She patted her stomach for emphasis.

"And you?"

Nora shrugged. "It's temporary. The problem should go away when the baby is born. No big deal."

His hand came to rest on her shoulder. "You've been saying that a lot lately."

"What?" Tension grew as she stuffed down her unease.

"No big deal. You'll be fine." He stepped away, settling Peyton into her high chair and pouring a pile of Cheerios onto the tray. "You need to give yourself some grace. Your dad died. That's tough stuff."

Nora turned away. The hormones made it hard to remain rational, to pull back the pointless tears. Frustration heated into irritation that boiled into anger. Why couldn't she get it together?

She spun around at his touch on her arm, the quick movement

turning the room into a carnival of lights and motion. In a flash, the anger was replaced with panic as she stumbled, using all of her resources to keep herself from tumbling to the floor.

"Whoa. Take it easy." Ferris led her to the couch and helped her onto the cushion.

She wasn't weak. But that little hiccup would do nothing to make that point to her husband. "I'm fine. Really."

Prying eyes bore into her.

"Don't go all supercop on me. It's just a temporary situation. The doctor says I'll be fine and so will the baby." How many times could she tell herself and Ferris these exact words before they felt believable?

"Did he say what caused it?"

She shrugged. "Just bad luck."

"Daddy!" Gwendolyn ran across the room and launched herself into Ferris's arms. "You're home early."

"I thought I'd stop in and see my girls, but I'll have to head back before long." He tapped her nose. "Are you and Peyton taking good care of Mommy and your baby sister?"

"She takes care of us." Gwendolyn snuggled up on his chest.

"Yes, she does, but even moms and dads need some help now and again." Ferris's eyes, staring straight at Nora's, spoke more than the words out of his mouth.

She looked away.

"How about we get that mess under the table cleaned up?"

Gwendolyn hopped off his lap, suddenly ready to do anything as long as it was with her father. That was one thing Nora had in common with her daughter. It tugged at her emotions, the beauty of their relationship. She was torn between frustration that she and Gwendolyn didn't seem to get each other—already—and fear for her daughter. Someday, she would be left behind without her dad, just like Nora was now.

# 5

If Cassie's time staring out at the endlessness of the Pacific hadn't been enough to convince her to move home permanently, the meeting with the hospital's social worker certainly would have. Shasta had finally relented and given the medical staff permission to talk with her, no small miracle.

Janice Herrera was a middle-aged woman who seemed to be in better shape than Cassie. She didn't bother to cover silver highlights running through her dark hair. When she spoke, each word punctured the air with crisp enunciation even as she managed to retain a tone of compassion and support.

The fallout was more than Cassie had been prepared for. Shasta's Parkinson's diagnosis was already five years old, yet Shasta hadn't bothered to let Cassie in on the secret. Yes, it was likely that Shasta was trying to protect her, but it still stung Cassie's heart. What worried not only the doctor but also Janice was the stroke that had landed her aunt in the hospital bed. But the part that shook Cassie to her core, the piece she wasn't ready for, was the mental aspect of the disease.

"Your aunt first came to the doctor when she found herself struggling to find the right words in everyday conversation. Though she's had relatively few physical symptoms of Parkinson's, she has dealt with loss of strength and dexterity in her right arm." Janice took a breath and rolled her pen between her fingers. "Lewy body dementia doesn't happen with everyone. That's one of the reasons families are so surprised. They expect the tremors and stilted walk, but memory loss, confusion, and hallucinations—those things are even harder for most people to manage." She pulled a pamphlet from the binder on her lap and passed it across the conference-room table. "Your aunt has been having trouble with recall for years now. There's no way to know how far this will go, but we've seen at least two incidents of hallucinations while she's been here. I don't want to frighten you, but Lewy body dementia"—she glanced at Lark, as if making sure she wasn't paying attention—"is fatal."

A little buzz shot up Cassie's neck.

"I want you to have all the information before you make a decision on her care."

"The decision has been made by Shasta and by me. I'm moving home, and I'll take care of her myself."

Lark slid from her seat, snaking between Cassie's feet as she drove a toy car along the carpet. Her motor sounds grew louder, until Cassie cringed and patted her daughter's arm. "Shh. Lark, please play quietly." Of course it made no difference.

Janice wrung her hands, as though washing them with invisible soap. "I understand your desire, but this is a 'round-the-clock job, and you have your hands full. There's a facility just down the road."

Cassie couldn't listen to another word. Her own doubts were enough to bind her stomach into a knot so tight she might never again manage to have a full meal. Allow Shasta to die in a facility? It wasn't her way. "I'm not trying to be a martyr. It needs to be like this." Cassie forced her spine into a straight line, hoping her posture would convey her intention in a way her voice wasn't able to do. Shasta, all free-spirited and artsy, had taken Cassie in and raised her as her own. As far as Cassie could tell, Shasta had never had the desire to live the life of a mother. She could have put Cassie in the system, let her bounce around from one foster home to another, but Shasta had made the hard choice. Cassie could do the same for her aunt now.

"Keep in mind, these beds aren't always available. If you should change your mind, it could take time to find her a space." Janice slipped the brochure into an oversized envelope with all the other information she'd presented and handed it to Cassie, along with yet another copy of her business card. "We're here to help. There are details about the support group for patients and their caregivers in the packet. Please give it a try. Sometimes talking with others who are experiencing similar situations can be more helpful than anything else."

Cassie pictured herself in a room, chairs in a circle, each one containing a person at least forty years older than she was. These would be people who knew who they were. They'd lived life and held the wisdom that seemed to come with age. She barely knew how to take care of herself and Lark. "Thank you. I'll look into it." But even as the words drifted from her mouth, she knew making that call was highly unlikely.

After the meeting, Cassie took a few minutes to chug down a cup of lukewarm hospital coffee and hand Lark another granola bar, then popped a mint into her mouth so she wouldn't have to explain her breath to Shasta. Her aunt would adamantly refuse to let this poor-quality java pass her own lips. After years as a student, Cassie could get past the bitterness and flavor of whatever was available and cheap as long as there was caffeine in her cup.

She needn't have worried. Shasta was fast asleep when they entered her room. Cassie set her bag on the floor and lifted Lark onto her lap. They sat together, watching Shasta.

"When is my Shasta coming home?" Lark ran her hand softly up and down Cassie's arm.

"I'm not sure, but I think it will be soon. We're going to need to help her. What do you think?"

"I can do that." Lark pulled her blankie over her face the way she did when she grew tired.

Shasta breathed in and out, her body peaceful. It was now that Cassie could see the difference Parkinson's was making in her aunt's life. All the movements and repeated mannerisms disappeared while Shasta slept. She looked like the calm and patient person Cassie had always known. If only she could stay this way, but eventually she'd wake up, and again her thumb would rub against her first two fingers. Then the thin hospital blanket would begin to shudder with the twitching of her leg.

Cassie gently placed Lark over her shoulder and eased out of the room, only relaxing when they were safely inside the elevator heading back to the ground floor. There were adjustments that had to be made at the house before she could bring Shasta home. A new beginning that would culminate in loss.

~

The pamphlets of information for caregivers seemed designed to push families toward shopping for nursing homes. If Cassie had ever thought childproofing was complicated, she gave up that notion as she worked through the checklist of suggestions, grateful she'd already tackled the area rugs.

The medications were up so high, Cassie would need a step stool to reach them, but that apparatus—another safety hazard—was tucked safely under her bed. She packed away the extra clutter that had been reproducing since she'd left for college. That box, however, was now too heavy to lift. With a dolly, she could maneuver it into the studio, but that would mean running around town to beg for the helpful equipment.

Instead, she sat on the ground, shoving the cardboard beast down the hall with her feet, one inch at a time, only reaching the doorway as sweat dripped along her temples.

Drawer locks, night-lights, and shower rails were all on order and should magically appear in two days. So much for buying local. Yet if she had taken Lark into all those shops, Cassie would be done for, conquered without Shasta even leaving the hospital.

Lark tossed down her crayon. "I need to go to the beach. And I miss Terri. When are we going home?" She hopped off the chair and stomped to Cassie's side. "I have an ouchy when I blow my nose." As if to demonstrate, she blew out a spray.

Cassie wiped droplets from her arm. "Lark, that's gross."

Cassie's cell phone buzzed.

"Can you color for another minute or two?" She turned her attention to the phone. "Hello?"

"Hi, Cassie. This is Janice from the hospital."

Cassie rubbed the tight muscles along the back of her neck. "What can I do for you?" She kept her voice light, trying to prepare for another list of reasons Janice would push for the care facility.

"I just wanted to let you know your aunt had a setback after you left."

Alarms blared in Cassie's head. "What happened?"

"She had an episode of hallucinations. The doctor wants to keep her another night as he works with the medications."

She spotted Lark chewing up a crayon and spitting it onto the table. Blue chunks clung to her chin. "Is she okay? I can be there in half an hour." Cassie scooped midnight blue slime from her daughter's mouth and deposited it on a napkin.

"Actually, she's sedated now. If you don't have care for your daughter, I'd recommend waiting at least a day to be sure we have this contained. This kind of thing can be frightening to a child."

It could be downright horrifying to an adult too. Cassie turned away from Lark as she blinked back the emotions that swelled like the incoming tide. They flowed over her head, pressing down with the weight of her aunt's and daughter's needs. But failure wasn't something she could accept. She'd done plenty to disappoint her aunt already. This was Cassie's opportunity to make Shasta proud. It was actually her last opportunity.

She thanked Janice and disconnected the call, then stared at the screen. Reality could not be denied. They were going to be here in Gull's Bay for as long as Shasta was still with them. The certainty drained Cassie's energy. She sank into a chair to FaceTime Terri.

When her best friend's face appeared on the phone screen, it almost undid her.

"Hey there. How are my favorite people?" Terri's dark eyes squinted with her grin.

In the background, Terri's boyfriend made a snarky quip about not making the list.

"We're good." Cassie forced her own smile.

"How about a bit of truth there, roomie?"

Though she blinked fast, Cassie's emotions rose faster still. "It's tough." She got up and walked to the windows.

"I won't eat the crayons, okay?" Lark hollered after her.

"Listen, we're going to stay. My aunt needs me. I can manage the rent for a couple of months. I'll Venmo you like always."

Terri shook her head. "Nope. In fact, I'm sending you a refund for this month. I had a feeling you were needed in Oregon. You know Jack's sister has been staying with him until she could find a place. I told her she could have your room. I hope that's okay. I didn't want you to feel pressured by anything here."

"Jack must be thrilled."

"More than any of you will ever know," he yelled from somewhere offscreen.

"Yes. I think he's pretty happy. Greta isn't you, but she'll be a fine roommate."

Jack's shaking face popped onto the screen. "She has no idea what she's talking about."

The warmth of Terri and Jack's relationship came through as if they were there in Gull's Bay. They were everything Cassie wanted, yet she didn't harbor the slightest bit of jealousy. Terri deserved perfection. She had earned the happily ever after while Cassie had gone off the rails at her first taste of freedom. "I can't tell you how much I appreciate this."

"Please let me know if there's anything else I can do from here. You know I'm praying for all of you. I love you!"

"I know. Thank you." Cassie hadn't put much stock in prayer for a long time, but Terri had grown closer and closer to God as she'd gotten to know Jack, a strong believer.

A crash startled Cassie. She fumbled the phone and looked over at Lark to find the cookie jar lying on the linoleum, shattered.

"I've got to go. Motherhood calls."

"Okay. Have the little squirt call her aunt Terri sometime. I miss her. And keep me up to date on all the happenings."

She scooped Lark into her arms. "Will do." She disconnected, severing the lifeline with the only person she could really talk to.

As Cassie contained the mess and her daughter, her gaze caught on the stack of mail she'd brought up from the shop earlier. There in the middle was a bulging manila envelope that had made her curious at the time but was quickly forgotten when they reached the top of the stairs and life took over.

She settled Lark on the living room floor in front of Daniel "the free babysitter" Tiger. Cassie swiped up the crayon mess and tossed away the chewed pieces.

Sliding the mail off the larger envelope, Cassie took a moment to examine the package. It was addressed to her—odd that anything other than the occasional piece of junk mail should arrive here. The lack of a return address ramped up the mystery. She checked in on Lark, then entered her old bedroom, where she scooted onto the mattress.

The space was crowded with a mix of Cassie's childhood

treasures and her current belongings, Lark's things, and the portable crib her daughter found so offensive. At some point, she'd have to move her clothes into the closet and dresser instead of living out of crumbling cardboard boxes.

Cassie slipped her feet under the blankets and adjusted the pillows behind her back. Closing her eyes, she thought about how easy life had been growing up here, yet she hadn't recognized the comfort until long after she'd moved on.

"It's over."

Cassie jumped up, holding a hand over her chest. "You startled me."

"You're welcome." The exchange made little sense, but Lark's face showed great satisfaction.

"You know what time that makes it, right?"

"Time for the ocean." Lark set her fists on her sides in a way that made it very clear she knew exactly what time it was.

"Nope. It's rest time."

"I don't need rest. I'm big now. I don't even go to my school anymore."

Cassie had started referring to day care as school a few months earlier, when Lark insisted she should go to class on her own.

"Maybe so, but I still need you to have some quiet time. Come on. You can lie on my bed."

Lark cocked her head. She was bright, a genius even.

"Please."

"Okay. If I can read books."

Cassie blew out an exaggerated sigh. "Okay. You win." She set five children's books on the bed and lifted Lark onto the mattress. After hugs and kisses, she left her daughter happily "reading" a story to a stuffed rabbit.

Lark was the opposite of everything Cassie deserved. She was a true gift.

Cassie settled onto the couch with her laptop to send another email to her advisor. Shasta's time was the most important factor right now. Cassie had given up her room in California, so even if she could go back, there were complications. It was time to be real and leave the doctoral program, as well as her job teaching undergraduates, something she'd been surprised to love. And it meant losing that meager income.

Just as she set down the computer, ready to tear into the envelope, something pounded on the wall outside the door. Waiting a minute, she dropped her feet to the floor. Then it came again. She walked over and flung the door open, nearly screaming when she found Marshall on the other side, a cordless drill in one hand.

"What are you doing?" Her words were a harsh whisper.

Marshall held the drill higher. "Working."

"By my door?" The guy had all kinds of nerve and very few boundaries.

"Okay, okay. I can see where you're coming from." He leaned back against the wall. "I'm not used to you being here. I guess we should have mentioned what we were doing before getting started."

"Mentioned . . . or even *asked*."

"You really don't take help well, do you?" Marshall pulled a flat pencil from behind his ear.

"Marshall, quit flirting and catch this." Mr. Watkins appeared around the corner, then tossed a measuring tape to Marshall.

Cassie's face burned. Flirting? No way. Marshall would never look at her, the mother of a four-year-old, as someone to flirt with, and she was not even slightly open to any kind of romantic relationship.

"How ya doin' there, Cassie? It sure is nice that you're back home. Shasta has missed you fiercely, even if she'd never say so." Mr. Watkins pulled off his cap and scratched at the top of his wisp-covered head. An oversized quilted flannel nearly swallowed up his slight frame.

"You know her well, Mr. Watkins. It's sure good to see you

too." Being home, with her people, gave Cassie the same feeling she got sipping rich hot chocolate on a stormy night.

"We'll be out of your hair in no time. Just wanted to get this second railing up before Shasta gets back. She'd have a fit if she knew we were doing it. That woman won't take nothin' from nobody." He shook his head.

Marshall crossed his arms. "Must be a family trait."

It wasn't easy, but Cassie chose to ignore him. "Thank you, Mr. Watkins. This is way too kind of you. What can I pay you for your work and supplies?"

"Not one darn thing. This is what friends do for each other." He tipped his head and pressed the worn cap back on. "Shasta and I have been acquainted since we were kids. It's my privilege to help out."

"Well, you're appreciated by me. Thank you." Waving, she clicked the door shut. Mr. Watkins was a man of deep generosity. Yet his help made her feel as though she was failing. Cassie melted back into the couch cushions and slipped her finger under the seal of the manila envelope, lifting it open. For the briefest second, she considered biological warfare and anthrax but then dismissed those fears because, really, who would target her?

Inside was a thick stack of papers. They were numbered and rubber banded together. The top sheet had a simple message. *Read my story with an open mind and an open heart.*

Cassie snapped off the band and fanned through the papers, finding no way to identify the writer.

"Mama, I'm hungry." Lark dragged her blanket behind her. One side of her hair stood straight up like an eighties new-wave band member's. A crease lined her cheek. Quiet time was never quite long enough.

The strange manuscript that was probably intended for a completely different Cassie could wait. She picked up Lark and held her warm body tight as they snuggled.

Cassie's own eyes were growing heavy. Lack of solid sleep was taking a toll. She'd just decided to lie down on the couch for a minute when someone knocked on the door. Expecting Marshall, Cassie pasted on a smile she hoped would show how little his insertion into her life bothered her. Instead, she found Aubrey on the other side.

She rubbed the skin above her right eyebrow. "Hey. I'm sorry. Shasta wasn't able to come home today."

"I know. I was just there. It's been a tough one for her."

Cassie glanced at the clock on the wall. "I should be there." The guilt and embarrassment grew until they stole whatever strength she had left.

Aubrey seemed to take this move as an invitation. She stepped in and went right to Lark. "Hey there, little one. I'm glad you're getting use out of the blankie."

Lark held up what was left of the once-purple fabric.

The memory flew to the front of Cassie's mind. Aubrey had made the blanket for Lark right after she was born. The pregnancy had been a secret, kept tucked under oversized T-shirts until the last month. At that point, no layer could hide Lark's plan to change the world. Thoughts came of that hospital visit the first day and Shasta and Aubrey there with gifts, pretending they weren't completely disappointed. That's when Cassie became determined to distance herself from Shasta and Gull's Bay. They'd already taken in one little girl. She wouldn't have them feeling the burden of her daughter too.

Aubrey sat on the floor next to Lark. It was truly impressive the way she stayed in shape, able to get on and off the ground like a teenager, while Cassie was already feeling age creep into her joints.

"I was just wondering if I could take this sweet girl to the beach for a walk; then maybe we could have a special treat at the bakery." Aubrey looked to Cassie, her eyes sparkling with excitement. "What do you think? Could you use a little time to yourself?"

The answer was of course yes, but Lark was *her* daughter. She was supposed to be able to handle all the care that went into raising her. "That's really kind, but I don't want to put you out."

"Seems like I was the one who offered. And look at this sweet child. It would be such a blessing to spend time with her. I promise not to take my eyes off her."

"I need to go to the beach." Lark hopped up and collected her flip-flops, forgetting it was much chillier on the Oregon coast.

"Are you sure?" Cassie bit her bottom lip.

"I am." Aubrey touched her forearm. "Please let me help. Shasta is part of all of us. I need to feel like I'm helping too."

The conversation had grown heavy. Cassie's shoulders tightened under the weight. "All right. I could use some time to get the rest of the house ready for Shasta."

Aubrey looked around. "It seems ready to me. Why not take the time to do something you love? Draw. Write. I don't know . . . something that feels indulgent." She grinned. "You deserve a break."

Lark held Cassie's cheeks in her hands and kissed her face. "Bye, Mommy. I'll see you after I'm good and done."

Emotion came with Cassie's smile. "You have all the fun, okay? And listen to Aunt Aubrey."

Lark signaled with a thumbs-up, then headed down the steps with handrails on both sides now, Aubrey a step ahead in case Lark fell, just the way Cassie would do it.

She shut the door and walked into the kitchen that overlooked the living area. After starting to load dishes in the half-sized dishwasher, Cassie remembered the mysterious papers, still unread.

# 6

How many times was I supposed to lose everything and still keep moving forward? I think that's the question I'm attempting to answer by putting my story onto these pages. Maybe by taking it all in, putting the pieces together in one flowing story, maybe then I'll be able to see the whole of it. All my pain in one place. All my wanderings and wonderings sewn together. Maybe it will be here that I find my peace in the storm that has raged over my life.

If you are reading this, then you are meant to have these words. They may be part of your story too. At the very least, I'm praying that, in knowing where I've been and how I ended up where I am today, you, the reader, will be blessed with a deeper understanding of the love our God has for each one of us.

All I ever wanted was a child. As a little girl, I carried my baby dolls with me wherever my mother dragged us. When we moved, which we did on average every six months, I made certain that each of my little replicas of a person had a safe place in the car, no one left behind in another life that was meant to be forgotten. My plans for motherhood were being established even then, at the beginning of my memories. I would do it differently than the way

I'd been mothered, and I would do it well. Being a mother was my identity long before I was old enough to make it reality.

The first part of my plan began to take shape in high school. I didn't date, though it wasn't because I wasn't asked. More than anything, fear kept me away from boys and on the path to my planned future. My picture-perfect future had been carefully plucked from television families and magazines. I poured myself into my studies. To meet a man who could support a large family while I stayed home and mothered my growing children, I would need to attend a good college. To do that, scholarships would be a must. And I earned them. Many of them. I received enough in grants and scholarships to pay my way through UCLA. I was living the dream I had designed for myself, every little detail falling into place.

While my studies were in psychology, my true aim was the now-scoffed-at MRS degree. I wanted the other half of my perfect equation. A man who would stand by me while we built a family like those on the evening TV shows. I was to be the matriarch of a modern-day, financially stable Walton family. How satisfying it would have been to fall in love with a man who had that last name!

I was halfway into my sophomore year when Topher asked if I would want to catch a movie with him sometime. My heart must have tried an actual flip-flop. Topher was the image my mind had glued together as my other half. He was tall but not awkwardly so, came from a family that wasn't lacking for anything, had a solid future, and those crystal blue eyes—those were the end of me.

It took a couple of years to convince Topher that I was everything he needed, but I set my mind to the task and accomplished the goal. Two months after my undergraduate graduation and Topher receiving his master's, we were married. No one from my family was in attendance, but it didn't matter to me. They were my past. Topher represented the future.

I reluctantly agreed to hold off on children for a couple of years. Topher was busy making contacts and a name for himself in the world of corporate business. I worked for a local nonprofit, helping at-risk youth find enrichment activities while encouraging them to pursue their dreams. The job was better than anything I'd hoped for with only a bachelor's degree, but my hopes of children were never far from my mind.

Two years passed, yet my husband still wasn't ready to add to our family. Topher's answer to my increasing maternal cravings came home with him one day in a crate. It wasn't even a dog. I'd always pictured a yellow lab or a golden retriever as part of my perfect family. Topher, however, brought me a cat. Not a kitten or a cuddly companion either. She came with papers, her lineage laid out as if she were the product of a royal line. And she hated me as much as I resented her.

If his plan was to get me to question my ability to care for a living creature, he almost won. Mavis—that's what I called the possessed creature—made me very aware of my lurking sin nature. She shredded anything fabric—my clothing, the curtains, the upholstery. Many mornings, I'd wake early to have my quiet time with the Lord, only to find Mavis in my chair, as if she felt my dedication to my faith was as superfluous as Topher did. The first time I tried to remove her ended with three angry red lines etched down my forearm and my Bible study taking place at the kitchen table. After that, I used the broom to retake my cozy seat by the window.

~~

Aubrey and Lark's return startled Cassie awake. She jumped up, wiping drool from her cheek as she rose.

Lark had a brown line around her lip that she kept swiping at with her tongue. Leftover spaghetti wasn't going to sound at all tempting for dinner now that she'd been to Mrs. Collins's bakery.

Grabbing a paper towel, Cassie ran the tip under the tap, then bent down in front of Lark. "Did you have a good time?"

"All the way. Aunt Awby got me these boots." She kicked

up a foot clad in purple plastic with silver glitter. When she stomped, lights lit up around the sole.

"You didn't have to do that." Cassie looked to Aubrey as she twirled one of Lark's brown curls around her finger. "I would have gotten her some soon."

"Then I'm glad I did it when I did. Cassie, sometimes—and by sometimes, I mean all the time—you try to do everything on your own. If you don't loosen your grip, you're not going to be any good to Shasta or to this sweet girl." She pulled a paper bag out of her purple tote. "This is from Mrs. Collins. She says for you to stop by soon and be sure you're getting enough to eat."

The scent of fresh pastries contacted Cassie's nose before she could reach for the sack. "That was so nice of her."

Aubrey shook her head, still looking at Cassie. "Pride. That's the beast you need to conquer." She leaned down to hug Lark and received a chocolatey kiss on the cheek as a reward. Aubrey gave Cassie a quick squeeze. "Let these people love on you, okay?" she said as she jogged down the stairs like a teenager heading out on a date.

*Pride?* Cassie closed the door. She was a lot of things, but prideful was not one of them. "Come on, Lark. You need a bath." She ushered her daughter down the hall, wondering what could possibly make Aubrey think she was prideful.

# 7

Nora would never admit it to Ferris, but she sometimes relished the nights when he worked late. There was no doubt that she loved him, but when he was away, once the girls were in bed, it was like her own personal vacation.

Usually, she'd pour herself a drink and snuggle onto the couch, the remote in her hand, and watch whatever she wanted, typically a crime drama that Ferris would tear apart as totally unrealistic. But tonight, she had another matter to attend to, one she wanted some privacy for.

It was a weak substitution, but Nora brewed a cup of peppermint tea to sip while she sifted through the results of the DNA test. For the first time in months, the laptop booted up quickly. A click on the link in the email, and she was face-to-face with the side of her she'd buried in an unmarked grave.

The first result was nearly ridiculous enough to make her laugh—nearly. Yes, she might have wavy hair. In fact, she did, but Nora could look in any mirror to find that information without shelling out a hundred bucks.

She sifted through the pages of useless trivia dredged from her genes. While she was more likely to be diagnosed with Parkinson's, she wasn't a carrier of Gaucher disease—whatever that was. She sorted the results into two columns: from her father's side, or from the egg donor—she couldn't assign the label *mother* to someone who skipped town on a baby.

Running a hand over her face, Nora tried to remind her body how important it was to not let stress take advantage. She had no real way of deciding which gene mutation came from which contributor, even if she had a suspicion that every disease she carried was from the maternal side.

She skimmed through, not resting too long on any one segment. It would be too easy to let fear take over. Fortunately, nothing relevant to her current stage of life showed up.

Absently, she clicked to the next set of results. Yes, she had a high percentage of Scottish ancestry. No surprise there. Her red hair and green eyes told her that much.

She should have stopped there, closed the tab, maybe even dropped the laptop in the trash, never to open it again. But she didn't.

Nora clicked again.

Coastal Coffee was transformed for St. Patrick's Day. Green streamers decorated the wall, while a pot of gold coins took up a chunk of counter space. Cassie took in her daughter, wearing not a speck of the traditional hues, though Lark had managed almost every other color. Her legs were covered in red leggings topped with a multilayered tutu of pink and glitter. On top of that was a bright orange Oregon State University Beavers shirt, a gift from Shasta at Christmastime. Only Lark could be perfectly beautiful in colors that made Cassie squint.

If only Cassie were the sort of mom who was comfortable using a leash to keep her kid close. Lark had already decided that, with the coffee shop being downstairs of their home, she clearly owned that space too. She ran from one end of the room to the other, singing at the top of her lungs and leaping toward

the decorations, way too close to the mostly good-natured pa-
trons.

The only way to draw Lark near was to behave as if Cassie
didn't even notice her daughter's antics. Lack of attention made
the preschooler confident. On her next run by, Cassie reached
out and grabbed her. The squeals that resulted may have been
worse than the prior performance, but at least she was contained.

"Oh my goodness. Cassie?"

The voice froze Cassie in her movements. Nora had been
two years ahead of her in school, and she'd married the only
boy Cassie had ever had a crush on—at least until college. A
calming breath did not manage to alleviate Cassie's shock. She
took control of her expression before turning to see what waited
behind her. "Nora. It's been a long time."

Nora rubbed her protruding belly. Her red waves were wound
into a bun at the base of her skull. If Cassie had tried this, she
would have looked severe or matronly, but on Nora, the style
looked sophisticated. "I heard you had a little one. Isn't she
something."

As if looking for a compliment, Nora glanced now at her
own daughter, a girl dressed as if she were a miniature busi-
nesswoman, her strawberry-blond hair formed into perfect
ponytails. "This is my daughter Gwendolyn." She pushed the
stroller's visor back. "And this is Peyton, my other daughter."

Her children, or models she'd hired to play her kids? "Well,
they're both something too."

Lark thrashed side to side, nearly knocking Cassie off balance.

"We just stopped in to get their daddy a coffee." Nora patted
her belly again. "Will your daughter be joining the preschool?
The church has a great program. It's very important for children
to be socialized, but I'm sure you know all about that."

Marshall came around the counter and handed Nora a paper
cup with a brown sleeve. "There you go."

"Thank you." She took a sniff. "I miss coffee, but it's not

good for the little one, so I avoid all caffeine." There was a hint of something in her voice—a crack?

Cassie bit the tip of her tongue. It wasn't until after their conversation ended and Nora left, the bell on the door jingling, that she was able to relax.

"A friend of yours, huh?"

She leveled a cool look Marshall's way. "Not exactly."

"She was right about the preschool, though." He crossed his arms and leaned against the counter.

"Let me guess." Cassie stuffed her oversized wrap in her bag. "You work there too."

Marshall's laughter was deep, but not in the same way Mr. Watkins's was. There was a silliness in Marshall's tone.

Lark lunged for this stranger who seemed to be around every corner, and he took her into his arms without hesitation. "Funny," he said with a flatness that emphasized his sarcasm. "I don't work in the preschool, but since you're being so nosy this morning, I'll tell you why I know. When I'm not busy being the barista boss or taking classes, I volunteer to work with middle-school kids at the church."

Of course he did. "Interesting . . . I took you for a jock."

He cocked an eyebrow and held Lark back. "Did you hear what your mama just said? A jock? As if there's anything wrong with that."

"You're Marshall." Lark wrinkled her nose, the joke far above her knock knock–style humor.

"That's right. I think she's confused because of my swagger." He jiggled Lark around until she laughed. "But seriously . . ." He returned his attention to Cassie. "The preschool is great. The kids always seem to be having a blast. You should check into it."

She reached for Lark. "Maybe I will. But for now, we need to get to the hospital." Cassie followed Marshall's gaze out the front window.

Mrs. Collins pushed her way across the street through the wind, her umbrella about to turn inside out. The door jingled as she shoved into the coffee shop. "It's a blustery one out there." Cassie had always thought of the dear bakery owner as a character straight out of a classic children's novel. She was a bit plump, kept her hair in a bun on top of her head, and she almost always had an apron tied around her middle. Mrs. Collins wasn't nearly as old as she dressed—her flawless skin attested to that—but her hair had streaks of gray and her eyes tended to twinkle like a mischievous grandmother's. "Looks like I'm just in time." She tapped a palm on each of Lark's chubby cheeks, then dropped a kiss onto Cassie's. "I thought Lark and I could bake some cookies. I assume you're heading over to pick up Shasta today."

"I am, but I packed a wrap. I'm going to tie Lark to my back so I can have my hands free." Cassie had spent hours after Lark went to sleep perfecting the skill of tying a bag of flour behind her without tipping it over. Google had a way of making things look easier than they actually were.

Lark's nose wrinkled. "That sounds like a baby thing."

"It's used for children bigger than you." Cassie's voice sounded like a beggar's rather than that of a mother in charge.

"Nonsense. If I don't take my chance now, I'll have Shasta to compete with too. This town is full of grandmas wanting some time with this little one." She tapped Lark's nose.

Something odd was happening here. Had the town met and scheduled out Lark's childcare without even conferring with Cassie? Surely they wouldn't. . . .

"I've set out my entire collection of ocean-themed cookie cutters. There's even an octopus."

Lark drummed her fingers on her lips, her excitement filling the room.

"I can't very well say no to an opportunity like that, can I?" Cassie really wondered. *Could* she say no? But the chance was too good for her to snub. She could be there for her aunt, without distraction. The doctor assured Cassie there'd been no more issues with hallucinations. But what if they came back? How was she supposed to keep Lark from being frightened when the thought of seeing Shasta confused and disoriented shook Cassie, a supposedly grown woman?

When Cassie arrived in Shasta's room, there was no sign of agitation on her aunt's face. In fact, Shasta slept so peacefully that Cassie settled into a chair near the window, letting her aunt continue with her rest. The nurse had suggested she help Shasta get dressed while waiting for the doctor's final sign-off.

If there was anything Cassie had learned since becoming a parent, it was never to wake anyone . . . ever.

At the last minute before leaving the shop, she'd run upstairs and replaced the giant scarf with the manuscript from the envelope. The story had woken her up more than one time the night before with musings and suspicions about the next chapter.

As a child, Cassie had been an avid reader, but college and motherhood had stripped her of that luxury. This story was like finding a part of herself waiting for her return home to claim it.

She slid the papers from the bag and returned to where she'd left off.

As if having an absent husband and a cat sent by Satan wasn't enough, I also had another birthday coming just around the next flip of the calendar page. How a woman who'd planned her life around future children could be approaching thirty and still childless was a mystery that woke me up in the middle of the night with panic. I wasn't going to keep going like I'd been doing, year after year, waiting for Topher to finally be ready. No. The time had come, and no matter what Topher had for an excuse this time, I wasn't going to accept it.

The night of my birthday approached. Topher had made dinner reservations at my favorite beachside restaurant. He'd been asking me for days what I wanted, and I always said I'd answer that question while we were at my birthday dinner. Of course this made no sense to my practical husband. How could he provide what I wouldn't tell him until the moment he was to provide it?

As we sat on the terrace, our table lit by little white lights strung above us, I stared out into the ocean. The sun was setting, casting oranges and pinks along the water that crashed to the beach, the waves cresting and rolling over, brilliant white tipping the blue. "This is nearly perfect, don't you think?" I didn't look his way as I asked the question. I couldn't take the risk of seeing his eyes.

"It is. Happy birthday." Topher's hand rested on mine, the warmth of his palm a welcome feeling after a year that felt distant and cold. "Are you ready to tell me what you want this year?"

Nerves bubbled inside of me. "I'm thirty."

He chuckled. "Yes, I know."

"Do you remember when we were dating . . . the dreams we had for the future, for a family?" I might have imagined it, but the muscles in his hand seemed to tighten.

"I do. We were so young then. All those things seemed easy."

I pulled my hand free and ventured a look his way. "It's time now, Topher. I want children, and I'm not getting any younger." I took a deep breath, ready to fight for what I was demanding, but something about the look on his face stopped me.

"All right. Let's move forward." He leaned back. "I'm fairly established now. Our income is sufficient for us, and we'll be able to support a child, pay tuition, and that sort of thing. I agree."

It wasn't lost on me that my husband sounded like a man negotiating a deal, but I really didn't care why he was ready. He'd given the okay, and once we had that first baby, he'd fall in love with her. I knew he would. And that love would lead us to a happy houseful. I was still so foolish at thirty, naïve and hopeful. But that night stands out to me like a beam of light in a world that would turn very dark. I hold on to those moments when it all seemed possible, when my future appeared whole, and not a fragmented story with sharp edges.

"We have those discharge orders." The nurse swept into the room, waking Shasta and giving Cassie a thorough startle. "Oh. Not dressed yet, I see. Did you need help with that?"

Cassie hopped to her feet, shoving the manuscript into her bag. "No. I was waiting for her to wake up. Sorry about that."

"Okay. I'll be back in just a minute. I forgot something at the nurses' station." She bustled off, leaving a trail of disappointment in her wake.

"Cassie . . . how are you doing, sweetie?" Shasta's voice was thin, but she seemed coherent. "Are we going home?"

"Yes, we are. Let's get you dressed, and we can be on our way." Cassie pulled Shasta's clothes out from under the envelope of papers. Setting them on the edge of the bed, she tried to peel the blankets back.

Shasta's fingers worked the fabric as she held tight. "I can do it on my own."

"I'm sure you can, but I could also help." This was a negotiation Cassie was used to, having it daily with Lark.

Shasta ran her hand over her scalp in a jerking motion. "Just let me be." The tone had Cassie stepping back as if burned.

Shasta tugged at the gown, finally managing to wriggle the left sleeve over her elbow. For a moment, she seemed tangled, and Cassie fought her every instinct to step in and take over. "I don't want any fuss being made over me, you understand?"

"Of course."

"The kid is not with you."

"Lark? She's with Mrs. Collins. They're baking ocean-themed cookies." Cassie had never baked with Lark. Honestly, she'd rarely baked at all. The joy on her daughter's face at the opportunity to create sugary treats was easy to imagine.

The nurse stepped in. She observed Shasta's struggles and gave Cassie a questioning look. Without asking, she scooped up the T-shirt from the end of the bed and started threading Shasta's arms through the openings. With the nurse, there was no complaining. But if Cassie had dared to make a move like that, her aunt would have firmly put her back into place.

"I jotted down a YouTube channel that may come in handy for you. They talk about ways to make caregiving easier on the patient and the caregiver. There are videos covering everything from monitoring medications to choosing clothes that make dressing simple."

As the nurse adjusted the long sleeves of the T-shirt, it was obvious Cassie hadn't chosen well.

They went over the discharge orders; then Cassie was sent to move the car to the patient-loading area while a CNA prepared Shasta for her wheelchair ride out of the hospital.

As Cassie pulled the car around, she remembered leaving the hospital with a newborn Lark. She'd been unprepared, scared to death at the reality that this child's life was in her hands. Today didn't feel a whole lot different, except now she had Lark *and* Shasta to look after, and she didn't know how to handle either of them.

The drive was quiet, oddly so. Shasta stared out the window as if she were traveling through places she'd never been before.

They arrived in front of the shop, parking in the handicapped space, thanks to the new temporary placard they'd been presented. Quite a crowd was visible through the front window. Cassie glanced across the street at the bakery, wondering if she should get Lark first or help Shasta up the stairs before retrieving her daughter, finally deciding on the latter.

Leaving most of Shasta's things in the car, Cassie opened the door and walked alongside her aunt to the coffee shop. As they reached the entrance, it swung open and applause took over. Friends from around the community stood in the dining area, welcome home signs waving in the air. Even the woman who seemed to always be typing away on a laptop in the corner booth had looked up and smiled, an octopus cookie on a plate in front of her.

Lark sat on the counter, a cookie in one hand and a blue stain across her upper lip. "Happy birthday, Aunty Shasta." It wasn't even close to Shasta's birthday, but Lark had only seen gatherings like this one at those kinds of celebrations.

Shasta moved around the room, her hands gripped together in a tight ball. Her gaze shot like a missile to the corner booth. Her arm reached back, grabbing Cassie's and bringing her close. "Watch out for that woman. She's a spy."

# 8

Nora eased the door shut, the sounds of an audiobook playing in Gwendolyn's room. She'd probably drift off to sleep today after their walk and time on the beach. If she hadn't already worn her daughter out, Nora would have kept her up and skipped room time all together, giving herself the distraction she needed from the chocolate ice cream in the freezer and the laptop, with its frightening results haunting her.

When Ferris had asked how she was doing that morning, she nearly broke down and told him what she'd found, but old habits were strong. She'd kept it all to herself, needing to work through it alone before laying it out for her husband.

She grabbed a spoon, opened the freezer, and scraped a thin layer from the ice cream. The taste was better than she'd imagined—creamy and sweet. And now she'd need to check her blood sugar. And she'd need to have some protein. Everything around her had become complicated.

The laptop couldn't be avoided forever. She had school-board business to attend to, and she was the class mom for Gwendolyn's preschool class. The machine came to life, popping open the same page she'd slammed shut.

Half sister.

She had a sibling out there. It wasn't really a surprise. She'd wondered, especially when she was in high school and felt alone as the second half of a very small family. Yet nothing could have lessened the shock of seeing the words in front of her. She blinked away tears, banishing her weakness. It meant nothing. Just another person on this planet who'd likely been abandoned by the same woman.

If her father had been there, he'd tell her she was tougher than this. The results of a little DNA test could not hurt her. Of course, if her father had been there, Nora would never have sent in her saliva and placed herself in this position.

Clicking over to her profile page for the DNA testing service, she noticed a red number one in the corner. Nora stretched out her shoulders. Those numbers had always held power over her. She kept her phone messages read and her email inbox empty, which was why she had to click now.

Hello,

My name is Becca. I'm twenty-five years old, and I live in New Jersey. Finding a sister here, in this virtual world with only DNA to link us, is a shock, but I'm guessing you weren't expecting to find us either. Maddie insists we give you space to collect your thoughts, but know that we're here if you ever want to talk.

Becca (for our older sisters, Maddie and Lex, too)

P.S. Feel free to use my email address—beccasemail@gmail.com

Cassie released a sigh after inhaling the scent rising from the two full cups of mint tea. Lark, after a busy day of visitors, cookie devouring, and no nap, had gone to bed early without even the tiniest complaint. Downstairs, the shop was closed and everyone had gone home. The house was quiet, aside from the crashing of waves in the distance and the ticking of the large clock in the living room.

Setting the mug in front of Shasta, Cassie hesitated. Was she supposed to check the temperature? Was it too full? "Be careful. It's hot."

Shasta nodded, tapped her fingers on the cup's rim, then wandered back to the windows. She hadn't said much since coming home, didn't even mention the additional railing along the stairs.

Joining her aunt, Cassie sipped tea and stared out as the setting sun cast colors onto the waves. "I don't remember my mother." She hadn't planned to say it, but the words took control, and there they were. Shasta might not have much time to relay any memories about Diane. Whether it was her mind that betrayed her or the ability to speak clearly, both would soon be gone. "What was she like?"

Shasta walked away from the view, pacing back and forth in the living room. "Diane was my cousin. She had a baby, but then you came here . . . and you looked . . ." She scrubbed her fingers over her forehead. "I don't know what. Diane was my cousin. But you are my girl."

Covering her heart with a hand, Cassie curled her lips around dry teeth, emotions ready to take advantage of the need for a good night's sleep. The way Shasta had answered, her sentences broken by whatever was going on in her brain, made her question whether it was too late to get a deeper understanding of where she'd come from. Before she could ask Shasta another question, her aunt left the room, her cane making a *tap-tap-tap* across the bare floor.

The sounds of cupboards opening and closing came from the studio.

Cassie followed to the hall, trying to look interested in the painting on the wall and not as if she were a babysitter. After five minutes that seemed to go on for seven hours and came with a great deal of worry about Lark waking up, she gave up stealth and stepped into the room.

Shasta had removed everything in the lower cupboards, leaving a minefield of tripping hazards all around her. "I'm not sure what I came in here for, but it's important." She looked to Cassie, an expression that was so much like Lark's when she felt unsure and frightened creased into her face.

"Let's not even worry about that tonight. I can't believe how tired I am after so many visitors and all. You must be wiped out." She turned her body just a hair toward the door, hoping to initiate the plan.

Shasta nodded. "I want to go to bed."

"We need to get your bedtime medications taken first. Did you want any of your tea?" It had to be cold by now. "Maybe something to eat?"

Shasta shuffled down the hall and into the kitchen, where she found the plate of remaining cookies and ate two.

The screech of packing tape being ripped off cardboard woke Cassie. Her heart hammered so hard and loud that she struggled to listen for more sounds over the pounding. Maybe it had been a dream. Taking long, calming breaths, she relaxed against the half of a pillow Lark had left her. The steady roar of the ocean was the only sound now, so she let herself relax and drift back toward sleep.

Her thoughts slipped to undergraduate days and the lies she'd told Shasta to cover her rebellious behaviors. She'd been two hours away but felt the embarrassment as strongly as if she were standing in front of her aunt. Shame always took the upper hand when Cassie was vulnerable and tired, just as alcohol had been a convenient fix to her paralyzing shyness.

The *thunk* of something landing on the floor made her eyes

snap open again. Definitely not a dream this time. Someone was in the house. Cassie slid to the end of the bed, extricating herself from Lark and the blankets. Her search of the small room in the dim glow of the moonlight produced only a twisted metal curtain rod to use as a potential weapon.

She moved quietly, managing to avoid the plank that always screamed in the middle of the night. The door was cracked. She eased out soundlessly, though her heart jumped to her throat when she realized almost every light in the place was on.

The sound of movement came from the studio, like boxes being dragged across the hardwood. The door was open. Cassie lowered her flimsy club. A few more steps, and her suspicions were confirmed. Shasta was the vicious criminal mastermind she'd been so afraid of.

Cassie leaned the rod against the corner in the hall. "What's got you up so early this morning?" It could hardly even be called morning, as the sun was nowhere near rising.

"What is all this stuff? I don't know these things." She yanked Lark's swimsuit from a box and waved it around.

"That's Lark's. Remember my daughter?" It was like telling Shasta all over again that Cassie had gotten pregnant and would be raising her baby alone, no prospects for a husband or the traditional plan.

"I know who Lark is." She scowled, something she'd never done even when Cassie went through a sassy stage at twelve. "It's a mess in here. I can't find anything."

"How about we get you back to bed, and I'll clean this all up in the morning?"

Shasta ran her hand over the top of a box, rubbing it as if it were a pet. Without a word, she turned and shuffled toward her bedroom, then closed the door.

The brief interaction had snatched any drowsiness from Cassie, leaving her ticking off a list of worries. She'd barely made it as a single mother with a small income. Now she was the caregiver for two people, and her take-home pay was non-existent. The coffee shop had never provided a swell of money, but Shasta's artwork had kept the two of them afloat with a little extra money here and there.

A hot cup of coffee was what Cassie needed. So much so that she considered sneaking downstairs to make herself one. Then her stomach growled. She'd noticed a couple of extra scones in the display case. That was what her belly was craving.

Before committing to her plan, she listened at both bedroom doors to assure herself that Lark and Shasta were both sleeping.

Then Cassie padded down the stairs. The scent of freshly ground coffee beans filled the air day and night. It was enough to wake any bit of her that hadn't already given up on returning to sleep. She started up the espresso machine and retrieved a scone from the case, taking a bite before setting it on a plate.

As the espresso maker sputtered, she spotted the garbage bag she'd brought down earlier, meaning to take it to the large can at the curb. Now that they'd passed midnight, it was officially garbage day, and the truck often came before dawn.

Cassie tugged off her socks and stuffed them into the pockets of her robe, then hoisted the bag over a shoulder and walked out the front door. Thin clouds floated over the nearly full moon. It was an eerie kind of peace, the kind that sent a shiver down her spine but allowed her to breathe deeper than she had in days.

After depositing the bag into the bin at the curb, Cassie wrapped the bathrobe tighter around herself and stood mesmerized by the vast sky and the familiar sounds of home. Gull's Bay was more than a place to visit; a part of her had been waiting for her physical self to return here. The salt air, the sticky cold wind that whipped her hair—they brought her back to herself.

When she finally turned back to the building, their home and business, Cassie was ready to take another run at life. But when she reached for the doorknob, all positivity crashed. It held tight. She'd locked herself out with not even a cell phone to call for help.

The only option she had was to resort to a method she'd used a few times in high school when she'd come back after curfew and her aunt wanted to teach her a lesson.

Cassie glanced around before sliding between the warped wooden fence and the side of the coffee shop and gallery that took up the ground floor of the house. Wind whistled through the space, deafening her ability to hear anyone coming up behind her. Their little town wasn't prone to crime, especially when the tourists weren't packed in the hotels and Airbnbs, acting as if the locals of Gull's Bay were there only to serve them.

Her fingers trailed over the siding and guided her around the corner, where a faint glow from the apartment above cast a dim light across the postage stamp–sized yard. Cassie shoved a crate below the window she hoped still had a faulty latch and jiggled until she heard the *clink* of metal falling over metal. After that, the window slid open with ease. She extended her arms into the opening and stretched her fingers to find the edge of the counter. It had been years since the last time she'd attempted this stunt, and even though she was still in her midtwenties, the athletic feat was much harder than she'd remembered. Digging nails into the pressed board underneath the counter, Cassie strained with muscles that hadn't been tested in years. The lower casing scraped along her stomach, sending pain through her middle, but she was almost there.

As she lifted her right knee into the opening, a crash reverberated through the night. She shot forward as if blown from a cannon and landed in a pile on the hard tile.

The side of her face was damp with the cleaning solution they used to sanitize the floors at the end of the day. Cassie wiped herself dry, closed the window, and tried to right everything she'd wronged.

At least her life still held some form of adventure. By the

time she was upstairs again with both a coffee and a scone, any option to sleep had been erased. Instead, Cassie snuggled onto the couch, covered her legs with a soft blanket, and pulled out the manuscript. She'd been finding moments to read a page or two here and there, but she cherished the time to dig in. Yet a part of her struggled with guilt over this pleasure. After all, it had to be meant for someone else.

Month after month, my disappointment grew. I wasn't pregnant. As my half birthday came and went, I gained a growing sense of doom. Would God really have taken me this far just to have my dreams crushed?

Topher refused to see a doctor. He said if it were important to me, I could go ahead, but he was fine waiting until it happened. This should have been another clue to what kind of man I'd married, but I was a great deceiver of myself. I continued to believe that Topher would change when our child was born, that seeing his own eyes in his child would break open the tough layers of his heart. But I'd have to get pregnant for that plan to happen.

I scheduled an appointment with a specialist but couldn't get in for three months. The receptionist assured me they usually had patients try for a year to achieve pregnancy before being seen. She believed I'd be pregnant before my appointment time arrived.

That didn't happen.

The doctor was kind, an older man who'd seen the fertility game change a hundred times during his career. He took me through a typical examination, then ordered enough blood work to nearly run me dry, but I did everything he suggested with enthusiasm. This was the man who had the power to make me a mother. Maybe I was putting too much faith in a human being, but desperation was driving me, even then.

Topher assured me that there wasn't a problem and the tests

would come back normal. But if that were so, why wasn't I expecting a baby? My ability to put up with his nonchalant way of seeing our empty home began to wear thin. I couldn't hold back my discouragement and frustrations. This only led to longer days at the office, an increase in business travel, and few nights together.

I felt like I was losing everything I'd hoped to have without ever getting to experience that life. And Topher just didn't seem to care anymore. Had I overlooked who he really was in my effort to control my future? God had taught me many things over my adult years, but giving up control of my life to Him was still a feat I hadn't managed.

When, still not pregnant, I saw the doctor again, he dropped some heartbreaking news on me. Not only was there an actual cause for our failed attempts at making a family, *I* was the problem. My body was betraying me, leaving me, a young woman with depleted eggs, on the verge of menopause. Premature ovarian failure, or POF, he called it. All I heard was failure.

Upon leaving that appointment, I rushed into the restroom and vomited. Without the information I'd just received, I would have thought throwing up was a good sign. Instead, I crumpled onto the tile floor and sobbed until the receptionist knocked on the door to see if I was all right. I didn't have an answer for her. At the time, I thought I might never be all right again.

A few days later, I was contacted by the fertility clinic. I'd rushed out before the doctor could give me a list of options. The choices were limited, but they existed, and after another week or two of mourning my dream, I started to explore the possibilities.

Adoption seemed so obvious. Though I longed to hold a baby in my arms, I found I was also open to an older child, someone who needed a mother as much as I needed a child.

Our anniversary was approaching, so I decided to present this plan to Topher as we enjoyed our special dinner at home, food brought in from our favorite restaurant. In hindsight, I can see that I should have brought this up in a public place.

Topher listened to me talk, his face growing hard and redness working up his neck. When I finally asked what he thought, the cork blew. In one quick motion, he was out of his seat, his chair crashing to the floor. "I am not bringing someone else's child into this house. We're not running an orphanage here, do you understand me?"

That was the first time I felt afraid of my husband, but it wouldn't be the last.

# 9

Nora stepped into the kitchen just in time to see her husband delight the girls by pouring coffee from the pot into his travel mug in a lengthening stream. Why couldn't she do things that made them giggle? It was like she had a missing gene, one that controlled fun.

Gwendolyn slapped her hand onto the counter, smacking her spoon on the way. Soggy cereal shot sideways, hitting the wall.

A knot tightened in Nora's stomach. She hurried to the sink, wet a washcloth, and wiped up the glob as it snaked toward the floor.

"I would have gotten that." Ferris took the rag from her hand. He kissed the back of her neck, sending chills across her skin. "I can't wait for tonight."

Nora closed her eyes for a moment, picturing her calendar.

He twisted her around to face him, a giant smile lighting his features. "You don't remember what tonight is, do you?"

The scramble inside her brain was like a panicked toddler.

"Mom and Dad have the kids. It's our night out."

Of course. Where was her mind? They did this the third Friday of every month. She shrugged. "I know."

He slowly nodded, the twinkle in his eyes saying he didn't

buy that for a second. "You should just let me have this one. It's not very often I'm more on top of it than you."

Nora tipped her head. "Don't get cocky. I'm carrying a human around inside of me, and ninety-nine percent of the time, I have to remind you what's on the calendar." She kissed his cheek.

"That's gross." Gwendolyn climbed down from her seat at the counter. "I don't want any more cereal. It's mushy."

Nora sighed. "It's mushy because you take all morning to eat it."

The only answer her daughter gave was a nonchalant shrug that seemed too familiar for Nora's comfort.

"I've got to run." Ferris squeezed her hand, then kissed Peyton and Gwendolyn. "I'll see you tonight, at the restaurant?"

She nodded, her stomach growling as she thought of the desserts she wouldn't be able to eat. At least the news she had to share with him while they had the rare opportunity to talk uninterrupted would probably cause her appetite to flee faster than her mother had.

Ferris waved as he left. A second later, the wall rumbled as the garage door opened, then again as it shut after her husband drove away. He was a good man. Always careful, being sure they were secure, with the house closed to danger. Some days this rubbed her like sandpaper, but today, it felt like love.

"Come on, girls. We need to get Gwendolyn to preschool."

"I don't want to go. There's no one I like there." Gwendolyn crossed her arms, her face scrunched.

"I wonder if that's one of the lessons you're learning. How to make friends and get along with others?"

"Fine. But I don't like playing with boys, and that's not going to change." She huffed down the hall toward the room she now shared with Peyton so that they could use the other for the new baby.

Gwendolyn would change that attitude soon enough. Probably far too soon for her father's liking. Nora couldn't figure out what the big deal was. So there were a lot more boys than girls in the preschool. Seemed like a lucky break. Nora had always had a better time hanging out with the guys. Gwendolyn would learn that with girls came drama. Who needed that?

Maybe that was the answer to the question that kept Nora awake. Should she respond to the email? It seemed a logical way to fill in any missing health information, but the woman who'd sent it—Nora's *sister*—seemed like the kind of person who would want to develop a relationship.

Cassie woke to the *click-click-click* of Shasta in the rocking chair. As sleep fell away and the drowsy fog thinned, she remembered this wasn't just another carefree morning. Despite every internal instinct, Cassie was an adult, supposedly responsible and capable.

"Good morning." Cassie eased off the couch and knocked the papers from her lap to the floor, where they skittered in all directions. "Can I get you some coffee and something to eat?" It would have to be decaf, but Shasta hopefully wouldn't remember the doctor's orders. She'd always been offended by the idea of decaffeinated coffee, as if the modification was an insult to the original bean

Shasta rose from the chair on her own after three attempts, then stared down at the scattered papers. "What is that?"

"It's a . . . story. Just something I got in the mail. Actually, I'm not at all sure where it came from or who sent it. It's a mystery." Cassie shrugged.

The lines forming on Shasta's forehead resembled a painting of gulls far in the distance. On her knees, Cassie scooped the papers into a pile that would need to be organized later.

Lark dragged herself into the room.

"Morning, sunshine." The greeting was plump with forced cheerfulness, the best Cassie could manage with a kink in her neck and a strong need for a caffeine boost.

Lark looked up at her, a snarl on her face and her blankie hanging out of her mouth. The thing stunk so bad, Cassie could hardly stand to get near. It filled the space between them with a sour scent she feared would not come out in the laundry this time. Cassie had to sneak it away soon and throw it in the wash, where it would hopefully manage another trip through the spin cycle.

Lark took Shasta's hand and led her back to the rocking chair. When she'd gotten her great-aunt to sit, Lark climbed onto Shasta's lap and snuggled close, slurping the edge of the blanket, much the way she'd done with her pacifier as a baby.

The two of them together were a swirl of happy and sad. Even with limited visits, Lark and Shasta had developed a bond.

Cassie chewed her lower lip. How was it possible to love someone as much as she loved Lark, yet still feel a twinge of failure whenever anyone asked about her father? Cassie had given him what he wanted, keeping him off the birth certificate and out of Lark's life. The guy was a fool.

Cassie's head started to pound. "How about that coffee? And, Lark, do you want some cocoa this morning?"

Two sets of eyes peered at her through half-closed lids. Cassie had grown up feeling so different from her aunt. Shasta was tall, with a birdlike frame and blond hair. But Cassie was the opposite, dark hair and the short and stocky build of a gymnast.

Lark didn't necessarily look like Shasta either, but inside, they were so much alike.

Cassie opened the door and attached the child safety gate, then jogged down the stairs, leaving Shasta and Lark rocking and staring out at the Pacific.

Aubrey was at the counter. The kitchen behind her clanked and hissed as the cook made breakfast orders, the only time of the day they served freshly cooked foods. Aubrey twirled a pencil in her fingers, then stuck it behind her ear and looked up. "Good morning. I didn't see you there."

"I'm only here for a second. Could I get a couple coffees, one a decaf for Shasta, and also a kid's cocoa?"

"Of course." She didn't need to jot down the order. Aubrey was a pro.

Cassie eased toward the stairs again. "I'll run back down to get them in a minute."

"No, you won't. Remember my little rant about accepting help? One of us will bring them up. By the way, you wouldn't happen to know what took place in the kitchen last night, would you? It looked like a raccoon or some other kind of rodent came in the back window."

Cassie cringed. In all her rushing around, she must have forgotten to pick up everything she'd knocked over.

Another glance at Aubrey told Cassie she hadn't been fooled for a minute.

"Sorry. I locked myself out." Cassie's shoulders rose toward her ears.

"I figured. Old habits die hard, they say." Aubrey swatted the air with her hand. "Get on upstairs. Coffee will be up shortly."

As Cassie turned to start her ascent, her gaze caught on that of the woman in the corner, a regular in the coffee shop for many years. Neither looked away immediately. She nodded her head in a barely perceptible gesture, swept dark hair behind an ear, then went back to typing as Cassie returned to the apartment.

Scaling the gate, Cassie caught her toe. Three hops, and balance was regained, but she'd been noisy enough to garner stares from her aunt and daughter.

They both appeared fully awake now, maybe due to the thumping of Cassie's near collision with the floor. Lark edged up in Shasta's lap and planted a kiss on her cheek. The kid was full of compassion and empathy beyond Cassie's own capabilities.

True to her word and generous nature, Aubrey arrived not long after with a tray crowded with plates and cups. With her came the scents of bacon, maple syrup, coffee, and chocolate that had been present in hints before.

Now that some of her favorite treats had entered the apartment, Lark was filled with the energy only a four-year-old could manage. She really shouldn't have so much sugar, but that seemed like an issue to address later, when they weren't trying to find a new normal.

Shasta's thumb worked back and forth along her first finger, a sign Cassie needed to get the morning medications. She should have thought of that before coffee, yet lack of sleep was beating her over the head, and coffee was the savior she'd searched for. Snagging the frothy cup, Cassie sucked in a dose of caffeine, then went to dole out the meds. "Aubrey, this is so much more than you needed to do." She opened the cupboard and stepped onto the stool, reaching the high shelf where she'd stashed Shasta's prescriptions and the pill organizer that was as big as a plate.

"It's no problem." Aubrey unloaded the tray, setting dishes of food out to be served.

"So, I'm banished to the tower now, I guess." Shasta's mouth was a straight line as her gaze darted from one of them to the other.

The shock of her harsh words had Cassie fumbling the container that sounded like a maraca with all those pills inside. Shasta wasn't one to be harsh or accusing, but the woman before Cassie wasn't consistently the aunt she'd known. That Shasta was buried under dementia, Parkinson's, and a litany of drugs with names that repeated in Cassie's dreams. MAO inhibitors. Bromocriptine. Levodopa. Were these really medications, or words for ancient spells?

"You know that's not it." Aubrey rubbed her hand along Shasta's upper arm. "In fact, friend, this isn't even about you. I thought it would be easier for Cassie to have breakfast upstairs today. She's only been here a few days. She has to be exhausted."

Shasta leaned on the table and didn't make another comment as Aubrey helped her adjust her seat.

Cassie set a mug of water near Shasta, then took her aunt's hand and dumped four pills into her palm.

Shasta's attention was fixed on the medications as she brought her hand to her mouth in slow, measured movements. When she tossed them in all at once, Cassie bit back the urge to tell her to slow down, but Shasta wasn't a child.

Caregiving was a maze that surprised Cassie with new obstacles at every turn.

# 10

Moonlight illuminated the crests of the waves. Seated along an oceanside window, Nora waited for Ferris to arrive at the restaurant. It was the first time she'd noticed how the water at night resembled Gwendolyn twirling in her glittering black tutu. Helen had given it to Gwendolyn at Christmas, and Nora's first thought had been the lack of practicality. Yet her daughter wore it every chance she got, never concerned when the tulle tore or glitter dropped off.

"Hey there." Ferris surprised her out of her thoughts. "Sorry to make you wait."

She unfolded her napkin, placing it on her lap. "I went ahead and ordered for us."

"The salmon?"

The predictability of her husband was one of the things she loved most about him. No sudden twists in the plan. He was steady and unchanging. "Of course, with the rice pilaf and steamed veggies."

He scooted his chair in. "You know me well." He punctuated his statement with a wink.

Without warning, her eyes filled with tears. Hormones. Why now? It was as if the baby took up the space inside her where she usually stored emotions, leaving them nowhere to go but out in public.

"Hey." He reached for her hand, which only gave the tears permission to fall. "Are you okay?"

She nodded, her lips a tight line.

Ferris rubbed his thumb across the side of her wrist.

This was too much. Nora swiped the tears away with the back of her free hand. "I'm fine. Really."

Silence. Waiting.

She tilted her head, pleading with her eyes for him to move on, to tell her about his day, but Ferris was a master at investigation.

She broke. "I got the DNA test results."

"Was there an issue? Something you're worried about?"

She blew out a sigh. "No. I'm falling apart here for no reason."

The server arrived at the table, the worst possible timing, or maybe the best. Nora watched the dishes being served in the window's reflection.

Ferris thanked the server and gave her hand a tug. He said a brief prayer, then turned his attention back to her, not touching the filet of salmon in front of him. "Tell me what's going on."

Nora poked her tri tip with the tines of her fork. "It's nothing to worry about. No big medical crisis."

"Would you tell me if it was?" A dig at her evading the conversation about her doctor's appointment.

"There was a familial match."

His head nodded along, but he made no comment or murmurs.

"I have a half sister . . . well, three of them."

He nodded again.

Nora tossed her napkin onto the table. "I can't talk to you about this when you're staring at me like that."

Ferris cleared his throat. "Sorry." He stuffed a bite of salmon into his mouth, chewed, swallowed. "I was sure you were going to say it was your mother."

"Tammy." Women who abandoned newborns did not get a title. "If she'd wanted to see me or know anything about me, she already knew where to look."

"I don't know. There are a lot of people who come through the station having made decisions they never dreamed they would and doing everything possible to avoid the consequences. Logic isn't always part of it." He shrugged. "So what are you going to do with this information?"

"No idea. The youngest one sent me a message. I suppose I could get Tammy's medical information from her. That's all I want."

The way his gaze lingered, he clearly had more on his mind, but he made the wise choice to stay quiet. Ferris liked to get to the heart of every situation, but Nora was different. She wanted to move forward without looking over her shoulder. *The past can only hurt those who let it.* There might have been a few flaws in those beautiful words.

That Sunday, they did not go to church. Cassie managed this by not mentioning the day of the week to her aunt.

"Dead. Dead. Dead." Lark marched in a circle, her baby doll hanging over one arm. Death had been on her mind since discovering a deceased western gull on the edge of the sand.

Cassie cringed inside but forced a smile on her face. The more attention she gave this new word, the longer Lark's chanting would continue.

By the look on Shasta's face, she didn't see humor in Lark's remarks. "Who is dead?"

"No one." Cassie stepped closer, turning her back on her daughter, who'd stopped to bury a stuffed bunny under a sofa cushion. "It's her newest curiosity, that's all. Nothing to worry about."

"Your mother did this. I knew she'd done something." Shasta raked her gray hair with both hands. "She was always doing things, always getting into some sort of trouble. That poor baby."

"But, Shasta, I'm right here. Nothing happened to me." Cassie ached to hug her aunt, but the tension on Shasta's face made her hesitant to reach out. "There's nothing to worry about."

Shasta's gaze drilled into Cassie. "There are things you don't know. Things you can't know. I don't even understand what happened. But there are things." She looked around, moving as if a tsunami was coming for them. "Where's the little girl? Where is she?"

"Lark? She's right there." Cassie pointed toward her daughter.

"She needs to stay close. She's not safe out there."

"What do you mean, she's not safe?" Cassie's own tensions were on the rise now. Lark was close by, but the thought of her daughter being in any kind of danger sent a buzz through Cassie's brain that no amount of caffeine could ever compete with.

The scowl from Shasta radiated her seriousness. "You don't know everything. Do you hear me?" She shook an arm in Cassie's direction. "You need to listen to what I'm saying to you."

"I'm listening. I understand that you're worried." Cassie reached for the cupboard door, somewhat concerned that Shasta would come at her, though she'd never once hurt Cassie or done anything violent. The look on her face was one Cassie had never seen before and hoped she wasn't going to ever see again. When she didn't move forward, Cassie stepped onto the stool and retrieved the medication the doctor had prescribed in case of agitation. Funny, she'd thought that was silly, a thing she would never need to deal with. Once again, Cassie had been proven wrong. She poured a pill onto her palm and stepped down. "It's time for your medication. Can I get you some water to go with this?"

Shasta stepped back, leaning heavily onto the dining room table—perspiration sprinkled along her brow.

Cassie moved slowly as she poured a glass of water half full and handed it to Shasta.

She accepted the water and the pill, swallowing it down without another word.

Cassie's sigh was audible, leaving her asking God to not let Shasta notice.

Within ten minutes, the medication was making a difference. Shasta let Cassie guide her to her room, where she lay on the bed, staring vacantly at the wall of paintings. Her aunt was fading right before Cassie's eyes, as if her brain had been able to hold on only long enough for Cassie and Lark to return home.

He didn't hit me that night, though he squeezed my arm hard enough to leave a bruise. The next day, Topher was so sorry. I really thought his words were genuine, that it would be a once-in-a-lifetime thing, a bad move as a result of his disappointment. Somehow, I'd convinced myself that Topher was deeply heartbroken because we couldn't have a child together. That's how saturating denial can be.

His apology went so far as to be willing to look at the list of fertility options we still had. There were a couple that interested him, egg donation and surrogacy, also with a donor egg. We decided to move forward with egg donation, allowing me to be the carrier. It was a long shot too, but with hormone injections, we stood a chance.

I was surprised how little I cared that our baby would have no genetic connection to me. Oddly, I was kind of relieved. There was little from my own family I wanted to risk carrying forward into another generation.

We chose a donor with similar traits to my own, but I was only concerned about bringing a healthy baby into the world. Topher, however, quizzed the doctor relentlessly about the precautions the clinic had in place to be sure his sperm was used. He wanted no chances of another man's DNA getting mixed into what seemed to be a science experiment to him.

There were so many warning signs. It's taken me years to stop beating myself up about all the junctures at which I should have seen him for who he really was. I know now that it was my desperation for a child, a chance to do family right, that drove me forward.

On our third attempt, I got the news that I was pregnant. My world changed with the revelation. I felt like I was a whole new human being.

I told Topher the good news that night over a special dinner. He shrugged, congratulated me, and asked if I'd gotten his favorite IPA when I was at the store. I passed his behavior off as concern. This was a high-risk pregnancy—maybe he didn't want to get too attached.

There was not a day of my pregnancy that I didn't feel blessed and glowing. It might be hard to understand, but even when I was sick from morning until night, when I could barely keep down enough nutrients to survive, I felt joy about the child growing inside of me.

Topher didn't join me for any of the doctor's appointments. He missed the first heartbeat, the ultrasound. When I asked him to come along, his anger would flare and he'd become ready to blow at any moment, but I still didn't let it get to me.

I know now that I was scared to look too hard at what was going on with my husband. That, along with my years growing up in a dysfunctional home, allowed me to remain in my imaginary marriage.

My friends would check in on me, but I pulled away. It wasn't intentional, not at first. Topher criticized them, claiming one after the other was influencing me in a way he couldn't stand. I was so desperate to keep him happy that I backed out of lunches and canceled plans at the last minute.

Even though most of my days were spent alone in our large house, I wasn't lonely. I bought a special apparatus that allowed me to hear my child's heartbeat, and I used it daily, touching base with my unborn baby in a way that connected us even deeper than our shared body. I read stories to my growing belly, marked milestones in a journal, and studied everything available on pregnancy, childbirth, and newborns.

The nursery became my obsession. If there'd been Pinterest in those days, I would have gotten lost in the internet wonderland of nursery décor. After months of paint and fabric samples, I settled on a light blue with white trim and perfect pink rosebuds on the white curtains and crib bedding.

We hadn't found out if I was carrying a boy or a girl, but I knew it would be a daughter. My little girl. A child who would have everything she needed, but mostly, all my love and attention.

# 11

More than a week had passed, yet Ferris hadn't questioned her about the message. He was a wise man, but Nora knew this couldn't last forever. Eventually, the detective in him would require answers.

Nora answered a couple school-board emails, checked her Google calendar, and skimmed the online version of their hometown newspaper. This was why people had social media accounts—procrastination. She toyed with the idea of creating one. It would help her stay in touch with what was going on, but a town the size of Gull's Bay didn't have much trouble spreading gossip without the help of the internet.

Opening the email tab again, Nora started a new message. She entered the address Becca had left in her note, worried over a subject line for at least five minutes, finally settling on *Questions*, then stared, paralyzed, at the body of the email. Why did Peyton nap soundly today, the one day Nora would have welcomed her restlessness?

Dear Becca,

Was *dear* too personal? She punched the backspace button until the screen was empty.

Becca,

Thank you for your message. I'm not interested in anything personal, but I would like to have any family medical history you might have.

Sincerely,
Nora Milford

She backspaced over *sincerely*, leaving the email without the added touch of a closing.

And send.

Nora leaned back, inhaling as she tried to count to ten and only making it to six as the baby took up most of the room her lungs usually enjoyed. Had she been too harsh? She'd been accused of being cold, yet Nora preferred the word *driven*. She got things done without losing the time many women wasted on small talk and fluff.

She started when the email popped onto the screen. A reply so quick left her wondering if Becca had anything going on in her life. But no. Nora wasn't going to fall into wondering about Becca or the other two. She had a mission to retrieve medical information, and that was all.

Dear Nora,

I'm so glad you contacted me. I was afraid I wouldn't hear from you. This is thrilling! I only found out about you a couple months ago, and since then, I've been dying to get more information. I'm sorry to have to tell you that Mom passed away last spring. She had pancreatic cancer, but don't worry too much—the doctor says there's no reason for us to be concerned. I know you're probably disappointed that she isn't around. I'm sure she would have loved seeing you.

As far as medical information, I don't have much beyond that. I'll have to check in with Lex. She's the one who would know.

Well, I'd better get back to work.

Your little sister

P.S. I couldn't find you on Insta. Follow me @beccaboundforglory, and I'll follow you back.

Nora's mouth hung open until her tongue started to dry. What had she done? She'd have to change her email address, maybe even her name. How had a simple request for medical records turned into . . . this?

About fifteen minutes too late to save Nora from making a huge mistake, Peyton started to cry.

⁓

Cassie thought once again of Janice and that support group. In the nearly two weeks since her aunt had returned home, she had come to wonder if maybe they had the secret to keeping her sane.

She cringed. Calling Janice was like going up in front of a class to acknowledge she hadn't done her homework. Desperation never came without a large scoop of guilt.

She let her shoulders relax when the call went to voice mail, yet it might have been nice to unburden a few insecurities on someone who didn't know her and wasn't counting on her. "This is Cassie George. I have some questions about the support group you mentioned. If you could give me a call, I'd appreciate it."

As she disconnected, Cassie heard the echo of her failures coming back at her. The bait shop down the road was owned by a woman with six kids. Her husband had died of ALS after a battle that lasted many of Cassie's growing-up years. She could remember Shasta and a few of the other women from church always looking for ways to help out without taking any of the woman's pride. The last time Cassie had seen that family, they were laughing and working together at their shop. They didn't seem to have a care in the world, though they couldn't have had many extra conveniences. How had she taken care of her dying husband while managing to raise confident and happy children? It was beyond Cassie, who was getting swallowed up by the care of her two charges.

Lark ran in with her new boots, one in each hand.

"What a good girl you are." Sometimes the pride for this child was all-consuming.

"It's one of my grammy days. I'm *existed*." She twirled in a circle, the boots stretching to the last bit of her grip.

Cassie slowed her down and set her on the floor. "I think you mean you're excited."

"I *am* excited." Her tiny toes wiggled as Cassie worked mismatched socks onto her feet.

She'd overheard Mrs. Collins in the shop the other day saying what a blessing they all felt it was to love on Lark. She'd called them an eclectic bunch of grammies. It hadn't taken long for Lark to apply this title that had so far been unused in her life to a few of her favorite women. At last count, Cassie had heard her refer to Grammy Aubrey, Grammy Mrs. Collins, and Grammy Shasta.

Behind her, Shasta tried each of the drawers in the kitchen, but the safety latches seemed to be holding. She'd rattle each back and forth the inch or so it would open, then move on to the next.

Cassie had always wondered what it would have been like to have a grandmother. Thinking back, she probably wanted a grandmother more than a father. That might have been because a grandmother seemed so much more accessible. Shasta's mother had passed away only a year before Cassie came to Gull's Bay. She'd had the bedroom before Cassie, and Shasta often told of how her mother would have loved being there to help raise Cassie. It was like she'd just missed a person who would have wrapped her up in loving arms and made everything safe and warm.

No matter how much the women's help with Lark stole Cassie's self-confidence, for her daughter's sake, she'd let it go on. Lark deserved the relationships that were forming. And, Cassie hoped, they would soften the hurt that would surely come with Shasta's passing.

"What's wrong here?" Silverware clanked as Shasta yanked with a hand on each side of the drawer. She threw out a curse Cassie had never once heard leave her lips.

Shock drove Cassie's gaze to her daughter, who might not have even noticed if she hadn't reacted so wildly.

Lark's head cocked to the side. "What does . . ." She seemed to be studying the air, searching for the word she'd heard.

"Nothing. Grammy Shasta meant to say bummer."

"She never says that."

Why did her daughter always pick the most inconvenient times to be observant? Cassie hopped up, kissed Lark on the top of her head, and went to the kitchen. "What's going on? Did you need something?"

"I do." Shasta's eyes took on a distant stare, as though no matter how directly Cassie seemed to look into her eyes, Shasta was seeing something far off. "I need to get in there."

"Let me help you with whatever you need. That's what I'm here for." Shasta had been a strong woman, an amazing artist, a business owner, and the closest thing Cassie could remember to a mother. But now she couldn't be trusted to open the kitchen drawers without hurting herself or someone else with the contents.

For some reason, Shasta had taken to removing silverware and leaving it all over the apartment. Cassie had found knives in the disposal more than a couple times since Shasta's homecoming. Her aunt had bent a fork trying to pry up a window that wasn't meant to open. And honestly, she'd had some outbursts during which Cassie had felt safer knowing she didn't have access to anything with a point.

"That's it. I'm going downstairs. I need to see the shop. They don't know what they're doing." In all her anger, Shasta still couldn't manage to stomp from a room, but the cadence of her shuffle made the point even without the thumping.

"We'll all go down. Give me a chance to get Lark ready."

Shasta jiggled the doorknob, but with the child-safety cover, it was nearly impossible for even Cassie's non-Parkinson's hands to get out the door in a hurry.

Snagging the tiny purple raincoat from the hook near the door, Cassie hoisted Lark onto her hip.

Her daughter squirmed, wanting to walk on her own, but guiding both of them down the steep stairs safely was more to manage than Cassie could handle right now.

They'd only come down four or five steps when Lark started to flail. "Let me go. I can do it. I'm a big girl."

Cassie's grip was slipping, but she couldn't take her other hand off of Shasta as she moved down the stairs backward. A choice had to be made between Shasta's and Lark's safety. At that moment, the burden suddenly lifted.

"Hey there, Miss Lark. I could use some help." It was Marshall's deep voice behind them, his arms having removed Lark's weight from Cassie's hip. When they arrived on the bottom step, Cassie blew out a whistling sigh. Her T-shirt clung to her back with perspiration, and she could see from Shasta's reddened face that it hadn't been an easy trip for her either.

Cassie turned to see Marshall and Lark setting a table with napkins and silverware. He had a sweet way of giving her daughter much-needed independence while never making Cassie feel unsafe. "Thank you." She steered Shasta to the seat by the window. "I'd love a latte, if you don't mind."

"Whoa. Are you saying you'll let me make your coffee today without an argument?"

Cassie rolled her head around, stretching tight neck muscles. "You've broken me, okay? Are you happy?"

"Actually, yes, but I'm not working. However, for you, I'll let Lisa know." He tipped his head toward the counter, where the thirty-something blonde with the ever-present messy bun and smile helped a customer.

"What are you doing in here on your day off?" Cassie moved silverware out of Shasta's reach. So much silverware.

Lark returned to the table with her plastic tray and tea set that Aubrey had gotten for her to keep behind the counter.

Marshall motioned to the group of five or six teen boys in the corner. They sat around a square wooden box made into a coffee table, each holding a Bible and a cup. "Once a month, I take the guys out for breakfast. It's a great excuse for bacon." He winked.

The buzz that shot through Cassie's body was not at all within her control. She swallowed, hoping the feeling he'd just given her didn't show on her face. But then the heat rose up her neck and into her cheeks. She ducked her head. "Shouldn't they be in school?"

"Spring break."

She nodded. "Well then, don't let us get in your way. Thank you for helping with Lark. She really likes you."

"I like her too." His gaze was still on Cassie, bringing that sensation to the surface again.

What was wrong with her? The last thing she needed right now was a crush on a man who she knew nothing about. That was exactly how she'd gone down the wrong path before.

He pulled at one of Lark's curls. "See you later, stinker."

Lark giggled in a way that displayed love for him. "See you, Marsh L." *Great*. The possessive barista and all-around good guy had won her daughter's heart. That only made him harder to resist.

"Hi there, girl power," Cassie said to her daughter. "What are we going to eat this morning?"

Shasta's chair screeched back from the table.

"Lots of bacon and syrup." Lark poured pretend tea into a tiny plastic cup and slipped it Cassie's way.

The shop grew oddly quiet. Cassie looked around, trying to find what had extinguished the usual buzz. By following the stares of the customers in line, she found Shasta, tugging a notebook away from the woman at the corner booth. Cassie jumped up and rushed over. "What are you doing?"

Shasta's face was stony in the stare she unleashed on the woman Cassie had never personally met.

"Shasta?" She pried her fingers off the book, one at a time, releasing the belonging to its owner. "Shasta, what's wrong?"

"Maybe she should tell you." Her aunt shuffled back to the table.

The sounds of the shop started to rise again as Cassie turned to the woman with the computer. "I'm really sorry. Do you know what that was about?"

Her smile was pleasant but guarded. "I don't." She tucked the notebook under her laptop and dismissed Cassie by returning to her work.

Shasta's words about watching out for Lark niggled at the back of Cassie's mind. They had to be delusional, but the fear behind them seemed contagious.

# 12

It wasn't an easy pregnancy. The all-day morning sickness lasted well into the second trimester, my legs ached with bulging veins, and I lived with nonstop dizziness. On any given night, I was either fighting insomnia or so solidly asleep I couldn't be woken.

Topher's attitude didn't grow warmer as my belly expanded. More than once, I wondered if the pregnancy was forcing a wedge between us. He still expected me to be free for travel, dinners out, or intimacy. And while I didn't regret my little one at all, I was finding day-to-day life a challenge. Topher's needs were more than I could handle, which seemed to equate to rejection in his mind.

I was entering my fifth month when he came home excited about a business trip to Las Vegas. It took all of my energy reserves to paste on a smile and tell him I hoped he had a wonderful time.

The expression on his face—I will never forget that look. Apparently, I was supposed to go with him. It was a surprise for me, and I'd missed the point. Another rejection I'd inflicted on him without intention.

I could barely walk down the stairs from our bedroom without falling, thanks to the almost constant spinning of the world around me, and my husband wanted me to get on an airplane and party it up in Sin City.

Maybe it was the lack of sleep I'd had the night before, but at that moment, I hit a breaking point. "I'm not going." Those are words I'll remember until my last day because of what came next. Topher's arm swung into the air, then slammed across my face, sending me to my hands and knees. He wasn't the man I'd met in college any longer. Fire was in his eyes, and hate had replaced love.

I lay there, my face in the carpet, blood seeping from my mouth and nose, and I listened to my husband stomp up the stairs. It took only a few minutes for him to come back down. I stayed where I'd landed, afraid that doing anything else would earn me another blow.

"I'm going on my own. Don't wait around for me. I'm not sure when I'll be back." He spit the words at me as though I'd been the one to attack.

I wanted to rage at him, tell him how cruel he was being, how he could have hurt the baby, but I stayed wrapped up with my arms across my middle, feeling the kicks that told me that, even though my child was shaken, she was a survivor.

Cassie pulled up in front of the shop after Shasta's physical-therapy appointment. In the back seat, Lark slept, her breathing a steady rhythm in a chaotic world.

Shasta reached for the handle, ready to get out.

"Hold on a minute. I need to get Lark."

"I'm fine. I can go in myself." Shasta and Lark were sounding more and more alike each day.

There was little hope of Cassie stopping her headstrong aunt from exiting the car, so she jogged around to at least be sure she was safe. There were only about ten feet from the car to the entrance, but Cassie locked the doors before walking beside Shasta. Once they were inside, she waved at Aubrey to keep an eye on Shasta. Thankfully, she understood without explanation.

Aubrey and Shasta had been close since Aubrey moved to town years before and took a shift here and there at the shop. Lately, it seemed Aubrey had taken over most of the management duties and was behind the counter more often than not. But now those were Cassie's responsibilities. She was the one meant to be in charge, yet she'd continued to take advantage of Aubrey's generosity.

Cassie sighed as she slipped out and stood beside the back door of her car, looking down into her daughter's sleeping face. When Cassie was growing up, this town, especially during the off-season, was safe. People let sleeping children sleep, not worrying about kidnappers and sex offenders. Maybe Shasta's unwarranted rants about Lark's safety were getting to her, but that fifteen seconds she'd left her daughter in the car had scared Cassie to the point of perspiration.

Leaning against the warm hood, she let the salty mist of the Oregon coast sprinkle her face. Wind whipped her hair around until she pulled a scrunchie off her wrist and wrapped it into a tight bun. Above her, western gulls called, hoping she'd spare them a treat or two, but her pockets were empty. The chill worked its way into the fabric of her sweatshirt, and she shivered. Instead of discomfort, though, it felt like the hug of familiarity.

The road between their place and the beach sloped downward, allowing a wide view of the ocean and coastline. Someone walked along the edge of the waves, a now-recognized cap pulled onto his head. Marshall looked like a man in his own world out there. She knew that feeling. And she missed it.

The peace Cassie experienced in the ten-minute wait while Lark slept in the car was shattered as she stepped into the shop. While she held Lark, a drowsy anchor on her hip, her gaze met Aubrey's lined face. Had Cassie taken advantage of Aubrey's friendship? "What?" Cassie asked. Looking around, she spotted Shasta tapping at one of her paintings, but she didn't seem distressed.

Lark slipped down Cassie's leg as Cassie used her arms to check her daughter's balance as she went. Lark ran to the window where Bogart waited for his afternoon snack.

Aubrey shook her head. "Lillian McPherson came in today, chatting up a storm about you coming home and taking over where you left off. When I turned around, there was Nora, just as quiet as could be, sucking up information to feed the local scuttlebutt."

That woman gave Cassie the same off-putting vibe she had in high school. Her father had been the mayor back then. She'd not only been a cheerleader but also the captain of the dance team and a member of student leadership—associated student body president. Cassie had also been on student council, but her voice wasn't loud enough to be heard over Nora's.

Lark dug in a box of blocks.

"Mr. Watkins brought those in for her. I'll let him know she liked them." Aubrey gazed at Lark the way a grandmother should.

Cassie tucked wind-blown curls behind Lark's ears and thanked Aubrey. Her daughter didn't even give her a second look. In just two weeks, she'd adapted to this new life in Gull's Bay, and it suited Lark. She'd become a more adventurous child, as if she were coming alive here. Cassie had missed too much trying to get by in California. Maybe they both needed this detour.

"Head upstairs and give yourself a moment of peace." Aubrey pushed her reading glasses into place and opened a book, sitting near where Lark played.

Cassie jogged up the stairs. She'd have a minute to get lunch ready and go through the mail. Bills had begun to form a stack on the counter. She grabbed one with her name on it, surprised how fast she'd been found. Cassie yanked a sheet of paper out of the envelope. As if she weren't already overwhelmed, Cassie had just received notification that, by leaving her doctoral program, she would have six months before she needed to start making payments on her student loans.

She leaned her head back on the sofa. If only this were the only set of loans she'd taken. She'd need to consolidate, figure out her budget, and hope for a miracle.

In a moment of frustration, she wadded up the paper and threw it against the wall. If Cassie could scream and not be heard downstairs, she'd give it all her lungs could manage. Instead, she slipped on her shoes. Life didn't have any scheduled breaks for this season.

In the shop, she found Aubrey busy with a line of customers not typical for the afternoon. Lark was on the floor in the play area, building a tower with her new blocks, Marshall seated in a folding chair next to her.

Before she could approach, Shasta started to take the stairs. After the first two, she stopped to rest. Physical therapy sapped the energy out of her for most of the day. Shasta needed a rest, but could Aubrey manage the shop *and* Lark?

Marshall motioned to her to stay with Shasta. It took all the time Cassie had to help her aunt into the apartment. Shasta went straight to her room and lay down on the bed, her eyes wide open and staring at the far wall.

Voices startled Cassie as she left the bedroom. Marshall was at the top of the stairs, Lark on one hip, the large blue plastic bin full of blocks on the other.

"You didn't need to do that."

"It's no problem. I thought it would be easier than you taking another couple trips up and down."

"You're saying I couldn't carry the blocks and Lark at once?"

Lark started showing off her tumbling skills.

Marshall chuckled, low and rich. "I'm sure you could. From what I've observed, you can do pretty much anything."

Cassie cringed and felt a pang of regret at her irritated tone. "Not anything."

# 13

By my seventh month, I was confined to bed rest. This was made even more difficult because I was afraid to call in the help of the friends I'd alienated, and my husband cut back on the hired help we'd had around the house, even before I'd become pregnant.

Not only was Topher's anger growing, so was the time he spent away from home. For that, I was grateful. My husband, the man I'd once looked forward to seeing each night, was now a force I dreaded.

When I went into preterm labor, Topher was at an "important" business dinner. He arrived at the hospital around ten that night, saw that I was admitted, and went home to get some sleep.

I started thinking about leaving him while I lay there, the IV pumping medication into my body to keep my contractions from starting again. But I knew I couldn't do it now. I could barely walk across a room without the threat of bringing my child into the world too soon.

When I returned home, I started to make the plans. My embarrassment kept me from calling many of the friends I'd distanced myself from, but there was one I thought might understand, or at least have mercy on me. I contacted that friend who I'd treated horribly and let her know about the pregnancy complications. Carmen encouraged me, praying with me over the phone and sending flowers on more than one occasion. She'd come over when Topher was at work just to make sure the house was taken care of and I was doing well.

But I was a coward. I couldn't bring myself to tell Carmen the truth of what my marriage had become. Instead, I played the part of a loving wife with a doting husband and a beloved child on the way. How I was going to explain my leaving Topher after the baby came was a worry, but not something I let myself be concerned with at the time.

My plans were coming along, until they weren't. I'd made a call to a landlord about a small apartment I felt I could manage with the money I'd been smuggling away. I'd need a job soon, but I had to keep my child safe. Every single day I tossed between the plan I was developing and the idea that it would be better to stay with Topher. I mean, maybe after the baby came, he'd fall in love and be the man I'd always wanted him to be.

By the time the landlord called me back with details, I'd changed my mind. It wasn't the time to throw away my dreams, my family.

Topher arrived home from work early that night. I hadn't managed to put on makeup or comb through my hair like I tried to do each day about an hour before I expected him to arrive. I knew I was in trouble from the first glimpse of my husband's face, reddened, his jaw set. He moved into our bedroom, working his lips as if the very breath of the devil was held behind them.

I pushed myself up against the headboard, my arms wrapped around my baby belly, as if I had the strength to defend either of us.

His words are still crystal clear in my memory. "I hear you're looking for a new place to live. What? This house, all these things, isn't good enough for you?"

"What are you talking about?" I forced myself to look innocent, like maybe I could convince him there'd been a mistake.

"A guy I work with owns rental properties. Can you even imagine how humiliating it was to have him come into my office today and ask if we were related? I spilled that you were my wife before he told me why he was asking." Topher picked up the vase of flowers Carmen had sent and threw them across the room. The glass shattered, and water dripped down the robin's-egg blue walls.

A piece of me became resigned to my death that day, but Topher didn't even touch me. What he did was so much worse.

Cassie didn't want to stop reading. But the alarm she'd set on her phone chimed. She got off the couch and checked in on Shasta, who slept flat on her back, like she was ready to meet God whenever He chose to come for her.

A peek in Cassie's own room found Lark on her stomach across the entire twin mattress, her arms and legs outstretched, as if to lay claim to the bed that Cassie would have to somehow squeeze into later.

It wasn't that Cassie was doing anything truly wrong; she just didn't want Shasta to walk in and find her going through the studio. The details of the past and present were a mix in Shasta's mind. Cassie wanted to see if there were pictures somewhere, things that might help Shasta connect to who she still was. Maybe even get her mind off the insistence that the woman in the coffee shop was some sort of threat to Lark.

She crept back to the studio, careful to avoid the squeaky planks as she snuck past Shasta's door.

The air had grown stale and cold in there with the heat turned off and the door closed to keep Lark from the paint and Shasta from rummaging. It was a clutter of boxes Cassie hadn't the space or the time to unpack, as well as canvas after canvas of Shasta's unfinished artwork.

For just a moment, Cassie wondered if she could manage to get any of these to the point at which they could be sold, but painting wasn't an artistic ability she had. These were Shasta's and like pieces of her heart. It didn't make a difference that

Cassie was about to come face-to-face with a mountain of student loans, money that she'd used to keep Lark fed and housed for the last four years. That was her debt, not Shasta's.

Shasta kept an old stereo cupboard, long and heavy with doors that slid open, beneath a window along the far wall. Next to that behemoth, reaching to the ceiling, were shelves with drawer inserts scattered around open sections. It all looked random, but she'd had a way of organization. Unfortunately, Cassie had never taken the time to understand Shasta's layout.

Two hours passed as Cassie shuffled through stacks of paintings, sorting the seascapes from the others. She lost time flipping through the photos she discovered, so many of people Cassie had never met but knew of from Shasta's stories. Exhaustion and hopelessness took their toll. She set aside anything she thought would bring her aunt happy memories.

She stood back and evaluated the room, which did not look at all as it had when Cassie entered. It was then that she pushed aside a box with her foot, near the clean canvases. It was something she hadn't seen in years, never thinking much of, though Shasta had always kept it on the top shelf, an ornamental box that seemed more decorative than utilitarian.

When she shook it, things slid around inside, but there didn't seem to be an easy way to open it. Using the flashlight on her cell phone, Cassie searched the inlaid wood for grooves or hinges. It shifted in her hands, a dark piece sliding from side to side. From there, she found another and another, until Cassie had removed all the sections that acted as locks. The top slipped off.

She sat down on the floor, letting her fingers sort through the contents. Everything inside seemed to have some connection to Cassie. Her mother's birth certificate, letters from Diane to Shasta, and faded photographs.

There they were. She pulled the picture from the middle of a stack—her mother, father, and Cassie. They stood on the pier in Seattle, Diane holding Cassie in her arms, but the baby was looking over at her father, who'd ducked his head, the photo blurring as if the move had been made just as the shutter clicked.

Cassie had seen this picture before, when she was much younger, but she remembered it with him smiling at the camera. A creation of a hopeful mind. The image she had of her dad was of a man who looked just like her, down to the odd crease in her right cheek. Probably the blurry remembering of a lost dream.

At eight, Cassie had started asking Shasta all sorts of questions about her parents. What had they been like? Where were they from? Where was her father now?

The only information Shasta had was about Diane, Shasta's own cousin and Cassie's mom, yet what she shared had seemed filtered.

Aside from that picture being different than she remembered, there was one Cassie had never seen before: Cassie as a baby in her mother's arms. She must have been only weeks old, wrapped in the blanket she still had in the top of her bedroom closet. There was no doubt that the quilt was something handmade, bright colors forming beautiful and unique designs. Cassie always cherished this as something special that maybe her mother had made.

Standing up, she stretched tired muscles. Her body, eyes, and mind all screamed for sleep. Instead of packaging everything up again, Cassie tucked the pile back into the box and stacked the pieces together, taking it all with her to her bedroom, where she'd hide it under the bed until she had a chance to look further.

Lark's claim to the bed left Cassie with few options—moving her and taking the chance that she'd wake up, or sleeping on the third of the mattress that remained available. She chose to take what was left.

But even as tired as she was with the clock shining three in the morning, she couldn't sleep. Her thoughts shifted from her parents to the woman in the story. There weren't many pages left, and Cassie had found herself reading only when she could give her full attention to the words on the page. Was this fiction or someone's life story? She ached to reach in and save the woman from her husband and the fear that must have come with that marriage.

# 14

Cassie sat bolt upright in the dark. Lark still snoozed beside her, but she was sure she'd heard something, though her mind couldn't make out what it had been. Easing off the mattress, she padded into the hall and grabbed her trusty curtain rod on the way.

All was silent, but that feeling kept niggling at her nerves. Cassie flipped on the light in the kitchen, somehow surprised and relieved at the same time not to find a burglar standing there. Back through the hall, she peeked into Shasta's room. The night-light near her bathroom illuminated a few feet into the room, but not enough to see her in the bed. Cassie stilled herself, listening for Shasta's deep breaths, but the room was silent.

Her pulse began to beat behind her ear. She snapped on the light. Shasta was gone.

Picking up her pace, Cassie checked on Lark again—still asleep. Going to the studio, she saw it was just as she'd left it. Then, after checking every corner, she stood in the living room and stared at the door. "Oh please, please, please, let her be in the shop."

Quietly, so as not to wake Lark and traumatize her with

Cassie's own fear and panic, she eased down the stairs. It was dark in the dining area, the only light coming from the security lamp in the kitchen. She searched the walk-in refrigerator, the restrooms, but Shasta wasn't there. That's when she saw the back door. It was pulled nearly shut, but a gap of about half an inch remained.

Cassie looked back toward the register, thought of her sleeping daughter upstairs, then slipped into the cold night. Wind whipped salt-laced ocean air around her face, and a damp chill wove beneath her T-shirt. The moon was dim, only lighting the crests of the waves ahead. "Shasta." Cassie's voice died on the roar of the water.

Rushing toward the front of the store, she hoped she'd be able to see her aunt in the light of the streetlamps. Cassie ducked under the branch of a tree but she misjudged, her head smacking into the bottom of the limb.

A zing of pain shot through her skull. Her hand instinctually reached for the point of contact and found her scalp sliced open. Within a second, her palm filled with blood. Dizziness tried to take Cassie down, but she couldn't buckle, not with her daughter alone upstairs and her aunt somewhere out there in who-knows-what kind of state.

Cassie stumbled to the street, scanning up and down the road, her eye catching on a distant figure. "Shasta?" Jogging forward, every strike of her feet against the pavement sent jolts of electric pain through her head. When she caught up, Shasta looked at her as if she shouldn't be there. Confusion settled deep into her aunt's gaze. "Shasta . . . what are you doing out here?" Cassie kept one hand tight against her wound while using the other to turn them both toward home.

"It's strange," she said. "I thought I heard my mother out here calling for me." Shasta looked up into the dark sky. "Did you hear her?"

"I'm sorry. I didn't." They walked up the hill. "Can you tell me about her?" Mist clung to Cassie's face, but she was unable to wipe it away.

"She was a gentle woman, caring. She took care of my aunt when Diane and I were small. You know, Diane's mother wasn't well. She had . . ." Shasta rubbed her hand hard against her forehead. "She couldn't think of things."

Cassie's head throbbed.

"She couldn't take care of your mom. She was so sad. She cried all the time."

A shiver ran over Cassie's skin. "Why was she so sad?"

Shasta stopped and looked at Cassie as they approached the light outside the coffee shop. "She was losing something special . . . her memories." A tear clung to Shasta's bottom row of eyelashes.

Cassie let her hand find its way down Shasta's arm to her fingers. And they stood there, connected in the dark, trying to figure out what to say next.

Cassie sat in the living room with a kitchen towel on top of her head and a bag of peas topping that. Stitches were not negotiable. Hopefully she could at least keep her hair. The sun rose slowly, but it was still dim when the sounds of the coffee shop opening gave hope that she'd make it through this disaster too.

Using her free hand to scroll through her phone, she called Aubrey.

"Good morning. You're up early." Her voice was so awake, so chipper, so very not what Cassie felt up to at that moment.

"Good morning. I need some help. I was wondering if you could watch Shasta and Lark for me?" The pain worked its way behind Cassie's eyes, expanding.

"Oh, honey, I'm sorry. I'm actually in Newport. I'm checking in on a project here. What's happening?"

Cassie had always known Aubrey's work at the coffee shop was more of a hobby than employment. She did some kind of nonprofit work, but Cassie had been self-absorbed enough not to pay much attention to that part of Aubrey's life. "It's not a big deal. I smacked my head and thought I should get it looked at, but it can wait." Of course, that wasn't really true. She couldn't even fake smile without starting the flow of blood again. "I'll see you when you get back."

After disconnecting the call, she tried to lean back, but her neck had turned into a series of tight bands. There was no ignoring this situation, but she questioned her ability to get Shasta and Lark into the car without passing out in the process.

She was about to give in and call down to the coffee shop when someone pounded on the door. At this early hour, the intrusion was startling. The knocking came twice more before she could get there.

On the other side, Marshall stood, his face lined with worry. "Are you okay?" He took hold of her arms and guided her to the couch. "What happened?"

"How did you know there was a problem?"

His eyebrows rose. "You left blood all over the shop."

The moan that came from her chest wasn't voluntary.

He rubbed his finger and thumb against his forehead. "I'll be honest. I was scared." His gaze lifted to the ceiling as if he would find God there on the drywall stained by too many tall Christmas trees.

"It's nothing, really. I just hit my head on a tree limb."

"Let me take a look." He peeled the towel away from her scalp, then whistled low. "That's actually something. A big something. You need all kinds of stitches." He shook his head and looked away for a moment.

"You're not too good with blood, are you?"

"Nope. It's my kryptonite."

Cassie put the rag back onto her head. "Wow. Comparing yourself to Superman. That's bold."

He smirked in a way that tempted her to lean on his chest. She was tired and in pain, all reserves on low.

"I'm calling in backup." He scrolled around on his phone, then lifted it to his ear. "Mrs. Collins, Cassie's had an accident. I'm going to take her into the emergency room to have her head looked at." He pulled the phone back for a moment, frantic sounds coming through the earpiece. "No. She'll be fine. I just think she needs some stitches." He laughed. "Yes, I can handle it. Yes, she already knows I'm not good with blood. Would you be able to take Lark for a bit? I don't think she needs to see her mom in pain."

He put the phone back in his pocket. "She'll be over in just a few minutes. She's just giving Harold the instructions for the morning."

"I can't go." Cassie's mind sped over the climbing mountain of bills she was acquiring.

"You can. Lisa can handle checking in on Shasta. Lark will be thrilled to spend the morning with Mrs. Collins." He stood and took his jacket from the hook by the door. "Let's get you ready so we can go as soon as she gets here. I think stitches are supposed to happen fairly soon after the cut."

"You don't understand. I can't afford this." Just forming an expression sent pain rocketing across the top of her head.

"Listen, I understand where you're coming from. I haven't always been so flush with cash as I am now as a college-student-slash-barista-and-youth-volunteer, you know." His smile made her a little more dizzy than before. "Let's give this one to God."

"Well, that sounds great, but it doesn't pay the bills." Cassie had grown up hearing about faith, about God coming through even in the darkest situations, but she'd made some real missteps in college, and He had left her to pay the price.

"What would you say to Lark if she were in this situation?"

The fight fell out of Cassie. "I'd tell her to go to the hospital, not risk infection or whatever might happen without medical care." And Cassie could tell her daughter all that because Cassie would find a way to take care of her. But who was left to take care of Cassie?

# 15

Nora stretched, the Braxton-Hicks contractions having ramped up after her morning walk. In the weeks since her gestational diabetes diagnosis, Nora had mastered the art of testing, changed her diet, and gone back to regular exercise. She'd never felt better—or worse.

She stepped into the front door and sat on the bench, slipping off her tennis shoes and storing them on the shoe rack.

"How was your walk?" Ferris carried a still-sleepy Peyton.

She forced a smile. "It served the purpose it was designed for." She held her hands out, and Peyton leaned forward into her arms. When had her daughter grown so heavy? Nora settled onto the couch.

Ferris picked up the assorted books Gwendolyn had left behind. "So, I haven't heard anything else about your sisters." He kept his gaze on his reshelving, as if that would take the sting out of his comment.

"Well, I think the one who reached out might be crazy, so I haven't opened any more emails."

When he turned around, his face was serious, but his eyes sparkled with humor. "Crazy, huh? Maybe a family trait?"

"Ha-ha." Nora rolled her eyes. "We're not family. She's nothing more than a stranger who happened to come out of the same woman as I apparently did."

"Did she say anything about this *woman*?"

Nora covered Peyton's ears. "She's dead."

There was one way to assure the attention of a four-year-old—whisper. Gwendolyn poked her head around the corner. "Who's dead?"

"No one." Nora gave her husband a look-stare.

"I heard you say someone was dead." Gwendolyn's face flushed as if she were going to cry.

"It's no one we know." Nora grunted as she got up with Peyton, then handed the child to Ferris and took Gwendolyn's hand. "We were talking about someone far away who we've never met."

"I bet her family is very sad about it."

Nora looked at Ferris. For the first time in her life, Tammy seemed like a real person.

There was nothing better in life at that moment than the lidocaine numbing the top of Cassie's head. It didn't even bother her when the nurse spent over forty minutes scrubbing away dried blood, moss, and bark from her scalp. They wouldn't have to cut her hair, but Cassie didn't even care about that anymore.

Marshall didn't seem to be handling the situation as well. He sat in the corner of the examination room, his hands folded together and his head ducked as though he required constant prayer for enough strength to remain this close to her open wound.

Cassie closed her heavy eyelids, letting all thoughts drift away from the sanitary examination room with posters warning about the danger signs of strokes. She wondered about the story in the pages she'd read. About the baby and if it came into the world safely. She wondered about the box Shasta used to hold her photos and paperwork. And she also wondered what would happen if she couldn't comb through all of them.

That's when the tears started to roll.

The nurse patted Cassie's arm. "Are you doing okay? Are you feeling this?"

"No." Cassie swiped at a tear. "Just tired."

"Well, I'm about done with this part." She cleaned up her supplies. "The doctor will be in soon to stitch you up."

"Thank you." Cassie's voice sounded thick in her own ears.

Marshall sat down on the side of the bed. "You know, there are middle schoolers who talk to me. I think that's a good indicator that I'm a capable listener."

Their gazes met, his intensely deep brown eyes undoing the rest of her reserves. Then he wrapped his hand over hers, and she let a single sob free. The words that fell out of her mouth took on their own life as Cassie dumped out her fears about being a capable mother and taking care of Shasta. She told him about the student loans coming due. And—the biggest one— what would she do without Shasta?

He tipped her chin up, genuine concern in his eyes. Maybe it was the lack of sleep, the trauma to her head, the buildup of stress, but for that moment with Marshall, Cassie could see a way clear of it all. Like nothing would matter if they were . . .

"Well, good morning."

She tumbled out of her addled fantasy world and back into the medical environment and reality, promising herself she'd do better at getting sleep so she wouldn't be caught this vulnerable again.

The doctor stepped closer, her blond curls pulling away from a bun at the nape of her neck. She was both beautiful and natural, much like Shasta and nothing like Cassie. "I see they did a great job cleaning you up." She poked and prodded Cassie's numb scalp. "You must have hit that limb hard. Can you tell me what happened?"

This must have been the fifth retelling of the incident. It was beginning to feel like she was being interrogated, with the authorities looking for the slightest differences in her accounts. She replayed the night's events, leaving out her daughter sleeping alone in the house.

Sixteen stitches later, Marshall was a good deal paler than before, and Cassie was ready to go home. Not that she had the energy to jump back into the role of parent and caregiver, but those were two things that would not wait for her head to heal or her energy tank to refill.

Marshall helped her into his vintage Bronco even though there was nothing wrong with Cassie's legs. The hospital was about twenty minutes from the shop along the coastal highway. Cassie watched the wind-curved trees swish by and waited for Marshall to have his say about all she'd dumped on him, but he remained silent except for the tap of his finger on the steering wheel in time to a folksy seventies tune.

The rumble of the motor and his deep tenor singing along to the radio lulled Cassie into the state somewhere between consciousness and sleep. She found herself lost in the world of her marine birds, animals she understood better than humans.

Marshall turned off the road and drove in alongside the house, close to the tree she'd fought with the night before.

"Thank you for taking me in." The space between them seemed awkward and off-balance now, as if she'd poured too much of herself out to a man she knew little about. Marshall held all the power, and Cassie was exposed.

She came into the world on November 19, 1997, three weeks earlier than my due date but brimming with health. My daughter, Ainsley

May, perfect in every single way. Her chin had the softest cleft, and her dark eyes looked intelligent from the moment they first opened. She was the image of her father, and I hoped seeing her would put us back on the path toward the happy family I'd prayed for.

With Ainsley's early arrival, Topher had missed the birth, being out of town on business in Seattle. He'd been there almost every weekend for the last month and a half. I knew he was stressed with whatever project it was that had him flying back and forth from LAX to SeaTac. Maybe now, with Ainsley here, he could settle into being a father. I truly believed his priorities would shift when he saw her.

I heard him outside my hospital room. I had just finished changing my daughter and kissing her on the softly raised strawberry birthmark along her rib cage. My love for her was so much deeper than anything I could have imagined.

He came in with a bouquet of roses, his tie loosened, and a soft smile on his face. I didn't say anything as he walked closer and saw her for the first time. I was confident that no one could ever turn their back on a child who was so wonderfully created.

Leaning down, he kissed me gently on the forehead, much like he'd done before we lost our way. In that kiss, I found all the hope I needed to keep going, to keep fighting for our family and our marriage.

When Topher held Ainsley for the first time, I saw his love for her. It wasn't my wishful thinking. The pride in his eyes was complete and genuine. I could have missed that moment if I'd left him. That thought would haunt me in so many ways in the coming years.

Topher stayed for hours that day and returned in the morning to bring us home. We spent night after night staring into the face of our daughter, watching her sleep. She was the miracle we needed, the glue I couldn't even have dreamed of. As if the last months had never existed, we drew closer to each other.

Work kept hounding my husband. His company mobile phone would go off at all hours, Topher excusing himself to deal with whatever tragedy was befalling. But he always returned to us, and he'd stopped traveling as much as before.

A couple of days after Christmas, Topher let me know that he would have to make another trip to Seattle. It would be my first time at home alone with the baby overnight. I was scared, insecure, and I begged him to stay. There was something about this trip that made me nervous, as if he wouldn't come home again. That maybe our being apart would end the fairy tale we were living.

Topher, never one to like being held back, stepped away from me. He said I'd have to understand—this was his work, the business that supported us.

As much as I wanted to do as he said, I couldn't help thinking there was more to these trips than work.

~

Cassie ran her finger over her own cleft chin and looked across the room at Lark, seeing the same groove on her face and the dark eyes she'd inherited from Cassie. The similarities rattled her. But the baby in the story had been born a month before Cassie's birth on December 27. Though she still didn't know where the manuscript had come from or why, the commonalities were just a coincidence.

And there was the fact Cassie didn't have a strawberry birthmark. So why did she feel like her world was sitting on a fragile sheet of ice?

She did what she always did to calm anxiety: she Googled. Her first request from the vortex of knowledge was about strawberry birthmarks. Images of raised brilliant red markings filled the screen. She would know if she had something like that. But then Cassie read something that denied her explanation: These types of birthmarks faded until they were often unnoticeable.

Shasta shuffled into the room and stood in front of the window, her fist tapping on the inside of her opposite palm. They'd never had a television. Shasta said it ruined the mind by taking away the opportunity to think for oneself. Somehow, she'd raised Cassie alone without stooping to the use of an electronic babysitter. Cassie, for her part, considered Daniel Tiger to be a friend of the family.

She stretched her neck. The muscles ached, and she was still as tired as ever, but her brain refused to shut off. "Shasta, do you remember much about me when I was a baby?"

She turned, not just her head—she seemed fused together now in some ways. "I do."

"Do you remember if I had a birthmark?"

Her lips curved as if seeing something pleasant in her memories. "You were so perfect." She tapped her chest with an open palm. "My girl."

A bit of the tension holding Cassie captive to her fears and worries drifted away. Shasta's words, few as they were, touched the soul. They were what Cassie needed to hear to bring her current days into perspective.

Lark ran in from the bedroom where she'd been playing with yet more toys given to her by the grammies of Gull's Bay. In her hands were a small plastic saucer and a matching cup.

"Is that tea for me?" Cassie asked. It always was. She'd sipped thousands of gallons of invisible tea in her short years as a mother.

Lark's eyebrows wrinkled. "This isn't tea. It's coffee, and it's for Grammy Shasta." She held the offering up to Shasta, who took it and drank the imaginary drink like it was the best coffee ever brewed. This was why coming home was right and good. It filled the empty spaces in their lives. Cassie didn't need a doctorate in a field she'd be surprised to find work in, especially since she was both scared to be out on the water and had a tendency to become horribly seasick. What she did need was to spend however many more days Shasta had left with her and to see her daughter enjoy the privilege of knowing her great-aunt.

With both of them busy at the work of playing, Cassie snuck off to the bathroom. There, she pulled up the hem of her long-sleeved T-shirt to assure herself there was nothing to the worries. And though she knew her own body, she sighed in relief when she didn't find a strawberry birthmark staring back from the reflection.

But then . . . it was too small to really take notice of, and she wasn't sure if it was really anything. Cassie took out her cell phone and snapped a picture of her rib cage as it curved into her back. Staring at the image, she expanded it. There were just a few tiny pink dots.

They proved nothing.

But what if the manuscript had come from her mother? And what if she was still alive?

Cassie had never been one to watch soap operas, and she'd never fantasized about her mom coming back from the dead. She'd grown up happy, not even remembering Diane. The need for love had been filled by Shasta.

Yet questions pounded at the surf of her soul. What if Cassie's mother hadn't died? What if she just hadn't wanted Cassie anymore and tossed her at Shasta, faking her death?

It wouldn't explain everything, but if her mother was the woman in the story, maybe this was her only escape, the way she found to get away from her father.

A tiny bit of forgiveness entered Cassie's heart. She'd grown up safe. If this really was from her mother, then it could have been her way to keep her daughter far from Topher.

# 16

Nora's cell phone chimed. Another email. She scrolled to the settings and turned off the notifications. Becca was more than Nora was prepared for. After a week without a reply, she still didn't get the hint.

The girls giggled from the kitchen, where they baked cookies with Helen.

Before Nora's restrictive new diet, she'd never been held captive by sweets. But now, her mouth watered at the smell of sugar in the air. As if the baby were reminding her of the rules, Nora felt a tightening across her belly. This contraction was stronger than the Braxton-Hicks she'd been experiencing. And it held on.

"We have cookies." Helen's singsong voice carried across the living room.

"Do you want one?" Gwendolyn's face lit up with her smile.

"No, thank you." Nora scooted to the edge of the couch.

Her words took the grin off her daughter's face.

"I'm sorry, Gwendolyn. I'm not feeling well."

"You don't look good at all." Helen came close. Too close. Her perfume clawed at Nora's stomach. "I'd better give Ferris a call."

Nora shook her head. "I'm fine, really." Then another twinge took her ability to speak.

Marshall's knock on the door had become familiar to Cassie, strong and bold yet not provoking the normal feeling of intimidation she often had with men. She flung it open, surprised to find Aubrey with him. They both carried bags of takeout, and the scent of burgers from the pub down the road floated in front of them.

"Come in, please." She pressed her hand against her salivating mouth, hoping she hadn't let on how eager she was to tear into those sacks.

"We thought it would be fun to have dinner together." Aubrey set her package on the table, then went to the kitchen and washed her hands.

"Are there French fries?" Lark tugged on Marshall's clothing, once again an athletic, casual look that made him seem like he'd stepped right off an NBA court.

"Hey, little Larkie, would I forget your fries?" He shook his head and gave her a smile that made Cassie wish she hadn't been looking. They were all getting too attached.

Aubrey set the table with real plates and utensils, something Cassie had only done a couple of times since being home. She poured water in glasses for all of them, always one to be sure they didn't become dehydrated.

Cassie guided Shasta to her seat. When their gazes met, Cassie tried to express herself without words the way Shasta often did.

Her aunt tapped Cassie's cheek with her palm and kissed the air between them.

Cassie's stomach growled loudly enough to call everyone's attention her way.

"When was the last time you ate?" Aubrey set a napkin beside a plate.

Cassie shrugged. "I guess I forgot."

"But I bet Shasta and Lark were fed, weren't they?" She lifted one eyebrow.

Heat worked its way up Cassie's neck.

Aubrey squeezed her in a quick side hug. "You're becoming more and more like Shasta every day."

Cassie blinked hard. Compliments like that were too much of a good thing.

As they settled into seats, Shasta on Cassie's left and Lark on her right, the room grew quiet except for the hungry sounds of Lark, eager to get her hands on French fries. They were ready to pray, and Cassie was out of practice.

Aubrey reached out and took Marshall's and Shasta's hands. Wondering what Lark would think about this, Cassie did the same. Her daughter didn't hesitate to join in the circle. After a prayer that reminded Cassie of all the things she had to be thankful for, Aubrey said *amen*.

Cassie wished she could shrink. Praying had left her with an irrational anxiety, as if everyone could see how she'd stopped trusting God, stopped even thinking about Him at all. Yet she still believed. She and God hadn't come to terms in quite a few areas, and Cassie really wasn't ready to do that work.

Marshall set a ridiculous pile of fries on her daughter's plate, then added a pool of ketchup beside them.

Lark's eyes were round and excited. She dug in as if she'd never seen a treat like this one. The nutrition game needed to be upped around there.

Aubrey passed out hamburgers. "I wanted to get together and talk out a few things."

Cassie's appetite shriveled.

Aubrey placed a hand on Shasta's arm. "I promised Shasta that, as things changed with her health, I would never leave her out of a discussion involving her." Aubrey looked at Cassie, who felt the weight of everything pressing down. "You're doing a great job, and I know how important it is to you to shoulder the load, but you should also know that this community is a kind of family. We want to help. It's not a failure to let us step in, and you're not making up for any self-inflicted guilt by doing it all yourself."

It was bad enough thinking of her aunt having to hear about her own fragility, but Cassie was getting a major dose of that discomfort as her own issues were laid out on the dining room table for Marshall and everyone else to hear. She swallowed a bite of hamburger, not fully chewed, then washed the lump down with water.

Aubrey bit off the end of a fry, then grinned at Lark, who had ketchup spreading across her mouth like lipstick. "I don't want you to feel attacked."

Well, that was just great. Cassie did feel attacked but couldn't put her finger on why.

"We've put together a schedule." Aubrey pulled a paper out of her purse and slid it toward her. "It's not exhaustive, but it would make us all feel like we were helping, and that's important to us. We don't want to be left out. Do you understand?"

Cassie dropped her gaze to the plate, nodding but unable to speak.

Rubbing her fingers along the edge of the paper, she pulled it into her line of sight. There were times set up for Lark to spend with her grammies and times for Shasta to be with friends, often with activities attached. Aubrey even had her helping out in the coffee shop for two one-hour shifts per week. Thursday nights were left open for Cassie to have a few hours to herself, something she honestly couldn't remember having outside of work and class. Every other night, dinner would be provided by one of the trusted community members. "This is a lot."

"Not so much. We love Shasta too. It's our chance to spend

time with her, a privilege, and I don't think you understand what a blessing little Lark has been to all of us."

"She's a blessing," Shasta repeated, her fingers working her napkin.

Marshall cleared his throat. "The church has a preschool slot available for the kiddo starting next week . . . if you want it. No charge."

"I couldn't accept that." Lark kept asking about kids to play with, but they weren't a charity case. At least they weren't yet. That very well could be the future they were heading toward.

He swallowed a bite and wiped his face with a paper napkin. "Do you know how many art classes and supplies Shasta has donated to the church preschool? This is far from a gift. It's more of a payback."

Shasta smiled, as if remembering a peaceful time.

"Lark." Cassie turned to her daughter. "Would you like to go to preschool?"

She covered her hand with her mouth the way she'd seen Mrs. Collins do. "Oh, I would like to. Are there kids there?"

"A whole herd of them." Marshall's eyebrows rose. "It's loud and crazy. Totally your jam."

She clapped. "I want my jam. Can Marshall take me there?"

How quickly her daughter replaced her! "We'll see," Cassie said.

"I'll start tomorrow," Lark declared.

Lark's overabundance of confidence often surprised Cassie, who'd been desperately shy at this age. But unless something changed, Lark didn't have a thought about not fitting in. She was who she was, and that was perfection. "Not tomorrow. I'll have to check into it; then I'll let you know."

"Marshall can fix it." She returned to the hamburger patty she'd pulled out of the bun.

"Where does this hero-worship thing come from?" Aubrey laughed.

Marshall rubbed his fingernails against the chest of his T-shirt. "We're more of a dynamic duo. I'm the tall and mighty sidekick."

Cassie's face felt like a painting of contradictions. She smiled, rolled her eyes, and cringed as it all tugged on her sutures.

After the meal, Aubrey and Cassie cleared the table while Shasta watched Marshall and Lark build a town out of blocks for Lark's Polly Pockets.

Cassie ran hot water into the sink and added dish soap. "Aubrey?"

"Hmm?" She laid a bright orange dish towel on the counter.

"What do you remember about me as a baby?"

Aubrey cocked her head. "What do you mean? I wasn't here when you were that young. I can tell you that Shasta considered you to be a blessing she hadn't expected or even known she needed. But she wouldn't trade you, and now Lark, for anything."

"That's strange. It seems like you've always been here. I don't remember a time before you." Cassie slipped dishes below the surface of the sudsy water. "When did you move to Gull's Bay?"

"I think you were just starting fifth grade. I'm not surprised you don't remember." She disappeared for a moment, then returned with water glasses. "I hope you didn't feel like we'd overstepped with our little plan."

She did, but Cassie also felt cared for, something she was beginning to realize had been missing in her life. "Not at all."

# 17

Topher returned home on New Year's Day. He was distracted, as if he'd only come home physically, but mentally, he was still handling the business in Seattle. It didn't take long for him to increase his travel schedule again.

I had my daughter now, and Topher, while absent most of the time, clearly loved Ainsley as much as I did. He treated me better too, though in a more platonic way than he had before. Maybe that was a normal transition for a couple as they became parents.

We went about our lives, creating our new dynamic until the night Topher was called away in the middle of the night. I was sure I'd heard a woman crying through his mobile phone, but he insisted it had only been a man from the office, and I'd been dreaming and thrashing in bed when he got the call.

When he came home almost a week later, he seemed tired, drained. As if he was getting sick or had just survived a battle with the flu. Over the next couple of months, I noticed that he never seemed to recover fully. He'd hold Ainsley extra long and as tight as she'd allow, as if he thought she'd slip away from him. I imagined being away from her so much while she changed so rapidly must be hard on him.

We were in the heart of summer when Topher suggested a family vacation to San Diego.

126

I can't explain how happy this made me. We'd be together for more than an entire week, walking the boardwalks, sitting in the sand, maybe even a trip to SeaWorld. Ainsley was eight months old and really beginning to explore her world, curious about everything.

We lived only two hours away from our destination, but it felt like we were traveling to another world, our little family together with no distractions for ten days.

Ainsley took to the beach as if she were born to live on sand. She grabbed it by the handfuls, watching it escape her tiny fists and sprinkle onto her legs. Topher scooped her up, taking her to wade in the shallow waves, but she screamed as the water touched her toes and held on to him as if she were in danger.

I pulled out the lunch we'd brought with us and set out a picnic on an oversized beach towel. Within seconds, we were spotted by a nasty horde of seagulls. They swooped and cawed, hoping for a scrap or two of our food.

My frustration shifted to delight as Ainsley reached for the birds, doing her best to mimic their calls. We spent the next thirty minutes tossing our lunch to scavengers and being rewarded by our daughter's laughter. My sweet girl.

I'll treasure that summer day for the rest of my life. It was the last time I'd be blissfully ignorant about the evils of the world.

What did Nora get for her seven-hour trip to the emergency department? Rest and a silly diagnosis—downright embarrassing. It wasn't preterm labor causing the pain. Nora had managed to pull an important ligament, and it was angry.

Along with the rest came help from her mother-in-law and the loss of control over Nora's own life and the lives of her family members.

Maybe she would open an Instagram account. She could always delete it when she was free again. Nora wasn't about to let a thing like social media take her away from the tasks she valued.

She scrolled around the app store, found the app, and downloaded it. Instagram was a deep dive into parenthood, mommy life, and productivity hacks. How had she not known the benefits that could be mined there?

She'd followed over fifty people when her very first follower popped up. She'd been found by @beccaboundforglory.

~

On Thursday night, Mrs. Collins arrived just as expected. She carried with her a warm dinner and a bag overflowing with knitting supplies.

"Grammy Mrs. Collins!" Lark cried as she dove off the couch, where she'd been listening to Cassie read a book.

Mrs. Collins untangled herself from the bag and set the food on the table, then lifted Lark as if she were accustomed to handling this kind of weight. Maybe she was, considering the industrial-sized flour and sugar sacks in the bakery kitchen. "Oh, sweet girl. I've missed you."

"Are we going to bake?" Lark wriggled free and ran to the bag of yarn.

"Not this time, I'm afraid."

"Lark." Cassie removed her daughter's hands from things she had no business getting into. "That belongs to Mrs. Collins. You need permission before touching other people's things."

"Oh, she's fine." Mrs. Collins waved it off. "Lark, I could use some help from a big girl like you to get dinner set out."

Lark never missed a chance to act the part of an adult. Cassie was glad she'd be starting preschool soon. There was plenty of time in her future for being a grown-up, but childhood washed away with the tides.

Shasta came out of her room, looked from Lark to Mrs. Collins, and scowled. Cassie's evening out—even if it was just to go to a support group, of all things—was slipping away. Shasta could be weird about Lark and other women. It was never as bad as her reactions to the one who frequented the coffee shop, but it was there. So was her undying fear that something horrible was going to happen to Lark. Those concerns were contagious when Cassie failed to intercept them early enough in the process.

"Shasta, I'm heading out. Is there anything you need before I go?" Cassie stepped between her and the others.

Shasta shook her head. "I'm hungry. It smells good."

"It should," Mrs. Collins said. "I made chicken and dumplings from your recipe."

The expression on Shasta's face relaxed, as if the words brought her back into the reality of her longtime relationship with Mrs. Collins. Cassie thought back, wondering when Mrs. Collins had appeared. It was before Aubrey, but not much before. She'd been widowed and moved to Gull's Bay for a fresh start in life, but aside from that, Cassie knew little about the woman's life beyond the bakery, her frugality, and her involvement in everyone's lives.

The support group was held in a classroom at the high school of a neighboring town. The smell, somewhere between foul body odor and cleaning products on steroids, made Cassie wonder if this was where teams came to watch film after practice too.

The chairs had been arranged in a circle so haphazard it would have caused her geometry teacher to faint. Eight of these seats were already taken. Cassie found a spot with an empty space on either side and sat there, wishing she'd gone to a movie or for a walk on the beach instead of coming here. After all, she had a support group of her own made up of people who loved her aunt nearly as much as she did. What was the point of talking through her struggles with strangers who most likely had much harder situations in front of them?

Cassie nearly gasped when Chloe Bassett, the woman who managed Shasta's physical therapy, walked in with a stack of papers. With the anonymity gone, Cassie struggled with vulnerability. It wasn't like this was Alcoholics Anonymous, but she'd thought the people would be strangers, making it easier to blend into the background and listen.

A woman stood up. With snow-white hair and a cane to help her balance, she must have been in her eighties. Cassie hadn't realized Parkinson's patients would be present. "Welcome to the caregivers' support group, with a focus on Parkinson's." Her voice was strong, unwavering. "For those I haven't met, my name is Priscilla. My husband, Henry, was diagnosed with Parkinson's disease almost ten years ago. I am the current president of our little group, which means I get the honor of introducing our guest speakers." She smiled at Chloe. "Many of you already know Chloe Bassett, as she specializes in the treatment of people with Parkinson's." Priscilla started to clap, and the small group joined in.

Cassie could have slithered away. If a woman Priscilla's age could care for her husband for over a decade and also run the support group, she had nothing to complain about.

Chloe passed out a few papers, then took her place at the top of the lopsided circle. "Thank you for inviting me to talk with you. I know many of us have had conversations about your loved ones and their physical needs. Tonight I want to talk about how we can keep them strong and prevent possible injuries. After that, I will spend some time talking about you as the caregiver and how you can keep yourselves healthy."

She went on pouring knowledge over them until Cassie had filled five pages with tiny printed notes and couldn't take in another drop. Plans raced through her head, ways to get Shasta out of the house and moving while remaining safe. Fear had caused Cassie to keep her in the apartment as much as possible in the name of safety. But there was hope.

As Chloe left, Cassie started to pack up her own area, then noticed she was the only one making a move.

Priscilla asked everyone to introduce themselves.

She'd missed her chance to leave, and now Cassie was about to be looped into one of the social interactions she hated the most. There was so little about her that was worthy of an introduction. She listened intently as the people before her did their bits.

Margaret was caring for her sister, a woman who had streaks of violence with her hallucinations. Mr. Miller's wife had passed away, but he kept coming to the group for the company of the friends he'd made here. Nicole's father had very few of the physical symptoms, but recently he'd started thinking he was back in Vietnam.

But the woman who went right before Cassie nearly broke the room. Cora announced to the group that she and her husband would be moving into a care facility because she had just received her own Parkinson's diagnosis. She went on about how they trusted God to carry them through this trial.

It was tempting to rush to the hall and scream at God. If Cassie had thought He'd treated her unfairly, she was mistaken. How could a God who supposedly loved His people allow for both a husband and his wife to contract this horrible death sentence?

When the room fell silent, she knew without looking up that it was her turn. "I'm Cassie, and I'm very fortunate." She dared a quick glance at Cora, who smiled as if she were there to care for her. "My aunt raised me, and now I have the honor of caring for her as she goes through this. I have a daughter who's almost five, and a lot of people who are willing to help me out. That's how I could be here tonight. Thanks for having me."

131

She expected the man on her other side to start talking, but he didn't.

Priscilla cleared her throat. "Cassie, how are you doing with getting enough sleep? Nights can be hard with a Parkinson's patient."

She wondered if news had traveled this far about her run-in with the tree limb or her search for Shasta, but that was silly. "I'm tired. But I'm doing okay." She forced a smile.

"Honey." Cora wrapped one hand over the other. "You look like you're wound as tight as a . . . Hmm, I can't remember the word I was looking for, but you know what I mean. We're here to help one another. I commend your love for your aunt, but you're looking at a future without her. I know what that feels like."

Cassie's throat clenched until she thought she wouldn't be able to get enough air to survive. She couldn't look that far into the future. Shasta's doctor had said she had anywhere between three months to three years, with three months more likely, but Cassie wouldn't be ready to live without her for at least three centuries.

Mr. Miller walked over and took one of the empty seats beside her. "Don't feel like they're trying to make you sad. They want you to be open about how you're feeling, how you struggle. It's only by being open and honest that we can help each other. Trust me, we all think about the end. Sometimes, it's scary, and other times, it's almost soothing. There's nothing wrong with any of it—just acknowledge your weakness. No judgment here."

He patted Cassie's arm, and his touch brought forth the tears she'd been biting back.

"I don't feel like I can do a good job, even with the help."

# 18

I don't know if you've gotten my emails, so I'm messaging you here. I'm really sorry about not having much medical information for you. Lex is . . . well, she's kind of stubborn. The thing is, she remembers Mom being gone that year. I think it left a scar on her heart. She and Mom were always tense.

But I don't want you to think Mom was mean or anything like that. She was a great mother to me, always compassionate and loving. She came to every single one of my games; Maddie's and Lex's too. She always seemed to be trying to prove something. Lex thought she was trying to make up for leaving that year, but then we found out about you. Now she thinks you were what Mom was trying to make up for. Not that you're a mistake or anything like that.

I really would like to talk in person. This is so difficult to communicate.

Cassie stayed awake after Shasta's five a.m. wandering, taking time to go over the budget, the shop receipts, and payroll. The schedule for the day was typical: full. Shasta had a morning doctor's appointment, and Cassie was to swing by the emergency department for a quick removal of her stitches.

But of course they could only find one of Lark's shoes until Cassie finally got down on her hands and knees and located the other, wedged under the couch. As she stood again, she heard the clatter of Lark's cup hitting the floor and liquid splashing. That required a new outfit for Lark and a near nervous breakdown for Cassie, but she didn't let it show. If she had, they'd never leave.

Lark's ordeal was quickly matched by Shasta, who tried to pour iced tea from the heavy pitcher kept in the refrigerator. The endeavor resulted in a flooded kitchen and another ten-minute cleanup. Somewhere in this madness, Mrs. Collins texted to ask if Lark was ready.

Cassie and Shasta pulled into the hospital parking lot ten minutes late for Shasta's appointment, a fact that turned out to not matter when Cassie called to let them know they were on the way up. The doctor had been called out for an emergency, and they needed to reschedule. At least she could get the itchy stitches removed from her head.

She rebuckled Shasta's seat belt and drove to the handicapped parking space near the emergency entrance. "Looks like you're getting a break. I'm the one seeing the doctor today." Cassie flashed her aunt a smile that was returned with an expression of fear. "Nothing to worry about. They're going to take these stitches out." She tucked her chin and pointed to the top of her head.

"Diane did that?"

A shiver ran through Cassie's middle. "No. Diane is dead. It's just you and me, remember? And Lark."

Shasta nodded, but the tension lining her forehead didn't agree.

Cassie kept her hand on Shasta as they entered the building. The second set of doors slid open, and a woman with her face bent over a cell phone nearly plowed into them.

"Oh, excuse me." Nora's eyes went round with recognition.

"No worries." Cassie steered Shasta forward.

"I sure hope everything is okay."

Cassie turned back. *Show no weakness.* "We're absolutely fine. I hope you're okay." Her voice carried a sticky sweetness Cassie wished she could take back. Nothing tasted worse than stooping to the level of implied nastiness.

"Came in for an ultrasound. All's well."

"I'm surprised Ferris isn't with you." Cassie could have slapped her own face. When had she become so condescending? She and Ferris had been friends in high school, and if Cassie was honest, she'd admit to having had a crush on the older guy then. But he'd never been more than a friend to her—and then Nora had caught his attention and he'd only had eyes for her, which hadn't made an ounce of sense to anyone. Sure, she was beautiful, but bossiness was her overriding quality.

"We came in separate cars. Ferris headed back to work." She tipped her chin as if to issue a challenge.

"Have a nice day." Cassie and Shasta stepped into the reception area.

Shasta immediately took a seat in front of a television playing an old rerun of *The Price Is Right*.

When the nurse called Cassie back, she signaled that Shasta could stay in the waiting area.

She started to let Shasta know she would be gone for a few minutes, then thought better of it, thinking Shasta was as mesmerized as Lark would be.

The stitches came out faster than they went in, and with much less trauma. "Everything looks good up here. How have you been feeling? Any headaches or dizziness?"

"No." Cassie hesitated. "Actually. Would you mind looking at something? It's just that I can't see it." She lifted the side of her shirt. "Can you see any red marks, maybe where there used to be something?" At this rate, they'd soon have Cassie on the same medications as Shasta.

The nurse flipped her glasses back into place and bent close, then swung the light into place. "I think I see what you're talking about. It looks like the remnants of a strawberry birthmark, but I'm not a dermatologist. Is it giving you problems?"

Cassie pulled her hem down. "No. I was curious, is all."

"Okay then. You're good to go." She slid open the curtain and waited for Cassie to exit. Or was she really Cassie? She needed help sorting this out. Luckily, she had an old friend with the knowledge and experience to shine a light on her situation.

# 19

Message from @beccaboundforglory

I hope it's okay that I passed your email address on to Maddie and Lex. Maddie doesn't do anything without Lex's approval, so I don't expect you'll hear from her for a while. I want you to know that Lex is really a great person; she's just very suspicious. Not everyone can have my trusting nature . . . wink, wink.

I saw that you finally posted some pictures. OMW, your girls are gorgeous! The little one looks just like I did at that age. Post one of yourself. I'm dying to see what you look like!

Nora stared at her reflection in the bathroom mirror. Even with her pulled ligament healing, this pregnancy had taken more out of her than the first two combined. How could she post a picture when she looked all puffy and exhausted? And why was she even considering this? Becca was a stranger. Even with shared DNA and closeness in age, they seemed like complete opposites.

Tipping closer to the mirror, Nora shined her cell phone flashlight on her hair. Three gray strands popped up like defiant, wiry flags. She plucked them each out, cringing as the sharp pop sent zings of pain through her scalp.

⁓

Cassie was surprised when Ferris Milford offered to meet her at the coffee shop late that very afternoon. Bringing him into her suspicions would either uncover the truth she might not want to know, or reveal her to be a paranoid maniac unsuited for motherhood and caregiving. Hopefully there was a rule against sharing information with wives, even though she'd specifically asked him not to make this police business.

She had nearly come to the end of the story, but instead of rushing through, Cassie found herself scared to read another word. If Lark were in this situation, she'd tell her daughter to put on her big-girl pants and dig in. But Lark would never have doubts about where she came from. Her father wasn't a secret; he just wasn't around.

"Cassie George." Ferris held his arm out, embracing her in a side hug. "It's been way too long. How are you?"

She tipped her head. "Okay."

"I guess we wouldn't be here if everything was great." He pointed to the back of the room.

They slid into seats, Cassie facing toward the front of the shop so she could keep an eye on Lark and Shasta. "This is off the record, right?"

"I'm not a reporter. There's no such thing as off the record with detectives."

"You know what I mean. Can you keep this between you and me?" She tapped her index finger in a fast rhythm on the edge of the table.

"As long as there isn't a crime involved." He laced his fingers, rubbing his thumbs back and forth. "I did some quick digging, and you're not going to like what I've found." He passed her a copy of a death certificate for Cascadia George. Cause of death—sudden infant death syndrome.

Her face tingled. There had to be a mistake, but what were the odds of someone having the same name and the same birthdate? Yet this had to be wrong. "No. This isn't mine." She dumped the contents of her sack onto the table. "I have all this. There has to be plenty of evidence right here to prove I am who I say I am."

"I really hope you're right. Take me through it." He pushed the papers and photos into a stack.

She swallowed, trying to force steadiness into her voice. "Most of this seems to be stuff my mother sent my aunt—actually her cousin, though I've always called her my aunt. There are letters here. I've had a chance to read a couple. My mom talks about my birth, my father. There's a mention about her moving here and asking Shasta to keep me while she packed up our place in Seattle. I was only a toddler when I came here. My mom was supposed to join me in a couple of days."

Cassie's mind shifted to the story, as if the words typed onto those pages could actually be a piece of her life. She wasn't ready to tell Ferris her worries that her mother had been running to escape a dangerous man. What if all of this brought Topher—or someone like him—to her door? She needed to work out this issue, but more than that, she needed to protect her daughter.

"Tell me about the accident." He stared at a picture of her mom and aunt together on the beach.

"There's not much to tell. She was in an auto accident. My aunt said the doctor assured her my mother died quickly. She probably didn't even know what happened—just there one minute and walking into Heaven the next."

"It must have been horrible for you. I don't remember you ever mentioning it."

Cassie shrugged. "I don't remember much about it, but

Shasta said I cried for my mom for the first few weeks." Outside, the rain was falling again, matching the mood of the conversation. "I feel bad for not remembering her. If something happened to me, I'd want Lark to be happy most of all, but I'd hope she could recall a few things we'd done together . . . special moments."

"I have no doubt she would. You seem to be a wonderful mother." He twirled a pen around his index finger in a fidgety habit that made her crazy.

"Milford, you'd better be careful. You're starting to sound like a reasonable person with a heart rather than a cold-blooded detective."

He shrugged. "There's no hiding anything from you."

Lisa came by the table and set a coffee in front of Cassie and another by Ferris. "I thought you might like these." She picked up a stray napkin from the floor and headed back toward the kitchen.

"I wouldn't worry about that too much. Most people think of guys in my position as one step away from an IRS auditor. Let's see what we can find here to help your situation." He pulled out the picture of Cassie with her parents. "What was your father's name?"

She shook her head. "I'm not sure. I've never seen it on any of the documents or pictures."

"But you know this is your dad?"

Cassie turned it over, pointing at the words, *Me, Cassie, and her daddy.*

"It seems rather unusual that she didn't use his name here." Milford tapped the photo.

Warmth wrapped around Cassie's neck. "They weren't married or anything." *Like mother, like daughter.* "I've always wondered if he was married, maybe had another family. I've thought about doing a DNA test and seeing if I could find him, but what would the point be? He had to know my mom died, and he still didn't come to get me." An idea popped into her mind. "What about DNA? Couldn't I prove that I'm who I say I am that way?"

"I thought of that too. But you'd need a closer relative than your mother's cousin, or direct DNA from your mom," he said.

She handed him another photo. The one of Cassie's mom in the hospital with her. "That was with the letter my mom sent to my aunt right after my birth."

He nodded. "If I can take these, I know a guy who could possibly say for certain that these are both you. The remains of the child listed as you were cremated. There's no record of where the remains went after your mother picked them up from the mortuary."

Cassie tipped her head back. "My mother didn't pick them up—I'm right here."

"She did have a stone placed with your name and dates carved into it." He tapped the side of his head. "Seems like a lot of trouble to go through if your child is alive and well."

His sarcasm settled in her gut like expired milk. "I have an idea. It's not impossible for her to have had two babies . . . could I be a twin?" It didn't explain the name, but desperation sometimes led to brilliance.

Her twin explanation sounded both ridiculous and genius at the same time. It would explain an awful lot, except why there was only one baby in the picture sent to Shasta. Another wave of dread pulled Cassie down.

Milford shook his head. "The hospital records were sent to my office just a while ago. I've been able to scan over them, and the birth was listed as a singleton. Honestly, I thought of the twin thing too, though it should have already come up."

"So, how do I prove I am who I say I am?"

"Do you know your blood type?" He checked something on his phone, then set it back on the table.

Cassie reached for her purse, shuffling through the clutter, in search of her wallet. Once, not long after high school, she'd given blood. The Red Cross card was probably still stuffed in a slot. She set ChapStick, a novel she'd forgotten about, and two of Lark's toys on the table before finding what she looked for. "Okay, here it is. I'm O positive."

"That's a match."

She clapped her hands together. "See. Does that clarify this mess?"

The way he sighed told her all she needed to know before he even uttered a word. "That's the most common blood type. It's a good start, but it really would have only cleared things up a bit if it hadn't matched."

"You mean, it would have told you my aunt was a liar?" She took a sip of her coffee to keep her tongue busy.

"Listen, I've begun looking into kidnappings. I need to do more digging, but so far, I can't find a child anywhere near Washington that matches your description."

Cassie's nerves actually hummed. "I'm not a stolen kid. Trust me. There's just been a mistake." She'd never wished her mother were still alive more than at this moment.

"Daddy." A child jumped onto the seat beside Ferris.

A moment later, Nora stood at the end of the table with a stroller.

Cassie scooped up the items on the table, shoving them into her bag. "Well, Ferris, it was so great to see you again. Nice catching up. I should be getting Lark and Shasta upstairs." She hoped her eyes were saying what her mouth couldn't. *Please do not say a word about this to your wife.*

She walked toward the kitchen, not looking back.

The more Cassie thought through the possibilities, the more she felt secure in the story she'd been building in her head. Cassie's mother was the woman in the manuscript she'd been sent. Somehow, at some point Cassie hadn't yet come to, her mother had gotten away from Topher. She must have changed

Cassie's name. And Shasta had to have known at least a portion of the situation left in the shadows.

～

Nora pounded the skillet onto the burner. She flung open the refrigerator and retrieved the chicken breasts and vegetables. With the slam of the door, magnetic letters slid to the bottom, a handful coming loose onto the linoleum.

Walking in as if he'd done nothing wrong, Ferris had the nerve to cross his arms and lean against the wall, an amused expression on his traitorous face. "You know you're being ridiculous, right?"

She looked at him, felt the words she shouldn't say rising, and tipped her head away just in time.

"She needs my help on something."

"Well, isn't Miss Cassie lucky to have you running to her aid." Nora doused the pan with olive oil, which sizzled on the overheated surface.

"You make it sound like I came riding in on a white horse to save her."

She didn't know what he'd done, and that was the part that frazzled her.

Ferris came up beside Nora. "Babe . . . if I could tell you, honestly, I would." He rubbed circles in her tight lower back.

If it didn't feel so good, she'd push him away. "She better be in big trouble—that's all I have to say about it. I expect to see Cassie's face on the county jail roster by the end of the week." Knowing her reaction was overblown, she tossed chicken into the pan, where it snapped and popped. Back in high school, it had taken her a year to pry Ferris's gaze away from Cassie. And maybe more than that, Cassie had never seemed to care what anyone thought. It made Nora crazy then, and it made her crazy now.

His laughter crawled up her spine.

It's not like she really thought little-Miss-Gull's-Bay had done anything prison-worthy, but seeing her all snug in the booth with her husband didn't sit well with Nora. And Ferris refusing to give her the details added to the bad flavor in her mouth.

On the third day of our vacation, we decided to go into Mexico. From San Diego, it was only a half-hour drive to Tijuana. I'd never been, but the idea of a day over the border was exciting.

We arrived at around ten in the morning. The streets were crowded, with bright colors bursting from street vendor stands. Ainsley seemed overwhelmed by joy at the surroundings. We placed her in the stroller, stuffing her diaper bag into the compartment below.

It must have been the stimulation of the sounds, smells of spicy foods, and intense colors that put her to sleep earlier than she'd usually go down for a nap. I draped a light blanket over the stroller to provide her with shade while we shopped.

We wandered around, turning onto a street with green and white flags waving overhead. Music played and people bumped into each other as we walked. I checked on Ainsley then, afraid the noise would wake her, but she slept deeper than I'd ever seen her do at home.

"Do you think she's okay?" I asked Topher.

He nodded and added something about me seeing trouble where there was none.

Topher led us into a shop, where he took the stroller and told me to pick out something to remember our trip by.

I made my way through hand-woven textiles, pottery, and jewelry, looking for just the right thing, an item I could display at home to remind us of our rebuilt family. I found the perfect item, a painting on cloth of three tropical birds, the colors in neon shades and black. When I turned to show the find to Topher, he and the stroller weren't behind me. I found them near the back of the shop, looking at clay figures.

My first instinct was to check on Ainsley, but my husband stopped me. "Don't keep messing with her. She's sleeping." He then pulled me into a hug, his arms tight around my waist, and kissed me. I know it sounds simple of me, but I got lost in that kiss, both consumed and safe at the same time.

We made our purchase and went on down the street. I felt as if I were walking through a celebration. An hour must have passed before we stopped for lunch. We'd sat down at an outdoor table, Topher pulling the stroller along his side.

"I can't believe she isn't awake yet." I'd been Ainsley's primary caregiver, and letting Topher take control and be so involved made me squirm.

"I'm sure she's just fine. Traveling is exhausting, even for a baby." He tapped the handle of the stroller.

Before he could stop me with another line of male reasoning, I hopped up and walked around the back of his chair, squatted down, and gingerly lifted the edge of the blanket.

And I screamed.

The sound of my own wailing still wakes me in the middle of the night.

I'm not sure what happened next. It's a blur of color and sounds and the explosive crash of my heart.

My daughter was gone.

Cassie bolted up from the couch.

Both Shasta and Lark looked at her.

She smiled and tried to appear as if her heart wasn't pounding out of her chest. The answer she'd created about who she was and how she'd gotten here crumbled with the information presented in this chapter.

She ran the name over and over again in her head. *Ainsley . . . Ainsley.* It was a name she'd considered for Lark, but that had to be just another coincidence. So many coincidences were piling up that Cassie was standing before the Mountain of Happenstance.

Ferris would need to be told, but there was a part of her that wanted to keep some of it to herself, even though he was on the same side.

Someone knocked on the door.

Cassie's mouth fell open, and she stood there in a state of utter fluster, as if she no longer had access to the proper etiquette for the situation.

"Mommy." Lark's cocked head looked like a puppy evaluating something new. "The door is knocking."

"Sure. Yep." She blew out a long breath, trying to regain composure, then opened it.

Mrs. Collins stood on the other side. It was her night to bring dinner. Cassie hadn't realized it was that time already.

"Come on in. I'm sorry. I was reading, and I'm having a hard time returning to the real world."

Their gazes met, with Mrs. Collins seeming to evaluate her, though as a huge reader herself, she should surely understand.

Cassie took the casserole pan out of her hands and set it on the dining room table. It was warm and smelled of garlic and love.

From the bag on her shoulder, Mrs. Collins pulled out bread, surely freshly baked, and then a bowl with a plastic lid, green salad showing through the clear glass.

"You don't have to go through this much trouble. We're happy to eat ramen noodles and frozen peas." Cassie lifted the plates from the cupboard and set them out.

"Nonsense. Statements like that will get you an extra vegetable dish next week." She smiled, but Cassie didn't doubt her commitment to their healthy eating habits. Mrs. Collins was a woman with a lot of love, and she tended to provide that through her kitchen.

"Would you please stay and eat with us?" Cassie placed the extra plate in front of her, emphasizing her determination.

She looked around the room and watched Lark guide Shasta into the bathroom to wash their hands. "You have a beautiful family here." Her eyes glistened with tears. "It would be my pleasure to spend some extra time with you all."

"I've been wondering about something."

"Yes?" She stood behind her seat, hands gripping the chairback.

"Where did you live before coming here? It's hard for me to remember when you came and, I'm ashamed to say, I don't know much about your story." Cassie chewed her top lip. It felt so wrong to ask personal questions of people a generation above her, but it also felt selfish that she'd never gotten to know any of the people in their community aside from the support they'd always offered her.

Mrs. Collins's knuckles turned white as she held the chair tighter. "There's nothing all that interesting about where I was before. I moved here to get away from my mistakes. Gull's Bay welcomed me, and now I feel like I've always been here. Whatever happened before is in the past, lessons to be learned from, but fears that are no longer welcome."

Cassie let that sink in. Her own past had a way of following her around, reminding her of all the places she'd failed, the people she'd let down, and the corners she'd cut. How could Cassie turn those fears into lessons and take away their power?

She was trying to find a way to ask this when Lark ran into the room and lunged at her. "All clean." She looked at Mrs. Collins. "Grammy Mrs. Collins, it's my birthday coming up."

"Oh my. What should we do about a cake?" The tension in

the woman's face had faded, replaced by the love Cassie often saw when her daughter was part of any conversation.

Lark's eyes lit up. "I want it to be purple with sparkles and a unicorn on top. And candy." She clapped her hands.

Shasta laughed. She spoke less each day, but her laughter warmed Cassie.

"That sounds like a great project. I might need help." Mrs. Collins winked.

Lark raised her hand. "I can help. I'm a great baker."

"Yes, you are. And a blessing to me in ways you will never know." Mrs. Collins tapped Lark's nose. "Let's eat this food before it gets cold."

It was Cassie who offered the prayer that night, the first time since she'd left for college.

# 20

All around Nora were Ferris's family—his mother, father,
brothers. They were a force. The only relative outside of her
daughter whom Nora could begin to claim was a woman whose
words on the screen seemed to bounce. That level of perkiness
was exhausting, yet her daughter Peyton showed signs there
could be a genetic connection.

Nora stood in front of the open refrigerator. Nothing had felt
right since finding Ferris with Cassie George earlier. He was a
sucker for a woman who needed saving, and Nora wasn't that
kind of person. Maybe her years of independence were wearing
on him. Or maybe it was the endless pregnancies, the swollen
ankles, the stretchmarks.

She had no doubt she could manage just fine if her husband
ever took off with another woman, but she wasn't sure she could
handle it if that woman was Cassie. That crush he'd had on

her in high school was still a bit of a splinter in her heart. It didn't make any sense. Maybe it was the relentless hormones, or the surprise of seeing Cassie again, but Nora felt as insecure as a teen.

Nora wasn't one for flowery declarations, but she loved Ferris more every passing year. And she knew he deserved her trust.

The next hours were a blur of unfamiliar people asking questions in a language I didn't understand. When we were finally connected with the Mexican police, they took us to their headquarters and started the investigation by interrogating both me and Topher.

I was furious, screaming at whoever would listen that my child was gone, and they needed to be out there finding her. *I* needed to be out there.

Hours passed before I was reunited with my husband. He assured me that he'd talked to an officer about calling in the FBI—that they could come over the border and help in the search. But what evidence could there possibly be? Our child had been snatched right out of the stroller.

"How could you let this happen!" I screamed at Topher until I couldn't breathe, my throat raw and my voice going hoarse.

We stayed in Mexico that night and for the next week. The FBI requested the stroller and obtained it from the Mexican police but were concerned that it hadn't been kept covered. They asked us a million questions about our families, our marriage, everything. But we hadn't done this. Mexico hadn't even been on the plans for our trip.

I retold the entire story a dozen times.

We'd left for Tijuana in the morning. It was a last-minute decision. We'd been having a wonderful time together as a family. We crossed the border around ten in the morning. Ainsley had been unusually tired, I assumed from the travel and all the stimulation

150

of Tijuana. She'd fallen asleep, and I'd covered the stroller with a light blanket.

They asked about the seat belt inside the stroller—had it been buckled?

It wasn't. I knew this specifically because I was the one to unhook it. I'd wanted her to be comfortable while she slept. The stroller was tilted back, and she liked to snuggle onto her side, pulling her feet in.

Her tiny little feet—I could hold them both in one of my hands. Her dark hair was beginning to curl over her perfect little ears. She knew me. She needed me. What had she thought the moment she woke up in the arms of a stranger? And what could that horrible person be doing to my daughter?

At some point, I was given medication to make me sleep, but even that was fitful, as my brain tried its best to keep me conscious to find my baby before it was too late.

We were in Mexico, in a hotel room with no air conditioning, a stain on the ceiling, and a door with a tricky lock, watching people walk by down on the street, wondering who had our child and why they'd taken her. Was she okay? Was she even alive?

The doctor came in and visited me every day, often giving me more of the medicine that made me lose my focus and drift away. But none of it completely relieved the pain. Nothing ever would.

Cassie threw the pages across the room, where they scattered into a mess of paper. She wanted no part of this story, yet Cassie *was* Ainsley. As much as she didn't want to believe it, it had to be true. Maybe that was the explanation for why she'd never really felt grief over her mother's death. But why wouldn't she feel the loss of the mother who had so obviously loved her before she was taken?

Cassie paced back and forth, anger flushing hot across her

skin. There was no good answer. Either she was who she'd thought she was, despite no proof, or she was an abducted child who didn't know where she belonged.

And what about her mother? If the woman who'd written the story was really the woman who'd given birth to Cassie, where was she now? And how had she found her? Why wouldn't she just come forward and tell Cassie the whole truth rather than sending a mysterious manuscript?

Maybe she'd seen Cassie and felt disappointed in who she'd become. Maybe she just didn't care anymore, but she'd loved baby Ainsley. That fact was certain.

Cassie pressed the button on the side of her phone, bringing the screen to life. Contacting Ferris would be easy; he'd take over and find the answers. But she couldn't get her fingers to make that connection. This was personal. She needed to find out as much about who she was as she could before bringing anyone else in again.

Outside the window, the sun had gone down, but the moon was still low on the horizon. How would she ever explain to her own daughter that she didn't know who her true grandmother was? Especially when Lark herself had never had a father either? Cassie's life kept stealing—it had taken from her, and now, it tore away the foundation for her child.

Cassie ran her thumb over the screen. She opened a new text and selected Marshall's name, but there was nothing to say. She needed a friend, and she felt like Terri was a lifetime away.

Shasta's door squeaked open at the same time Cassie's phone beeped to signal the alarm. Cassie had the app set to go off every minute until she dismissed it, that way hopefully avoiding another middle-of-the-night chase through Gull's Bay.

Shasta shuffled into the room, tapping every horizontal surface as she moved past.

"Did I wake you?" Cassie looked at the papers strewn across the floor, then back at Shasta.

A wave, like a chill, ran over her body. "I'm . . . drink."

"You need a drink? Let me help." There was a fine line between treating her aunt like an infant and giving her the care she needed. Cassie could never tell which side she was falling on. In the kitchen, she pulled out a chair so Shasta could sit, then half filled a plastic cup with water from the tap. She placed it in front of Shasta and took the seat next to her. "Shasta, where did I come from?"

Her face wrinkled. "God made you."

Even in the midst of confusion and frustration, Shasta's answer brought a smile forward. "I mean, when I came here, did I really come from Diane, or was someone else involved?"

"Your mother left you. I loved you." When she spoke now, her voice had a rasp that made her sound as if she'd smoked a pack a day for decades, though Cassie had never known her to pick up a cigarette. Each word was pushed out with effort, as if it was a chore to communicate.

Laying her hand over Shasta's, Cassie felt the thin skin, the bones moving beneath her touch. "Shasta, do you believe Diane was my real mother?" The words hung in the dimly lit room, bringing tears to Cassie's eyes and a blanket of fear over her life.

Shasta looked at her through eyes that continued to grow deeper and more veiled with time. "No." Then, forgetting the water she'd come for, Shasta stood and went back to bed without another word.

Cassie wanted to stop her, to mine for the whole story—everything Shasta had buried about Cassie's early life—but the weeks had made her wiser. To push too hard would be to lose forever the answers she needed so badly.

The next morning, the papers were still all over the living room. Instead of doing the responsible adult thing and picking them up, Cassie got herself, Shasta, and Lark ready for the day—give or take a few steps—then headed downstairs to the coffee shop.

As long as she was in the same place as that manuscript, all Cassie could think about was baby Ainsley and her mother. Cassie couldn't have gone on if something happened to Lark. Yet somehow, the woman in the book had. She'd written her story. But Cassie didn't have that kind of strength or the faith to withstand the disappearance of her child. Lark was Cassie's very own heart, beating outside of her body. Without Lark, Cassie ceased to exist.

The morning rush was in full swing, giving a lively hum to the air that transported Cassie to better times, when she knew what she was doing and what came next. Much of her high school homework had been done here, the sounds and smells giving her the feeling that what she did was important and would set her life on some kind of invisible track toward perfection.

If only high-school Cassie had known the truth—outside of these walls, she'd had no idea who she was or who she could be. Cassie had crumbled once away from the familiar faces and solid guidance. When no one she really knew was looking, she'd let herself go, drinking within the first term of college, and on and on.

Lark let go of Cassie's hand and jetted toward the counter, her usual starving self.

Cassie's stomach twisted when she saw Marshall come to the register. They'd shifted from speaking easily together, more so than she had with any man in years, to hardly seeing each other. Who could blame him? What man would want to get involved with a single mother who didn't know where she came from, had a towering mountain of debt, and a dying aunt to care for? Honestly, if he had been interested, she would have wondered what was wrong with him.

The look he gave her was deep and serious, not his usual quirky smile. She'd pushed him too hard by dumping her stuff in his lap. From what she'd seen, Marshall was a free man, no complications or responsibilities beyond college, work, and his volunteering. "The cook just got in. There was an accident up the highway, and he was stuck in the traffic. It could take a bit to get your food out. Would you rather have it upstairs?"

Little bubbles started bursting in her stomach. This was still her home, her shop, her community. If he thought he could just get her out of his sight so he wouldn't have to deal with her, well, that wasn't going to happen. "We'll wait." Cassie crossed her arms tight over her chest.

"Would you mind writing down your order so I can keep the line moving?" He slid a tablet across the counter.

Cassie glanced behind them. Only one couple waited, tourists. "Sure. Customers should come first." She hoped he caught the barb. Shasta was the owner, but Cassie was second in command around here, and he didn't need to forget that just because she'd had a blubbering meltdown in front of him.

The pen was still in her hand when Shasta started tugging on her sleeve.

"What is it?"

"She's the one." Shasta lifted her arm toward the woman in the corner. When would this stop?

Then Cassie's heart dropped into her shoes. What if Shasta meant the woman in the booth was the one who sent the manuscript, the one with the answers? What if *she* was Cassie's mother? Donated egg or not, shouldn't Cassie have known and felt some kind of connection with the woman who'd brought her into the world?

Cassie stepped away from the counter, guiding Shasta with her. Lark had already gone to her toys. "Do you mean she knows about where I came from?"

Shasta's clouded eyes stared through her, tears pooling, but she didn't answer. She didn't need to. Shasta was scared. Cassie couldn't be sure, and she couldn't trust that her aunt's statement about the woman was true, but she had every intention of finding out when Shasta wasn't with her.

"Okay. Let's not worry about that right now. What's important is the three of us: you, me, and Lark. We're family no matter what happened in the past. We'll have our breakfast and worry about all that later."

Shasta nodded.

A booth opened up, and they took their places on the benches. It wouldn't take long for Shasta to grow restless and start wandering the shop, but for a moment, she was there with Cassie, the one person who would always love her, sitting across the table.

# 21

Marshall came by the table as Cassie was sticking the last bit of cinnamon roll into her mouth. He gathered the dishes, keeping his gaze away from hers. *Fine.* She didn't need this from him or anyone else. Cassie certainly hadn't come home to find a man. In fact, she was perfectly well suited to live life single forever. Back in her youth-group days, they'd talked about Paul saying singleness was a great thing. Well, that was one biblical reference she could get behind. Bring on the single life.

He came back a minute later, before they could escape. "Hey." Marshall leaned down toward her ear. Too close. She could smell the men's bodywash lingering on his skin. "I'm off work in a few minutes. Could we talk?"

Cassie glanced back at Lark, syrup in her hair and a chunk of egg on her cheek, and Shasta, not much cleaner. "I'd better get these two cleaned up. Don't worry. You don't owe me anything."

He straightened. "Oh. It's going to be that way?"

Cassie's expression probably screamed, *"Don't you dare start this here."* "Fine. If you have something to say, you can say it upstairs to the three of us." She kept her voice all sing-songy, so Lark wouldn't become concerned.

"Well then, I'll see you up there as soon as I freshen up." His response mimicked her tone so perfectly it nearly got her to crack, but she wasn't about to let this man off that easy. There'd been something going on between them, and if all this was too much for him, she could understand that, but he ought to have the decency to say it to her face.

Shasta had gotten up during their back-and-forth. Cassie spotted her heading toward the woman in the corner and popped out of her seat, pushing past Marshall.

"Shasta." She slung her arm around her aunt's shoulder and guided her in a half circle. "It's time for us to go upstairs and get Lark washed up."

It wasn't surprising that Marshall caught up with them before they made it to the landing by their door. He scooped Lark into his arms, tickling her until she burst into giggles. It made it a lot harder for Cassie to keep her anger burning.

Inside, Shasta shuffled off to the bedroom and Lark bounced around, showing Marshall every ballet move she was sure she'd acquired through sheer desire to be a ballerina. Nothing would distract her from the attention of their visitor aside from Daniel Tiger, so once again, Cassie gave in to the screen.

When Shasta came out, she went to her puzzle. Cassie laid it out near the window on a high table so Shasta could stand as she worked the giant pieces, a little something Cassie had learned at Thursday's support group.

"I have to get the laundry in. If you'd like to talk, you can follow me." Without waiting, she started for her room, where she picked up a basket and went back to the hall, opening the closet doors that hid the washer and dryer.

Marshall stood with his hands pressed down into the pockets of his sweatpants. "Listen, I can see you're mad at me. Do you want to tell me what I did?"

She dropped the basket onto the floor at her feet and raised the washing machine lid, careful not to give in to her temper and slam the lid into the cupboard above it. "You didn't *do* anything." The water started to pool in the bottom of the tub, and she wanted to shrink down and crawl in. But of course, Cassie did what was sensible and tossed in a detergent pod, then the clothes. Once she closed the machine, there was little choice. His body blocked the hall so that she had to look at him. What a mistake that was.

"It's because I haven't been by or texted, huh?" He had the good sense to look down at his very clean shoes.

"I just thought we were friends, you know? I'm embarrassed. I shouldn't have dumped all my stuff on you. I know I'm making it hard right now. It's hard for me to be that real with anyone, and even harder when the other person isn't ready for it." Perspiration dampened the hair at the top of her neck. She tugged at the collar of her T-shirt, not a square inch of her body anything less than squirmy.

"We are friends." He shifted his weight from one foot to the other. "It's . . . I'm not ready to tell my story. I know that makes me sound like a big baby, and maybe I am, but I need more time. I came to Gull's Bay to sort out some things about myself, my family, and who I want to be. I didn't expect to love living with Mr. Watkins, to find myself connected to the people." His chin lifted, and his deep coffee eyes looked straight into her. "I didn't expect to find you here."

She hadn't expected to find him either. And wished she hadn't. Marshall, with whatever secrets he was holding on to, was a risk Cassie couldn't manage right now. "I understand." But truthfully, she didn't. She wanted to know everything that had brought him to this place and time, to the point where their paths crossed, leaving them awkwardly staring at each other in silence.

Then he reached out and put his palm on her crossed arms. It sent a shiver through her, both exciting and frightening at the same time. "I really like you. Can you be patient with me?"

Cassie shrugged, keeping her hands tightly tied to her elbows.

He moaned and tipped his head back. "Before I was a jerk, did you like me at all?"

And he had her again. A smile broke through Cassie's armor, shattering the effect of strength she was going for. She released her grip and set a hand on his. "I can wait. You don't owe me your story, and I'm really not in a position where I can spare a friend."

When his gaze came back, it sent waves through her stomach.

Cassie swallowed. "Friends." Taking a step back, she tried to form a boundary between them. She had a very young daughter. Any man who thought he could become anything deeper than a friend would need to pass a rigorous background check.

The first thing Cassie did once Lark and Shasta were asleep was make a call to Terri. No FaceTime for this conversation. They'd been doing a lot of texting, but for this, she needed to hear Terri's voice.

When she answered, tears sprang to Cassie's eyes.

"I think I was kidnapped, and my real name is Ainsley."

There was a beat of silence; then Terri cleared her throat. "What are you talking about?"

"It's that envelope I told you about . . . the weird one that showed up. It's the story of a woman who wanted a family, a baby and all that. Her daughter was kidnapped in Mexico. I think that's why I'm supposed to read it."

"That's a stretch. Maybe it's just fiction."

Cassie's mouth fell open. She'd always been prone to falling into whatever story she was reading, but this time felt different. "I don't know. The way it's written, I think it has to be her story."

"Okay, but then why do you think the baby in the story is you? Did you ask your aunt about it?"

"I did, but I'm not sure what to make of the things she says. The dementia is getting worse by the day."

"Is it possible—now hear me out on this—could you be feeling scared that you're about to lose the only family you have? I mean, you have Lark and me . . . but Shasta has basically been your mom since you were tiny. Seeing her like this has to be very difficult."

Cassie rubbed her fingernails up and down her jaw. "I'm more scared than any time in my life, even when I found out I was pregnant, but I do think there's more to this." Her breath lifted the hair off her eyes. "I asked a guy from high school, a detective, to look into a few things. He found my death certificate . . . I mean, Cassie George's. She's been dead since 1998." A cynical laugh jumped out of Cassie's throat.

"That's super eerie. Do you need me to fly up there? I'm worried about you."

"No, you're coming up on finals. Though I wouldn't say no to a visit after the term." The thought of Terri coming here made Cassie smile through the dark cloud of everything that seemed to be falling on top of her.

"Plan on it. I can't wait to see you. And in the meantime, have you Googled this missing baby? Maybe they found her, and this is nothing."

"I haven't had the courage. Plus, I don't even have a last name. I'll let you know what I find out."

Before she could launch into her situation with Marshall, a crash came from Shasta's room. "Oh no. I have to go."

"I'm praying for you."

Cassie blinked hard. "I know you are."

~

We'd been in Mexico for three weeks when Topher told me it was time to go home. How could that be? Without my daughter, there could be no home. I'd been walking up and down the streets day after day, looking for any sign of Ainsley. I distributed flyers and begged people to call the number if they knew anything. All this I did in the Spanish I'd learned for the purpose of bringing my daughter back to my arms. To this day, all I can say in that language is, "*Ayúdame a encontrar a mi hija.*" "Help me find my daughter."

We drove back in a haze of grief so thick I can hardly remember passing from Mexico into the United States. What kind of mother leaves a foreign country without her baby?

A couple weeks after that, Topher went back to work, and I started my weekly trips to Tijuana. The authorities approached me many times, asking me to stay out of the more dangerous areas, but that only pushed me toward them. The kind of person who would snatch a child from right under the nose of her parents was not the kind of person I expected to find on the safer blocks.

News got back to Topher that I was doing this. He was furious, claiming I was trying to get myself killed, but that wasn't true. I still had hope that Ainsley would be in my arms again.

Our marriage had returned to the condition it had been in when I was pregnant. The only difference being me. Now, I screamed back at my husband. I blamed him for not watching the stroller close enough, though there was no way to tell if she had been taken under my watch or his. I insisted he didn't love her the way I did, but I knew that wasn't true either. Basically, I stripped him of everything: I wanted to hurt him, to see that he was in as much pain as I was, but no one could understand what I was going through. My very heart was missing.

Topher began his regular business trips again, each one lasting longer than the one before. I knew I still needed him, but I couldn't bring myself to tell him that. Everything in my life felt fragile and vulnerable.

It was April of 1999 when the Seattle Police Department sent a local officer to my house with the news that would make it all worse. While Topher was standing outside of a restaurant on one of Seattle's piers, a truck had come careening through the crowd. The driver was unconscious due to a medical crisis, and, his foot on the gas, he ran straight into the side of a building. On his way, he'd hit seven people. Four had died of their injuries. Topher was one of those four.

I woke up in the hospital. There was a point where my mind and body could take no more, and I'd met that point. They kept me there for a few days, saying my exhaustion was at a dangerous level.

My friend was there with me most of the time. She was the one who made the arrangements to have Topher's body brought back to California. She started the plans for the memorial, and she let people know what had happened.

In late April, we had a service for both Topher and Ainsley, as the Mexican authorities had informed me only a week after Topher's death that the bones of a baby had been recovered. They felt sure this was my daughter.

I stood over my husband's grave, having lost everything, and tossed a handful of dirt on a casket that held only one of the two I grieved.

In the coming weeks, I waited for Ainsley's bones to be sent to me. I'd planned to have her buried next to her father, but they never came. The FBI questioned the Mexican authorities, who finally admitted that they didn't know what had happened to all that was left of my baby.

When the gravestone arrived, I was there alone, watching them set it into the spot above Topher's final resting place. Both of their names were carved into the granite, but it was the dates of Ainsley's life, from birth until the day she disappeared—that short time defined by a single dash—that broke me. I wept there until the sun went down and the groundskeeper asked if he could call someone to come get me. Then I went home alone.

That was the day I began to plan the end of my own life. I couldn't go on and didn't want to go on without my family. Each day I sat in my chair, the Bible beside me collecting dust, and watched out the window, hoping something would happen to kill me so I wouldn't have to do it myself. Yet I kept feeding that uncaring cat.

My friend checked on me regularly. I made an attempt to sound like I was getting better so she wouldn't feel she had to watch my every move. I regretted what I was going to do to her, the guilt I didn't want her to feel, but knowing her as I did, I knew she would.

My doctor had given me sleeping pills after Ainsley's disappearance. I took every pill in the bottle and washed them down with a Diet Coke.

That should have been the end for me, but it wasn't.

# 22

Nora lined the girls up in front of the rhododendron and snapped a photo in the perfect natural light. Within a few minutes, she had it posted on Instagram, applying a few appropriate hashtags and tagging the local shop where the clothes had been made from fabric she'd chosen herself.

This social media thing wasn't so difficult. Likes popped up almost immediately. She refreshed the page again, finding it up to fifteen. When she checked who the likers were, she found it disappointing that @beccaboundforglory was not on the list.

Gull's Bay Community Church was a place Cassie had loved growing up. It was where she felt safe and connected. But she hadn't been back since finding out she was pregnant with Lark. Every time Cassie tried to make another step toward God, the shame took her down. She hadn't followed the example she'd been taught. Maybe God could forgive her, but she wasn't sure she wanted Him too.

The plan this Sunday morning was to walk from the shop to the church, only the equivalent of a few blocks. Exercise for all three of them was a priority that had been pushed aside, but since the support group meeting it was at the front of Cassie's thoughts. There were two ways to get to the church: one was flat until the stairs that Shasta had fallen down; the other had a slight incline, but no steep steps. She decided on the slow-and-steady strategy.

Lark bounded out of their room wearing not the simple dress and tights that Cassie had set out, but a combination of colors and textures that could make the wildest teen cover their eyes. She'd managed to pull the tutu from her dress-up clothes over a sparkly purple skirt. Her orange shirt hung down, half covering the tulle. A green sweater covered her arms, and she'd donned her rubber boots to complete the look.

"Wow, Lark. That's quite an outfit. Did you see the clothes I put out for you?" Cassie started toward the bedroom to retrieve the outfit that wouldn't call all attention their way.

"It's pretty." Shasta rubbed her hand over Lark's curls. "Perfect."

There'd be no going back now. Lark was heading to church looking like a parade float.

Cassie's phone buzzed with a text from Aubrey, who offered to walk with them. Cassie had made the mistake of telling her they were going this week; now she had to follow through on the commitment. She texted back that they would appreciate the company. What Cassie really meant was she could use the extra hands, but admitting her shortcomings had never been easy for her.

When Aubrey arrived, she helped Shasta down those horrible stairs while Cassie carried Lark and her bag of distractions. Outside, the air was crisp and clean. The wind was a salt-laced breeze—a blessing in their little town that commonly felt whipped around by the ocean air.

The farther they went, the more Cassie's legs ached to really move. Though the last weeks had been exhausting, it was a mental fatigue. She'd never been a great runner, but with the sun shining, she longed to let go and push her muscles to the limit.

Lark bounced along in front of them, following the paved path. She sang a song she'd learned from Aubrey about baby turtles finding their way across the sand and into the sea. It was a catchy tune, almost too catchy. Cassie had found herself humming it when Lark wasn't even around.

Shasta and Aubrey were about twenty feet behind, their one-sided conversation a happy sound, though too distant for Cassie to make out the actual words. Shasta's face was flushed, but she was smiling.

When they turned the corner and could see the church in the distance, Cassie called Lark to her. Holding hands, they waited for Aubrey and Shasta to catch up, then let them take the lead as Cassie held back Lark's enthusiasm that was in complete contrast to her own reluctance.

Cassie had miscalculated the amount of time the trip would take. Music and voices already came from the door.

Lark jumped like a kangaroo with a belly full of sugar. She hadn't stepped foot in a church her entire life, but that didn't stop her from thinking it was akin to Disneyland.

The church had a small but eager congregation. They were welcomed at the door by familiar faces who acted as if Cassie had only been away on a brief vacation rather than run for distant lands.

They followed Aubrey to the row of cushioned chairs where Marshall was already seated next to Mr. Watkins. There were so many things Cassie loved about small-town life, but when it came to relationships with men, the tight quarters weren't always helpful. It wasn't her choice to be seated next to him, all dressed up like he was ready to model for J.Crew, but that's where she ended up. As if the scent of his soap wasn't enough to break down her walls, the deep timbre of his voice booming out the worship song nearly took her balance. Thanks to Marshall,

Cassie was taking another run at crushing on the tall guy from the football team. Any assumptions she'd made about maturing since she'd been in college washed away. Inside, she was regressing into the boy-crazy younger self she'd made fun of.

When the music ended, they took their seats, Lark tucked between Cassie and Aubrey. This was a risk, but Cassie wasn't ready to hand her off to the children's program, not when she was starting preschool the next day. Being together all the time—like they'd been since coming home—had given her an appreciation for the moments with her daughter. As a mom who'd previously been gone nearly sixty hours a week, the feeling that four hours three times a week was going to break her heart came as a surprise.

"I'm hungry." Surely Lark's whisper was loud enough to hear from any location in the sanctuary.

Cassie tapped her finger on her lips, then opened the bag and found the sack of Cheerios she'd packed.

Lark responded with a wide but silent grin.

And then she crunched.

Cassie looked around, but no one else near the second-to-last row seemed to notice the way her daughter's mouth sounded like a dinosaur chewing up a bone. The sermon might as well have been given in Hebrew. Cassie's mind was preoccupied with crayons rolling under the seat in front of them, a water bottle dropping, and the rough scratching of Lark's pencil as she shaded in the picture on the front of the bulletin.

When the prayer was said and they stood to sing the final song, Cassie held back her own scream of *amen*. Amen that they'd made it through, and amen that no one had outright turned in their seat and given her the why-did-you-bring-a-child-to-service stink eye.

Outside, Cassie stared out at the ocean while Lark ran circles in the grass.

"She did so well in there." Aubrey patted the back of Cassie's arm. "Not even five. I hardly heard a peep the whole time."

Cassie turned, eyes wide and mouth open. "Seriously? That was insane. I'm sure I lost a year off my life."

Aubrey shook her head. "Mothers hear their children through amplified ears. Really, she did well. You should be proud."

That was a funny thing about parenting: Parents were proud for reasons that made no sense. Cassie's daughter had been quiet, but was that what she was aiming for? Cassie had been so concerned that people would judge her because her daughter made noise, that they would have reason to say she couldn't handle motherhood and shouldn't be raising a child on her own. But what she really wanted for Lark in life was to have a voice and use it—maybe not in the middle of a sermon, but at the right time and place.

Nora squeezed her fingers into fists as Cassie yammered on with person after person after church.

"Don't even ask me." Ferris lifted Peyton into the stroller. "I'm still not going to tell you what Cassie and I were talking about."

"Ferris Milford, that is just ridiculous. You made a vow to me."

"Yep. And I made a commitment to my job too. You know I'm not doing anything wrong." He kissed her cheek. "I guess you'll just have to trust me."

Nora bit at her bottom lip. It wasn't Ferris she didn't trust. If she were the kind of person who analyzed her feelings and reactions, she'd have to acknowledge that she really didn't trust women in general. The reaction might be irrational, but the circumstances that led her to that way of thinking . . . maybe Ferris was right when he told her to stop beating herself up.

I woke up in the hospital, disappointed. The last thing I remembered was lying down, my mind going foggy, knowing I'd be with my daughter any minute. I hadn't even remembered that the lady who cleaned our house had changed her schedule. She'd found me unconscious and called 9-1-1.

The taste of tar filled my mouth, and agony throbbed under my skull. The pain I'd been feeling seemed intensified now that everyone knew how deep my grief ran. I could physically feel the missing parts of me. Breathing was a kind of suffering I couldn't force my body to stop.

I wasn't surprised when my friend appeared next to my bed. I'd become a child in so many ways—people shared my information and took turns caring for me. I didn't want any of it. I wanted to die and be whole again.

Closing my eyes, I turned to the side, acting as though it was still too much effort to stay awake.

She dropped something heavy onto my lap.

My fingers grazed over the surface. It was familiar, like something that had once been part of me. I opened my eyes to find my Bible on the white sheets that covered my legs.

Her hollow stare probably mirrored my own. I couldn't tell if she was angry or disappointed. "You don't have to open that. You can choose to lie there and pretend that you're all alone. I'd probably do the same thing if I were in your shoes. But I'm hoping you'll open the pages and read your own notes in the margins." She eased into a chair she'd pulled over to my bedside. "I understand you're in the middle of great pain, but when I got the call from your housekeeper, it . . ." Her voice grew raspy, then faded out.

I reached my hand toward her, the IV draping over the bed railing. "I'm sorry. I didn't mean to hurt you."

"I'm not trying to make you feel guilty. You have enough pain, but God still has a purpose for you."

Those words attached themselves to my heart. God still had me here for some reason. I didn't understand it, but maybe someday I would.

There had been a point in college where Cassie had thought about what it would be like to die. She wouldn't say she was suicidal—more like desperate. If Cassie had lost what the author had, she wasn't sure she could have gone on. But that woman had a faith that was tested and strengthened.

Cassie tucked the pages back into the envelope. They didn't come together with straight sides anymore, the papers creased and worn.

The time had come to let Google have a swing at her concerns.

Cassie opened her laptop. The first thing she searched for was *missing Ainsley Mexico*. The results were a hodgepodge of cases, none of which seemed to match. She added *baby* to the criteria.

That's when she found the grainy photo of an old flyer. There'd still been a part of her hoping to find this was all a work of fiction, but there they were, and she knew the eyes she was looking at. They were the eyes of her own daughter, the trait everyone said she'd inherited from Cassie. Baby Ainsley wasn't a story. She wasn't a murdered child. She wasn't even missing. Baby Ainsley was her.

Cassie slid the laptop onto the couch and melted to the floor. Everything she'd known in her life was a lie, but who had initiated her false story? What if Shasta were behind it all? How could Cassie stay here and care for someone who very well might have been part of her kidnapping?

A scream grew in her throat, but she swallowed it down where it would have to reside with all her other feelings of betrayal and loss. Until Cassie had more information, this would stay with her alone.

The healthy thing to do next would have been to drink a glass of water and go to bed. The action she took was to Google her "mother." Though Cassie had no personal memories of Diane—and by the looks of the information piling up, the woman could possibly have been a kidnapper—she still had a twinge of guilt. It was odd, but giving up a lifetime of considering a particular person as one's mom didn't happen with ease or immediacy.

The first page of hits offered things she'd seen before in her absent-minded Googling, but this time, Cassie dug deeper. She wanted to know about who Diane was, what she'd been doing in the years after leaving Gull's Bay, and more about the accident that took her life.

Cassie had read her obituary before, but she pulled it up onto the screen again. Diane George died in an automotive accident in Seattle, Washington, on April 11, 1999. A connection popped into place. Topher, her father, had died in Seattle. Had he been searching for Cassie? Did he know she'd been there too, or was it just a coincidental business trip?

There was little about Diane. No birth announcement for her child, no story about her death. Just an archived bare-bones obituary. Cassie couldn't find that Diane had ever done a thing worth mentioning. Maybe it was the anger that steamed in her veins, but this realization that Diane's life had no moments worth memorializing on the internet did not surprise her.

She needed more help from Ferris, but this was getting into an area that tipped into police business.

# 23

Nora folded the towels straight from the dryer. She couldn't stand the way Helen dumped laundry on the sofa to handle again during her television programs. Efficiency was the key to life that so many people were missing.

Her phone buzzed on the kitchen counter. Closing the dryer door, she stepped in from the garage and checked the number. Not an Oregon area code. "Hello?"

"Nora, this is Maddie. Becca is refusing to come to Easter if Lex doesn't talk with you. Is there anything you can do about that?"

Nora pulled the phone from her ear and looked at the display again. "What?"

"I know it's asking a lot, but this is our first Easter without Mom, and I just don't want us to fall apart."

"I'm not sure what this has to do with me, or how you got this number."

Silence stretched out until Nora wondered if the call had dropped.

"I thought Becca had told you all this. Aren't you chatting with her?"

"Chatting? That's an exaggeration. We've exchanged a couple messages. Listen, I don't know you, and I don't know your sisters. I was only looking for some medical history, and I'm beginning not to care about even that."

"Oh dear. I think I made a mistake. You just can't understand what it's like for us. We're all we have now that Mom and Dad are both gone. Lex feels like she has to keep us together. I mean, what would happen if we let some rift get between us now?"

Nora tucked a loose clump of hair behind her ear. "Well, I guess you'd be like me." She disconnected the call.

Lark stood by the door of the apartment, bouncing up and down for ten minutes before it was time to head to preschool. Though Cassie found their time together since returning to Gull's Bay to be a beautiful bonus, Lark was all too ready to spend time with new friends her own age. Lark had not inherited an ounce of Cassie's introverted personality.

Aubrey had volunteered to hang out with Shasta while Cassie took Lark in for the first day, but the plan was to have the three of them make the walk together starting Wednesday.

Cassie moved Lark away from the door, explaining to her for the seven hundredth time that it could open and knock her down, but Lark rolled her eyes like a professional doubter.

"I'm going to be late." Her hands planted on her hips, she tapped one foot on the ground, as if keeping the beat of a very irritating song.

"If we leave now, you'll be far too early."

"But not late." She raised her eyebrows.

Cassie needed to get this sassiness under control, but she knew exactly where Lark had picked up her attitude. Lark was her reflection.

"She should stay here." Shasta pounded a fist on the table. "She stays."

Cassie rolled her neck, stretching stiff muscles. "She's going to be fine, Shasta. It's just preschool."

"She needs to be here." Shasta's face twitched with unease.

Lark left her post near the door and put her tiny hand on Shasta's fist. "Grammy Shasta, it's okay." Her voice was smooth, like warm maple syrup. "I love you, and I'll be back soon."

Shasta did her best to rub her hand over Lark's curls. The tremors seemed to be getting worse, going from manageable to out of control in a matter of a few weeks. Cassie would call the doctor as soon as she dropped off Lark.

Aubrey tapped on the door as she came in. "Lark, today is your big day." She went straight to the little girl, squeezing her in a hug. "You and Mom have a wonderful walk to school. The sun is shining bright, and the birds are talking."

"I hope no one fed Bogart yet. He likes me to do it. Marshall told me I'm his favorite." She hopped up on her toes and kissed Shasta's lax cheek. "See you later, Grammies."

Cassie caught herself mid eye roll. If she wanted her daughter to drop the habit, she would need to do it first.

It wasn't long before Cassie received her first opportunity to gain control of her own formidable sass. They found Marshall downstairs, serving customers.

Lark bounced across the room as if she were Rabbit and she were Tigger coming for a visit. "I'm going to school, Marshall."

"That's the rumor I heard." He bent down to her level. "I wonder if you need something special for your first day."

"Like chocolate?" Her eyes went wide.

Marshall stuck his hand into his apron pocket and pulled out a woven purple bracelet with silver accents.

"That's so pretty." She stretched out her little arm like a princess. "Can I wear it?"

He looked to Cassie for approval, as if she could deny it even if she wanted to. "Of course. That was so kind of you."

"It's nothing. I saw it and thought of her."

Lark turned her wrist one way, then the other, letting the light reflect off her new jewelry. "What does it say?"

Cassie hadn't noticed the small beveled plate on one side.

Marshall leaned his elbows on his bent knees. "It says *Hope*, because no matter what the situation, we always have hope because of Jesus."

Lark narrowed her eyes. "You're going to have to tell me more about this guy." She hugged him, then took Cassie's hand. "I can't be late to my first day. Thank you, Marshall."

They had begun to walk out the door when Lark stopped and turned back. "Don't forget I'm having a birthday."

"I would never forget such an important occasion." He held the door for them. "Cassie, I know you have your support group on Thursday night, but I wondered if I could drive you there. I'd like to talk . . . maybe spend some time together."

Cassie swallowed and looked down at Lark for a distraction, but when she needed her daughter's interruption, the girl was silent. "Okay. That would work." They walked away, Cassie's gaze remaining forward until she heard the door shut. When she looked back, he was still there, standing on the sidewalk, all tall and dark and handsome.

Cassie accepted Aubrey's offer and took the long way back, walking down to the beach and along the shore. Above her, gulls cried, their familiar high-pitched longings resonating in her heart like the call of lifelong friends. An adult female flew over her head, floating in the air above her, the white belly as smooth as the silky clouds beyond.

She'd never been sure what had drawn her to study marine birds, especially those in the Pacific Northwest. Looking back over her educational decisions, she questioned going on for graduate degrees in a line of study that could never put her in a comfortable living situation.

Yet to her, the birds were part of home.

She sat on the damp sand, the cold working through the seat of her jeans. Sandpipers skipped along where the waves had just vacated, looking for a treat. A western gull inched its way closer, his friends farther off. Cassie dug bare feet into the sand, scraping the surface with the tips of her big toes. The waves crashed and roared; the wind hummed. The coast wasn't the California definition of tranquility, but for her, this was peace.

The last time she'd happily spent with her parents had been on a beach. Maybe somewhere inside, she remembered the birds flying overhead, or the sound of the water. But she did not remember her mother or father. Like a fading dream, they weren't even there.

Tears blurred her eyes. She was alone on this stretch of sand, yet Cassie was safe, protected, embraced by her surroundings. She felt God here. And to her surprise, that feeling was one of love and welcome, rather than condemnation.

As she'd read through the pages of the story, Cassie had often been drawn into the way the writer immersed herself in faith, until she didn't . . . and that was when the woman had cracked. Cassie had been coming apart along the edges for years, always trying to mend her own wounds with academic accomplishments. Biologically, the writer was not her mother—an egg donor somewhere out in the world had that title—but still, the woman who'd given birth to her was the one whose life was speaking truth to her heart. Cassie needed to find her.

She picked herself up, dusted the wet sand from her jeans, and jogged alongside the ocean, feeling the air burn her lungs, legs aching with the exertion. Picking up speed, she pushed on, past driftwood and beached jellyfish. Her unbound hair blinded her as it blew in front of her eyes, snapping its ends against chilled cheeks.

When she reached the rocky outcropping only passable during low tide, Cassie fell against it, the cold surface rough on her face and hands. Holding on to this familiar landmark, she no longer questioned her purpose. God would use her the way He'd designed, regardless of the years she'd gone the other way. Cassie was like Jonah, and this was the beach on which the Lord had spit her out.

# 24

As if the pestering "sisters of shame" weren't enough, Nora had to listen to Gwendolyn the entire walk home, retelling every wonderfully perfect thing about her new friend, who happened to be Cassie's daughter. She wore clothes that looked like those of a princess. She told the best jokes. She was Gwendolyn's best friend.

Not for the first time, Nora's mind swirled with the dangers that could accompany Ferris's secrets. The other moms went on and on about how interesting it must be to have a detective for a husband. She let them have their delusions. In reality, the parts of his job that he didn't share with her were the things that had Nora awake and anxious in the middle of the night. Having Cassie George on the other side of something confidential made her skin crawl.

Shasta's face was pale, her body a collection of tremors and uncontrolled movements. When Cassie touched her forehead, she snapped her hand back in surprise. Fever.

Lark hopped into the bedroom and climbed up on Shasta's bed.

"Come on, Lark. Grammy Shasta is sick. You need to stay out of here." Cassie lifted Lark and set her on the floor.

Half a moment later, little Miss Nightingale was back on the mattress, making her own estimation of Shasta's health. "Oh, Grammy. I'm sorry you're sick."

Cassie picked her up again, this time depositing her on the other side of the door. All she needed was for Lark to get whatever Shasta was fighting. "Lark, go color at the table. I'll be there as soon as I can."

She stomped her foot twice, then turned and did as she'd been told.

Cassie had never been a germaphobe, but the desire to Lysol the entire apartment itched at her fingers.

Her phone wasn't in her pocket. She searched around, then went to the living room, finding it on the windowsill.

Lark looked up from the coloring page she'd been scribbling black. "I want to have Gwendolyn at my birthday party. She's my new best friend." Her gaze dared her mom to argue this fact, as though Cassie would. Somehow, a week at her new preschool had instilled even more confidence in her daughter.

"Okay. I'll find out who her mommy is and invite her."

"You know her mom. It's that lady from your school." She ripped the page out of her coloring book.

Cassie's stomach twisted. Of course her daughter would make friends with the child of the one girl Cassie could not tolerate in high school. She should have expected it when Lark started preschool with Nora's child. "Lark, I need to call the doctor. I'll work out the details of your party as soon as I can." Or they could cancel the whole thing due to sickness so Cassie could avoid the judgment of Supermom for a less-than-perfect gathering. If only that was an actual option.

The call to Shasta's doctor went to a recording rather than the service she'd gotten before. Cassie didn't think this was a 9-1-1 situation, but she needed to talk to someone soon, or she was afraid it could become one. There was an urgent care in the town to the north of them. She Googled until she found the information and made the call.

"This is Beachside Immediate Medical. How can I help you?"

"My aunt is running a fever. I'm not sure where the thermometer is, but she's definitely hot."

"What is your aunt's date of birth?"

Cassie rambled off the date she knew better than her own at this point.

"Can you put her on the phone?"

"No. She has Parkinson's and dementia. Whatever is going on seems to be making her symptoms worse."

"Have you spoken to her doctor? We would recommend getting their input before bringing your aunt here. They might prefer her to be seen at an emergency department."

"I called, but there wasn't an answer." Her foot started tapping.

Lark looked over, her expression lined with worry that shouldn't have been on a child's face.

"I'd try again. This time of day, you can catch them as they're closing but before the answering service switches over."

Cassie took what was supposed to be a calming breath. "Thank you. I'll try again." With her neck beginning to ache, she redialed the first number. This time, there was an answer. The woman assured her a doctor would be in touch within twenty minutes. If they weren't, Cassie should give her another call. It didn't seem that their track record for callbacks could be too great if she had to add that amendment.

Cassie's body was feeling the effects of this Ping-Pong game, bouncing back and forth between Shasta's room and checking on Lark. Her back and neck felt as bruised as if she'd been in an accident. Then the room took on movement of its own. She reached for the counter, balancing herself as she fought the nausea that rolled in hard.

At the sink, Cassie turned on the tap and filled her palms with cold water, then dipped her face into the pond she'd created. It didn't take much for her to go from fine to ready to hurl. Even looking at the ships out on the ocean did Cassie in. And, as she knew from Terri's bout of food poisoning, she had a very sympathetic stomach.

"Mom, you're all drippy." Lark curled her lip.

Cassie swiped a finger under one eye. It came back smudged with mascara. The one day she put out some real effort, and she wound up looking like a rabid raccoon.

Twenty-three minutes after she'd hung up, there still hadn't been a return call from the doctor's office. Shasta was now shivering no matter how warm Cassie made her room. She couldn't wait another twenty minutes, but Cassie called the office again to let them know she hadn't heard anything and that they were heading to the hospital.

The phone rang again before she could find her tennis shoes.

"This is Dr. Edwards." Her voice was bright and cheerful. "I'm on call today. I understand you're Shasta's niece and caregiver?"

"Yes. I was about to take her into the ER. She's shivering and has a fever."

"I think that's wise. An episode like this can be very scary for everyone involved. I'd like to meet you down there, if that's okay. Parkinson's patients have a few different needs than you and I do."

"That would be wonderful." For the first time that day, there was a sense of hope. As soon as she hung up, Cassie remembered she hadn't yet gotten a sitter for Lark. She typed out a group text to everyone she trusted enough to take her daughter.

Marshall was the first to reply. He was finishing up a meeting with some boys in the shop and would be right up.

Counting on him so much was dangerous. It made her heart vulnerable, allowing her to get attached to someone she had no claim on. But Cassie needed the help. That had been the verse and chorus of her life since returning home. She couldn't do it all on her own.

True to his word, Marshall's distinctively masculine knock sounded on the door moments later.

Lark recognized the sound and leaped to answer.

"Hold on. You're not allowed to answer the door by yourself." Cassie gave her the stern-mommy look.

"But I know it's Marshall."

"You do not know that. You *think* it's Marshall, but it could be anyone." Cassie opened the door, and there he was.

"I told you so." Lark jumped into his arms. "What are you doing here, Marshall? It isn't my birthday yet."

Cassie shook her head. Everything in Lark's world came back to her birthday. What would she do when her special day was over? Hopefully not start a countdown to the next one. "Marshall is going to stay with you while I take Shasta to see her doctor. Is that okay?"

She pumped a fist in the air. "It's super great. I have the stuff to make slime. Grammy Aubrey brought it to me. Want to make it?"

Marshall made a squeamish expression. "Slime?"

"It's all the preschool rage these days." Cassie spoke over her shoulder as she made another run to Shasta's room.

She was awake but barely. Cassie helped her to sit up, easing her feet into the slippers with the secure fastenings that she'd ordered online. "Let's just put a sweater over your pajamas."

"They will find out." Shasta's voice was thin and shaky. "They're coming for her. I've seen them."

On her knees, Cassie looked up into Shasta's eyes. With the stooped posture that had been increasing at an alarming rate, her face was cast down in Cassie's direction. "Who's coming?" She tucked loose hair behind her aunt's ear, pulled a tissue from the box on the nightstand, and dabbed at Shasta's chin.

Her eyes closed, and Cassie thought she was falling asleep even while sitting, but then she opened them again and pinned Cassie with her intense stare. "I have always loved you." Her words were clear to Cassie's heart, though they would have been slurred to an outsider.

She had to look away to keep her emotions under control. Taking Shasta's hand, she squeezed. "I love you too. You've been the best mother I could have asked for." Her greatest desire was to just lie in the bed next to Shasta, like they'd done when she was little, talking about art, movies, the future. Nothing had turned out the way Cassie had imagined back then, but she was so blessed to have Shasta.

# 25

The doctor guided Cassie out of the room where a nurse was fitting Shasta with an oxygen mask. "I've seen this in my patients who have severe dementia as part of the disease. They can decline quickly, and often at very unexpected times. We can treat the pneumonia, but I'm afraid the blood work is showing decreased liver function too."

"What does that mean? Can you change her medications to help?" Cassie rubbed her arms. The hall felt as if someone had switched on the air conditioning.

"I'm afraid not. This is part of the disease. It would be best for Shasta to see her regular physician, but from what I'm seeing in the notes, she's taken a significant turn for the worse. You may be looking at hospice care."

The floor shifted beneath Cassie. She reached out and placed a hand on the wall for balance. "That can't be right. It's been only a month."

The doctor pulled her white coat around her chest. "Her chart says it's been five years since her diagnosis. If she hadn't been struck with so many of the cognitive issues, I would have guessed she'd have another ten years. It's not the Parkinson's that's the biggest problem. It's the Lewy body dementia. I'm sorry." She glanced over her shoulder, as if expecting someone to be there. "Look, we can help you find a secure facility to take care of her. You can be there as much as you want. There's a beautiful hospice house down the road too. Many of my patients have gone there. We want to help you however we can."

Cassie nodded but couldn't look up again. Instead, she stared at her shoes, one with untied laces hanging to the floor. There were decisions to make. If it were just Cassie, she wouldn't hesitate, but what about Lark? Was it fair to her to have her Grammy die under their roof? Would it traumatize her daughter to lose someone so connected to her? "Thank you. I'll give what you're saying some thought."

The doctor touched Cassie's arm before clicking down the hall on perfectly balanced heels.

They met in the coffee shop, everyone who cared about Shasta. Aubrey had arranged the chairs so they could all see one another, but Cassie wasn't sure she could look at their faces and keep her emotions in check.

Mrs. Collins handed around a basket of warm croissants. Her eyes were rimmed as red as Cassie expected her own were.

In the corner, Lark watched Daniel Tiger while acting out the scene with her miniature versions of the characters.

Marshall turned the sign on the door, closing the business for another day, then came to sit next to Mr. Watkins.

Their little meeting felt like a funeral, and in so many ways, it was. They were facing the truth of Shasta's situation, and doing it together. Cassie called this meeting because she knew she needed everyone here, but more than that, Shasta did. Maybe Cassie had the biggest claim to her, but they were family too.

Aubrey didn't sit. She stood behind a chair, her shoulders stooped, her arms rigid, as if the chairback was all that kept her from crumbling.

Cassie told everyone what she'd heard from Shasta's regular

doctor, who had confirmed the information given to her by Dr. Edwards. Whether they were ready or not, they were facing an end. Shasta's body was starting to shut down.

"We have some decisions to make. I'm not trying to get out of making the final choices, but I know you all love Shasta too. Whatever is best for her is what we should do. There's a hospice house down the road. The doctor said we can get a room there as things progress, or we could try to find a way to keep her here." With the espresso machine off for the night and the room empty of customers, the silence spoke too loudly.

Finally, Mr. Watkins blew out a breath. "I've been trying to come up with a plan for those stairs. The incline is too steep for a ramp, and I'm not sure one of those seats that goes up and down would be stable enough for Shasta. I talked to an engineer buddy of mine a couple weeks back, and I think we've come up with a plan. It's a kind of platform that works on a pully system. We can fold it up when it's not in use, so the stairs are usable for the rest of us." His head bobbed. "Just thought you should know. I can get it going in a day or two."

"I've got a couple college kids coming in for the summer." Mrs. Collins dropped her knitting into her lap. "They'll be helping out at the bakery. I'd be honored to help out with Shasta's care."

"We could get a hospital bed, when we get to that point, and put it in the living room. I think she'd enjoy watching the ocean." Aubrey's bottom lip quivered. "I just can't stand to think of her dying outside of Gull's Bay."

Cassie felt the same way. This was home. Maybe life wasn't always perfect, but for someone like Shasta, the right to die where you were loved seemed important and right. Just like she'd given Cassie a life filled with love and freedom, Cassie wanted to give Shasta the best she could manage. And with all this help, she was starting to feel like keeping her at home was doable.

Pastor Stewart stepped into the entryway, shaking rain from his coat. "Hey there. Sorry I was late." He came over and took the last seat.

Mrs. Collins gave a run-through of the conversation so far.

"Sounds like you've got a lot of obstacles worked out. I think the church can help with a few others. I sent out a message to the hospitality team. The response was amazing. Everyone loves Shasta." He grinned. "We've got a weekly grocery shopper, meals, and someone who'd like to come in and clean each week."

"That's too much." Cassie held up a hand. "I can do a lot of that myself."

"No one doubts that you can, but we all know how precious time can be. You need to take care of yourself and Lark too."

The love took on a suffocating quality. "It's just that I don't think it's needed. I'll handle the house. Having someone pick up groceries would be wonderful, and"—Cassie looked around the room—"a few meals, with the understanding that it would give everyone else here a break too. I think what I want most is for all of you to have time with Shasta. She's always loved her deep conversations and friendships. She might not be able to hold up her end of them anymore, but I think she'd cherish the time with each of you."

～

When it seems like you have nothing, giving can be the thing that brings you hope. The poor care for the poor, and while I was financially stable, I lacked almost every other thing needed for a happy life. If not for volunteer opportunities, I might have slipped back into the depression that had already tried to kill me.

I found my reason for being when I met a young woman named Stella in a homeless shelter. She was eighteen, technically an adult. But she'd spent much of her teen life in foster care. Though she'd worked hard to keep her grades up so she could attend college, adult life was more than she had expected.

Her foster mother allowed her to stay on through graduation, but Stella had to find her own way after that. She worked two jobs to pay California rent, but when classes started in the fall, she couldn't keep up. Finally, she made the hard decision to take the little bit of savings she'd been able to squirrel away and buy a car, which she moved into.

Stella might have made it living like this, showering wherever she could, but trouble kept coming. She was carjacked, the criminal making away with everything she owned, from her identification to her textbooks. She had the bare minimum in car insurance, so the theft wasn't covered.

She'd managed to move up from a hostess position at the diner where she worked to a server. But the two uniforms had gone with her car, leaving her with a debt to her employer. Stella was fortunate. She'd been able to hold on to her job. She slept in the shelter whenever she could and took the bus to work, picking up any extra shifts she could get.

Week after week, I watched Stella as she did everything she could to get back on her feet, only to be met with one complication after another. She had a strength inside of her I envied. And I knew I could learn from her as much or more than I could ever help her.

Stella moved into my house the next week. It was less than a month later when Tricia joined us, a kid who hadn't aged out of foster care but who might have been better off if she had. Then, over the next year, came Samantha, Kat, and Cory, all with their own personal stories of tragedy and trauma.

I found solace in mothering my girls and giving them a place to call home for as long as they needed. Every day, my heart ached to hold Ainsley just one more time, but they gave my stifled love somewhere to go. They gave me purpose.

Stella stayed with me until she completed her undergraduate

work. From there, she went on to a full-time position as a director at a nonprofit working to better the lives of children in foster care.

We lost Samantha to an overdose, her body found in the middle of a park. And even though that loss hit me hard, I had the success stories to keep me strong.

I started traveling, helping other people and communities implement programs to allow youth to reach their potential and step out of unhealthy dysfunctions.

All the while, a verse played in the back of my mind, Psalm 113:9, a song of the Lord's sweet remembrance. *He settles the childless woman in her home as a happy mother of children.* That promise rang true in my life, and I was content.

Lark tucked a doll into a cardboard box bed. She cooed to the toy, which had been Cassie's at that age. It was easy for Cassie to recall the disappointment and fear she'd experienced when the pregnancy test came back positive. There were even times, though not many, when she'd considered terminating so no one would find out how stupid she'd been. She covered her mouth with one hand, contemplating the emptiness that would have haunted her life if she'd given in to that choice.

Cassie picked up the stack of papers again, determined to finish the mysterious manuscript today, before Marshall picked her up for their . . . outing.

Her phone chimed the sound of a FaceTime call. Her friend Terri's image flashed on the screen. Cassie swiped it on and genuinely smiled. "Hey there. What's up?"

Terri's face burst with excitement; then she thrust her hand in front of the camera. "Look!"

Cassie sucked in air. "Oh. My. Goodness!" They squealed together like tweens at a slumber party. "You're getting married."

Lark climbed onto the couch back and looked over her shoulder. "I want to be a flower girl."

Cassie had no idea Lark even knew what a flower girl was, much less anything else about weddings.

Her heart sank.

"What?" Terri's expression matched hers. "Aren't you happy?"

"I'm so thrilled for both of you. I just don't know when I would be able to leave here." The picture of Terri's wedding was clear in Cassie's mind. They'd been planning it since the day after she went on her first date with Jack. They'd created Pinterest boards and surfed through photos of venues. It had always been the two of them, and now Cassie would miss that special day. "Shasta isn't doing well. I can't leave her."

"You're not getting off that easy." Terri's eyes went wide. "I did not mean that how it sounded."

Cassie gave her a forgiving smile. Terri had never been purposely insensitive. "Are you sure you're not going a little Bridezilla on me?"

She chuckled. "Not yet, but I reserve the option. Listen, having you and Lark at my wedding is very important to me. Jack fully understands that. We talked to my parents, and we've all decided that the wedding should take place on the coast. It's only an hour drive for my grandparents and two for my parents."

"And a state away for Jack's family."

"Bride rules."

"Are you sure about this?" Cassie had to bite her lip to keep it from quivering. "I might not be much help in the planning."

"What's to plan? We've had this locked up for a couple years now."

"I love you."

"Me too." Lark's hold on Cassie's neck pulled her hair, but her daughter's smile reflected on the phone screen made the pain worth it. "When you come to visit, you can meet Marshall. He has love eyes on Mommy."

The rough thing about FaceTime was the little image of one's own face in the corner of the screen. Cassie saw her skin pale and her mouth fall open.

"Hmm. That's interesting news, Miss Larkie. Tell your aunty Terri more."

"No way." Cassie pulled Lark onto her lap. "Marshall is just a friend. I have no idea where she got that idea."

"Grammy Aubrey and Grammy Mrs. Collins say it. I don't think they'd lie." Lark broke into giggles.

Terri tapped a fist on her chin, then wiped a tear from her eye. "Lark, you're the one I will get all my information from, okay?"

Lark grinned as Cassie squirmed inside. "Okay, that will do. I have to get ready to go, but I'll call you later. I'm so happy for you and Jack."

"Marshall is coming!" Lark made kissy lips.

Cassie shook her head. "I don't know where she gets this stuff."

Terri responded with her own kissy lips, then waved goodbye and disconnected.

# 26

Message from @beccaboundforglory

Oh, I could just die. I'm so sorry about Maddie! She feels really bad. Even Lex feels bad, and that's not an easy accomplishment. I want to make this all up to you somehow. I'm going to tell you more about us so that you can see we're not judging you or anything. We're just . . . a bit crazy.

From what I understand, Mom was hard to pin down. She had big dreams of travel and all that. But then she got pregnant with Lex when she was a teen. I guess her parents didn't take it too well. She married Dad when Lex was four. He was twelve years older than she was. I'm not sure how they met, but they really didn't have much in common. Dad was a professor of European literature, and Mom was a photographer . . . like me!

They had Maddie not long after they were married. And then—I really don't know much about this part—she ran off, leaving Maddie and Lex with Dad. A year later, she was back. I only learned about this after she passed away. Maddie doesn't remember it, and Lex DOES NOT like to talk about it. From what I gather, Dad just welcomed her home, no questions. Side note: Isn't that weird? And then I arrived ten months later. Proof they made up.

I think Lex feels like she wasn't enough to keep Mom happy. She's kind of bitter, and now that she's in the middle of a divorce, it's hard.

I'm hoping you can forgive us. We're all sisters.

♥

Nora didn't have any kind of sibling relationship to compare this mess to, but this couldn't be what sisterhood was all about. And if it was, she was not climbing on that crazy train. Becca seemed nice enough, but she'd get over this. Nora was not her sister. They shared a bit of DNA but not a drop of experience. Becca was the baby Tammy had stayed for. Nora was the cast-off.

Cassie's stomach did a happy turn when Marshall opened the passenger door to his Jeep. She didn't even have to ask if Thai food was stashed somewhere in the back. Turning to him, she licked her lips. "Nice move."

"I thought we could eat before your meeting. And I remember you saying something about missing spicy food since Lark won't touch it."

In a perfect world, there would be room in her life for a relationship with Marshall. And there would be room in her heart to give him what he deserved in a partner. She just wasn't sure she had the ability to do that for him, Lark, *and* Shasta.

Cassie climbed in and buckled her seat belt before he got into the driver's side. "It's the perfect night to watch the sun go down over the ocean. I know a place, if that's okay with you."

He wouldn't be able to take her anywhere she hadn't already been around here, but Cassie nodded, letting him take the lead. About ten minutes later, they were parked at the lookout perched high above the beach. The sun had just begun its descent, the bottom of the orb touching the horizon.

Marshall reached behind her and brought forward a white bag. He set it on the console between them, the scents of basil and curry filling the space. "I got two dishes. I thought we could share, if that's okay with you."

Cassie rubbed her hands together. "Sharing is good."

"I'm so glad you said that. Whichever one I ended up with, I'd be dying for a bite of the other." He pulled out the to-go boxes and settled them in the middle. "We have spicy basil green beans with chicken, and chicken red curry. I'm kind of into chicken. Hope that's okay."

He seemed nervous, as if they hadn't seen each other almost every day for weeks and he hadn't kept her at arm's length. The thought of that did a great job of curbing Cassie's appetite, but only for a moment.

"I have forks and chopsticks. Which do you prefer?"

"Hmm. I'll use chopsticks if you will."

He elevated his eyebrows. "You don't think I can. Well, Cassie, I believe you're about to be schooled." He handed her a pair, then slid his from the paper wrapping and snapped them apart. Swirling the chopsticks around the basil dish, he chose a bean and a chunk of chicken, then folded them into his mouth. A dribble of sauce wove down his chin.

Cassie picked up a napkin and, without thinking first, wiped away the mess. The act was intimate in a way she hadn't meant it to be. "I'm sorry. I do this for Lark and Shasta all day."

He took the napkin and rubbed it against the back of his hand where another drop had landed. "Forks?" His smile made her shiver, but in a good way.

"That might be better at keeping your car and the front of my shirt clean. So, you were going to tell me something about yourself." She scooped a bite of curry into her mouth, sending her taste buds into a state of absolute joy as flavors covered her tongue.

Marshall leaned back in his seat, the basil chicken dish in his hands. "I like you."

"I like you too—what's wrong with that?"

"Nothing is wrong with it. I don't know. I mean, I love being here in Gull's Bay. Most of the time, I feel comfortable, but it's really different from where I grew up."

"Where's that? I assumed you must be somewhat local."

He grinned that perfect smile that made her crazy. "You assumed I was one of the six black men who've always lived on the Oregon coast?"

"Oh, come on. There are more than that."

"You're right, but it's a smaller community. It's taken a lot of getting used to."

"So, you don't plan to stay around here?" The last bite didn't sit well in her stomach. Why was she letting this man get under her skin? Cassie hadn't even looked at a guy since finding out about Lark. Why now? Why him?

"Nah. I like it here. And I've met some guys farther south. It's, like I said, an adjustment." He closed the lid and handed the basil chicken to Cassie.

She took one more taste of the curry before giving it up. "Tell me about your family and where you're from."

He didn't touch the dish in front of him. "I was raised by my dad in downtown Portland until he died. I was sixteen—not a good time in a guy's life to be alone."

"Didn't you have other family?"

"Nope. My dad and I moved out here from Chicago. He wanted a better life for me, and he did a great job giving me every opportunity. He worked hard all day and went to college at night when I was little. By middle school, he had a good job, and I was going to a private school in Portland, on track for an academic scholarship." He shrugged. "When Dad died,

I did some dumb things, ended up in the juvenile version of probation. Luckily, I got connected with some people who got me back on the right path and helped me to see I was throwing away my dad's legacy to avoid my grief."

"Wow. I'm so sorry." Her body felt heavy with his emotions. "I didn't even know my mom, so I guess I don't really understand that kind of loss."

He turned his head her way. "Yes, you do. I see it in your eyes when you're with Shasta. Moms don't have to be the ones who gave birth to you."

She ran her fingers through her hair. "Or even biologically connected, as it turns out."

"I thought she was your mom's cousin."

She shook her head. "It's not true. A detective friend found Cassie George's death certificate. We're still trying to uncover the truth." She touched his arm. "Please don't mention this to anyone."

He nodded, his eyes round. "Are you sure this isn't some kind of mistake?"

"Unfortunately, I'm sure." It was her turn to lean back in the seat and gaze over the ocean. The light had turned pink and orange, with brushstrokes of clouds crossing the distance. "Looks like I was kidnapped. And just as surprising, I think my mother is right here in Gull's Bay."

He set the fork full of food back on the container. "You're kidding me. You are, right?"

"I wish I were. I think. I'm not sure about anything right now." She turned back to him. "I'm taking over the conversation again. Please tell me more about your father."

The expression on his face was doubtful, but Marshall knew her deeper than she wanted him to. He could tell she was still moving the pieces of her story around in her head, trying to find their logical order. "Well, my dad was a good-looking man." He winked.

"Is this where I'm supposed to give you a compliment?"

His laughter filled the Jeep, stripping away a layer of worry from her heart, allowing her to spill everything she'd discovered.

Five years had passed when I finally went through Topher's things. I was ready to take everything that could be used again by someone and donate the items. Maybe one of Topher's many suits could help a man find a job or bring back confidence that had been beaten by circumstance.

I stood in front of his closet for ten minutes before stepping over the threshold. We each had a walk-in, so I'd managed to stay out of this area, avoiding the loss that would come with seeing all of his things in one place.

The suits were well designed and fine, but ultimately, they were just pieces of cloth. They were not part of my lost husband any more than the car I'd donated to charity years before. I started with one of his favorites, deciding to take on the challenge rather than save the hardest for last. There were butter rum Life Savers in his pocket and a ChapStick, evidence that he'd been there. I decided to leave them where I'd found them. Someone else could toss those things in the trash. I slipped the suit into a box I'd brought upstairs for the transport, took a breath, and went for the next one.

Two hours later, the clothes were packed, and I was left with all the miscellaneous belongings. Most of this stuff would find its way into the garbage, a statement on our priorities, to be sure. Sometimes we cherished our items above even the people in our lives, but in the end, they were meaningless without the love and devotion only we had for them.

In the back of the closet, behind a series of books about business and leadership, I found a box. Wondering if it contained our letters back and forth while we were in college, I sat on the closet floor and opened the lid. What I found drained the blood from my face and left me numb, though I wasn't at all sure why. There was a picture of a baby, a child that was not Ainsley, in the arms of another woman. The woman looked so familiar, yet I knew I'd never met her.

I turned it over, looking for a message, maybe a name, but there was nothing. Deeper in the box, I found another picture. This one of Ainsley and Topher. But she seemed older than when we'd lost her, as if my memories were already betraying me. Her curls were over the top of her ears, and I didn't recognize the background.

My stomach clenched, and I shot from the floor, barely making it to the bathroom before I vomited. Ainsley had never been away from me, not until that horrible day in Mexico. How could there be a picture of my daughter in a place I'd never been?

I abandoned the project, going to my bedroom and laying the photos in front of me. I couldn't place the woman in the first, but I knew I'd seen her somewhere, and I had a sad feeling when I looked at her.

Comparing the picture of Ainsley to the photos taken on our horrible vacation, I found the differences were slight. I wasn't sure I could convince anyone else that the one I'd just discovered had been taken later.

It didn't matter. I had to try. I called the detective who'd helped us out before. He wasn't impressed by my find but said he'd take a look. The case was, however, closed. They had documentation from Mexican authorities that my daughter's body had been found. Once again, I was the grieving mother whom everyone treated as if she'd gone crazy. To an extent, I probably had. Who wouldn't?

I ended up not taking the photo to the police department. Years had passed, and I realized what I was saying was ridiculous. After all this time and trauma, I couldn't testify to every place I'd been to with my child.

It was a full two weeks later, after having sifted through every bit of Topher's closet, that I placed the woman in the image. Her identity was another drop in the bucket of information I would need to find out what my husband had really been up to.

She'd been one of the victims of the runaway truck. It had never occurred to me that Topher could have been there on the pier with someone else. He'd always loved the water, and I assumed that was what had called him there that day. But she was the real siren, and I wondered how many times she'd sung her song for him before.

I stomped around, angry, letting my emotions dictate my moves for far too long. Then one day, I thought about the baby with her in the picture. I wondered what had happened to that child, and honestly, I wondered if my husband was the father.

The woman's name was easy enough to come by. It was listed with Topher's and those of two other victims in the newspaper article about the accident.

Though I tried for months, I couldn't find a single other detail about her. She hadn't done anything newsworthy until being run down by an out-of-control truck. I did what I should have done in the first place: I hired a private detective.

Someone who worked out of Seattle seemed to be the best choice. The guy I found was supposed to be great at his job, but there was a waiting time while he finished up cases ahead of mine, likely situations that were more pressing than finding out what a husband had been up to when he died years earlier.

I'd let the whole thing out of my conscious thought when I finally got the call from him. "Well," he started, "you're not going to like what I have to tell you."

I was in the middle of a grocery store when he called, deciding between pineapples. It seems so odd now.

"The woman in the photo and your husband were in fact in a relationship. They had been for a few years from what I can figure."

"What about the baby? Do you know if it's his?"

"Yes." He hesitated for far too long. "I believe the child in question was his biological daughter. He was not listed on the birth certificate, but they were together months prior to the time she

200

would have been pregnant, and there doesn't seem to have been any disruption in their relationship except about a month in November, just before the child was born."

"That's when our daughter arrived." The only thing that held me together at that moment was the scene I didn't want to make in the middle of the produce section.

I ended the call. It was more than I could take at that moment. But I kept wondering, what had happened to the baby?

*That's it?* Cassie flipped the last page over as if it would contain all the answers, but there was nothing.

# 27

Cassie came back into the shop after dropping Lark at preschool. The conversation with Marshall the night before, as well as the words written in a story that was now clearly part of her own, pushed Cassie to do something.

She'd always loved the way it sounded in the shop when the tables were full and the espresso machine hummed and sputtered, music floating above it all. Cassie loved the call of the barista to the crowd and the scent of baked goods and coffee. She loved that the shop was always a little warm and a lot cozy, and that the people who gathered seemed to be connecting with friends over mugs of latte or tea.

Until Cassie read the manuscript, Coastal Coffee provided a special place for people to be who they really were. In the corner, the woman sat like she did almost every other day, typing away on her keyboard. Was that really Cassie's mother? Had she been watching for all these years? In a sideways stare, Cassie tried to see if there was any resemblance between them, but then remembered that she'd been the result of an egg donation. Her legal mother could be anyone who walked into the shop.

Her chest tightened. In a situation like hers, how could a person be sure they weren't dating a cousin or a sibling, even? She rubbed her temples and looked back at the counter.

Marshall gave a little nod, encouragement to keep going, to come clean about what she knew and find the truth that maybe this woman, and this woman only, could give her.

Cassie shook out her arms and stepped toward the back booth that should have the woman's name carved into the wooden table for as often as she was stationed there. The closer Cassie got, the more she felt anger rising up. Maybe this woman was the one who'd given birth to her, but did that give her the right to stalk another person? Why hadn't she just come right out and told her story?

The woman looked up from her keyboard. "Yes?"

All of Cassie's muscles went rigid, freezing into masses of unmoving tension.

"Can I help you?"

Cassie swallowed. "Just wanted to see if you needed anything?"

She tipped her head at her coffee and smiled. "I'm good. Thank you."

"Well, that's great, then, isn't it?" Her words were laced with sarcasm.

The woman's expression changed to one of concern.

Cassie backed way, turning as she ducked by Marshall and into the kitchen. "Oh my goodness. Oh my goodness. Oh my goodness." She leaned her forehead against the cupboard.

"Hey. What happened?" Marshall covered her shoulder with his palm.

She looked up at him, lunging into his chest.

His hesitancy was obvious, but he caught on and wrapped her in his arms.

"I couldn't do it. I totally chickened out."

"That's okay."

"No, it's not. I stared at her without saying anything. What if she's some kind of creepy stalker? What if Shasta is right, and she's here to steal Lark?" Cassie pulled back and looked up into his eyes. "This is making me crazy, but with all she's been through, it's quite possible she's even crazier."

"You know, my dad used to warn me about girls."

Cassie cocked her head. "What's that supposed to mean?"

"Nothing. I'm just trying to lighten the mood. I don't think she's going anywhere, even after your weird creeper moment."

"Thanks." She beat her head against his chest. "You're a big help."

"Is that sarcasm I'm hearing?"

"Oh yes." Cassie pulled back. She'd overstepped the level of their friendship, and awkward feelings were setting in. "I'll get the dishes going back here and check the supplies."

"Mr. Watkins and his buddy are coming in after the morning rush. I'm going to try and help them out as much as I can so we can get that contraption up and running before Shasta's released from the hospital."

The front door jingled, and they both leaned to the side to see who'd come in or left.

She was already walking down the sidewalk past the large shop windows. Cassie had actually managed to chase off the woman from the back booth.

Lark and Cassie picked up a few things at the grocery store on their way home from visiting Shasta. Cassie held the bag on her hip and let Lark through the door ahead of her.

Mr. Watkins was pounding away on the wall that ran along one side of the stairs. There wasn't a customer in sight, but there was a man Cassie had never seen before who shuffled in through the back with a large sheet of plywood.

"What are they doing?" Lark tugged at her arm.

She set the sack on an empty table. "They're making an easier way for Shasta to get up the stairs."

The man turned to Cassie, lifted his safety glasses, and held out a hand. "Hello. You must be the beautiful Cassie I keep hearing about."

She stumbled for the right words. He was good-looking but also the kind of man who clearly knew it. "Hi."

"They did not do you justice." He shook his head, looking at her a little too personally for comfort.

Marshall came in, a drill in his right hand. His gaze bounced back and forth between Cassie and the guy, but then he set to his work as if it didn't matter to him.

"I'm Frank. I can't believe we haven't met before."

"All right, Frank, that's enough flirting with the lady. Let's get back to work." Mr. Watkins stepped between them. "What do you think so far?"

Cassie tried to picture what they were creating, but at this moment, it looked like a mess. "I'm sure you know what you're doing." The warm coffee smells had been replaced by the scents of fresh-cut wood and working men.

He shrugged. "We should be done this afternoon. That will give us time for a few trial runs before Shasta comes home tomorrow. Aubrey says she's getting grumpy in there. I'd say that's a good sign."

"Aubrey was being kind. Lark and I stopped by after preschool. As Shasta would say, she's fit to be tied." The spunk her aunt had even in the face of this hardship made Cassie happy all the way through. If only she could become a woman with just half that strength. "Why don't you go over and see her? She'd love to have you visit."

Suddenly, his shoes were more interesting than looking Cassie in the eye. The toe of his boot scuffed along the wood floor. "I don't know. She'd probably rather I didn't."

"I'm sure you're wrong." Mr. Watkins had been around all of Cassie's life. He'd been married for a long time, raising five sons, but his wife had passed on many years ago, and his boys were grown with families of their own. Until Marshall moved in, he'd lived by himself in a cabin that overlooked the rocks near the beach.

He picked up a measuring tape and started back to work, only to turn to Cassie again. "Hey, you wouldn't need a twin bed, would you? I was helping a guy out with some remodeling. He asked me to get rid of one even though it's practically new."

Cassie stretched the stiff muscles in her shoulders. "That would be great. Sharing with Lark is tough."

Lark heard her name from where she was helping Marshall mark something on the wall. "I want my own bed, please. I'm too big to share with Mommy."

"Truly. She takes up the whole mattress." Cassie smiled. "How can I make the arrangements?"

"It's in the back of my truck. I'll get these young guys to bring it up to you."

"Thank you." Cassie had no idea where she'd be putting the thing, but even if it was in the middle of the kitchen, she'd be thrilled to get a full night's sleep. "Come on, Lark. We've got some things to do upstairs."

For once, her daughter didn't argue. Preschool must have worn her out, but she made sure to give Marshall and Mr. Watkins hugs on her way. For Frank, she had a side-eyed look that matched Cassie's own reservations about the man.

Upstairs, Lark asked if she could have some screen time, and Cassie gladly allowed it. If she moved quickly, there might be a way to make enough room to put the bed in the studio. She couldn't bear to dismantle Shasta's art or her space. She might never paint again like she once had, but Cassie could still see her in there with her easel. Did it hurt Shasta to know what she was missing? It certainly cut Cassie deep.

She bundled her daughter up on the couch and turned on a show for her to watch. Lark held her favorite stuffed animal in the crook of her arm. From the telltale signs of tiredness apparent in the drooping of her eyes, she'd be asleep soon. Before Cassie took on her next task, she knelt beside Lark, rubbing a hand over the top of her head, feeling the warmth of her sweet skin. Then she kissed her daughter's forehead, overwhelmed with the depth of her love for her child. Lark was the best of Cassie.

Lark patted Cassie's cheek, her gentle way of dismissing her mother so she could focus on her show.

In the studio, Cassie collected paintbrushes, gathering them together in a couple of wide-mouth jars. There was plenty of light in here, enough for her to work without turning on a lamp, though Shasta would often drag her easel out into the living room and paint while staring out over the ocean. The one thing this room didn't have was that view.

Standing next to the resin table in the middle of the cluttered space, Cassie turned a circle, evaluating the room and its contents. An idea struck her, one that might give Shasta a bit of herself back.

Cassie removed the painting from the easel and slid it next to others along the wall, then folded up the wooden contraption and moved it to the hall. Next, she went through all the paintbrushes, weeding out the tiny ones and collecting those with wide handles. She found Shasta's tabletop easel in the closet and set that with the other one.

With a load of art supplies in her arms, Cassie crept into the living room. Lark was sound asleep, the edge of the blanket hanging on her bottom lip. Slowly, Cassie deposited the items and returned to the studio.

The resin table could come out to the living room too. It would hold the smaller easel and the art supplies Shasta would need to paint alongside Lark. Later, when the two of them worked side by side, the fact that Shasta had lost so much in the way of motor control and verbal ability wouldn't matter as much to her. Instead, she could smash Play-Doh, color with crayons, and even spend an afternoon digging her fingers into slime. Being with Lark would be enough.

Cassie's daughter was doing so much good for her great-aunt, but what was the loss of someone so close going to do to Lark? As if Cassie's own impending grief wasn't already a heavy burden, the thought of Lark hurting in that way broke her open. She would gladly endure any pain to keep it far away from her child, but she was helpless to save Lark from the future.

# 28

Lark was awake and bouncing around the improved studio space when Cassie heard the knock at the door.

"Settle down for a minute, okay? This might be the new bed."

Cassie opened the door and found Frank standing there empty-handed. "Hey there. I thought I'd let you know we're about ready to bring the bed up, if that's okay." He looked over her shoulder, as if trying to get a look at the apartment behind her.

Shifting, Cassie used her body as a wall to block his view.

"Are you an artist?"

The question was momentarily confusing; then she remembered the hodgepodge of supplies in the living room. "No, my aunt is. So, you're ready to bring up the bed, then?"

"Yep." His head bobbed in a way that somehow seemed suggestive.

"Thanks." Cassie started to close the door.

"Don't miss me too much."

She shoved it closed the rest of the way with more force than was needed, then twisted the dead bolt. Did guys like that really get anywhere with women? But she knew they did. She'd been a very naïve young woman when she left her protective home for the first time, and she'd fallen for men who came on to her with lines so much worse than anything she'd heard from Frank thus far.

In the kitchen, Cassie pulled out leftovers for dinner even though she had no appetite, knowing Lark's was intact. Cassie had never been afraid of men before college—the only ones she'd known well were honorable, like Mr. Watkins and their pastor. Frank had shaken up her security again, robbing Cassie of the comfort she should have felt in her own home, even if he really hadn't done anything truly out of line.

The next knock on the door startled her so much that a short scream jumped out of Cassie's mouth. She covered her heart with a hand and took a couple of breaths. Before she could get to the door, Lark was there turning the lock.

"Lark, I keep telling you not to open the door. That is an adult job."

She huffed. "I didn't open it." Her hand was still poised in the air, ready to grab the knob.

Cassie scooted her away, relieved to find Marshall on the other side, a mattress balanced against his leg. Frank must have been down the stairs on the other end of the thing. Mr. Watkins had been right. It looked as if no one had ever slept on it. Bedtime could not come soon enough. "Come on in." She held the door open and made herself small against the wall so they could come into the living room.

"Where do you want this?" Marshall's voice had a frosty edge.

"Down the hall. I've made room in the studio."

Frank scratched his jawline. "Better leave this here while we get the frame installed." He winked at her. It was like he couldn't catch any of the very obvious signals she was throwing back at him.

They returned five minutes later, Marshall carrying both a small headboard and footboard, while Frank had the easier task of the side braces.

After showing them where she wanted it set up, Cassie decided to leave them to the work rather than risk another interaction with Frank. She set Lark at the table and put her dinner in front of her. They prayed, and Cassie picked at the leftover spaghetti while trying to stretch her neck enough to get a look down the hall where all the action was taking place.

The men didn't talk as they worked together, except for the occasional directional order. If this had been the way the construction of the lift had gone, Cassie was glad she'd had no part in it. They came out and picked up the mattress, threading it down the hall. A moment later, Marshall was ushering Frank out the door. He started to go too, but Cassie stopped him by taking hold of his upper arm.

The look he gave her was cold and out of character for the man she was becoming so comfortable with.

"Hey, if you could stay a minute, I need some help with something up too high for me to reach." She couldn't help the look she shot Frank. Being mean wasn't necessary, but she hoped he got the point. Cassie was not interested, at least not in Frank.

Marshall tipped his head back in the casual way he had of answering in the affirmative, but his face remained hard and set.

"Frank, thank you for your help with the bed and with the lift."

"Anything for you." He winked again, and she closed the door.

"What is with that guy?"

Marshall shrugged. "I guess he likes you."

"That's no way to get a woman to take interest in you. He's obnoxious."

"What would a guy need to do for you to notice him?" His head tipped to the side.

Cassie grinned, then went to check on Lark. She was covered in spaghetti sauce, and some noodles had managed to get woven into her curls.

"Well?"

Turning back to him, she shook her head. "You're jealous."

Marshall tapped his fingers against his chest. "Jealous? No way."

"Way." Cassie pulled Lark up from her chair.

"I'm still hungry." Her red face stared up at her mother.

Marshall was in the kitchen with the spaghetti, ready to dish her more before Cassie could even settle Lark back in her seat.

"That's it." Cassie pulled a piece of pasta off her daughter's head.

Marshall scooped more noodles onto Lark's plate. "What?"

"That's what a guy needs to do for me to notice him. He needs to care about my daughter. And care about me."

He picked up Cassie's hand and pulled the noodle out of her grip, then wiped sauce from her palm, his gaze locked on her eyes.

Cassie's heart pounded in her chest. Who was she becoming? She'd never been the kind of girl who swooned over anyone. But Marshall . . . she could really get hurt here. Not the kind of hurt where she felt the burn of rejection, the feeling that, once again, she was just not good enough. With Marshall, so much more than her ego was at stake. This man could break her heart.

Nora typed her daily tip for mom-life success into the design on Canva, then downloaded it for posting on Instagram. Later, she would snap a picture of the hanging pocketed organizers she used to set out the girls' clothing for the week.

Growing up, Nora had created an image of what a mother would look like—a good mother. She'd be the head of the PTA, the one in the concession stand, the mom organizing school events. All things she'd seen the mothers of schoolmates busy doing. And Nora had planned to do all those things, keep her house tidy, make healthy meals, and always be smiling.

The reality was much harder than the fantasy.

But this new Instagram hobby gave her the chance to use her marketing degree in a fresh way. Not only did she feel like she was helping others, but there was a nearly immediate boost of gratification.

She switched over to her analytics page. Up seven more followers just that day, bringing her total to one hundred fifty-seven.

Now, if only she could find a tip for dealing with husbands who had secrets with other women.

Saturday morning, Cassie popped into the little office next to the shop's kitchen, posted the next week's schedule, and grabbed the receipts. The business account was thin after Cassie cut the payroll checks, which meant she needed to pick up more shifts, leaving less for Marshall and Lisa.

All this effort might keep the coffee shop open and their stomachs fed, but it certainly wouldn't make the payments on Cassie's mountain of student loans.

Ainsley.

She wondered how life would have differed if she'd grown up with that name. Would she have made the same mistakes, or possibly a whole different set? Ainsley wouldn't have had to worry about financial aid. She would have driven a car she could rely on. Ainsley would have studied something in college that would have given her a career. But Ainsley wouldn't have had Shasta, and she probably wouldn't have had Lark. She was the fork in the road, the life never lived.

Coming around the corner, Cassie nearly crashed into Aubrey. "Sorry."

"It's all good. I thought I'd help with the party decorations. Is the birthday girl at the bakery?" Aubrey pulled her arms out of her jacket and hung it on the peg.

"She sure is. Lark woke me up at 5:45 this morning, asking if it was time to decorate the cake." Cassie tucked the receipts into a manila envelope.

"Beverly and Lark have a special connection, don't they?" She tugged her T-shirt down to cover her hips.

"Mrs. Collins lets her bake and eat sugar. She's a four-year-old's dream."

Aubrey waved five fingers in the air. "She was five as of 6:45 a.m."

Cassie looked up, really taking Aubrey in. She was the same woman Cassie had known for most of her life, but Aubrey's face was aging, showing lines that creased around the edges of her eyes. "I can't believe you remember what time she was born."

"Of course I do. Shasta and I were so excited. You know, we wanted to be there."

"I . . ." The memory hurt. "I couldn't. I was scared and ashamed. I had let Shasta down."

"Those are lies you let get into your heart and mind. You were so worried about what everyone else thought, even when you were a kid. It was like you were always trying to make up for something, and all the while, you were loved perfectly for who you were."

"What if I'm not who anyone thinks I am? What if I'm not Cassie George?"

"Isn't Cassie whoever you are?" Aubrey tied an apron around her waist. "Cassie, you are who God designed you to be. You are growing and changing all the time, and it may seem like you're lost in all of the mess of life sometimes, but your identity is not in your name, your hair color, your job, or your academic achievements. It's in your heart." She tapped her chest with an open palm. "It doesn't have to be so difficult."

If Aubrey had even a nibble of what was going on, she wouldn't be so quick to say a name was just a name. The fact that Cassie's name belonged to a baby who'd died complicated everything. It wasn't like this identity was something she could share with a lost child. "Thanks, Aubrey. I'll keep that in mind."

But she wouldn't, because no one, no matter how well-meaning, could understand what she was trying to wrap her mind around. Cassie wasn't Cassie, and she didn't know who she really was. She carried a last name that she had passed on to her daughter, but it wasn't hers to give. Cassie needed to find the only woman who could help her put the pieces together.

As she headed out of the shop, Cassie looked back at Aubrey. She was sliding tables together to form a larger area for Lark's party. Aubrey and Shasta told each other everything. They'd been as close as sisters for as long as Cassie could remember. Shasta's communication had gotten weak, but Cassie was sure she understood much of what was being said to her. If Cassie opened up to Aubrey, she might tell Shasta. That couldn't happen. No matter what, Shasta was going to enter Heaven's gate without this worry.

~

Shasta's color was still dull, and she seemed to have lost more weight, but she was fever-free and breathing as well as ever, so the doctor had signed her release. It was a blessing not only in her increased health, but in the fact that she wouldn't have to miss Lark's party.

They ran through the hospital routine, with a CNA bringing Shasta down to the car in a wheelchair. Shasta's doctor had written orders so they could have one for home use, a thought that both terrified Cassie and comforted her at the same time.

Cassie had picked up a latch to secure high on the doorframe but hadn't gotten around to the installation. She needed a few tools and worried that Mr. Watkins would take her asking to borrow the items as a request for yet more help. She was so deeply indebted to him already, yet she couldn't stop the vision in her brain of that wheelchair hurtling down the stairs.

Once Shasta was buckled into the car, Cassie thanked the CNA, then pulled away from the curb. "What do you say we stop for some super-greasy hamburgers and fries?"

"Yes." Shasta rubbed her hands together.

"It's been lonely without you. I'm so glad you're coming home."

"You have Lark." That rasp in her voice would always make Cassie worry about pneumonia from here out.

"I do. But we both missed you."

Shasta's eyes glistened.

"Do you know that I love you?" Cassie stopped at an intersection and waited for a clearing to pull into traffic. "You're the best mom I could have asked for."

Shasta's fingers came to rest on Cassie's arm. "You are mine." It didn't take a chapter's worth of words to say what they meant. Those three told Cassie everything she needed to know. They reassured her that, even if she was supposed to have been raised by someone else, the woman who'd filled the role was a perfect match.

They pulled into the only Burgerville on the coast and maneuvered along the drive-through lane. Cassie ordered two Northwest Cheeseburgers, fries, and fry sauce. A person couldn't go to Burgerville and skip their famous fry sauce. After receiving the order, Cassie pulled into a parking space, and they ate in the kind of silence that was neither awkward nor lacking—they just enjoyed being together.

# 29

Lark's party went off exactly as planned. She arrived with Mrs. Collins to find the shop transformed by sparkles and streamers. Unicorns and fairies decorated the walls and the tables. She squealed and spun in circles, a new dress Mrs. Collins had sewn for her spreading out in the most child-like twirl that had ever been seen.

Only a few minutes after Lark arrived, her friends started to file in, joined by their parents. Cassie had wanted to set a limit on the number of invitations, but Lark had informed her that it would be rude, and kids could get their feelings hurt if they were left out.

She'd been hoping that since Lark had only just joined the preschool, there wouldn't be many kids in attendance. But every last one of her twelve classmates arrived, bringing the volume in the shop to a level that would have drowned out fireworks.

Since they couldn't afford to lose much business, they hadn't closed the shop, but Marshall had hung a sign the day before, letting people know there would be a party and apologizing for the expected increase in noise.

Lark sat at the head of the table, a party hat perched on

her head and a grin brightening her face. She glowed in all the attention, a stark contrast to Cassie's own childhood. Her birthday parties had consisted of two or three friends, a movie, popcorn, and cake after. She would have crawled under the table if her fifth-birthday celebration had been even half this size.

Nora shifted her weight from side to side, her hands over her pregnant stomach. If Cassie could avoid a conversation with her, she might make it through the event.

The door jingled, and Marshall pushed through, stacks of pizza boxes in his arms. "Who's ready to get their grub on?"

Kids clapped and cheered as he set the food out on a nearby table.

Cassie snagged the party plates and started dishing up slices of pepperoni, Hawaiian, and cheese pizza, then attempted to get each flavor to the proper kid.

Her gaze kept drifting to Shasta. She'd been worried about the intensity of the day. The party had been planned before she'd gotten sick. One of the drawbacks to preschool was Lark learning to understand the days of the week and how to count down to her big day. Moving it would have broken her heart, not to mention the difficulty of getting the word out.

Shasta's chair was at the other end of the table, giving her a straight view of Lark and the festivities. Aubrey sat nearby, and they both seemed entranced by Lark's joy. The wheelchair had been delivered, but it was still in the back of the store. Cassie wasn't ready to see it yet, nor to let it be a new reminder of the slope they were living on. Right now, her daughter was turning five, and she was surrounded by the best community ever.

Cassie ducked around the corner to find the lighter she'd stashed earlier, then lit the candles. As she walked out, the sounds and excitement died away, replaced by an off-tune rendition of "Happy Birthday." The best things in life had flaws.

The illness, leaving the hospital, Lark's party, and that very first and exciting trip with the new stairlift had not only wiped Shasta out, they had sapped Cassie of all energy too. Lark, however, was ready for another party.

While Aubrey watched and laughed, Lark bounced around the living room, asking Marshall to open one box after another. With patience that could only belong to a saint, he unraveled, cut, and snapped the millions of fasteners manufacturers seemed to believe absolutely necessary for securing children's toys.

Cassie took Shasta back to her room and started their evening process. The first few times she'd dressed and undressed her aunt had felt awkward, as if she were humiliating her more than the Parkinson's, but now it felt like a natural extension of her love for Shasta. She wondered what it would be like someday when Lark had to help her, and she immediately felt the need to protect her from that challenge. Yet Cassie was honored to help Shasta and thought it a privilege to be able to step in. Why would that be so different for her own child?

Shasta patted her lips with her fingers. It had become a form of sign language, replacing words when she couldn't find them in the maze of her mind.

"You're thirsty?"

She nodded.

"I'll get your pills and a glass of water." Cassie helped her to scoot farther onto the mattress, then went to the kitchen.

Lark sat on the floor with a pile of tiny dolls, dividing them amongst the three of them. There was a purple ribbon hanging out of Marshall's hair, and Aubrey wore a hat made of extra wrapping paper.

"Do you need any help?" Aubrey asked, her hat toppling as she turned.

"I've got it. You're actually helping me in the best way possible right now."

Shasta had started to drift off before Cassie returned to the room. Her body leaned over on the mattress. "Hey there. You need to take your medicine first."

Her eyes fluttered.

Cassie shifted her upright, wedging her own body beside Shasta's, and handed her one pill at a time, each followed by a drink. When she was done, Cassie kissed her cheek and helped her to get under the blankets.

She waved her fingers in the air, calling Cassie's attention to her face. "They will care for you."

"Who?"

Her eyes blinked, then shut. A moment later, her mouth had fallen open, and soft breathing sounds told Cassie she was asleep.

She rested her hand on Shasta's face and thanked God for the time they'd been given, however short it might be.

When Cassie returned to the living room, Lark was curled into Aubrey's arms, listening to a story from a book Aubrey had gotten her. There was a time when Cassie might have felt a touch jealous of her daughter's love and affection for others, but this was a beautiful picture. She wanted Lark to grow up surrounded by people she could count on. She wanted her to have other adults to ask questions of, to get opinions from. As Lark became independent and started that search for who she was, they could be guides, examples, and safety nets.

Marshall joined Cassie, standing at her side along the border between the kitchen and the living room. "Hey, I wanted to talk to you about something." His gaze didn't turn her way.

"What is it?" Little alarms went off. She was always ready for him to say she didn't interest him, yet she was never fully prepared.

"Mr. Watkins needs me for a few shifts at the hardware store. I'll have to cut back here, if that's okay."

Cassie wasn't fooled for a moment. "You don't have to do that."

"The hardware shop gives me a chance to try something new and put away a few extra dollars for tuition. I'm starting online classes again next term."

"That's great."

"Looks like one more year, and I'll have my master's finished. Then I'll be qualified to take Mr. Branson's position once he retires."

"I still can't believe you love working with middle schoolers that much. And being their counselor—that seems intense."

"It helps that they speak at my comfort level."

Cassie did something so bold at that point, so out of her own character, that it sent chills over her skin. She wove her pinky finger around his while she stared at the darkened window.

⁓

Having her own room had its advantages. Cassie could stretch out on the mattress, read in bed, and get up without worrying about waking Lark. But it also allowed her to get lost in the black hole of Google when she should have been sleeping.

The tiny clock on the bottom of the screen read 2:11 a.m., and Cassie was wide awake, having lurched out of a dream. There'd been a crowd of people standing outside a restaurant when a truck came hurtling down the road, across the sidewalk, and through the people. It hadn't slowed, only gained speed, and the crowd had nowhere to go.

Her body had quaked with the vivid images, until she took what felt like control. Cassie typed *Topher* and *accident on the pier of Seattle* into her search engine. When the results came back with only current stories, she added the year, but that didn't help.

She continued trying all sorts of combinations, never finding a mention of the accident that must have taken that man's life. Maybe it was just fiction after all. Diane had been killed in a car accident. No one had ever told Cassie she was a pedestrian.

Taking a couple melatonin pills, Cassie thought she'd try sleeping again, but as she closed her eyes, a thought jumped to her mind. She sat up and typed in a search for the Seattle newspaper. From there, Cassie was able to find archived articles from that far back.

"Fatalities in Runaway Accident."

She clicked on the link. The image showed paramedics working on the site of the collision, the truck stopped halfway into a restaurant, and people being held back by police. The text didn't give the names of the victims or any real information about them, but she found a follow-up article talking about the heart attack that led to the driver losing control of the truck. In this report, there were images of each victim. There was no one named Topher, but there was a Christopher Reynolds, and two names below him was the one that would keep her up the rest of the night.

Diane George.

The truth had been weaving itself together, but there were questions that could not be answered by digging through newspaper archives. For the details she craved, Cassie needed to talk with the woman who'd sent her the chapters. She couldn't call her *Mother* yet, though it was clearly not her fault that any of this had happened.

Cassie's whole life, she'd lived with the understanding that the woman who'd *claimed* Cassie was her daughter had died in an automotive accident. While that was technically true, Cassie couldn't understand why Shasta never told her the full story.

There'd never been a better Sunday to watch church online. Though the sun shining through the windows made a walk tempting, her body was exhausted, and Shasta was still recovering.

Lark had gone right to her new toys when she woke up. It was Shasta's door alarm that roused Cassie from restless sleep, hours before she'd had enough shut-eye to make it through the day.

Shasta shuffled around the room, going from the window to the painting area, as if trying to put together the plan Cassie had laid out. The wheelchair remained downstairs. It was still something they could get by fine without upstairs, but any trip outside the house, and they'd be forced to use it.

That was another reason Cassie wanted to avoid church. She didn't want Shasta to have to arrive in that thing. It was another step toward the end, another blaring sign that this disease was real and deadly and winning.

"Who's up for cereal?" Cassie's voice was so singsong that it sounded as if it belonged to someone else, someone like Mrs. Collins, who seemed to always see the good when surrounded by bad.

"It's a church day." Lark hopped up, bringing an armful of Polly Pockets to the table. "I'm going to wear my new dress."

"You wore it yesterday. I think it's got frosting on the sleeve, and I thought it might be a nice day to stay home and watch church together online." Her daughter was beginning to talk like a grown-up, which had its benefits, but again Cassie was grateful for preschool and Lark's time with kids her age.

"We should go. All our people will be there." She set up her dolls around her bowl. "Grammy Shasta wants to go."

Cassie bent over, resting her elbows on the table next to her. "And how do you know what Shasta wants?"

She shrugged. "I just do."

The sun was beautiful as it sparkled off the ocean. Cassie

sidled up next to Shasta. "Would you like to go to church today or watch from home?"

Shasta lifted her hand, no longer using her finger to point, but indicated something outside the window. And Cassie knew Lark was right. Shasta loved Sunday mornings. She always had. This was the time when she reconnected, taking a moment out from all the work of the week. Church was followed by lunch with friends and long walks on the beach. It was tradition, family, and faith, all together in a way that lifted her up.

Until college, Sunday mornings had been a precious time in Cassie's week too. But then she'd bought into the idea that she needed to find out who she was aside from what she'd been taught.

Cassie guided Shasta to the table and sat her in front of her cereal, then poured a very small amount of milk on top. Digging around in the cupboard, she found the French press that was Shasta's only acceptable form of coffee maker and scooped in a Nigerian coffee they hadn't tried before. When it had steeped in the hot water long enough, Cassie slowly pressed down the plunger. She poured half a cup into Shasta's new heavy-bottomed mug and a full cup into her own.

When Shasta took a sip, her delight was evident in her eyes. She let out a long sound of enjoyment that made Cassie want to grind enough coffee to supply her with another cup every hour.

Cassie held her mug up, clicking it against Shasta's. "So, we're heading off to church in an hour. Shall we give the new wheels a try?"

"What wheels?" Lark asked.

"Shasta has a new wheelchair downstairs. I might need some help pushing it up hills."

Lark swiped at a milk drip on her chin. "Can I ride with Grammy Shasta?"

Cassie was about to say no when Shasta reached out and tapped Lark's hand with her own.

Message from @beccaboundforglory

I talked to Lex again. I'm sorry. She's being ridiculous about contacting you. I'll see what I can pull together and send it myself. Please don't take it personally. Lex is . . . well, she's not easy for anyone to get along with.

# 30

That week Lark asked to go to Sunday school, and Cassie was ready to let her go. It wasn't fair to hold her back for the sake of her mother's insecurities. When the final prayer ended, Cassie went to get her daughter while Shasta's friends came by to greet her.

Cassie had a plan but wasn't sure it would work yet.

Lark saw her at the half door and hugged Gwendolyn. "I'll see you at preschool. I love you super much."

Gwendolyn smiled shyly and waved good-bye. Cassie couldn't help really liking that child and assumed her personality had been acquired from Ferris. With Lark's hand safely in hers, they walked down the hall to join Shasta. The bathroom door swung open, and Nora walked out, her gaze low.

"Are you okay?" Cassie wished she hadn't asked, but the words were out before she'd thought better of them.

Nora nodded. "Just allergies." Her nostrils flared, and she curled her lips between her teeth as tears gathered in her eyes.

Lark pulled on Cassie's hand, urging her forward.

"Go ahead and stand by Shasta." Cassie let go, and Lark was off.

"Do you want to talk? I'm an okay listener."

Nora fanned her hand in front of her eyes. "No. Everything is good. I couldn't possibly unload my silly problem on you when you have so many larger ones."

The sting of her words didn't strike Cassie the way they had in the past. There was a desperation in Nora's voice. "Well, if you change your mind, you know where to find me."

"Thank you, but really, I'm very blessed."

Cassie faked a smile that helped her hold back her tongue. If she were any less genuine, the woman would turn to actual plastic.

Her head was still shaking when she joined Shasta, Aubrey, Mrs. Collins, Mrs. McPherson, and three other women all in a circle around Lark, who was belting out a worship song she'd learned in preschool. When she finished, Lark bowed, and the entire group burst into applause and accolades. If Cassie wasn't careful, her daughter was going to grow from confident to an egomaniac.

Cassie took Shasta's blanket from the back of her chair and wrapped it around her legs, tucking it in so the coastal wind wouldn't uncover her. "We're going to take a little walk near the beach."

Shasta's eyes met hers. "Yes." She went on, but the rest of her mumbles and sounds didn't form actual words.

Before Cassie could stop her, Lark had climbed onto Shasta's lap, snuggling under the blanket.

"Hey, I can't push you both the whole way." Cassie was already thinking about the bumpy, cracked sidewalk they'd have to use. Marshall would have been a huge help, but he was taking a group of middle school kids to lunch.

"Just a little bit?" She fluttered her eyes at her mom. She must have learned that somewhere, and Cassie was going to be sure and ask about it later.

"Five minutes." Cassie turned to the rest of the group. "Would anyone like to join us?" There was a bit of relief when no one volunteered. If her idea was a failure, she'd rather face it on her own than with the eyes of Gull's Bay following along.

After their good-byes, Cassie, Lark, and Shasta started for the path that led to the beach. As they neared the edge, the paved section curved, keeping a ten-foot parallel to the sand. At one time, this had been a pleasant stroll, but the weight of the cement on a less-than-solid foundation left the surface crumbling in places.

Lark bounced along in front of them.

"Be careful. I don't want you tripping."

She twirled around like a ballerina, wearing the dress from yesterday, frosting still clinging to the sleeve. "I won't fall."

And then, of course, she did.

Lark was sprawled out on the ground, her hands in front of her like Superman with no ability to fly.

Cassie clicked the locks on the wheelchair and ran to her, pulling Lark up and checking her knees and palms for blood.

Tears washed down Lark's face.

"Are you okay?"

She didn't answer, just grabbed hold of her and clung like an octopus.

Cassie tucked Lark's head under her chin, inhaling the sweet scent of her daughter. If tripping on a sidewalk made her ache this deeply for Lark, how was she ever going to handle Lark's bigger bumps? Someday, a boy would break her heart, and she wouldn't get picked for a team. And her Grammy Shasta would pass away.

Like only a child could, Lark was ready to run and jump again before Cassie was ready to let her go.

They hit a particularly rough section of sidewalk, but up ahead, Cassie could see her goal. "Don't worry. I'm going to tip the chair back a little so I can get over these bumps."

Shasta's fingers curled around the armrests.

There was sweat on Cassie's brow and her hands ached from

the tight hold on the handles, but they made it over the crumbled chunks of cement and onto the highest point of the path. Here, the dunes separated, leaving a gap in the beach grass and a perfect view of the ocean.

The roar entered Cassie with each breath of fresh, salty air. It empowered her, reminding her of who she was, not who she thought she should be. It made her feel alive and hopeful in a way that was reassuring.

Shasta closed her eyes and raised her arms, her body in a posture of complete worship. What would that doubtless devotion, that ease and carefree nature, feel like?

What came for Cassie was doubt. She had no memory of rejection, but faith and security were not a natural part of her either, and they refused to be forced.

Yet Cassie was sandwiched between two people who seemed to have been born with the confidence she had searched for her whole life. Why did it exist for some but remain hidden for others?

"Look, Mom." Lark popped out of the sand and pointed to where she'd been. A heart was carved into the surface. "I love you."

"Oh, Larkie-bird, I love you too. More than you could ever know."

~~

Nora ran a large bunch of organic green grapes under the water, then set them on a paper towel. She retrieved the cutting board from its home beside the microwave and picked out her favorite knife. One by one, she sliced grapes in half, dropping the less-fatal-to-toddler versions into a bowl while, outside, the giggles of her daughters mixed with the laughter of her husband and in-laws.

The baby inside of her twisted, as if realizing she was missing something by being stuck inside with her mom.

Nora had been Tammy's third daughter. She'd been the one worth sacrificing. Tears came again. Her unborn child had taken over her body and stripped Nora of her normal self-control. Crying never did a thing to solve a problem, and it wouldn't help her now.

A wave of nausea hit her when she thought about her run-in with Cassie. It was bad enough she'd had to excuse herself from church, but then to be caught in her fragility? That was just cruel.

She wiped a stray tear with the tip of her middle finger, careful not to upset the makeup she'd reapplied.

What if there was some genetic code hidden in her body? The kind of ticking bomb that exploded when a woman gave birth to so many daughters? The comparisons between her life and Tammy's kept hitting her. They came full force as she tried to sleep at night, and they assaulted her anytime the world around her was quiet enough for thoughts to form.

Nora ran another bunch of grapes under the water.

Imagining herself as a third-born when she'd always been an only shook up every story she'd ever concocted about her mother and what her life was like somewhere beyond Gull's Bay. There was one thing Nora knew for certain: She would not be having a fourth daughter. There wouldn't be a @becca boundforglory under her roof.

Cassie scrambled around Monday morning, getting Lark ready for preschool, Shasta fed and dressed, and her daughter's toys into the cardboard container that acted as a toybox. Today they were scheduled for the first visit with the home health nurse.

Her purpose was to monitor Shasta's health, but Cassie couldn't help but feel as if she was about to endure some serious judgment. She scanned the living room. It seemed passable. Shasta slumped on the couch, exhausted from all the hurried activity.

Cassie checked the kitchen, where Lark was scarfing down her breakfast in preparation for Aubrey's arrival and escort to preschool. Below her, Cheerios were scattered on the linoleum, only a few of which were from that morning, or even from Lark. What Cassie needed was a dog that didn't require walks, bathroom breaks, or attention.

When Cassie heard the knock at the door, she hollered for Aubrey to come in, having already unlocked it while tidying over there.

"Hello?"

Cassie snapped upright, seven shrunken Cheerios in the palm of one hand, a stray hair pretty clutched in the other. "Hello." She swallowed. "Please come in."

A badge hung from a lanyard around the woman's neck, and a bag from her shoulder.

Cassie's face must have been scarlet with the rush of heat and embarrassment. She used an empty chair to help her stand and slipped the ancient cereal into the trash.

"Who are you?" Lark asked.

Cassie slapped a hand onto her forehead. "I'm so sorry." Turning to her daughter, she gave Lark that behave-yourself look she never seemed to pick up on. "Lark, this is Aunt Shasta's home health nurse."

The nurse reached her hand out to shake but hesitated, then pointed to Cassie's forehead.

Reaching up, she quickly found the problem. Another Cheerio, stuck to her face. If there were deeper depths of mortification, Cassie had not met with them . . . yet. "Would you excuse me?"

In the bathroom, she gave herself a thorough check and found no more food stuck to her skin, but hair that was looking mighty ratty after months with no haircut. Cassie ran water on the brush and forced it through, transforming curls into frizz. With a yoga breath, she altered her face with a smile she inspected for obvious signs of manipulation, then returned to make her second impression on this woman.

With feigned confidence, Cassie stepped into the room, head high and acting skills on point. "Hello. You must be Anna-beth." She held her hand out as if she hadn't already tried this and took it as a good sign when the nurse shook it this time.

"Please, call me Anna." She seemed to relax. Perhaps Cassie's chaos hadn't made her physically uncomfortable. "Is this Shasta?" Her head bent toward Cassie's aunt.

"Yes. She tires easily." Cassie sat next to Shasta and gently nudged her arm.

Her eyes fluttered, then snapped open, a look of shock on her face as a stranger stared down at her.

"Shasta, this is Anna. She's a nurse, and she's here to check you out." Cassie patted her hand.

Anna knelt on the floor in front of the sofa. "I understand that Shasta has given you power of attorney?"

Cassie nodded.

"Then I'm going to need your signature on a few forms." She pulled out a clipboard, snapped some paperwork in place, and handed it to Cassie, along with a pen. "There's also some information about the services we provide and how long we can accommodate a patient." She laid another stack of papers on Cassie's lap. "And the doctor asked that I give you this packet about hospice. I understand they may be called in soon."

Cassie's stomach dropped like it always did at the mention of hospice.

"Now, I don't want you to get worried because we're talking about that step. Hospice is in place to help. I've seen many patients live much longer than the six months we expect when they're assigned. I've even seen a few taken back off of hospice. I think you'll be surprised how helpful the program can be and how much it improves the lives of patients."

Another knock at the door. This one had to be Aubrey. "Lark, can you let Aubrey in, please?"

Her daughter cocked a hip and gave Cassie the are-you-crazy stare. "I can't. I'm not allowed."

"It's okay. I know who it is, and I'm right here." Cassie looked from Lark to the papers all over her lap.

Lark shook her head.

Anna talked to Shasta about getting vitals while Cassie tried to communicate with her five-year-old through telepathy. She could, of course, call for Aubrey to come in, but that hadn't worked out well the time before.

Cassie shuffled everything into one stack on top of the clipboard and set it on the far cushion, then let Aubrey in.

"I thought I'd missed you." She held her hand out to Lark. "I'm sorry I was late. I got a call as I was walking out the door. Come on, Lark. We'd better get going if we don't want to be tardy to preschool."

Aubrey had the ability to get Lark going in a hurry, whereas when Cassie tried, she was met with slothlike movements from her daughter.

"There's hardly even a crackle in her lungs. That's impressive this soon after a battle with pneumonia." Anna patted Shasta on the leg and stood. "I understand you have a wheelchair available?" Her eyes seemed to be searching for it.

"We keep it downstairs. There's not much need for it up here."

"I understand. That may or may not change. It's hard to tell with these things. Do you mind if I look around? I might be able to give some thoughts on equipment and supplies that may help make this time of life easier on both of you."

"Sure." Cassie was doing her best to keep the place safe for Shasta, but honestly, they were dealing with an overflow of clutter. Her room had been kept as she left it, all of her high-school possessions still taking up the same space they had when Cassie thought every one of those things was necessary for life. Lark and Cassie had come home with not as much stuff as the typical American, but it was a great deal to add to an already full space. And Shasta had lost the art of tossing unneeded things. The three sets of salt and pepper shakers were a testament to that. "What would you like to see?"

"The bathroom is always a good place to start."

Cassie was sure her eyebrows rose an inch. While she'd been able to convince Lark to stop leaving her clothes in there, she hadn't been able to keep up with Shasta's dropped hand towels and her need to keep moving items from the kitchen into the bathroom. It didn't make a lot of sense, but this one-little-thing-at-a-time adjustment seemed to give her satisfaction, and Cassie wasn't going to stop it when it wasn't causing any real problems.

She ushered Anna down the hall and pointed into the bathroom. "We just have the one."

The way she nodded, her expression like a schoolmarm with a white glove, had Cassie chewing away at her inner cheek. "It's not usually this cluttered."

After looking behind the shower curtain and under the sink, Anna stepped back into the hall. "And where does Shasta sleep?"

Cassie pointed, letting Anna go in first.

She stopped in the doorway and stared at the alarm system, writing something in her notebook.

In high school, one of Cassie's teachers had been going through the process to become a foster parent. She told them all about the background checks and home inspections. Cassie wondered now if this was how she'd felt, like she was being searched by a stranger.

Anna examined the power cord that ran to the digital clock and tucked it behind the nightstand, then turned to Cassie. "It looks like you're doing a great job. Some rails could really help in the shower. It must be difficult to get her in and out of that tub."

"We have a method that's working, but yes, the rails would be helpful, mainly for me." Cassie had nearly slipped more times than she wanted to tell Anna about while attempting to help Shasta in the shower.

"If you move forward with hospice, there will be someone who can come out and handle bathing. A lot of caregivers really appreciate that bit of assistance."

"Really? That would be amazing. She's my aunt, and I love her, but it's awkward for us."

"I'm sure it is. I think it's a relief to a lot of patients when they can have someone else take care of those kinds of intimate details too. No one wants to think about their loved ones having to care for them as they age. It's often a thought that people avoid. Then time sneaks up, and they need help."

Someday, Lark might have to do these things. It broke Cassie's heart to think she could become a burden, yet she hoped they would have the kind of relationship Cassie had with Shasta.

"There's a group that helps coordinate home health supplies. I'll write the number down for you. They can usually provide grips and handrails for the shower."

Cassie thanked her, handed over the stack of papers she'd filled out and signed, and took the card with the number she'd mentioned.

When Anna left, Cassie dropped onto the sofa. *Hospice* felt like a dirty word on her tongue. It was connected so closely with death, with endings and grief. Yet the way Anna had spoken,

Cassie could see that it might bring some life into these days too. Caring for Shasta, no matter how much longer she lived, was something Cassie wanted to do. She wasn't the same person who had cried on the drive back to Oregon, scared she might have to stay here. Aside from being Lark's mother, tending her aunt was the greatest honor of her life.

# 31

The internet of 1998 had been scant. Only those obsessed with technology had seemed to do anything beyond the range of email. And while Amazon was a thing, no one had really known about it yet. So finding information on Christopher Reynolds would take more than a quick Google search. The average person who died before 2000 barely even existed online.

These were the lovely thoughts sorting through Cassie's mind as she waited for Shasta's platform to bring her down the stairs to the wheelchair. Even after more than a week, it always felt like a show when they did this, the bottom of their apartment access being in the center of the dining area of the shop. When the motor clicked off, Cassie held back the temptation to give a bow to all the folks who had watched the snail-paced program.

Mr. Watkins was bringing Lark home today, and Cassie was taking an extra shift as a barista.

Cassie checked the locks on the chair before helping Shasta over to her "chariot," as they'd started calling it. "How's that? Are you comfortable?"

Her gaze swung to the back booth. Seeing the place empty, she nodded, a look of victory playing briefly over her features.

The mystery woman hadn't been in since the awkward stare

down. Cassie was embarrassed at having frozen like a fool, yet also relieved not to have to face the woman she suspected of sending the chapters.

What kind of person did that make her, having no compassion or care for the woman who might very well have given birth to her? How could Cassie not feel a connection with her? Shouldn't there be a magical thread that connected them, something that tied them together from the moment Cassie was forming inside of her? Cassie often felt that way for Lark, as though she didn't have a choice in how devastating the love for her could be.

Cassie wasn't one to think DNA glued a family together. Shasta had only been her "mother's" cousin, yet Cassie loved her as much as if she'd been her biological mother. It was hard to displace her understanding of who they were together, knowing she wasn't the girl Shasta thought she was. Though Shasta hadn't known it, there was no obligation on her part to raise Cassie. Yet Cassie struggled with the fact that she was grateful Shasta *hadn't* known. Somewhere out there, a woman had grieved for Cassie, but if that woman had known where Cassie was, Cassie would have missed out on this. She leaned down and kissed Shasta on the cheek.

Stationing Shasta where she could greet customers, Cassie stepped into the back and washed her hands.

Lisa had just finished putting the last of the breakfast dishes on the shelf. "The dry-goods delivery came in about an hour ago. I haven't had time to unpack it. Would you like me to stay after my shift and get that done?"

As much as Cassie wished she could say yes, financially, it wasn't possible. "No. Go on home and enjoy your time off." There was an hour until the lunch people started to show up. Cassie could get everything prepped so maybe she could maintain a bit of control throughout that hour. The boxes would have to wait until after.

Then Cassie did something that was out of character—and probably frightening to anyone who knew her: She hugged Lisa. "Thank you for all you do around here. I really appreciate you."

Lisa's smile was both sincere and questioning, but Cassie didn't wait for a reply. The door had again jingled with the reminder to check the counter. Sure enough, three women stood staring up at the menu. Life wasn't giving Cassie much time to stand still, but maybe that was for the best. Too much time contemplating both the past and what was to come would have weakened her in the heart and legs. Work soothed the soul in a way fear and regret could not.

"How can I help you?"

After they rattled off their coffee orders, each one stopped to greet Shasta, one even leaning down to hug her. They were locals, women Cassie recognized but couldn't call by name. And they bestowed on Shasta a joy that she didn't possess when held upstairs like an aging Rapunzel.

By half past noon, Cassie was damp with sweat and craving a drink of her own. Lillian McPherson had been through and was kind enough to help Shasta get situated with her lunch at the table they kept reserved for her, with one side empty for easy wheelchair access.

Cassie slapped a turkey sandwich together, plopped on a pickle, and dropped the plate on a tray as another customer came in the door. Without looking, she hollered over her shoulder, "I'll be with you in a minute." Then she took the tray to table five, where she'd already served two iced teas and a scone.

When she turned, there was a grinning Lark, high on top of Marshall's shoulders. "What are you doing up there?" She glanced at her watch. Mr. Watkins should have had her back half an hour earlier, and Cassie had been too busy to notice he hadn't come.

"I hope it's okay. I switched with Mr. Watkins. One of his

sons came into town, and I thought they might like some time together."

"That's great. I wish I'd have known. I could have gotten her."

He glanced around. "You've got that Superman thing going, right, where you can just fly out of here, then show up ten seconds later?"

"No. But it's my responsibility. I don't want anyone feeling like they have to drop what's important to them to help me out."

"You are important to them. So is Lark." He lifted her off his shoulders and set her on the floor. "You're both *very* important to me."

The way he emphasized *very* sent tingles over her skin. "Thank you."

"You're welcome." No one had ever said those words with such depth—at least not to Cassie.

She shrugged off the feelings for Marshall, trying to remain in a neutral stance. Going all head over heels for this man was going to knock her clean off the carefully balanced life she was trying so hard to maintain.

Aubrey came up to the counter through the kitchen. "Cassie, are you about ready for a break?" The way she said it was laced with accusation.

"It's my shift."

"And I'm here to tell you to have lunch." She looked at Marshall. "Let me tell you, if I had a man that handsome standing next to me, I'd find a way to take a break and spend a little time with him."

Cassie's mouth fell open. "Aubrey."

She shrugged. "I'm just saying."

"I hear what you're saying. It's not like that."

Marshall mimed a stab to the heart.

"You know what I mean."

"I'm taking over." Aubrey tied an apron around her waist. "You two go join Shasta and Lark." She indicated the table where Lark was pushing her art projects from preschool in front of Shasta and her sandwich. "Or . . . you could take the empty table in the back." She winked.

*Wow.* Cassie could have been scooped up and thrown out the door without the slightest bit of argument. She'd never be able to look Marshall in the face again. At least not today.

∿

Christopher Reynolds had married Amanda Gray on February 7, 1989, in Santa Barbara, California. It wasn't a lot of information, but that's all the marriage certificate she found online told Cassie. But now she had her name. The woman who had given birth to her, unless this whole thing was someone's sick joke.

Cassie searched Facebook for Amanda Reynolds and Amanda Gray. The results for either name were endless. None of them claimed Gull's Bay, Oregon, as her current location. Most seemed her own age or younger. She scrolled through page after page of Amandas, clicking on each one who looked as if she could be over forty, though the woman would be in her fifties by now.

Hours later, her eyes had grown weary, and Cassie was still sorting through timelines, looking for any mention of an Ainsley or a Topher, with nothing to show for her time. There were too many pieces missing from this puzzle. Had she remarried, changing her name again? Did she go back to her maiden name? Had she remained in Southern California to be near the resting place of her husband and daughter, or was she somewhere closer?

The online White Pages weren't much more help. There was no listing for Amanda Gray or Amanda Reynolds in any of the towns near Gull's Bay. And the search in California brought up so many, she'd need a way to narrow the parameters.

Cassie's phone buzzed with the opening of Shasta's door. This was her third time out of bed that night. Closing the laptop, Cassie set it on the shelf near the head of her bed. Finding Amanda could wait. After she got Shasta back to bed, Cassie needed sleep. Working and caring for Shasta and Lark were taking a toll on her ability to function and think.

She found Shasta in the kitchen, attempting to open the drawers.

"Are you having a hard time sleeping?"

She started and looked at Cassie as if they were strangers.

"Shasta? It's me, Cassie." She stepped forward, hesitant to make physical contact.

Shasta's eyes were open but unfocused, as though she were still asleep, yet not fully. She went back to yanking on every handle, as if she needed something but wasn't sure where to find it.

"Can I get you a drink?"

"You can't take her. She's mine." The rage that burned in her eyes with those words forced Cassie back a couple steps.

"Take who away from you?"

"You know." Her voice was a low growl that seemed to rise from deep in her abdomen.

"I don't. I promise you, I don't understand what you're saying."

Shasta's arm swept across the counter, sending glasses across the surface and onto the linoleum floor. They shattered into sharp pieces.

"Don't move. I need to clean this up." Cassie stepped over the mess and reached for the broom, but Shasta pushed past her, going straight through the shards.

She cried out in pain and tumbled to the floor near the hall.

That's when Cassie saw Lark standing in the hallway, the

moonlight illuminating her tears as they coursed down her cheeks, her hands held tight to her chest. They both needed so much, but Cassie needed someone too. She sank onto the floor next to Shasta and held her arms out for Lark. The three of them cried out their ugly tears, filling the night with their mourning.

"It's going to be okay." Cassie kept repeating this through her own gasping sobs. "I promise you both. I'm going to make this all okay." But she didn't know how to fix Parkinson's or the consequences of Shasta's stroke, and she didn't know how to take away her daughter's fears. She could barely keep them in a place where they weren't having to file for bankruptcy.

The cuts on Shasta's feet wouldn't need stitches, but they would surely be uncomfortable for the coming days. And Lark would likely remember this night, the one where she had to see her mother and her grammy cry out the fears and hurts until they were wasted and empty. She'd remember the blood too, but Cassie prayed she'd also remember that they were together and love would see them through.

In the morning, Cassie would pack away all the glasses, and they would replace them with plasticware. It was another tiny thing, but it was all she was able to do to bring safety and security to their lives.

# 32

Mrs. Collins was upstairs, making a pie crust with Lark and Shasta. She was convinced that this was something they both could do, and the end result would be utter happiness for all involved. After last night, Cassie was ready for any ideas.

Cassie walked down the stairs, her left hand riding along the railing Mr. Watkins and Marshall had put up, back when Cassie still saw Marshall as a threat to her independence. *Grateful* wasn't a big enough word for how she felt for them now. Her exhausted body could have tumbled down the steps as easily as Shasta's. Maybe she should have taken the slow, mechanical ride.

At the bottom, Cassie stopped to indulge in a giant yawn and stretch. As her eyes opened, they caught on the booth. She'd assumed the woman was gone forever, at least until Cassie hunted her down and insisted on answers, but there she was, typing away again.

*Enough already.* Cassie shook out her arms and headed that way.

The woman's gaze shot up. She slapped her laptop closed.

"I need answers. This may seem harsh, but I can't go on pretending you're not here."

The woman swallowed, then started to pack up.

"No." Cassie slammed her hand down on the counter, then looked around. She'd caught the attention of half the shop. Easing her way into the booth, she spoke in a hushed tone. "Did you write the story? The one about . . . me."

Her stare was as blank as Shasta's had been the night before.

"Listen. I get if you don't want to tell me, but I need to know. Who are you?"

Her forehead creased. "I'm not sure what you're talking about." She dropped her gaze. Something seemed off, but Cassie couldn't put it together.

"I may be wrong, but could you tell me what you're doing on your computer all the time?"

"Is this a normal question you pose to your customers? It seems that what I'm doing is my business, and none of yours."

"Do you know who I am?"

She didn't answer.

Aubrey appeared at her side. "Cassie, could I talk with you in the kitchen? There's a bit of a problem."

"Can it wait? We're in the middle of something here."

"No. I think now would be the perfect time." She gestured with her hand for Cassie to lead the way.

"Okay." She turned to the woman. "I'd like to pick up this conversation soon. And I'll find you if you don't come in. This is a small town."

Aubrey grabbed Cassie by the elbow and tugged her away.

Once they were in the kitchen, out of the sight of customers, she turned Cassie around. "Have you lost your mind?"

Her mouth fell open, but she stumbled over her words. That question was becoming hard to answer. "Maybe, but that was why I was asking that woman questions. You don't know what's been going on around here."

Aubrey cocked her hip so much like Lark that Cassie had to wonder who was influencing whom. "Sometimes it's hard to see the crazy when you're all up in it."

Cassie crossed her arms. "And that little fortune cookie gem means what?"

"It means you were very rude and abrasive. Cassie, if you don't know someone's story, you have no business making judgments about them. Mandy hasn't done a single thing to you, yet you're over there talking to her as if she's hurt you in some way."

Mandy.

"Short for Amanda?"

"What?"

"Her name. Is Mandy short for Amanda?" Cassie pulled her sweater tight. The temperature in the kitchen had gone from toasty to chilly.

The door did its jingle. Cassie didn't even have to look to know it was Mandy leaving.

"Listen. I'm just asking you to leave her alone. You don't know her story."

"What if I did? Would that make a difference?"

Aubrey filled a cup from the valve that supplied nearly boiling water, then dropped a chamomile tea bag in. "If you knew her story, you wouldn't be hounding her like you were."

"Okay." Cassie cut her hand across the air between them. "Let me have it. Tell me the story that means I should keep my distance." She couldn't wait to hear how poor Mandy had been watching her for years rather than coming out and telling her the truth.

Aubrey handed her the tea. "This is for you. Take a minute and regain your senses, please."

The warm mug was soothing to her palms. Cassie set it down. She wasn't ready for comforting or calming—she wanted answers.

"Mandy's story is not mine to share. If it were, I guarantee you, I'd tell you. I'm not sure why Shasta has gotten it in her head that Mandy is dangerous. I don't believe that for a minute. And I'm shocked that you're falling into this hallucination too.

You know Shasta sees things that aren't there." She picked up the mug and handed it to Cassie again. "There are things done in this town that are the way they are for good. If we went around chattering about it all, that good would be ruined. I want you to trust me on this, and let it go."

Shasta had never given Cassie this kind of talk, not even when she was a snotty preteen. The tone hit hard. Aubrey could be right, but what if she wasn't? "Look . . . I think she's my mother."

Aubrey's face broke into a smile. "What? You're kidding me, right?"

"No. I've been reading this story, and it lines up."

"That Mandy, the woman who sat in that corner booth every day until you and Shasta finally scared her away, is hiding the fact that she's actually your mom?" Aubrey's gaze rose until it found its destination on the ceiling. "Please believe me on this: If Mandy had any living children, she wouldn't waste any time telling them they were hers." She looked back at Cassie. "I have a meeting, but when I get back, I'll keep Shasta and Lark down here for a couple of hours. You need to get more sleep." She snagged her sweater off the hook and walked out.

Cassie checked the mailbox but only found a circular for their little grocery store and the electric bill. For some reason, she'd been sure more chapters would arrive, but they hadn't. Despite Aubrey's words, this only supported her assertion that Mandy had a secret, and Cassie was part of it.

*If* the story she'd written was accurate. If she'd only lost Ainsley because of the kidnapping, then why wouldn't she want Cassie to know? She had nothing to lose, unless she'd watched Cassie long enough to wonder if she even liked her, much less loved her. Was it possible that their lack of genetic connection had resulted in no maternal feelings for the woman Cassie was today?

Yet, how could Cassie judge her harshly? The way Cassie had stood over her, questioning what she was doing—there'd been no sweetness on her part either. It was only when Aubrey laid into Cassie that she felt desperation to regain respect.

She should give Ferris a call, see what he could dig up on this woman. But Aubrey's words stopped her, leaving the feeling that bringing in the local detective was another overstep.

Tossing the junk mail into the recycling, Cassie moved through the shop, startling Shasta as she started to push her toward the stairs. "Sorry. I should have told you we were about to move."

Her chin nodded forward again. The day had worn on her, as they did more and more. The three of them had taken to quiet afternoons of Shasta snoozing on the couch while Lark snuggled beside her, enjoying her allotted screen time.

That time would have been a great opportunity for Cassie to rest too, but her mind was on fire with all the what-ifs that had surrounded her life since returning home. The chapters weren't there by accident. Someone had gone to the trouble of typing out the pages, printing them, and making sure they were delivered.

At first, Cassie had read them with curiosity, unthinkingly leaving the pages lying around when she moved on to something else. What if Shasta had read them? It would have devastated her to know Cassie didn't truly belong here. Yet somehow Shasta sensed that something was off with Mandy. She knew some piece of this puzzle, but it was stuck in her mind, behind a tongue that couldn't form the words to let anyone know.

Upstairs, she helped Shasta get comfortable, then placed a fuzzy blanket over her lap. She knelt down, her face close to

Shasta's, and spoke in a hushed tone. "Shasta, do you know where I came from?"

Her face was blank, and Cassie thought she hadn't understood, but then a hand came up, her fingers tapping her chest at the location of her heart.

There were more questions, ones Cassie should have asked earlier, ones she'd always had and ones that were new. And it was too late for all of them. She would spend the remainder of her life knowing she should have listened better to Shasta, taken in everything she had to share. Cassie should have asked about Shasta's story, as well as her own. Someday, Lark would have questions Cassie wouldn't be able to answer because she'd been so saturated in shame that she'd missed her chance.

But she would teach her daughter that shame stole. It took away the light they were created to live in and tricked them into hiding while they should be out living, breathing, and growing. Shame removed the ability to accept oneself as a person who was changing and becoming, instead inserting hopelessness. Cassie would teach Lark to cast off shame, and she would teach her by example how to move forward, learning to be better, kinder, and more compassionate to all those around her.

As if it had been directly messaged to Cassie's heart, she knew what she had to do. She needed to apply these thoughts to her life by giving Mandy grace. Cassie had served the woman shame, and she knew how bitter that tasted.

When Aubrey came by so Cassie could nap, she begged off sleeping and told her she'd be better served by a walk on the beach. It was a lie she'd have to face up to and ask forgiveness for sooner than she'd want to, but the need to apologize was heavy.

Outside, the air was warm for any day on the Oregon coast.

Cassie walked down the small street lined with local businesses, feeling as if everyone looking out their windows could tell she was up to something she didn't want to share.

For the first time in her life, Cassie was happy to see Nora coming toward her. She knew everything about everyone in town, and she had no reservations about sharing information.

Cassie waved, calling an unusual amount of attention to herself.

Nora squinted before finally returning the gesture.

"Hello. How have you been doing? Lark is really loving pre-school. Thank you so much for the suggestion." The smile on Cassie's face actually cramped her cheeks.

"I'm glad. Children need socialization, you know. It's important if we expect them to develop empathy. I think that's such an important trait, don't you?"

"I do. Where is Gwendolyn today?"

Nora patted her rounded stomach. "It's just me and this tiny one. My mother-in-law has my girls this afternoon."

Cassie could have been wrong, but it seemed as though Nora cringed just a little at the mention of her mother-in-law. Was it possible that not even Nora had a perfect life? "That must be nice."

She nodded but didn't offer anything further on the subject.

"I was just wondering, do you happen to know Mandy? She's a regular in the shop, a real sweet lady." Cassie tipped her head, trying to look casual as she mined for information.

"Oh yes, I know exactly who you mean. She lives three houses down from Julie. Do you remember Julie from high school? That woman is such a dear. She has two perfect little twin boys and is married to an attorney. The man drives an hour each way to his office so she can remain here in our charming little town. What a dream."

"Isn't that something. An attorney." Cassie tapped a finger on her chin. "Now, where did you say Julie lives?"

"I didn't." There was a twist in her expression, as if Cassie had pushed this act too far.

"I'm just curious where people feel the best neighborhoods are these days. I assume Julie's would be at the top end."

A muscle in Nora's jaw pumped. "I wouldn't call it the top. We live on Jasmine. We have an unencumbered view of the ocean and all the houses are less than five years old. Julie's place is nice. It has . . . character. You know the area. She's the second house on LaComb. They have wonderful yards there, but the view isn't what most of us live here for."

Cassie had what she needed, other than a way to escape this mindless conversation. Where was her compassion, the new Cassie and all of that? "It's been really great chatting with you. I need to get moving. Aubrey is taking care of Lark for me right now so I can get some exercise and fresh air."

Nora nodded. "It must be very difficult for you, being alone and all."

Cassie pressed a fingernail into her palm. "Yes, there are difficult times, as there are for all moms, but I wouldn't trade any of it. I'm sure you know exactly what I'm talking about."

Nora's smile faded for a moment. "Yes . . . of course. Have a nice walk." She readjusted her purse strap on her shoulder and started back up the street.

Was it worse to have struggles everyone knew about, or to feel forced to always appear as if you had none?

With the information gathered, Cassie crossed the street, heading directly to LaComb, a classic neighborhood that must have had a beautiful view before the newer homes popped up between it and the ocean. If Julie was two houses in, Mandy had to be the fifth, being three past Julie. Cassie's life was becoming one logic puzzle after another.

Her confidence grew when she walked past the house she assumed was Julie's, a white colonial with large pillars outside the double front door and matching tricycles near the garage.

Three houses farther on, she found a smaller house, painted almost ink blue. The curtains were closed, and no car was parked in the driveway. It wasn't uncommon for the people in Gull's Bay to walk more often than drive, even when the weather wasn't cooperative, which was a great deal of the year, but it could also mean that she wasn't home.

Cassie looked down the road. Maybe Aubrey was right, and she'd lost her mind. But the flutter of the curtains falling shut again in her peripheral vision told Cassie she'd been caught. Going back now was creepier than going forward.

She reached the door and said a quick prayer before knocking.

It took three more attempts before Mandy came to answer. She opened it but left the security chain engaged. "What do you want?"

"I'm here to apologize. Could I come in?"

The look she gave Cassie through the gap was similar to the one she'd gotten from Aubrey.

"I promise, I'm not crazy. I made a terrible mistake. I just want to talk."

"Is anyone with you?"

Cassie looked around, as if needing to check for herself. "No. It's just me." She held her hands out, palms toward Mandy.

The door closed.

It seemed like minutes went by before it opened again. "Aubrey is a very good person. I'm only letting you in because I know she trusts you."

Cassie's stomach sank. If Aubrey could see her now, that trust would evaporate.

Mandy let her into the living room. It was sparsely furnished, with a couch and a single chair. A fold-out TV tray sat by the seat, suggesting this was where Mandy ate most of her meals. There was a small television on a pressed-wood stand and one clock. As if she'd just been dropped here out of nowhere, the walls were vacant of pictures.

"Have a seat." Mandy took the chair, folding her hands together in her lap.

The couch wasn't meant for regular company. It sank down in the center, throwing Cassie's hips out of alignment. "I wanted to come here and apologize for my behavior."

"How did you know where I live? And how do you know who I am?"

Cassie scrubbed a hand through her hair, searching the room for the answers. That's when she noticed the door that must lead to the garage. Beside it sat two suitcases. "Are you going on a trip?"

"That doesn't concern you."

"You're right. I deserve that. But I wish you wouldn't go on my account."

"You haven't left me much choice, now, have you?"

Cassie had been horrible to Mandy, but this reaction was extreme even to Cassie, who'd been known to go overboard. "I'm not sure I understand. I shouldn't have pushed you." The words were all tied up in her chest. "I have questions. Something weird has been going on. Did you come here to find me? And if you did, why leave without even talking?" A deep shame started to climb into her soul.

Mandy evaluated her as if Cassie was a book she was considering, but the back cover copy left her more confused than intrigued. "Why would I be looking for you? I don't know you."

Cassie's pulse pounded behind her eardrums. "Are you from California?"

"Why?" Though the reality that she might have made a huge miscalculation was staring at Cassie with questioning eyes, she had to concede that Mandy was about the only person she'd met who could come into a situation as defensive as Cassie could.

"Did you write to me?"

"No."

"Okay. May I ask why you sit behind your laptop every day in our shop?"

She raised her chin. "Aubrey didn't tell you anything about me?"

"She didn't. She wouldn't, in fact." Cassie lowered her gaze. "She'd be after me if she found out I was here."

"Look. I'm going to have to leave here now anyway, so we might as well be honest with each other."

"That's all I'm looking for."

"My name isn't Mandy. I'm not going to tell you what my actual name is. You don't need that information, and it would only increase the risk. My ex-husband wants me dead. He will kill me if he finds me. In the last ten years, this is the place I've been able to stay the longest." She blinked away tears. "Until you and Shasta started questioning me, I thought I'd found a place I could stay."

"Are you saying you're in some kind of witness-protection program?"

Her laugh was dry and dull. "More of a grassroots program that helps domestic violence survivors. You can't mention this to anyone. Do you understand?"

"I won't. I promise."

"There are others here in Gull's Bay. If something were to happen to them, their blood would be on your hands."

A wave of dizziness swirled around in Cassie's head. "But . . . why were you in the shop? What were you doing with the laptop, if not writing your story?"

"What makes you think I wasn't writing what had happened to me? If I don't survive my ex, I want the world to know exactly what he was capable of and what he's done. And . . . I don't have internet here in the house. It's too risky. I come to the shop to browse around online. Sometimes, I just need to see that the world is still turning for the people I love. If he ever found out, if I made direct contact with my sister or my mother, he would have them killed or do it himself."

"I'm so sorry." Cassie might not have much in the way of family, but Shasta and Lark were there with her. She'd never have to run away and leave them behind. "You don't know anything about a baby named Ainsley, do you?"

"I've never even met anyone by that name."

Cassie deflated as she exhaled. Amanda Reynolds had an Ainsley. She'd met Cassie. Somewhere deep inside, a bit of Ainsley still lived. Cassie had to believe that, yet she wasn't sure why.

# 33

Nora had the house to herself, a rare luxury. She opened her fundraising notebook, ready to make a few calls to raise money for the peddle-car track the committee had decided to build for the preschool.

First, however, she took a look at Instagram. The photo she'd posted of Peyton and Gwendolyn in their newest dresses had garnered quite a bit of attention. She'd have to post a follow-up.

The number one hovered in red over the message icon. It had to be Becca. If that woman talked like she messaged, even Cassie's daughter wouldn't be able to get a word in edgewise.

Message from @beccaboundforglory

You should follow my friend Juniper @Juniper_Junction. She asked me why I'm so obsessed with you. I had to give that some thought. Here's what I came up with:

1. You are so much closer to my age than Maddie and Lex. I've always felt like they were a team, and I was the extra.

2. There's something missing here. I know it's because Mom and Dad are both gone. I've realized how important family is.

3. If it weren't for you, I never would have been born. It's pretty obvious that Mom had me to make up for leaving you with your dad.

I don't know if you want anything to do with any of us, but I hope you do. I'm sending you all of our phone numbers . . . just in case. If you're ever in New Jersey, you have a place to stay.

Nora punched the number for Lex into her phone. It rang three times before a voice that sounded oddly familiar answered.

"Hello?"

"Lex, this is Nora."

"I assumed as much from the Oregon number."

Nora hadn't thought of that. She'd wanted to catch this woman off guard, the way Nora had felt when this all started.

"I want you to know that I'm a human being, and even if you'd rather I didn't exist, I do." Heat pulsed along Nora's skin. She walked to the kitchen, where she paced from the oven to the refrigerator. "I asked for a simple thing, medical records for Tammy's side of your family. I want nothing else from you. Nothing. Do you understand?"

"I do." Her voice was small now, like the power had drained away. "I'm really sorry. It's not you. Becca has been rubbing me the wrong way since she found out about you."

"Since *she* found out? Did you know before she did?"

A long sigh filtered through the line. "When I was ten, I found a letter between your dad and my . . . our mom. I never told her I'd seen it, but it messed with my head, you know? I was always worried from that moment on that she'd leave again. That you would be more important than I was."

Nora nodded along as if Lex could see her.

"I've been really unfair. Becca let me know all about it in her five-page letter. Seriously, *five* pages."

A bubble of amusement tickled Nora's throat, but she swallowed it down. No way would she share in some kind of sisterly moment with Lex. "I don't want to come between any of you.

If you could just send me the information you have . . ." Nora pushed her back against the corner of the wall, working out a knot that seemed to be growing faster than her belly. Liquid ran down her leggings, filling her socks. "Oh no."

"What?"

"My water broke." She disconnected the call.

Nora looked all around her. Where was her cell phone? In her hand. She needed to call Ferris. This wasn't how the other labors had begun. Her water had never broken on its own. This baby was throwing out the normal process of being born within a couple days of the due date. She wasn't supposed to be here for three more weeks.

A contraction hit. She stopped moving, waiting for the grip to release, then pounded out a text to Ferris and waddled to the garage for rags. They didn't even have a name. Lexie had been high on the list, but that was before she knew about Lex. How many other names of unknown relatives should she avoid? Another contraction managed to stop Nora before she could get the towels down from the cupboard above the dryer.

~

Cassie couldn't look Aubrey in the face when she returned to the apartment. Though she thought she may have talked Mandy into staying, she wouldn't blame her if she was already traveling down the highway toward a new life. Cassie was doing her best to shake off shame, but guilt was another layer, and she probably deserved the heat it was piling on.

Lark ran out from behind the counter, launching herself into Cassie's arms.

Cassie kissed the top of her head and snuggled her close.

"How was your walk?" Maybe Cassie was projecting guilt into her daughter's voice, but it sounded like condemnation was painted all over her words.

"It was . . . good. My head is much clearer now."

Shasta stood near the window, staring out at the waves the way she used to before starting a new painting, as if she were seeing something no one else could imagine.

Cassie pulled out the easel and positioned it beside Shasta, then prepared some paints in greens, blues, and a blob of white. Guiding her to the chair, Cassie settled her by the canvas and placed the brush in her hand.

Shasta closed her eyes for long enough that Cassie thought she had drifted to sleep, but then they opened with a clarity that hadn't been present in weeks. The tip of her brush dipped into the blue, mixing it gently with the edge of the green, and then played it across the canvas like a dancer across a stage.

The movements were not the same as they'd been before, but the love and passion her aunt had always displayed as she worked lit up the room.

Lark watched with an intrigue deeper than she gave to Daniel Tiger.

"Would you like to paint with Shasta?"

Her eyes brightened. "Yes. Can I?"

With the other easel settled in on Shasta's right, Cassie gave her daughter a variety of colors and let her go to work on her own canvas.

Aubrey had disappeared somewhere, and Cassie wished she'd been beside her to see Shasta and Lark working side by side, creating the worlds they could see only within their own minds.

As she watched, thanking God for the beauty of the artists, Aubrey walked up beside her. She placed something familiar in Cassie's hand. It was her sketchbook. Cassie had never been a painter, though she'd given it many tries—that form of art didn't greet her soul the way it did for Shasta—but Cassie could spend hours with a pencil, using strokes to create the birds she loved, flying through the winds.

She reached around and hugged Aubrey. She knew her and being known felt like the way family should always feel.

Cassie snuggled onto the end of the couch, seeing what she wanted to create right before her. She sketched out the lines of Shasta and Lark, paintbrushes in hand, the window before them, gulls floating on the air currents outside.

✑

The shop was closed, and Cassie was ready to settle in for a movie with Shasta and Lark, when a distant pounding came from downstairs. Gull's Bay had a low crime rate, but the whole town had been talking about the home that was burglarized just down the road. Her first reaction was to grab her phone and start to type a message to Marshall, but she didn't want him to see her as the kind of woman who went running to a man every time there was a bump in the road. Before knowing him, she'd been perfectly capable.

Cassie stuffed the phone back into her pocket. "Lark, you stay up here with Shasta. Do not open the door."

She nodded but didn't take her eyes away from the puzzle she had strewn across the table.

The door clicked into place as Cassie took the first step down the stairs. The noise was gone, and she realized she'd overreacted, something she was becoming skilled at doing. As long as she was there, another cup of that chamomile tea would do her good. She padded into the kitchen and flipped on the light.

Marshall screamed.

Cassie held her hand to her chest. "What are you doing?"

He breathed in and out a couple of times. "Trying not to die of a heart attack at the moment."

"It serves you right, lurking around in the dark." She crossed her arms.

"I wasn't lurking. In fact, I was on my way out when you turned on the light. My goodness, how do you move around like that without making a sound?"

Cassie's vanity took a liking to this. She'd always seen herself as kind of clumsy, never the girl one would describe as graceful.

"I got worried about that window with the bad latch." He pointed at her emergency entrance. Installed there in the frame was a security lock.

Not having a father and having never been in a relationship with a man that went past the physical, she was stunned by the warm way this act made her feel protected and safe. She jumped into his arms and buried her face in his neck.

"It's just a lock."

Standing back, she looked directly into his eyes. "It's not. You were concerned about us."

He looked away. "I was. You heard there was a break-in, right?"

"So, if it's not too presumptuous, would you like to watch a movie with us?" Cassie flashed her sweetest smile, not even embarrassed tonight that he brought the girlie out of this empowered woman.

"Is it a Disney princess flick?"

"Nope."

"I feel like there's a catch here, but I'm in. You are three of my favorite ladies."

Cassie's hands were still on his biceps, and she couldn't help wishing he'd lean forward, maybe kiss her, but after waiting long enough to give Marshall every opportunity, she released him. If anything was going to happen with them, it needed to be about the long-term commitment, not hormones. "Let's go." She'd left Shasta and Lark unattended for about as long as she should allow.

At the top of the stairs, Cassie tried to turn the knob but remembered it was locked. She knocked, but no one came. "Larkie, can you let Mom inside, please?"

"I can't." Her voice was muffled, as if she pressed her mouth against the doorframe.

"Why not?"

"I'm not allowed to open the door."

Cassie scratched her pinky nail along an eyebrow. "It's okay, Lark. It's me."

"I'm sorry. You said it doesn't matter who's at the door. I should never open it without you."

"But this *is* with me."

"That doesn't seem right."

"Lark." Her temper was barely hanging on. "Please let us in."

Marshall held up a finger. "Lark, it's me, Marshall. I was really hoping to watch a movie with you. Could I please come in if your mom says it's okay?"

"Mom, is it okay if Marshall comes in?" Excitement was evident in her tone. Marshall had a way with the George girls.

"Yes, you may let Marshall in."

The lock clicked open.

Before Cassie could step in, Lark had Marshall by the hand, dragging him to the kitchen. "We're going to make popcorn. Do you like popcorn? Do you know how to make it? And we're watching *Annie*, the newer one." She turned toward him, her hands in the air between them. "It's so good."

Marshall looked over his shoulder at Cassie. "You said it wasn't a girlie movie."

She felt the grin all the way to her ears. "I said it wasn't a Disney princess movie. And it isn't."

He rolled his eyes and lifted Lark into his arms. "Do you know how to make kettle corn?"

"You can make that? I thought it only was at the candy store."

Marshall pointed to his chest. "Girl, I know how to make crazy-good kettle corn. If it's okay with your mom."

Cassie's mouth was already watering. "Please." She wasn't a huge fan of popcorn, but kettle corn and caramel corn were not just popcorn. They included one of her favorite vices: sugar. Cassie pulled the popper from the cupboard and set it next to where Marshall had deposited Lark. "You two have my blessing. Shasta and I will recline in the living room while you make our snack."

Cassie guided Shasta from the window to the sofa.

Her aunt's thumb rubbed frantically against her first finger. It seemed like they were making medication adjustments weekly now, and even if she showed some improvement in her symptoms, the changes didn't last.

Taking her hand, Cassie uncurled Shasta's fingers and massaged the muscles in her palm. "You're okay. Lark and I are with you. We won't leave ever again."

Cassie watched that booth in the back, praying, as she'd done for a week now, that Mandy would return. She also pleaded with God to keep Aubrey from bringing up the subject again. It would have been easy for her to sink into the guilt, but her schedule didn't allow for that kind of self-indulgence. The hospice social worker was arriving soon for the intake interview. With some prodding, Cassie had taken the step, accepting that they were ready for the hospice help.

The way it had been described to her, this was to be simply a getting-to-know-you-and-your-needs kind of meeting. But the word *interview* put a different twist on it all, leaving Cassie concerned whether she would be deemed good enough to continue as a caregiver.

She checked the till, thanked Lisa for all her great work, and went to get Lark from the table where she sat with Shasta and Mr. Watkins. "Come on, kiddo, time for you to report to work at the bakery."

She hopped up, kissed Shasta on the cheek, and waved to

Mr. Watkins. "See you later. Grammy Mrs. Collins needs my help with some pies today. Grammy Shasta, I'll bring you home a treat."

Shasta's crooked smile was as bright as any expression that had ever graced her face.

"Are you okay here for a few minutes while I take her over?" Mr. Watkins looked Cassie's way. "It will give us some more time to talk." His eyes went back to Shasta as if there was something there, something they were communicating that Cassie was not a part of.

She wrapped a hand around her daughter's and headed out the door.

Summer was on the horizon in Gull's Bay. It was a sparkly time of beauty, with the sun reflecting off the sand that had blown in all winter, dropping on the street, sidewalk, and storefronts. Tourists were expanding the population, especially on weekends, but that meant more business for the shop and more income to pay off some of the bills that rushed in like the tide.

Lark yanked on her hand, eager to cross the street.

"You forgot to stop and look both ways again. There's a lot more traffic now that the weather's getting nice. You've got to be careful."

Lark wrapped her free hand around their connected ones. "I'm sorry. I'm just really excited about today. I've been waiting ever since I got out of bed. That's a long time when you're little. Can you even remember what it's like to be little?"

Cassie blew out an exaggerated breath. "It's hard since I'm so very old." She pushed loose hair away from Lark's eyes.

They crossed the street and walked up the hill past a few stores until they came to the bakery. Mrs. Collins displayed her goods in a way that would have looked old-fashioned in a bigger city but seemed charming here in Gull's Bay. The front windows were filled with pastries, pies, cupcakes, and croissants. The scent of bread, fresh from the oven, seeped out the front door. Inside, customers pulled tags from a large red dispenser and waited for Mrs. Collins or her employee to call out their number.

Baked goods from this shop were not only sold in the coffee shop, but up and down the coastline. They were as much part of visiting the ocean in Oregon as saltwater taffy and Mo's clam chowder.

Praise and worship music played in here, dancing with the scents and creating a place of peace. For as long as Cassie could remember, she'd loved this store, using her allowance as a child to try different treats each week. It seemed like a man was always behind the counter back then, but she couldn't remember much about him.

When Cassie graduated from high school, Mrs. Collins presented her with a heavy box. Inside was every cent she'd ever spent in the store. Cassie had been shocked at both her generosity in saving it for her and the total amount she had handed over through the years, a dollar or two at a time.

"Well, good morning to two of my favorite people." Mrs. Collins wiped her floury hands on her apron. "I thought that might be my little helper arriving for work." She winked at Lark. "Head on back and wash up. Your apron is by the sink all cleaned and ready for you. Be sure not to let the water run, though."

Lark didn't need a second to reply. She dropped Cassie's hand and was gone from sight as she hollered back her good-byes.

"Thank you for having her. It's such a special thing for Lark, and it helps me out a great deal."

"You have no idea. Lark is the best part of my week. You're doing me a favor by allowing me to keep her."

Cassie twisted her toe around on the checkered flooring. "Mrs. Collins, do you know if there was . . ." She squished up her lips looking for the right way to ask this. "Was there ever anything besides friendship between Shasta and Mr. Watkins?"

Beverly Collins crossed her arms over her ample chest, whether a natural occurrence or the result of sampling years of amazing baked goods, Cassie wasn't sure. "I'm not one to talk out of school, but . . ."

The phrase caught Cassie by surprise—not that Mrs. Collins didn't often use old colloquialisms that were decades before her time, but this one Cassie had heard before yet never understood.

"I believe they were quite an item in high school, but she went off to art school, and he took up with someone else. Life does that. It goes on without us if we're not careful. Sometimes things that should be get lost to time." She sighed. "I'd better go check on my little buddy. We won't be done until after lunch. Can I bring her by then?"

"Perfect." Cassie waved as she walked out of the bakery, her mind forming images of a young Shasta and a young Mr. Watkins, in love.

# 34

The social worker sat across from Cassie, while their new in-home CNA helped Shasta get a bath. It was like their apartment was being invaded, and no matter how often people kept reassuring Cassie that they were there to help, all she could see was the control of her surroundings slipping away.

Cassie crossed her legs and tucked them underneath herself on the sofa, a throw pillow clutched in her arms.

"Is it okay if I call you Cassie?"

Cassie just barely caught herself before asking if she meant as opposed to Ainsley. "Yes. That's right."

"I'm Anaya. I won't see a whole lot of you after we get services set up, but I want to be available to you however I can be. The transition to hospice is sometimes difficult, even in the best circumstances. Are there any concerns you'd like to talk about?"

Aside from her aunt looking at the end of life without really understanding or knowing who she was, and Cassie facing debt that would make it hard for her to help her own daughter when it came time to pay college tuition? "No, I don't have any concerns."

Anaya's smile was too knowing, like she could hear the inner thoughts. "Can you tell me about yourself before you became your aunt's caregiver? What were you doing? What did you love about your life?"

"Um . . . well, I was a student, working toward a doctorate in the study of marine birds. I had my daughter, Lark, of course."

"I love that name. Did you choose it because of your love for birds?"

"Sort of. It's not like I could call her *Seagull*."

Anaya raised an eyebrow. "I've heard of celebrity kids having crazier names than that."

"I suppose you're right. Seagull is a better name than Blanket."

"What did you do in your spare time back then?" She lightly tapped her pencil on her finger.

"I didn't have any. I went to school, taught undergraduates, took care of my daughter, and worked on my studies." She shrugged. "Honestly, I feel like I have more time now than I have in years."

"That's wonderful. As we come to the end of a loved one's life, it's good to have time to reflect on our relationship with them. I like to encourage my clients to tell their loved ones how much they have meant to them. I understand your aunt raised you from the time you were very young."

"That's right."

"It sounds like she's acted as your mother. Would you say that's correct?"

"I would." It really didn't matter at this point who Cassie's actual mother had been. Shasta was the one who'd raised her. She'd loved Cassie through all the hard times and celebrated with her in the good times. "She's the only mother I can remember."

There was a sadness in the way Anaya nodded, as if she'd felt the grief Cassie was doomed to endure. "When your aunt has passed, do you plan to return to California and your studies?"

Cassie shifted in her seat, moving her gaze to the window

where the sun shone, though it was only about sixty degrees. In California, everywhere she went felt lonely, as if it were a place she'd never been before, a place that didn't know her from any of the other people rushing here and there. But in Gull's Bay, Cassie was known. She was surrounded by neighbors who cared about her and Lark. Being known trumped hiding from mistakes. "I think we'll stay here."

"And do you have a plan for what you'll do?"

"I'd like to teach. I think I'd like to teach high school biology." The words slipped out of her mouth, and she learned her plans at the same time this stranger did. "Yes. I'd love to be a high school science teacher. I have a master's degree. I've done a lot of teaching at the college level. Maybe I can help kids to see the beauty we have all around us here." Her volume increased as she rambled on. Cassie had a plan, a future, a goal that finally made her feel complete and excited. And it had risen out of nowhere.

Cassie burst into the hardware store, a brown bag with two turkey sandwiches in one hand and a latte in the other.

Marshall looked up from where he was making notes on a legal pad. "Hello there. You're a beautiful sight."

"You're going to like me even more when you see what I have with me." She dropped the bag on the counter and handed him the coffee.

He took a sip, then gave an approving nod before pulling out the food. "Smells great. I'm so hungry. I think every cabin owner in the county came back for the first time this week and found winter had left them with plenty of house projects. I haven't had time to grab a snack all morning."

Cassie unfolded the paper on her sandwich and took a bite. There was something very satisfying in a lunch made with all the yummy additions she had access to in the shop. Alfalfa sprouts, tomatoes, pickles, and pepper jack cheese. This was more than a sandwich—it was a culinary feast.

He wiped a drip of mustard from his lip. "You look all kinds of excited about something. Spill the tea."

"The social worker for hospice came today. Most of the meeting was really tough, but she asked me about what I was going to do after . . . you know, when Shasta is gone."

His eyes clouded. "And?"

"I want to stay here. I think, actually I know, I'd like to teach biology. It may take a while to get a job close-by, but I'm willing to wait. Maybe I can be a substitute while I get my license. There's a temporary one I qualify for. I can work in the coffee shop until then. Lark will be starting kindergarten in the fall, and I think this is a great place to grow up. And . . ."

He had come around the corner while she spewed all her future plans. And he was so near, she could smell the rich scents that always clung to him. Cassie's mouth went dry, and a light swirl of dizziness wrapped around her. Looking up into his eyes, she swallowed her next words, helpless.

"You're sure?"

"I am."

He leaned down, his nose brushing against hers, his breath on her cheek, her lips. And he kissed her.

"Is that our Miss Cassie?" Pastor Stewart strode into the room, a bag from the bakery in his left hand. "I just saw your little one next door. She's quite the salesperson. I had no intention of buying a bag full of cookies."

Cassie stepped away from her biggest temptation, feeling the air touch her mouth where his had been. "She's been in training with Mrs. Collins."

Marshall slipped behind the counter. "Can I help you find something?" His cheeks were flushed with a red tinge. She hadn't thought he was capable of embarrassment.

"Don't let me interrupt. I can wait my turn." He stepped

a few feet closer, the scent of snickerdoodles emanating from the white paper sack.

"It's no problem. I was just dropping off some lunch for Marshall." Taking her own sandwich, she made room for Pastor Stewart.

He pulled a screw out of his jeans pocket. "I need a box of these, the same size. Can you help me out?"

"Sure can." Marshall's gaze stayed clear of Cassie, and she was more than a little bit grateful, as she couldn't seem to stop her own. He held his hand out for the screw. "What are you working on?" Marshall might not have grown up in Gull's Bay, but he knew how to talk to the locals.

"The railing on our porch is about shot. I find it's better for my marriage to fix things before they collapse." He raised the cookie bag to his nose and inhaled. "Anyone want a cookie? My wife is not going to be thrilled that I succumbed to my sugar cravings again."

Cassie waved him off. "I need to be going. I sent Mrs. Collins a text that I'd come get Lark."

Outside of the hardware store, Cassie walked about twenty feet, then leaned up against the brick of the next building. That kiss had been nothing short of magical, but to have it broken by Pastor Stewart was cruel.

Her lips hadn't touched a man's since she'd found out Lark was on the way. That's when she became certain a life with a man was not in her future. She had a child to care for and, honestly, no idea what to do with men. She'd proven that right off the bat in college, seeking their attention in any way she could get it.

Lark had saved her from a fate she didn't want to ponder. Would raising Lark the way she'd been raised, no man in sight, not understanding the first thing about dating or marriage, mean she would wind up with the same temptations and needs that haunted Cassie?

"Hey there."

Her heart skipped a beat, lurching her upward.

Pastor Stewart stood in front of her, a sack in each hand now. "That Marshall is such a great guy. We're really fortunate to have him here in Gull's Bay."

Cassie nodded. "Yes. He's been a great help to us."

"How have you been doing, Cassie? You and Shasta are often on my mind." He shifted so he held both bags in one arm up against his side.

"We're doing good."

"Being a caregiver is no joke. I've watched many people in the church go through what you're going through, but none of them were also raising a child. Are you getting the help you need?"

"I am. Everyone has been so kind and understanding."

He didn't say anything but stepped to the side, allowing room for a couple of tourists to pass by on the sidewalk. He crossed his ankles and pressed his side against the wall. "Do you have people you can talk to who are supporting you?"

Cassie gave that a moment's thought and nodded.

"Okay." He started to push away from the wall, then stopped. "Listen, you look like you have a world full of burdens on your shoulders. I'm not here to force you to talk about them, but I would like to help in any way I can."

Tears stung behind her eyes. "I have nothing I can complain about. I'm really fortunate to have Shasta still with me, it's just . . . I don't even know what's going on with me."

"You're carrying an awfully heavy load. I'm just guessing here, but I'd bet the weight is mainly coming from in here." He tapped at the side of his head.

She took a second to stare straight up, hoping that would keep the tears at bay. "Sometimes it feels like I've screwed everything up. I'm so grateful to be able to help out Shasta, especially with everything she's done for me, but everything I do seems like it's not as good as what she would do, or anyone else for that matter."

"That voice in your head that's telling you you're not enough for this, whose voice is that?"

She rubbed the tense muscles in the back of her neck. How could she know who it was when she wasn't even sure who *she* was? "I'm not sure."

"Well, I can tell you for certain it's not the voice of God. Is there a way you would be willing to hand over some of the pressure? Let God take the burden?"

She scrubbed a hand through her hair. "How? I know Scripture. I was raised in the church and I understand what I'm supposed to do, but I don't understand how. How do I lay my burden down? How do I forgive others? How do I forgive . . ."

"Yourself?"

Tension throbbed at her temples. "Yes. How do I find a way to move forward without looking over my shoulder at the past? I want so much for Lark. She's everything to me, but I don't know how to be the mom she deserves." Cassie looked around, suddenly aware she was about to lose her senses on the street where anyone could see.

"Cassie, you're an amazing mom. I've seen the way you and Lark interact. That little girl doesn't see you for whatever mistakes you've made along the way. To her, you are the safe place. Forgiveness isn't an easy one-step-and-done process, but don't give up. Maybe you could start by giving yourself the grace I know you'd give to anyone else."

She tucked hair behind her ear. "I'm so sorry about this. I guess it was all piling up inside."

"No worries. That's what I'm here for." He glanced at his watch. "But I've got to get going. Hannah has a shift at the hospital, which means it's my turn to watch the boys. Come by any time and talk. Hannah and I will do whatever we can for you."

"I know. Thank you."

He kicked a foot forward, pushed off the wall, and waved as he took a couple steps down the sidewalk. She thought their conversation was over until he looked back. "And Marshall . . . he's a great guy. I'm glad to see the two of you are hitting it off so well."

Cassie covered her face with both hands. The kiss hadn't gone unnoticed.

# 35

I found out why Gwendolyn was gone for so many days. Her mom had a baby!" Lark sorted through the assortment of items in her backpack until she withdrew a drawing. "See. She drew me a picture so I could see what she looks like."

Cassie examined the artwork. She could see that it was a baby, but that was about all. "That must be very exciting for them." She should at least get a card for Ferris and Nora. "What did they name her?"

"Nothin'." Lark dropped to her hands and knees and bucked, imitating the horses she and Gwendolyn made up at preschool.

"That doesn't sound like a very good name."

"They just don't know it yet. Gwendolyn will tell me when she knows."

Cassie hung the artwork of another woman's child on her refrigerator. Lark would notice.

"We could get a baby too . . . or a puppy," Lark said.

Cassie fluffed her daughter's hair.

Shasta stood at the window, her favorite place in the apartment. Every few minutes, Lark would stop her bouncing around the room to check the view, as if looking to see if she could find what drew Shasta's attention. Then she continued with her game, neighing and jumping like a horse.

The clock seemed to be counting time backward. Terri was due to arrive around dinner. Cassie hadn't been in the same room as her best friend since the moment life had turned sideways. With Marshall's kiss still very much on her mind, she needed someone who knew her as well as Terri to talk things through with.

But this weekend wasn't about Cassie. It was a chance for Terri to get a start on her wedding plans. Cassie couldn't wait to help her with the details, knowing all the while that Terri and Jack would have the perfect ceremony even if nothing followed the inspiration they'd collected from Pinterest.

"Lark, do you know what special surprise I have for you today?" Cassie plopped down on the sofa.

Her daughter trotted over and hopped onto her lap. "Are we going to Disneyland?"

"Nope." A niggle of guilt pinched her. Despite having lived in Southern California, Cassie had never taken Lark to the theme park. "It's better."

Her hands flung up. "Oh my goodness. Marshall is going to be my daddy!"

Cassie was shocked into silence.

"You're right. I'm so excited." Lark jumped on Cassie's thighs.

"Lark . . . that's not the surprise. Where did you get the idea that Marshall and I were in that kind of relationship?" Cassie wasn't even sure what turn they were taking, but they were nowhere near the long walk down the aisle.

"Gwendolyn has a dad. Everyone at school has one. And you're the right age, 'cause Aunt Terri and Uncle Jack are getting married. Why don't you want to do it too?" There was a sadness in Lark's eyes that broke Cassie's heart.

"Do you think about this kind of thing a lot?"

She nodded. "I love Marshall. I don't want him to go away."

Cassie wrapped Lark up in her arms. "I don't want to lose him either, but that doesn't mean we'll be getting married."

She tickled the tip of Lark's ear. "I still have that surprise. Do you want to know what it is?"

She wriggled free from the embrace, her expression having fallen. "What is it?"

"We have company for dinner. In fact, we have company for the whole weekend. Aunt Terri is coming for a visit."

Her daughter didn't respond with the squeal Cassie had anticipated. Instead, she let out a whinny that would have made a real horse startle. "I can't wait. Is she sleeping in my room? Will she get to see my preschool? Will she get to meet Marshall?"

Marshall was becoming a theme. One kiss. That was the only identifiable thing that had happened between the two of them, and Lark didn't even know about that, yet she was probably already adding his name to their Christmas cards. "I'll let Aunt Terri have my bed. She has to go back to California before Monday, and I don't know if she'll meet Marshall," Cassie said.

"What about Uncle Jack? I think Marshall and Uncle Jack would be great friends, just like me and Gwendolyn."

"What makes you say that?"

She looked at Cassie as if she was missing an obvious connection. "They're both boys."

"Yes . . . I guess that would make them besties."

"I'll ask Aunt Terri to bring him next time." Lark trotted off to the window and stood next to Shasta to relay all the news that had already been spoken within her earshot.

"What do you ladies think we should have for dinner?" Cassie pushed herself off the couch.

Lark turned to her. "Macaroni and cheese from the box."

"I don't think so. Terri has been traveling all day. We can do better than neon cheese powder on pasta with a cardboard aftertaste."

After staring at her mom for a few seconds, Lark went back to giving Shasta the rundown.

In the kitchen, Cassie searched through the refrigerator and freezer. She was no chef, but they weren't going to starve. Her phone buzzed, and she scooped it up, for some reason expecting to see Marshall's name on the screen. Instead, it was Terri. She'd gotten in safely and was midway on the drive over from the airport. On schedule like always, she'd be there in an hour.

Nora wrapped the blanket snug around the red-faced baby. *Vivian. Dakota. Bonnie. Jade.* No, not a one of those would work. She'd felt brief excitement at the name Milly, but then Ferris had pointed out that the baby would be Milly Milford. That wouldn't do. *Ava. Poppy. Mia. Henley. Bailey. Brooklyn.* How were they supposed to settle on a name when Lennon/Blakely/Willow wouldn't stop crying?

They'd been prepared for sleepless nights before Gwendolyn was born, but she'd been as regulated as her mother. Everyone said the second was a handful, but Peyton might have been easier than Gwendolyn. Nora had gotten cocky. She'd assumed she and Ferris only made relaxed and scheduled babies. Until number three showed up weeks early and appeared to be allergic to sleep.

She picked up Avery/Phoenix/Maren and patted her back as she walked back and forth in the nursery, the baby's wails vibrating her eardrums.

When Cassie heard the knock on the door, bubbles of excitement went off in her chest. The table was set for the four of them, and the house smelled of garlic, bread, and tomatoes, even if the scents came from a frozen store-bought garlic loaf and spaghetti sauce out of a jar.

She wiped her hands on a dish towel and jogged to the entrance, opening it without asking who was there. At first sight, they were in each other's arms, so much relief washing over Cassie that if they hadn't been tangled together, she might have fallen.

Lark used her little body like a wedge, forcing herself in between their legs.

Stepping back, Cassie let her have a turn. "I'm so glad you made it. Lark, let Aunt Terri in."

Lark grabbed Terri's hand and tugged her to the couch, where Shasta sat covered in Polly Pockets. "Aunt Terri, do you know my sweet grammy?" They'd been working on how to introduce people at preschool.

Cassie covered her mouth with her fingers, hiding the smile that Lark would surely find offensive as she displayed her new skills.

"Why yes, I do." Terri sank onto the cushion beside Shasta and took her hand. "It is so nice to see you again."

Shasta didn't often attempt speech anymore, especially with those outside her closest circle. The work of it was exhausting for her, but the smile in her eyes warmed Cassie's heart. She'd always been so welcoming to all of her friends. Cassie needed to remember that when Lark went on and on about Gwendolyn. It wasn't the girl's fault her mother was . . . rigid.

"It smells delicious in here. My little Larkie-bird, did you make dinner for me?" Terri stood and lifted Lark into her arms. "My goodness, girl, you are growing. I won't be able to lift you much longer."

Lark's face was all light and excitement. "I have a job in a bakery, and I work very hard."

"Your mom sent you out to make a living, huh?"

Lark's head bobbed. "I work with Grammy Mrs. Collins. She really needs me at the bakery. People buy a whole lot more when I'm there."

"I think Lark eats most of the profits, though." Cassie filled glasses with water.

"Grammy Mrs. Collins says it's good for someone my age to get extra treats. She says she doesn't want me being all skin and bones and flying away. We get a lot of wind around here."

"Well, it looks to be doing you all kinds of good." Terri set Lark near the table. "What can I do to help?"

"I've got it all ready." Cassie went to Shasta, helping her off the sofa that had just a bit too much give. Then she sent Lark to wash up while she used a washcloth on Shasta's hands.

They formed a circle around the table, ready for the prayer.

"Mom, at preschool we get to make asks for the prayer."

"Did you have something you'd like to pray about?"

"Yes, could you please ask God to give me a you-know-what?" She tipped her head as if emphasizing her point.

Cassie shrugged. "I'm not sure what you're talking about."

Shasta released her hand and lifted her napkin, clearing her throat. In a husky whisper, she said, "Marshall."

They were ganging up on her.

Cassie woke up from a disappointing night to the scent of coffee and bacon so much closer than the smells that wafted up from the shop. Rolling on the couch, where she'd gotten very little sleep, she peered over the back and found Terri and Lark whispering to each other as they flipped a pancake.

"I'm awake." Cassie stretched and let out some of the tension that had invaded every single one of her muscles. Last night had been a tough one for Shasta. She'd gotten up and roamed the house at least eight times. With the nighttime issues starting before they could pop the popcorn and get settled, Terri and Cassie hadn't even gotten the chance to talk after Lark went to bed.

"How are you doing?" Terri handed her a very large mug of coffee with just the right amount of cream to change the color to her perfect caramel. It nearly matched Marshall's skin, but she kept that observation to herself.

"I am so sorry about last night."

"No worries. To be honest, traveling exhausts me. The sleep did me good." She set plates on the table.

"I don't know how we've survived without you. Breakfast smells amazing." Cassie's stomach growled, reminding her that she'd saved room for that popcorn that never arrived. Her phone jingled its alarm tone. A swipe of the screen, and she saw her programed reminder that Shasta had her bath helper coming in that morning. "Any sounds from Shasta?"

"Not a peep. I imagine she's mighty tired."

Lark climbed up on a chair and pointed out the syrup for Terri.

"Barbara will be here in thirty minutes to help her with a bath. I'd better get her up and moving." Even Cassie's feet ached when she pressed them into the floor to stand. "You really didn't have to do this. It's your vacation."

"I'm glad to. And I can't take much credit. It was Larkie-bird's idea."

Lark looked up at the mention of her name. Cassie decided not to say anything about having just spied her sticking a finger into the powdered sugar.

She bent over, taking in a breath and letting it go as her body hung limp from her hips. After relaxing into the stretch for a few counts, Cassie curled back up one vertebra at a time, until her tired neck lifted her head. Stopping in the kitchen, she gave Terri a quick side hug and kissed the top of Lark's curls. "I love you both."

"We know." Terri dipped her own finger in the powdered sugar and dotted it on Lark's nose.

In Shasta's room, Cassie found the curtains closed. She'd pulled them open at least five times during the night. Shasta rested on her back, a position she'd never slept in before Parkinson's, her mouth open and her breathing labored. Cassie sat on the edge, watching her sleep, letting her remain in this place of peace for a moment longer, then set her hand on Shasta's arm. "Shasta? It's time to start waking up." In the future, she'd need to see about having Barbara come later in the day, if that was possible. It wasn't like Shasta usually slept late, but having to wake her felt cruel.

With no response yet, Cassie gently jiggled her shoulder. "Shasta?" Her heart started to pound, as if she'd run up the stairs. "Shasta, can you hear me?"

Her eyes fluttered, and Cassie breathed in relief, surprised by the tears that came so quickly. Lack of sleep wasn't something her emotions handled well.

As Shasta awakened, Cassie could see a difference from all the night's events. Shasta clearly knew her now. Her face was relaxed, her eyes focused.

Cassie covered her cool hand with her own warmer one, rubbing the skin gently to get circulation moving. "Barbara will be here soon for your bath. I thought you'd want to be up before she gets here."

Shasta pulled a hand free and nodded with it, a gesture that had become a common acknowledgment.

Cassie stood and collected her robe from the hook near the closet, then pulled the lace-up slippers with the traction soles from beneath the bed. After helping Shasta to sit, she threaded her arms into the robe and her feet into the slippers. "Lark and Terri have made us a wonderful breakfast. Let's get you some food too."

Another hand motion indicated she was on board for food, though Cassie knew she'd eat very little.

Cassie kissed Shasta's cheek before helping her to stand and guiding her out of the dark room and into the brightness of the rest of the apartment.

# 36

What could Nora have done to deserve what was happening around her? Ferris's dad had brought the big girls home the night before due to his wife's nasty head cold and migraine. Then Ferris was called into work at 3:17 in the morning because someone had burned down the rec center in the town next to them. She knew exactly what time it had been because Ava—at least she was pretty sure that's what they were going to call her—had been screaming so loudly that Ferris had nearly missed the ringing of his phone.

Now the big girls were eating dry Cheerios from the box while watching a cartoon. Peyton kept wiping her nose with the back of her pajama sleeve, but the baby was finally asleep. Nora collapsed on the couch, drifting away on impact.

But somehow, the baby knew. Screams scratched through the monitor. For the first time, Nora could gather a tiny bit of sympathy for her mother. If Nora had been similar . . .

*No,* Nora thought. She would never leave her child.

~

Cassie managed to get herself semi-presentable, Lark dressed and ready, and the kitchen cleaned up by the time Terri had finished her call with Jack. Barbara and Shasta completed the bathing process.

When Barbara walked Shasta into the living room, Lark had already slipped into her boots, even though the weather had grown warm for around there.

"She did a wonderful job today. And now she's fresh and clean." Barbara's Mediterranean accent made the words sound even more warm and compassionate. "Miss Shasta, I will be back on Wednesday afternoon." She helped Shasta to sit and patted the top of each of her hands.

"Thank you so much." Cassie walked to the door and held it open for Barbara.

"No need to thank me. I love my job. It makes me feel like I'm helping." When she smiled, her cheeks lifted and loose skin under her chin shook. "I used to work in an office. Every day I came home feeling like I'd spent my day on things that didn't matter. No more. Now I go home tired and happy." She winked.

"Barbara, please stop at the counter and order yourself anything you want." The woman started to argue, but Cassie lifted her hand. "Please, it will make me feel like I'm doing something and let me feel happy at the end of the day too."

Barbara looked over Cassie's shoulder toward Lark. "Your mama is a tricky one." Then she started down the stairs.

"All done." Terri came up behind Lark and hugged her. "Are you sure you can take me to the bakery? I could find my own way, or Lark could guide me."

"No way. This is a maid-of-honor responsibility." Cassie helped Shasta into her sweater. She always seemed cold these days, even when the temperature climbed to seventy-five.

Terri had so much more patience for the stairlift than Cassie did. She and Lark waited at the base of the stairs, making up a song to go along with the whirling of the motor. By the time they reached the bottom, Lark had brought out the wheelchair. Her five-year-old was sometimes responsible beyond her years.

Cassie hoped that wasn't out of necessity but from a deep-seated and growing level of leadership.

As summer approached, Gull's Bay became a far different environment than the sleepy town of the off-season. Tourists roamed up and down the streets, popping into stores and restaurants, some which only opened for the vacation weeks. On the beach, kites flew in the wind, something they had no matter what time of year it was, and a few people even braved the waves on surfboards. Of course, surfers there weren't anything like what Lark had seen in California. In Oregon, no one took a board into the water without the added insulation of a full bodysuit.

Lark was all excitement at the opportunity to take Terri into what she thought of as her place of employment.

The four of them crossed the street and went up to the bakery. Lark pushed through the door. Her squeal was more than expected, and it stole Cassie's breath. By the time she could get through with Shasta's chair, Lark was on Marshall's shoulders, practicing her introduction skills again.

"It's a pleasure to meet you." He held out his hand to Terri, who shook it as she shot Cassie a look—a look Cassie recognized right away. It wasn't like there was a woman in the world who would be able to miss how handsome Marshall was.

"The pleasure is all mine." Terri tipped her head. "Lark has told me so much about you."

He eyed Cassie. "Just Lark, huh?"

Cassie fanned her face before realizing how obvious that made her look.

Mrs. Collins saved her. She came out from the back, her silver-streaked hair tied in a bun at the top of her neck. "You must be Terri." She waved for them to follow. "Come on back."

Marshall started to put Lark down.

"Nonsense. You're coming too." Mrs. Collins hooked her hand through the crook of his elbow. "It's always best to get a man's opinion when tasting wedding cakes."

She took them into a room off the side of the kitchen entrance. Here, she had displays and photo albums she used to show off options for special occasions. While Gull's Bay had a tiny year-round population, it was a popular wedding destination, especially with the lodge that overlooked the bay, and no one got married here without one of Beverly Collins's famous cakes.

They took seats at the table—all but Lark, who must have thought she was on the clock. As if they had it all planned, Mrs. Collins pulled a small apron off the counter and wrapped it around Lark.

With Lark and Mrs. Collins standing on the other side of the table, the counter at their backs, Cassie felt like one of the judges on a cooking show.

"Terri, we are so excited that you came to see what we offer in wedding cakes." Mrs. Collins pulled Lark to her side. "Lark and I had a long talk about what you might like. Each time I make a special cake, I make a few miniatures and freeze them for tastings, so you see we have quite the assortment for today."

Mrs. Collins and Lark moved seven plates covered with opaque domes to the table, Lark licking her lips more than once. "Before we start the tasting, let's talk frosting. The naked look is very popular right now, and if you prefer less frosting in your bites, it's a good way to go. Personally, I find the look a little unfinished, but that's just me."

Cassie raised a hand as if in school. "What does that mean, naked?"

Marshall's low laugh rumbled beside her.

"Very mature." She elbowed his arm.

"It means leaving the sides nearly unfrosted." Mrs. Collins opened a photo album and pointed to a cake where the layers were visible. "There's still frosting between, but none around the outside."

Lark shook her head. "It kind of ruins the cake, 'cause all the yummy part is gone."

"I'm with Lark." Terri pushed the album away. "The more frosting, the better."

"Oh yes. I definitely want to be at this wedding." Marshall crossed his arms.

"Lark, can you tell them about the first cake?"

Lark tugged on Mrs. Collins's arm, and the baker bent down to hear the five-year-old's whisper before returning it with her own.

"This is the chocolate one. It's the best. I've tried all of them." Lark lifted the lid to reveal a tiny cake about the circumference of Cassie's favorite oversized coffee mug. "This chocolate stuff that runs over the side is so yummy. My uncle Jack would really be happy about this cake."

Cassie leaned back, enjoying the show.

Mrs. Collins cut the cake into tiny pieces, using up about half the work of art. She slipped slices onto plates, giving one to each of them, including her helper.

Cassie helped Shasta get a bite into her mouth before taking a fork to her own. The rich chocolate spread over her tongue as if it was melting in her mouth, but Cassie kept her opinion to herself. This was Terri's decision, and Lark was pushing an agenda enough for the both of them.

"Wow." Terri ran her cloth napkin over her lips. "That is amazing. Lark, your taste is perfect, and Mrs. Collins, I don't think I've ever tasted anything so luxurious."

A proud smile graced the baker's face as her posture confirmed her delight in the compliment. "But we're only just beginning. Next, we have our champagne cake." She revealed a cake with brilliant white frosting decorated with tiny shimmering pearls. When she cut into its several layers of light pink, it looked like a dessert fit for a royal wedding.

As with the last, Cassie loved the flavor, yet this one was almost its opposite, light and smooth.

"Okay." Marshall leaned forward. "I'm here for the guy

thoughts, right? The cake tastes great, but isn't it a little on the girlie side?"

Even Lark gave him a quick sideways look.

"I mean, it's pink. Guys don't usually like pink." He shrugged. "I don't know. I'm just saying, maybe not a pink cake. But maybe Jack likes pink."

Cassie laughed a little. Having Marshall, who was usually all confidence and swagger, pulled off his game tickled her more than it should.

"I hate to admit it, but he's right." Terri leaned forward, looking at Marshall past Cassie and Shasta. "Jack wouldn't pick a pink cake either."

They went on to try a vanilla cake decorated with a Pacific Northwest theme that included fir and pine sprigs. Then there was the chocolate raspberry that appeared to be wearing a fur coat of raspberry buttercream frosting. One taste of that slice, and Cassie nearly forgot her love of the first. The lemon-raspberry was elegant and not pink, while the salted caramel was so sweet, Cassie needed a drink of water to wash it down.

"We have one final cake for you to taste today. It's not a traditional flavor, but it's one of Shasta's favorites." Mrs. Collins uncovered a white cake with piped-on designs, ornamented with slices of orange. "This is an orange creamsicle cake."

Lark passed out the portions.

"Oh." Terri closed her eyes. "This is amazing."

Shasta waved her hand in the air. She'd managed to get most of her slice into her mouth with her fingers and indicated she'd like more.

Cassie really hadn't anticipated how much she would like this cake. It reminded her of the ice-cream cups they would have on the last day of school each year, but without the horrible wooden spoons.

They proceeded to retry every cake, until Cassie's head was spinning from the overconsumption of sugar. Shasta's body must have been a bit overwhelmed by the experience too, as she'd fallen asleep, her head tipped and resting on Marshall's arm. The man who would voluntarily prop his left arm on a wheelchair to provide a pillow for a woman he wasn't even related to had to be a good guy. Didn't he?

Terri scrolled through the photos she'd taken of each cake and sent them off to Jack. "Mrs. Collins, this was amazing. I'm torn between the chocolate and the orange creamsicle. Can I have some time to decide?"

"As long as I know within two weeks of the wedding, we're good. Lark and I have you on the schedule. Have you reserved the lodge? It's hard to get on a Saturday in the summer."

"I was actually thinking of something less formal, like on the beach."

Cassie wiped cake from Shasta's chin as she slept. "This isn't California. You know it will be windy no matter what day it is."

"I know. I thought maybe we could rent the coffee shop for the reception and do the ceremony on the beach. It's only going to be a few of us. What do you think?"

"Well, there is a little inlet where the beach expands during low tide. It's near the rock cliffs where they scoop over a bit, leaving a place where the wind doesn't come in as hard. That could be a nice location."

"Then that's what I want. As long as my people are there and the ocean is nearby, I'll be happy."

"And I'm the flower girl." Lark never wanted that fact to be forgotten.

Terri pushed back from the table and opened her arms to Lark. "That is one of the most important details."

# 37

After the cake tasting, it was clear that both Lark and Shasta needed a break. Cassie hadn't been able to get Marshall alone and really felt they needed to hash out whatever it was happening between the two of them. She had a child. That fact left her without the luxury other women her age had to casually see what happened. Lark had a way of getting attached to people, and Marshall had proven to be no exception.

They approached the coffee shop, Cassie's need to care for Lark and Shasta overshadowing her responsibilities as a maid of honor. "I'm so sorry about this, Terri. Can we give them a rest, then head back out in a couple of hours?"

"Of course. I might take a walk to see if I can locate the place you were talking about. I really want to see the location."

She had little chance of finding the path down to that part of the beach without Cassie's help. It was a secret the locals didn't advertise to tourists, so the trail was rugged at best.

They were discussing this when they stepped into the coffee shop. It was quiet, with the lunch customers already gone and the late-afternoon coffee drinkers yet to arrive. Lisa had everything in order as usual, and the scent of freshly ground coffee filled the room.

Aubrey sat by the unlit fireplace, going through a stack of papers on her lap. Cassie wasn't sure about the details of Aubrey's other job—she didn't often speak about it—some kind of social-service work.

"Hey there." She straightened her papers and set them beside her, then stood. "How was the cake tasting?"

"Mind-blowing." Cassie exaggerated her words by miming her head exploding. "That might have been too much sugar, even for Lark and Shasta."

Lark hung over Terri's shoulder. Shasta, while awake now, seemed more than a little out of it.

"The comedown has been rough." Cassie wheeled Shasta to the bottom of the stairs. "They're going to need a rest."

Aubrey came up beside them. "How about I hang out with Shasta and Lark while you and Terri get some time together? I bet you haven't had much of that."

Cassie gave in to the sudden urge to hug Aubrey. "Thank you." It was during this embrace that she noticed someone in the back booth. Mandy was right there where she belonged. Though Cassie ached to go over and thank her for the second chance, instead, she offered a smile. "That would mean so much to me."

"My pleasure."

Cassie had lent Terri one of Shasta's windbreakers, forcing her well outside the comfort zone of her usually neutral-toned clothing. She was now dressed in a purple so bright, it could have belonged to Lark.

They walked down the road and along the old sidewalk that paralleled the beach. Where it ended, they continued, until Cassie pointed to a path with pines growing up against its sides. Weaving through the trail single file, salal reaching out for their feet, they started the steep decline that curved around until—like it came out of nowhere—the ocean appeared in front of them. They emerged on a rocky shore, the ground covered in stones that were rounded by the waves over time. The rocks clinked as they crossed, their feet finally landing on sand.

Large pieces of driftwood were piled against the cliffs, and more salal grew from the side of the hill. With no wind to muffle the sounds, the ocean roared and crashed, exhibiting its power to Cassie and Terri, just beyond its reach.

"I've been in California too long." Terri stared out at the curling waves. "It's different here."

"Uncontrolled."

She turned to Cassie. "Exactly. It's not like the ocean down south isn't, but all the people and the deep beaches make the water seem somehow tame in comparison."

Cassie walked around an old log wedged into the sand and sat. "Are you sure this is where you want to get married? I'd totally understand if you and Jack wanted to have the ceremony somewhere closer to one of your families."

She joined her. "It's not about the ceremony, though I think this is the most perfect place I've ever seen. We're focused on the marriage that follows the party. My parents are going to love this place. My mom is all into hiking and exploring nature these days, and my daddy just wants what will make his little girl happy." She leaned her head onto Cassie's shoulder.

She breathed in a lungful of the ocean air. This place was so much a part of Cassie that she found herself questioning all she'd learned. If she was Ainsley, then this wasn't where she was supposed to have grown up, yet nowhere in the world could ever feel as much like home as right here on the beach.

"I want to hear all about Marshall and what's going on with the two of you. That guy snuck so many looks your way today." Terri squeezed her shoulder. "I think he's got a crush on you."

"He kissed me."

Terri's whoop was caught up in the growl of the waves running over the sand.

"I'm not sure it means anything. I don't know. It feels like there's something not being said. Maybe he doesn't like me that much, or he's not ready for the kind of package I come with. I mean, who'd blame him? Marshall is single, with no responsibilities. Why would he even give me a second glance?"

"There you go again, selling yourself short." She dug her toes into the sand. "Any man would be lucky to have you. You're the kind of person who will drop everything to care for those she loves. And what makes you think that all men want is a life without connections? Maybe he wants the wife, kid, and all that. Have you met his family?"

"He doesn't really have one. His dad died when he was in high school."

"Didn't he go to high school with you?"

"No. He just moved here a year or so ago."

She looked around. "This place is gorgeous, but it doesn't seem like the kind of town that calls people in as year-round residents without a reason. What brought him here?"

Cassie rubbed the skin beneath her eyes. "You know, I have no idea. I've been so absorbed in my own life, I've been a horrible friend to Marshall. He wanted to tell me his story, and he did share part of it, but since then, everything has been about me putting out fires." The smoldering embers of the manuscript burned in the back of her heart.

Terri stood, walking in front of Cassie. "Have you gotten anything more from the mysterious mother?"

"Not a thing. I'm beginning to think she'll never make contact again."

"I'm sure she will."

Tears rushed over Cassie's cheeks. She wiped them away and smeared sand across her face. "There are two child-sized graves out there. One with the name I was born with, and the other with the name I have now. How am I supposed to tell Lark about our family? I scared a poor woman who's only trying to stay hidden from her abusive ex-husband." She covered her face with both hands, her shoulders bobbing with sobs she couldn't get under control.

Nora woke to an odd silence in the house. She peered into the bassinet and found it empty. Ferris was gone too.

In the still-lit living room, she located both of them on the couch. The baby slept peacefully on Ferris's chest. His mouth hung open, his breathing deep. On the floor was the notebook he kept investigation information in.

Nora had never opened it, never overstepped in that way, but . . . before she could stop herself, she was flipping through the pages.

He was looking for Cassie's mother.

Enough. She set it back on the floor, shame burning her muscles. Maybe it was the sleep deprivation, but sympathy and understanding were upending her normal feelings for Cassie. After all, Nora sure wouldn't want Cassie to know about Tammy.

She brushed hair out of her eyes. The only person she knew who could maybe understand what Nora was feeling . . . was Cassie.

# 38

On Sunday, Terri left right after church. Where she'd been was an empty hole now, and without the secrets to fill the space inside, Cassie was empty.

Shasta was having one of her good days, painting beside Lark, an activity that seemed to give them both overwhelming joy. The shaking of her arms and the loll of her head told Cassie it wouldn't last long. Her aunt's stamina was dwindling.

In the kitchen, Cassie looked back through the pages of the manuscript. Why did they have to stop? She needed the rest of the story. If Amanda Reynolds knew she was here, why hadn't she come for her? Cassie kept coming back to the thought that maybe she found that Cassie wasn't worth her time or effort. Maybe her mother had come into the shop. They might have spoken, interacted in some way, but when she stood before her lost daughter, Cassie wasn't what she'd wanted, and she'd walked away, untying herself from Cassie's life.

Sharing all of this with Terri was supposed to ease the burden, but it hadn't. It had only worn away the edges, leaving vulnerability.

One thing was more certain than anything else: If they were going to stay here and make their lives in Gull's Bay, Cassie needed to know who this woman was and make contact. She couldn't live the rest of her life looking over her shoulder or wondering if the person who walked by on the sidewalk had given birth to her.

Marshall's knock sounded at the door. She ducked into the bathroom, checking her eyes to be sure her emotional state wasn't obvious, then went to answer. She shouldn't have bothered checking herself—as soon as she caught sight of him, her emotions blurred. She turned away, keeping her face from Lark and Shasta at the same time.

"Hey, Marshall!" Lark called. "I'm painting a giraffe in the snow."

"That's amazing, Lark. I'll come check it out in a few minutes, 'kay?"

"Yep."

He took hold of Cassie's arm and guided her into the kitchen, then held her tight against his chest.

Tears soaked into the front of his T-shirt, the same one she held on to as if the cotton was enough to save her.

His hand stroked the back of her hair, and his breath warmed her scalp. Cassie wasn't being fair to him; they had no commitment, and she was a horrible mess.

When she could finally speak without choking on tears, she pushed back, mourning the heat that had come from his embrace. "I'm so sorry. You don't have to stay. I'm fine. Just having a rough day."

"Why do you do that?"

"What?"

"Make excuses for having feelings. Do you want me to go?" His eyebrows pressed together as if he were experiencing her pain too.

Setting her hand on his damp chest, she shook her head. "I want you to stay, if that's okay."

"I'm done," Lark called from the other room.

Cassie covered her eyes, feeling the swollen hot skin.

"I got this. You go get cleaned up." Marshall kissed her on the forehead, the kind of kiss one gave a good friend, but not the kind Cassie had ever been given by a man. "Hold on, Lark. I want to see what you've got."

In the bathroom, Cassie ran cold water, forming a bowl with her hands and using it to dip her face. After a few minutes, she dabbed her angry skin with a soft towel. She still looked like someone who'd been crying, but if she didn't make direct eye contact for a while, maybe Shasta and Lark wouldn't notice.

She leaned against the wall and stared at herself in the mirror. Cassie had never been a crier. She didn't even remember if she'd cried when she found out she was pregnant. She'd been stunned, yes, but on some level, she'd felt she deserved to have the additional challenge. At the time, Cassie had no idea that the challenge would actually be the best thing that could ever happen to her.

So why was this undoing her? Why now, when she had limited time to spend with her aunt and didn't want anything to get in the way of what they had left?

If she hid out in the bathroom much longer, Lark would come looking for her. It was time to face the man she'd gone all sappy on and the issues that were spreading her far too thin.

A package sat on the table. She was sure it hadn't been there before. Cassie ran her fingers over it.

"Oh, I found that on the top step when I came up. Sorry, I forgot to mention it." Marshall settled on the couch, where he read a ballerina story to Lark.

There wasn't a name on the padded white envelope and no postage, so whoever left it had done so in person. Cassie tore off the top and slid another bundle of papers into her hand. As realization hit, so did the feeling that the room had begun to spin. She pulled out a chair and sat, the chapters in front of her, her head resting in her hands.

Part Two

I needed to see what had happened in Seattle. Was my husband living another life up there? Were there more children? And . . . was I the last one to know?

I posed as the sister of the woman, Diane, calling the utility companies to gain more detail on where she'd lived. As it turned out, she'd been in the last apartment only a few months and had made arrangements to end her electric service the week after the accident.

Next, I called the last landlord she'd had, using the same deception. I was surprised he remembered her after so many years had passed, but the circumstances of her death and the fact that her things had already been packed when he went in to check had left a lasting memory. He said most of the boxes were labeled with her daughter's name, as if the toddler had more than her mother.

I'd questioned him on this, having found out that the woman's daughter had died, but he assured me there was indeed a child—he'd seen her himself. He also told me that my cousin had come for the boxes and taken everything back with her to Oregon. He assumed she had the child too. That's when he got wise to my lie.

"Hey," he said. "If you were her sister, why don't you know about her kid? What kind of ruse are you working here?"

Before I could come up with an answer, the line went dead.

I had no knowledge of how to get more information, and I was running low on finances, having used much of the life insurance to pay off the house and help my teens become steady on their feet so they could move on to better lives. If I could have afforded more time with the private detective, I would gladly have hired him again, but his fee would mean turning away kids who needed help more than I needed answers about a dead woman.

The mission I'd begun with the youth who came through my home was so needed that I soon found myself struggling for time

298

and resources. It was at this point that I moved forward to make Ainsley's Hope a nonprofit. Money wasn't rolling in, but we were able to acquire grant money. Eventually we opened a home for young men with staff who were there solely to mentor young people who'd made some bad choices but had a sincere desire for a better life.

I'd nearly forgotten about Seattle and the other woman as I filled the next couple of years with building futures. The work was endless, leaving me little time to stew about what I should have known. But then I was invited to speak at a conference in Seattle. It was far outside of my comfort zone, standing in front of an audience, telling stories of how my kids were succeeding in building bright futures, but the importance of sharing what we were doing so the work could be duplicated elsewhere outweighed my reservations.

I thought this would be a one-time thing, but word spread, and a group up there decided to replicate our program under a different name. I traveled back and forth, training and working with the Seattle area director.

One afternoon, I found myself with the rare treasure of extra time on my hands, and I did something strange with it. I looked up the child the other woman had lost, and I visited her grave. Standing at that site, I realized that even if she had taken my husband's affections, we'd shared something deeper than that man's love: We'd both lost children.

My heart actually ached for her as I stood over the tiny marker with her baby's name engraved in granite. *Cascadia Marie George.*

Cassie woke up from a nightmare, soaked in her own sweat, gasping for air. She'd been standing over a grave—a grave with her own name etched into the stone—when the ground started crumbling beneath her feet. No matter where she stepped, she was pulled down, the grave taking her away from all she had, as if it had been searching for her.

As much as she needed the information on the new pages to make sense of what was true, Cassie couldn't handle knowing any of it. The words she'd read before going to bed had haunted her sleep, and now that she was awake, they grew more sinister.

She got up and padded through the house, checking the locks again. She'd gone downstairs twice before bed, just to be sure the shop was securely closed up. Yet Cassie still didn't feel safe.

In the kitchen, she drank a glass of water, then another. It wasn't cold in the apartment, but she shivered. Every sound made her feel like turning on all the lights and sitting in the living room with a butcher knife for protection.

She went to Lark's room and found her sound asleep, still holding her blanket close to her mouth, the way she had as a baby.

At Shasta's door, she clicked the alarm off and pushed it open. To her surprise, Shasta lay in the bed, her eyes wide open, her face illuminated by the moonlight streaming through her windows. Cassie sat on the side of her mattress. "What are you doing awake?"

She didn't answer but reached up and touched Cassie's face, tapping fingers below her eyes.

Lifting the blankets, Cassie crawled in beside her dear aunt Shasta. Tears fell again, but these were silent tears that wouldn't be held back.

# 39

When Cassie woke the next morning, her nightmares had come calling. Shasta, the only mother she remembered having, had somehow slipped silently into Heaven. Before it actually happened, Cassie had worried about how she would handle losing her. She thought she might panic and cause serious emotional damage to her daughter, but that's not what happened.

When Cassie realized Shasta was gone, she sent a text to Marshall and Aubrey, then did what she'd been told to do, even if the order wasn't correct. She called the hospice nurse.

Lark was still asleep when Cassie heard the first tap at the door. Opening it, she found Aubrey standing there, her face pale aside from the red rims of her eyes. "Are you okay?" She pulled Cassie into her arms.

Cassie nodded. "For right now, I think I am. The hospice nurse is on her way over. Lark is still asleep." She had to blink away tears then. It hurt to lose Shasta, but the thought of having to tell Lark that her grammy was gone snapped her heart into pieces.

"Do you mind if I have a few minutes?" Aubrey nodded toward the hall that led to Shasta's room.

The only response Cassie could give her was a forced smile,

but her meaning must have made it through the armor holding her upright.

Cassie paced the living room, picking up Shasta's paint-brush, the one she'd been using only hours before. On the canvas was a painting so different from the true-to-life style she'd always been known for. It was a mix of color—blues and yellows—that looked as if God himself was reaching down through the sky. There were hundreds of Shasta's paintings on display all over Gull's Bay. Yet none would ever mean as much to Cassie as this one.

When the nurse arrived, Cassie went back with her. She stood at the end of the bed, giving Aubrey another moment, then verified what they knew already: Shasta was gone. Only her body remained.

A large hand slipped into Cassie's as she stood at the foot of the bed.

She tipped her head onto Marshall's chest. Even if whatever they had never went any further, he'd always be the rock that had held her up when she most needed it. Cassie followed the nurse out of the room, her fingers still tightly holding on to Marshall's. She made the call for the funeral home to come by, thinking she'd fall with the way the room had begun to spin. They'd take Shasta's body. Wasn't it enough that her soul was gone? Shasta would never be in this apartment again. Cassie would never have her to steady the craziness, to encourage her, to be the place she could fall and be safe.

She didn't have living grandparents, and she'd never had a father. With Shasta dying, Cassie was alone on a level she hadn't anticipated. Loneliness seeped into her heart; it tore her open and stole the strength from her lungs.

Her body began to shake, and she struggled for air. She wasn't ready. She couldn't manage this on her own. Cassie was still a kid herself in so many ways. And then she heard the tapping sound of Lark's feet, always bare in the morning, coming closer. She needed Cassie as much if not more than Cassie needed Shasta. Somehow, Cassie continued to breathe. She dropped to her knees, Marshall's hand on her shoulder, and pulled her daughter close, then explained that her grammy had been called home to Heaven.

Life became a kind of heavy blur from there as Cassie was led from one step to the next. Downstairs, the shop was closed to all but their local friends, who came in and out, voices hushed, movements slow.

With Shasta's body taken from their home, the depth of grief found another trench to drop into. The farther Cassie descended, the heavier the weight of everything above pressed her down. There was no oxygen, no air, no light. Only the despair that came with losing one's lifeline to the surface.

If it hadn't been for Lark, Cassie could have lost herself in those depths and given way to the current that would push her away from land and never bring her fully back. It took all the strength she had to keep finding Lark, making sure that she was in the arms of someone important—and she always was. Mrs. Collins, Mr. Watkins, Aubrey, and Marshall took turns caring for Cassie's treasure.

Coffees and teas were set in front of her warm, then taken away untouched and replaced with fresh mugs.

Each time she felt her strength returning, she'd picture Shasta's room empty, her paintbrush never to be lifted by her crooked hand again, and she'd go back under.

Somehow, the day moved forward, though without Shasta, it shouldn't have been able to. Yet the sun set like it had the night before. Cassie slipped off to sleep, her body, mind, and heart so exhausted, she thought she might miss the whole next day. But she woke in a dark house, the ticking of the clock in the living room hammering the reality of her loss into her core. She couldn't go back to sleep, yet also didn't want to be awake.

The good thing about living with little family was that she

had never really experienced the loss of someone she loved. The other side of that meant Shasta had forged an extra bond of connection. Cassie had lost her mother, father, aunt, cousin, sister, all-in-one person, in a moment she hadn't been ready for.

Cassie sat up in bed, switched on the light, and stared at the papers still sitting where she'd left them the night before. It all seemed so trivial now, like whatever had happened in the past, whoever she was or wasn't, didn't matter in the face of life without Shasta.

Stumbling toward the kitchen, Cassie checked on Lark and found her sound asleep, Aubrey next to her. Cassie should have been the one to comfort her daughter. It was her job, but she didn't know how to put salve on Lark's wounds when her own were so open and raw.

She switched on the light above the stove, not wanting to face the harshness of the overhead, her eyes strained from tears that kept pouring like a river off a melting mountain. Would she ever have control of her emotions again?

A figure was sitting on the couch, back toward her. Cassie moved around the dining table to see Mrs. Collins, her hands folded together, her head dipped as if in prayer.

She eased herself down next to her. Her aunt's death didn't just belong to Cassie. It was a grief that would be shared by friends, the community, the people who had made up their family.

Mrs. Collins cleared her throat. "There's a Scripture I've held on to. It's walked with me through many deeply painful trials. Psalm 34:18: 'The Lord is close to the brokenhearted and saves those who are crushed in spirit.'" She wrapped Cassie's hand in hers. "I've held on to these words many times in my life. I know the weight of grief and what it's like to have your family ripped away. I'm always going to be here for you and for Lark. You're not alone. But more important, God, the Father God, is here right now for you too."

Cassie braced for the next wave of tears, but they didn't come. Instead, she breathed in and breathed out, something she would need to practice for the foreseeable future until this empty space became the new normal, and Cassie no longer tripped over the grief.

Cassie didn't have to ask Marshall to be near during the memorial service; he was simply there. And when they returned to the shop for another round of Shasta memories, he walked beside her.

Shasta had made all the arrangements years ago, when she first realized something wasn't right. Those little signs Cassie was too self-absorbed to see would be a regret following her until she found a way to cut them off.

More of Shasta's paintings had been brought out and hung around the shop, bringing so many experiences back. She'd captured a life. Mr. Watkins, behind the counter of his hardware store. In her image of him, he was a little taller, a little broader, his wrinkles not so very prominent, and his hair a bit fuller.

There was one of Lark as a newborn baby in Cassie's arms—she couldn't believe she'd never seen that one. Cassie could only take quick glances at it now or the emotion she was trying so hard to hold in place would burst through her restraint.

She could stare at the one of Marshall at the espresso machine forever. He had that sassy look, the one that warned of his teasing. It was exactly what she'd seen the very first time she'd met him. But in Shasta's version, there was a depth in his eyes and the set of his jaw, like a man who'd gotten to where he was by working for it.

Mrs. Collins came in the door, pushing the cart she used to move pastries from one location to the other. It was filled with orange creamsicle cupcakes. Aubrey took hold of the front, and together the two of them unloaded treats onto a table beneath the painting of Mrs. Collins biting into an éclair, flour dusting her face and pink tingeing her cheeks.

Mr. Watkins was the first to speak. "As many of you know, Shasta and I were sweethearts in high school." His stare rose to the ceiling, and he took a moment to compose himself. "We didn't break up because we fell out of love or any of that nonsense. No, we just had different ideas about what our lives should look like. Shasta went off to that art school, and I stayed here, met my Marianne, and raised our boys. Now I have Marshall. I've been very fortunate. Some men never know what it's like to love a woman. The good Lord blessed me with two." He lifted his glass of iced tea. "Shasta, my love, you will be missed until we meet again in eternity."

The group murmured in agreement.

Cassie sipped her water, pondering the things she hadn't known about Shasta, wondering what she'd been like as a child, as a teen.

Everywhere she looked, Cassie saw Shasta. She saw her love for their neighbors, the way she cared for Cassie and for Lark. She saw the ocean through Shasta's eyes, sometimes stormy and gray, the water swirling with rage, and sometimes light aqua blue, its waves lapping gently onto the beach.

It was all here, as if Shasta were still talking in her ear, still directing Cassie through the hard times as well as the moments of uncontrolled beauty. No matter where Cassie had come from, Shasta was part of her. She would be part of her for the entirety of her existence, and her influence would spill over into Lark, who would share it with her children.

People might not stay on this earth long in body, but when they gave their hearts to others, when they sacrificed for their well-being, a piece of them went on.

# 40

Grief was an unreliable counterpart.

The next days went by with some glimpses of normal, and some setbacks that knocked Cassie to her knees. She found herself dependent on prayer in a way she never had been before. Talking to God helped her through the times when life seemed pointless, when the space that taking care of Shasta had filled now seemed too open and empty.

Lark and Cassie walked down the path to the beach. They'd spent very little time without the ever-watching eyes of neighbors making sure they were cared for, eating, and getting enough sleep.

The tide was out, spreading the beach wide in front of them. Cassie guided Lark to the tide pools along the rocky ridge. "Be careful now. The rocks can be very slippery."

Little ponds of captured water were home to sea creatures. She pointed out an anemone.

"What's his name?"

"Do you mean what is it called? It's a giant green anemone. Don't touch it in the middle, or it will hurt him." Cassie took her hand and helped Lark drag a finger over his tentacles. The anemone curled in on itself, and Lark giggled.

"But what's his real name?"

*"Anthopleura xanthogrammica."*

She looked up. "I think he'd rather be called Alex."

Cassie's laughter felt distant, like it came from someone else. "Alex is a great name for an *Anthopleura xanthogrammica*. What should we call this, do you think?" She pointed to a sunflower sea star.

"This one has so many legs. What's its big name?"

*"Pycnopodia helianthoides."*

"Heather. Can I pick her up?" Lark slid down on her bottom to get closer.

"No, but I bet she wouldn't mind if you carefully rubbed her back."

"She's so bumpy." Lark flipped over on her belly, her eyes only an inch from the surface of the water. "Mom, do you see that they're all in families?"

Cassie got down on the jagged rock, careful not to tear the knee out of her jeans. Examining the tide pool through Lark's eyes, she could see what her daughter meant. So many different kinds of creatures, all living together in their own community. "It's kind of like all of us here in Gull's Bay, isn't it?"

Lark started renaming all her new friends with familiar names. Cassie had to laugh when the tallest of the anemones was assigned to be Marshall.

Lark pushed up and looked at her, her eyes giving away her sincerity. "Why don't you have a mom?"

Cassie pulled Lark onto her lap, rocking back and forth as she watched the ocean beyond them. She wouldn't burden her daughter with all the new questions that were arising about this very question, but Lark deserved an answer. "Larkie, I don't really understand that myself. But God gave me Shasta, and she was the very best mom I could ever have."

Lark wrapped her arms around her mom. "I don't want you to ever die."

"I don't want to die yet either, and there's absolutely no reason to think my time is coming. We have many years together still." Cassie kissed the top of her head.

"I have another question."

"Okay, shoot."

"Why do people need a daddy to have a baby?"

This was a loaded query—one Cassie had been afraid of since Gwendolyn's little sister Ava had been born. "Well, it depends on what you mean by that."

"Gwendolyn has a dad, and she told me you have to have one of those to get a baby. But I don't have one, and you don't have one."

"I see what you're getting at. It does take a man to make a baby, but sometimes children are raised by only a man or only a woman. It's very complicated, and I'm not sure I understand myself."

Lark nodded. "That's what I thought. I was pretty sure you would have told me if you knew. I'm going to ask Marshall about this. He's a guy, so it seems like he'd know. I'll let you know what I find out."

Cassie's mouth fell open, and she gulped a mouthful of sea air. Maybe she should warn him before the interrogation. "Slow down, kiddo. That might be a bit personal to ask him."

"What does that mean?"

"It means that Marshall is our good friend, but he's got his own life, and things could be different for him. He might have feelings about things."

"You don't know, do you?"

The tide was rising in front of them, announcing their time in the tide pools was coming to an end. A divine miracle in Cassie's eyes.

Cassie arrived back at the shop to find a pile of mail waiting for her. She'd come to the point of cringing as she flipped through the envelopes. There were always bills, so many of them. There were the bills for the supplies, invoices that had to be paid, medical bills—including for the stitches to the top of her head, the scars of which still itched from morning to night—and the five companies from which she'd taken out student loans. It had been foolish to take the private loans on top of the federally funded ones. Consolidation was the next step.

Lark spotted Aubrey in the kitchen and skipped off to join her while Cassie verified what she'd expected. Now that she was so confident in what she wanted, it seemed that all her foolish choices were going to ruin it. Gull's Bay was home, and she couldn't stand the thought of raising her daughter anywhere else, but going back to school seemed like the only answer. If she returned to the doctoral program, at least the bills would slow to their minimum payments. In the meantime, she could sell the shop and the apartment.

Large hands came around her shoulders, warming her at the same time they sent a chill over her skin. She turned and pressed into Marshall's chest. It wasn't fair of her to make such use of him, but he had a way of always being near when she needed someone.

"What's going on?" He stepped back. "Everything okay?"

"Honestly, I'm swamped with student loans. I don't know what I was thinking. There are cheaper ways to run away from shame than by becoming a professional college student."

"Ouch. Did you apply for a deferral?"

She rolled her head, stretching her neck muscles. "I need to look into that. The thing is, I've been taking loans to keep us afloat for years, sometimes taking more loans to pay the interest on the unsubsidized ones along the way. California is crazy expensive for childcare, rent, and tuition. I got myself into this mess. I'm going to figure out how to get out of it."

"Ah, there you are."

She cocked her head. "What do you mean by that?"

"I mean, you're back to the woman I met right here." He pointed at the espresso machine. "You can do it all on your own. No need for anyone else, just you."

"That's not true."

"Isn't it?" He crossed his arms.

"Wow. You hardly know me. What makes you think you can diagnose my issues, Dr. Phil?" Heat crawled up the back of her neck.

"Hardly know you? Fine. If that's how you want to play it, just forget I was here." He turned, heading out the door.

"Not a problem." Her words were too late for him, but saying them still gave her the last word. That used to mean something.

# 41

Looking back on the things I did and the choices I made, I can now see that I'd become obsessed with the woman who'd taken my husband's love. Yet it was more than that. We'd lost Ainsley, but Topher might well have lost two children. How had he kept moving forward after Cascadia and Ainsley were both gone?

Part of me relished in his suffering, but there was another part that was grateful he'd passed without knowing Ainsley had been killed. Maybe he'd still had hope that our daughter would be returned to us. I knew our time together before the disappearance was like a new start for our little family. He would have stayed with me and left her if only we hadn't lost our sweet daughter.

When I finally got up the nerve to visit the apartment building where she'd been living when the accident happened, I tried on a new ruse. This time, I was an old friend from college, looking to find Diane and reconnect. I knocked on five doors before finding someone who'd been there long enough to remember her.

"Whatever happened to her sweet little girl?" the elderly woman asked me. I was taken back by the question, knowing by this point that Cascadia had died prior to Diane moving here, but also fully aware from the landlord that he believed there had been a child.

"Are you sure we're talking about the same woman? I didn't think she had a child."

"Oh yes, such a sweet little thing. Cassie was her name, but I haven't heard hide nor hair about her since the older woman came to get the boxes."

I'd remembered the landlord mentioning a relative who'd moved out Diane's things. Maybe she also had this kid. A child who was likely also the offspring of my very busy husband and who shared a very similar name to Diane's deceased daughter. I needed to see this child, see if she had his eyes, his smile. What I really needed was the chance to see a little of my Ainsley again.

I was walking away, having finished my conversation, when the woman's door opened again. "I just remembered something. It may not help you much, but the lady who came was from a little town in Oregon . . . Gull's something. I'm really sorry you weren't able to see your friend again." Then she closed the door, not knowing that those last words would change the rest of my life.

Cassie stomped down the stairs. Her anger at Marshall and his know-it-all attitude wasn't softening with time. And maybe she was a little upset by the change in their schedule. Lark's preschool was having a summer send-off all the families were to attend, and of course, all Lark had now was Cassie. She'd spent the entire morning hearing from her daughter about how amazing it was going to be. She'd dressed in her best princess-like outfit and tried to sneak out of the house with a plastic wand. Now Cassie was about to leave for the program portion of the day and see her daughter's disappointment. It was just too much.

She waved at Lisa as she left the shop, trying to force a smile, but probably scaring her for a future with Cassie as her employer. She'd gotten caught up in the manuscript chapters and left a few minutes later than planned, so she started to jog. It took only a block for Cassie to feel the burn in her legs and lungs. She'd gotten so out of shape, Cassie would be needing to get that wheelchair back for her own use soon if she didn't get some exercise.

Stepping into the sanctuary, she could see that everyone had arrived before her. Nora sat right up in the front row, surrounded by her in-laws, her husband, and what were probably her neighbors. A toddler held on to the back of the bench, bouncing up and down. The new baby was asleep on Nora's shoulder. They looked like perfection . . . as always. Gwendolyn wouldn't feel a bit forgotten. Cassie should have made a sign. At least Lark could have seen that from the back of the room where her mom was going to have to sit.

Just then, the kids started filing onto the stage. Lark, all smiles and glitter, sparkled with her tiny graduation cap formed out of paper stuck to the top of her head.

Cassie's phone buzzed. In true great-mom fashion, she couldn't resist the temptation. She looked at the text. It was from Aubrey. *We saved you a seat.*

Her head shot up, and she looked around, spotting them in the second row on the other side. A crowd of them. Cassie made her way up, staying bent over, trying not to call attention to herself.

Mr. Watkins held his hat in his hands. He stood while Cassie shimmied down the row, settling between Aubrey and Mrs. Collins. The room was darkened with lights shining on the kids, but that manly soap scent announced Marshall was in the row too. He'd come for her daughter even if there was no future between the two of them, and she missed him all the more for that fact. Why did she have to be so stubborn?

When the kids were lined up in rows on risers—a real risk with preschoolers—and the teachers had each introduced themselves, the music began. Cassie had always been a shy child. Presentations like this one had been her least favorite thing of the year. She'd once faked a cold to get out of the Christmas pageant. But Lark, she was a seagull, never one to hide away. She soared up there, dancing to the music, expressing herself with grand gestures.

Both Aubrey and Mrs. Collins watched her with grins so wide they took years off their faces. Aubrey's phone was recording and centered on Lark. The attention egged Lark on to her full potential. She moved to the beat like she was the only star on the stage.

Next to her, Gwendolyn looked at her patent leather shoes, her hands clasped together as if she wished she could disappear. Cassie's heart went out to her. With a mother like Nora, not wanting to be the center of attention was going to be a struggle.

When they finished the songs, their row burst into applause.

The kids were each given a special certificate while the teacher remarked on what they'd brought to the class. When it was Lark's turn, the teacher laughed, going on about how everything in the preschool had gotten a little brighter when this child started. Lark shook her hand, accepting her preschool diploma, and they all clapped. Marshall let out a whoop, and Lark pumped her hand in the air in response.

That was Cassie's baby up there. But Lark wasn't just hers. She had a big family who loved her unconditionally.

Nora had seen the light go out of Gwendolyn's eyes when baby Ava started to fuss and Nora had taken her out of the sanctuary. From the little window at the top of the door, she tried to see her daughter get her diploma, but the view was blocked.

Ava's body trembled with anger. She could barely catch her breath. Nora had taken her to the doctor again the day before, but colic was still the diagnosis. What had they been thinking, having another baby? She and Ferris were outnumbered. How did Cassie George make parenting look so easy?

Nora snapped a selfie of her and Ava, the baby's face flaming red, her mouth wide with a scream, and tears evident in Nora's eyes. Before she could think better of it, she posted the picture to Instagram with the caption *Real motherhood isn't always pretty.* #momlife #colic #iamsotired

They gathered in Mrs. Collins's bakery after the big show. Cassie tried to keep her distance from Marshall, unable to look him in the eye for fear her embarrassment would show. There was this nagging feeling that what had happened between them—the argument and the coldness since—might have been her fault alone.

She bit into the perfect snickerdoodle and stared out the window, watching the vacation people go by, the ones who were here because they'd stepped away from their normal lives, their work and trials and struggles.

"Can we talk?" Marshall's voice was like melted chocolate, sweet, rich, and smooth.

That's when Cassie saw Ferris Milford. He stood on the sidewalk outside the coffee shop, his gaze sweeping the area like a man on guard. Before she could turn from the window, he spotted her. Tucking his hands into his pockets, Milford started to cross the street.

"I have to go. I'll come back for Lark. Tell Mrs. Collins." Cassie slipped out of the door and caught Ferris in the middle of the street. "What are you doing here?" She nodded toward the sidewalk he'd come from.

"I got word that you had a death in the family. Thought I'd better make sure you didn't apply for any survivor benefits."

"What?"

"Sorry. Dumb joke."

She shot him a glare that should have covered him with shame.

"Too soon?"

"There will never be a good time for that kind of joke." Looking back at the bakery, she could see Marshall watching them. "Come with me." She led him down the street and around a corner.

When they were out of Marshall's sight, she turned to Milford. "Seriously, what did you find out?"

"I got a call from the picture guy. He said there's no way that's you in the hospital. It has something to do with the ears. Personally, I can't see it, but it's not my specialty. It turns out the Mexican government has taken back their claims to have found Ainsley's body. I'm not sure why, but nothing else was done in the investigation. I can't find anything that says there was knowledge you were actually alive. And to be honest, we don't really know you are Ainsley. What we have for sure is that you aren't Cascadia George.

"The egg donation is another complication. I've made a couple of calls, but I haven't been able to find anyone who would have records about the donor. We'd need a court order for something like that anyway."

"So basically, I'm nobody right now?"

He shrugged. "I'm going to have to tell my boss what's going on soon. He found your name where I'd been doodling as I checked on some leads. I think the guy has the idea we're seeing each other on the side." He shook his head and rubbed at the dark circles under his eyes. "Ava doesn't seem to sleep . . . ever."

"I'm sorry. You do look wiped out."

"Nora is worse."

Cassie held her lips together tightly. What kind of person wanted to smile at news like that?

"Do me a favor and don't call any attention to yourself. I

317

have no idea how you've managed to use a dead girl's Social Security number all these years without some serious fraud issues arising."

"I need to consolidate my student loans."

His eyes were as wide as a man that exhausted could make them. "I know you want this kept quiet, but eventually, the government is going to get wise to you not being you."

She kicked a rock with the toe of her shoe. It skittered across the road and bounced off the opposite curb. "I'll lose the coffee shop if I don't get the loans worked out. And there's all the estate stuff."

"I'm sorry. There's nothing I can do. You might consider an attorney."

Cute. Tell the woman with no money to hire a lawyer. Here came another tsunami.

# 42

There was only one town in Oregon with Gull's in the name, Gull's Bay, a tiny hamlet that had grown up around a small bay on the Oregon coast. I had no idea what I would do once I arrived. Being the off-season, there were plenty of cabins available for vacation rentals. I didn't have a lot of savings remaining, but this was an investment I needed to make. If I could be close to someone, anyone who held a little shared DNA with my baby, I had to do it.

The town was quaint, like the kind of village one expected from a Hallmark movie, though I immediately questioned the motivation to live in a place with constant wind and rain that beat down like nails out of the sky. My California jacket was no match for the weather.

After driving all around the town, I parked and watched the rain snake down the windshield of my rental car. A group of people ducked into a coffee shop. It seemed like as good a place as any to warm up.

Inside, I found an atmosphere like nothing I'd seen before. The shop was filled with paintings of such quality, I wanted to fill my home with the images that made me feel welcome just staring at them.

A woman older than I was stepped up to the counter. "Hey there. By the looks of that jacket, you're not from around here."

I shrugged it off, suddenly self-conscious about the drips I'd been leaving on the wood floor.

She walked around, taking my coat and hanging it near a set of stairs. "Come on over here by the fireplace and get yourself warmed up. You've got to be chilled to the bone."

I was. The cold had seeped through me, and the wind had forced it farther in until I shivered in my damp shirt. "Thank you."

"Just sit right here. We'll get you taken care of."

Soon I had a hot cup of coffee, the flavor rich and earthy, the mug warming my hands. The woman jogged up the stairs and returned with a sweatshirt. "It's not much, but it will do while I throw your shirt in the dryer." She showed me where to change, and I gratefully followed directions.

I had never been part of much of a community at all aside from the work I was now doing, but this town was already weaving into my heart. I could see how a person might like this life where everyone seemed to know everyone.

As I sipped the hot drink, wearing clothes that didn't belong to me, I had plenty of time to watch people come and go, greeting one another as if they were all one family.

The owner of the shop came over and sat next to me. "What brings you to Gull's Bay?"

There was no accusation in her tone, just simple interest.

I was about to pour out another fabricated story when the door jingled, and in came a child dripping with rainwater, her backpack forming a hump beneath her raincoat.

"Will you excuse me for a moment?" The woman rose and embraced the child without regard for the wetness. They spoke for a moment, the woman handing the child a cookie; then the girl disappeared up the same stairs the woman had taken.

"Shasta?" A woman in a booth near the window raised her hand.

The owner walked over. "What can I do for you?"

320

"I'd love to get your sweet potato casserole recipe from you, dear. I want to serve it at Thanksgiving."

"Marianne, you know I can't do that. I won't even share that secret with Cassie until I'm dead and buried."

I coughed and choked, the coffee running down my esophagus. Before I could settle my thoughts, Shasta was at my side with a glass of water. "My goodness. You're having a tough day."

When I could talk, I asked her about the girl who'd come in. I hadn't gotten a close look, but she'd be about the right age. It struck me at the moment that I'd been expecting a small child, a toddler, not having given much thought to the passage of time. It was strange how things had changed since losing Ainsley—even years later, time didn't have the same meaning as before. In many ways, I was passing time in order to be with her again.

"Cassie is my niece. Well, technically, she's the daughter of my cousin. Diane passed away quite a few years back, and I've been raising her ever since. That girl is the greatest blessing the Lord has ever given to me."

The look on her face when she talked about Cassie made it clear she wasn't exaggerating.

As I sat there, waiting for my clothes to dry, I went back over all that I knew. Cascadia had died as an infant, yet here was a girl named Cassie who must have been Diane's daughter and looked the age Cascadia should have been. Maybe she'd been adopted, or Cascadia had been a twin. As a mother who'd lost a child, I knew how deep that hurt could run, but I couldn't imagine naming another baby anything like Ainsley. Ainsley was Ainsley. The name belonged to her.

I hoped Cassie would come downstairs again but didn't get another chance to see her, so I planned to come back the next day, near the time when school let out.

I'd become a regular by the time our paths crossed again. Cassie, it turned out, had after-school activities and volunteered time with an elderly woman from their church. The sun was shining the day she came into the coffee shop, no hood hiding her hair or face. And I saw it, the curly brown hair, just the way I'd assumed Ainsley's would grow to look . . . and the eyes. They were Ainsley's eyes, not a reflection of her in Topher's shared features. Ainsley's perfect brown eyes.

I called out her name. A few people looked my way, but she didn't. There wasn't the slightest recognition. Stepping closer, I complimented her on her sweater.

"Thank you. Aunt Shasta ordered it for my birthday. It's my favorite." They were the first words my daughter had ever spoken to me. I held back all that was pushing to come out. I wanted to hold her, to smell the baby scent of her, but those years were gone. Before me was an eleven-year-old girl on the cusp of her teen years. She didn't know me from any other stranger, yet my soul knew her.

I couldn't trust myself then, and I knew I needed to walk away before I traumatized my child. Maybe I was crazy. None of this made sense, yet I would need to put the story together if I was going to bring this to the police. If I took her now, I'd be put away for kidnapping and find myself trying to explain that she was mine to a psychiatrist. No one would believe me, and I didn't share the DNA to prove she was my daughter. I should have demanded information about the donor.

When I returned to the cabin I was renting, I cried. Not happy tears of the kind that I would have imagined. I cried for the years I'd lost. It was all about me, my misery, my longing to watch Ainsley grow, my thinking she was gone all these years when she was right here, growing up like any other child.

I didn't leave that cabin for five days. I'd been able to continue my stay by using a credit card to pay for another week. My phone rang and rang, people wanting to know when I would return. I gave them only enough to keep them from filing a missing person's report on me.

On day six, I watched the angry ocean fight the rocky cliff, the sky dark and the rain coming down at a sharp angle. Lightning lit the sky, followed quickly by the thunder echoing off the water.

The pounding on the door startled Cassie. She dropped the papers from her lap and jumped off the couch. Immediately, her thoughts ran to Lark. She was with Mrs. Collins, working out a new recipe for cookies, but Cassie's mind was able to come up with a thousand things that could have gone wrong.

Without even asking who was there, she swung the door open, the knob banging into the wall where there was already a hole forming in the drywall.

Marshall's face was weary, lines forming between his eyebrows.

At the bottom of the stairs, a couple sat at a booth, staring up at them.

"Come in." Cassie stepped away, making room for him to enter, then shut the door so they wouldn't become the community entertainment.

He went straight toward the window but didn't pass the canvases still standing where they'd been the last time Shasta and Lark had painted together. His T-shirt fit snugly, the muscles in his back an impressive display that made her want to look away or give in to apologizing. Anger flared in her chest, not so much at Marshall, but at herself. She honestly couldn't remember why she'd been so mad at him, but she wasn't ready to give it up. Not yet.

"Listen." He spoke with a voice of authority that resounded in the room even though he still did not face her. "My academic program requires me to attend my own therapy sessions. Until recently, I've found them to be insightful. I just came from my last required meeting."

"Congratulations?" She sat on the arm of the couch, something Shasta had scolded her for a hundred times. "What does this have to do with me?" The selfish tone in her voice sounded like a piece of gravel stuck under a door. She tried again. "I'm sorry. What did you need, Marshall?"

He sat on the opposite side of the sofa, elbows on his thighs, his fingers stitched together. "I don't want to walk away from what we have, but, Cassie, you need to give both of us some grace. I own my pride. I'm working on it. And I'm sorry I stomped out. It was childish."

They were silent for a long time.

Marshall cleared his throat. "Your turn."

Her eyebrows rose but so did the corners of her mouth. "I'm sorry. I was a horrible, filthy, terrible, no-good lout."

He slapped a hand down on his leg as he laughed. "I was expecting something like you were sorry for overreacting, but I'll take what I can get. And you're forgiven. I'm glad we could get you all fixed up."

She tugged at the end of her T-shirt. "There are so many obstacles. Lark, for one."

"Stop." He held up a hand.

"Well, that's not a very nice way for a counselor to talk."

"You're not my patient."

She pressed her lips together, breathing through her nose.

"Lark is an issue, but not in the way you think. I love that kid. I would never want to do anything that would hurt her."

Cassie's shoulders rose toward her ears. "You can't build a relationship out of protecting a child."

"No. You're right about that. What I want to say is that I'm committed to her, to both of you. My feelings for you—just you as a woman, not a mother, or Shasta's niece, or the owner of the coffee shop, but the person you are at your core—those feelings are very strong. That's not to say you don't drive me completely crazy sometimes." He rubbed both hands over his head. "But I'd like to be with you, and I'm trying to tell you that I know Lark is part of the deal but not a burden. She's a bonus." He shook his head. "Man, that girl is a bonus with rhythm. Did you see those dance moves? We've got to get her into a class."

"We?" There had never been a *we* when it came to Lark. Even with all of Terri's help, it had come down to just Cassie in the end.

"I don't mean to overstep."

"That's not what I meant. It's just a new idea. I'm not sure I know how to be part of a *we*."

"And I'm not sure how to balance my role with Lark, but I'm hoping we can do the work to figure this all out together." He reached over, wrapping his hand around her ankle, then tugged her onto the sofa cushion. "Didn't your aunt teach you anything? You can't go sitting on the arm of the couch. It's not made for that." His grin was all she needed.

Cassie lunged into his arms, feeling them surround her. The attraction toward Marshall was full and real, but there was more. They were becoming part of a team that could conquer their challenges—his, hers, and theirs together. For the first time since Shasta had left, Cassie felt the warm sense of home.

# 43

Between customers, Cassie dug into the search for financing to combine all her student loans into one payment. She could use the shop as collateral, but the payments would still be like a very significant mortgage. She couldn't live off what the shop brought in. Not if she wished to feed both Lark and herself. And not if she wanted to pay the crazy bill for simple stitches just to have her head held together. If she could have done that over, she would have sewn her own scalp shut.

On top of that, each time she filed for a loan, a job, a mortgage, she had to use her Social Security number. Sure, it had worked all these years, but knowing it wasn't hers now equated to fraud. That was a line she couldn't cross.

Cassie listed her car on Craigslist. It wouldn't bring much, but walking was a healthy decision, as long as they didn't need to go more than five miles. But maybe she could borrow a car when things like that came up.

Nora strolled—or rather, trudged—into the shop. Her face was pale, but Cassie chose not to mention it. "What can I get for you?"

"I would kill for an iced tea." She ran her palms down her face, readjusted her posture, then slumped again. The baby in the front carrier started to cry.

Cassie led her to the couch. "Let me get you a cookie and a cold drink." Something about the humanness she'd displayed made Cassie want to care for her. This moment was temporary. Nora would be back to her superior self by the time she walked out of the shop, but it helped to know there was a real person buried under all that perfection.

Nora took the offers with a weak smile. "I've really missed sugar." She bit into the double chocolate chip treat. "This is amazing." She sighed. "I came here on school-board business. We have a position opening up at the high school. Mr. Selby is finally retiring. I guess his wife convinced him they needed to free up time for the grandkids before they left for college. I saw that you'd applied as a substitute. Would you be interested in something full-time?"

"Are you serious?" Cassie sat down next to her.

Nora removed the baby from the carrier, patting her on the back. "As serious as colic. We have to put out the job listing, but as a local, you'd be a top pick. Can you get your resumé in soon? We're pushing this forward quickly."

"Absolutely. I can have it ready today."

She shimmied to the edge of the couch. "Great. Check the district site. The job should be posted this afternoon." She looked Cassie over as if making a final judgment. "I've got to make a trip to the girls' room. Would you please watch Ava for a minute? I just want to be alone. You know what I mean?"

"Yes. Sure thing." She scooped the baby into her arms. It had been years since she'd held a child so small. The baby wound up to scream again, but Cassie walked her near the espresso machine. The hums calmed the little body, and soon she was back to sleep.

Cassie looked around for someone to share the amazing job news with and realized immediately that it was Shasta she was searching for. A full-time teaching position gave her the possibility of a loan deferral.

Nora returned, a skeptical look on her face. "How did you do that?"

"I think she was just tired."

The air cooled between the two of them, and Cassie wished the baby would howl again before she handed her back to her mother. "Thank you so much for the job opportunity."

Nora lifted Ava into the front carrier, gave a nod, and headed out of the shop, leaving her crumbled cookie for Cassie to clean up.

It would take more than Nora's mood swings to bring Cassie down. She went through the kitchen to get more cream for the front. It was oddly quiet back there, something missing that she couldn't put a name to. When she yanked the handle of the fridge, the door opened easily. Inside, the air was cool, but not cold, and water dripped from the shelves.

Panic drove her to the electric box. All circuits were in order. The bells jingled. More customers. Cassie jogged to the counter, took orders, checked the supply they had in the tiny under-counter refrigerator, and realized the truth: She was going to have to shut down the shop early. Shasta had taught her much about running the business, but not what to do when a very major piece of equipment went down.

She turned the *open* sign on the door to *closed* and switched off the neon image of a cup of steaming coffee that hung in the window. "I'm sorry, everyone. It looks like we're going to have to close for the day. Take your time finishing your drinks."

I pulled myself together and went back to the coffee shop one sunny day. I was surprised to see Ainsley, or Cassie, behind the counter. I'd planned to lay my story out for Shasta. I'd call the police in if she became a problem, but I thought we could be reasonable. Ainsley was my daughter, after all.

I ordered a latte and asked Ainsley about her day, expecting a complaint about having to work when the sun was up. Instead, she told me about how excited she was. A group from her school was going to Washington, D.C., for spring break, and her aunt had given her permission to go, as long as she earned half the money by helping out in the shop.

"That's too bad you have to spend all those hours serving coffee. I bet you'd rather be out with friends."

She grinned. "I love doing this. And my friends come in and visit. Shasta says we can serve them for free." She shrugged. "We're a team. This is our shop, and it makes me happy to be part of something so big."

My child had grown into the kind of young woman I'd wanted her to be. She was caring and responsible, and her devotion to Shasta was evident. I opened my mouth to ask her about where she'd come from, but no words came out. As a mother, I realized I wasn't able to do the thing I needed most, because claiming Ainsley meant destroying Cassie. There was nothing I could offer her that she didn't have here with Shasta.

I walked on the beach for hours that day, pleading with God to give me the answer, but He was silent. The roar of the waves only pushed me farther down the shore. I could call in investigators, make my claim, but Ainsley wasn't a thing to be owned. She was a person, a young woman becoming who God had designed her to be. I'd never be able to walk away from her again, but to grab hold of my role as her mother would be to extinguish who she was.

Before I could move forward, I had to figure out how we'd ended up here. Back in California, I read back through all my journals from the time we'd decided—or I'd decided—to have a baby, up until Topher's death. I compared the dates of Diane's child's birth to Topher's travels. Everything was connected. My husband, the man I had vowed to love, had created another family in another state. And he must have loved her, because somehow, he'd stolen my child, the baby who was still alive and who shared his DNA. And he'd given her to his mistress.

I don't know what would have happened if Topher and Diane hadn't been killed that day. Would he have eventually left me to be with Ainsley and the other woman? If he'd been alive, I would have made sure the full force of the legal system came down on him. How could I have been so wrong? I'd married a monster.

But Topher didn't have to answer for his sins here on earth. That punishment was in God's hands. It would take years for me to find a path toward forgiveness, and I still wonder if I would have been able to get there if Topher hadn't been dead already. But giving up my list of grievances against him freed me to explore what would become of the rest of my own life.

The house in California sold quickly, leaving me enough to restart my life in Oregon. Gull's Bay became my home, and Shasta and Cassie were part of my family. I'd been using my mother's maiden name along with my middle name since the first visit, leaving Amanda in California forever with Ainsley.

Cassie set the papers on the counter, grateful for Marshall and Lark's appearance at the shop's door. Knowing Amanda was here, somewhere, and that she'd been watching her gave Cassie an unnerved feeling she wasn't sure she could shake off.

Marshall rattled the door.

Cassie slipped over and unlocked it.

"What's going on?" The skin along his forehead folded in concern.

"Major refrigerator malfunction. I had to close up. The repairman will be here Friday morning. Until then, we're out of business." She'd be busy from now until then tossing food that had gone too long at temperatures above those set by the state of Oregon.

"Is this it?" Marshall pointed to the chapters.

Instinct told her to change the subject, but she wouldn't continue hiding from life and risk. They were a team. "The pages that changed everything." She nudged him with her elbow.

"How about we talk more while we look at that walk-in?"

Lark was fully invested in the picture she was coloring in the play area. "Lark, we're going into the kitchen to work on the fridge."

"No kissing." She grabbed her tummy as she laughed.

"I don't know where she gets these things." Cassie led the way. "Do you know anything about walk-ins?"

"Not a thing." He opened the door, roamed around inside, and came back out. Shaking his head, he used the flashlight app on his phone to look behind the giant appliance. "Interesting."

"Interesting good or interesting bad?"

There wasn't enough room for both of them back there, yet she craned her neck, trying to see what Marshall saw.

"Did anyone use the ladder recently?"

"I did. I was hanging one of Shasta's pictures."

The refrigerator gave a deep belch; then the room filled with the beautiful sound of the appliance's hum.

"What did you do?"

He came out, turned off the light, and stuck his phone back in his pocket. "Thank the mad skills I've developed at the hardware store."

Cassie shrugged. "Seriously. What did you do?"

He pulled her to him, looking in her eyes. "I plugged it back in."

"What?" She swatted his chest.

"When you put the ladder away, it knocked the plug out of the outlet." His chuckle rumbled in his chest.

"I feel like such an idiot."

His finger lightly swiped beneath her chin, lifting her face toward his intense stare. They stood there for a moment, breathing each other's air. She licked her lips, letting them part slightly, feeling the rush of blood tingling her face. The touch of his mouth to hers was warm, gentle, and fully enveloping. She lost herself for a moment.

"Gross."

They jumped back from each other.

Lark's face was wrinkled. "Grown-ups are so sick." She stuck her tongue out and mimed a shiver.

Marshall tipped his head back and laughed. He scooped Lark up with one arm and brought Cassie close with the other. "How about I try to only kiss your mom on days that end in *y*?"

She grinned. "That sounds like a trick."

"There's no way to get anything by you, is there?"

She put her arms around their necks and pulled them close, then kissed each of them on the cheek. "It's okay. I love you both anyway."

# 44

I kept up my work as a mentor to youth up and down the coast, establishing nonprofits and working within the foster-care system to promote change, but that part of my life I kept separate from Gull's Bay. They were like two worlds, both of which I was a part of, although the two could not survive if they overlapped.

Until the day they did.

I'd traveled two hours up the coast to meet with a woman hiding from her husband. She was the mother of three children. The teen-aged boy was struggling, having been arrested for a theft. These issues were calling attention to the family, which had forced them to make this move to Oregon. I knew there was a group somewhere around here that helped women go into hiding when necessary, but I didn't know a thing about them.

We met at a McDonald's. No one takes notice of the people in a McDonald's. And that is where my mission slammed full force into my private life. The woman I'd been set to meet with wasn't alone. Shasta sat by her side.

The two of us stared at each other, gaping, until the woman's expression turned to alarm. She was jumpy, scared of every little move, and I knew she'd struggle to help her son when she required so much for herself.

Shasta and I went through the meeting, laying out plans to get this family safe and on a good path, never mentioning that we knew each other.

That evening, I came by the closed coffee shop. She seemed to have been waiting for me. We sipped coffee as we sat by the gas fireplace, and I spilled every drop of my story. To say we shed tears together that night would be like comparing the ocean to a gentle stream, but our love for Cassie was always at the center.

Shasta wanted to tell her, but I was the one who held back. We were at a point in our child's life where she was already in the midst of big changes. Cassie was only a couple years from graduating and leaving for college. I couldn't bear the thought of her going into the world with this burden on her shoulders. Her life was in front of her. It just didn't feel like the right time.

God had given me the gift of my daughter, not once, but twice. He had been close to me when my heart was broken and my spirit crushed. Knowing that, I would sacrifice whatever I needed to just to see her happy.

The time was never right.

Not long after Lark's birth, Shasta got her diagnosis. We decided at that point that life was not to be taken for granted. It was Shasta who insisted I write it all down. Shasta wanted to be sure that if something happened to us, Cassie would know the entire truth.

So, here it is. Cassie, you have always been loved. You are a light in this world that has touched many lives. Shasta and I were blessed to watch you grow into the fine woman you are today.

I hope you can forgive us for keeping this secret. Just know, I will always be here.

Cassie flipped over the last page, expecting a name, an address, something, but there was no indication of the sender anywhere, only a Bible reference. The sun was just beginning to color the sky, not yet day but no longer nighttime. Just the lightening of the black to gray, the stars no longer visible.

This lack of information could have left her angry, but she

didn't feel the slightest bit of rage. Cassie waited for the hurt to arrive and unravel her world, but it did not. Now that the story had been laid out, all she saw was a deep love and tremendous sacrifice. She tried to put herself in the position of the writer. Would she have been strong enough to stand back and let her daughter grow up outside her arms? She doubted it. But her mother had given it all up so Cassie could live without the painful knowledge of the trauma she had endured.

Cassie's pacing grew faster as thoughts swirled in her mind, moments becoming clear with the missing pieces now slipping into place.

She went to Lark's room and scooped her still-sleeping body into her arms. Lark moaned but snuggled her face into Cassie's neck. "We have to go somewhere, but you can stay asleep."

Slipping on flip-flops near the door, Cassie opened it and started down. Light clatters came from the kitchen, where Aubrey was preparing for the day.

She walked around the corner and their eyes met, Cassie's going damp. It felt like years passed as they stared at each other, trying to communicate without words.

Aubrey spoke first. "You know?"

Cassie lifted her chin.

She closed her eyes and carefully lifted Lark from Cassie's arms, then kissed Cassie's cheek.

The chill in the early morning air poured over Cassie. She wasn't sure she could do this. Crossing her arms over her chest, she curled forward. There were times when life could be too much, too heavy, too complicated.

Aubrey nodded toward the door. "You can do this. You were made for this."

Cassie blinked away tears. There was a time for weakness and giving in, but now was not a time like that. This moment was about restoration, about reaching out, and about saying thank you.

# 45

~

Gull's Bay was the home of early risers. From fishermen to local businesses, it was a kind of tradition in these parts to get up and see the sun rise over the coastal range to their east. Cassie folded Aubrey's sweater tighter around her as she watched the first rays of light shoot out over the mountains.

In the distance, gulls cried, probably begging at the docks while bait was set out for the day's fishing excursions. The call of the sea lions echoed up from the bay. A garbage truck rumbled down the road, a guy she'd graduated high school with behind the wheel, giving her the morning salute as he passed.

She embraced this moment before her world took another huge turn and watched the waves from their little hill perched above the shore. A flock of seagulls dotted the beach, and just beyond them, light glimmered off the water, giving testimony to the sun rising again.

With her lungs filled with sea air, Cassie stepped into the bakery. Mrs. Collins came out from the kitchen and set a hot pan of croissants on the counter.

"I don't know how to call you mom." Cassie's words hung in the air, supported by the rich scents of freshly baked goods.

The woman's shoulders slumped, and she pulled the mitts

off her hands. "It's enough to know that you know me: who I was and who I am, and especially that you are loved."

"'The Lord is close to the brokenhearted and saves those who are crushed in spirit.' When I read the reference, Psalm 34:18, I knew it was you."

She touched Cassie's arm, and the warmth of her skin brought life.

"I want you to know that I can give you my deepest gratitude. You've always been part of my family. I'm not sure how this changes anything, or what you need from me."

She handed Cassie a warm pastry. "I thought you were dead. When I saw you in the coffee shop, it was like God had brought you back from the grave. I believe He guided me to you and allowed me to be part of your life. I always thought I'd know when the time was right, and it is now . . . but I sure thought Shasta would be here too." She pulled out a seat near the window, and Cassie sat across from her. "I didn't want to tell you about your dad and what he did. Maybe I was wrong, maybe you would have been better off knowing you had a father who had you kidnapped in another country than no father at all. It was easier to put off the decision than to tell you and be wrong."

Cassie reached across the table and held Mrs. Collins's hand. "We'll figure this out as we go along."

"What are you going to tell Lark?"

"Just what I already have. Grammies come in many different forms. It just so happens that one of her grammies is actually her mother's mother." She shrugged. "How terribly traditional of us."

Beverly—Cassie could manage that for now—laughed, her face beaming in the morning light.

They sat there for an hour talking, until customers started coming in to be served breakfast treats. Then Cassie returned to Lark. Oh, the stories they would share in the coming years. She held no hard feelings about not being told the true story, but she wouldn't lie to Lark. Her daughter was a different child than Cassie had been, and they were all here, surrounding her with so much love, that she would thrive in the transparency.

~

They sat at the picnic tables overlooking the bay following church. Their first family meal, and hopefully the first of many more to come. It was potluck style, with a range of options that included a dish not traditional for the end of summer, but still the first thing Cassie planned to scoop onto her plate. Mr. Watkins had come with this sweet potato casserole so clearly Shasta's that it seemed obvious he or Marianne had figured out a way to coax the recipe from her.

Lark and Gwendolyn chased each other through the grass, Nora being glad to let Cassie take Gwendolyn with them, as she was obviously exhausted with a colicky baby. They were waiting for Marshall, who was lining up a meeting with some boys in the youth group.

From the other direction, Marshall came hiking up the hill, a bag of fun-sized Kit Kats in his hand.

Mrs. Collins stood and began uncovering dishes.

Marshall looped one leg under the table and straddled the bench beside Cassie. "My offering to the potluck." He dropped the candy in front of her.

Mrs. Collins mussed his hair. "Kid, I know I taught you better than that."

"Yes, ma'am." He winked at Cassie, sending shivers down her arms. "I'll do better next time."

Cassie called Lark and Gwendolyn to the table, where they all prayed together. At the amen, she opened her eyes and caught Lark staring at the candy. "Food first."

Lark licked her lips. She had a sweet tooth that rivaled her Grammy Collins's.

"Beverly, tell us all about how you met Marshall here." Cassie leaned into his chest.

"Well now, it was quite a few years ago. I was helping a group in Portland get established with mentoring programs and things like that. And this young man came up to me. He said, 'Ma'am, I'm graduating soon. I've made some mistakes, but I'm working hard to fix what's broken.' I took to him right away. I mean, look at that face."

Marshall shook his head, but his eyes were all smiles.

"I knew this kid was going to be something special. I asked if I could write to him while he was in college. And he allowed it. Soon the boy was coming home for holidays and helping me in the bakery and staying with this lonely old man I know. I couldn't be prouder of the man he's become. And to think you two would wind up together." She patted her heart and looked up into the sky. "It blesses me."

Mr. Watkins wiped sweet potato from his chin. "He's okay."

Aubrey shook her head. "Old man, you couldn't get through a day without that boy. What are you going to do when he finishes school?"

"Hire Lark, of course." He tipped his head toward Cassie's daughter.

Lark's eyes went as round as saucers. "Two jobs!" She rolled her eyes. "You all need a lot from a little girl."

Cassie laughed so hard, she nearly lost her bite of casserole.

Sneaking out of the nursery, Nora stepped into the bathroom and doused her red and puffy eyes with cold water. Ava had finally fallen asleep after two hours of wailing.

"Hey, are you okay?" Ferris rubbed circles in her tense shoulders.

"Yes . . . well, no." She shook her head. "I didn't hear you come in."

"I didn't want to step in and start the whole process over again. I know getting that kiddo to sleep is harder than anything I've done so far in my life."

"I miss being part of a family." She leaned her head back onto his chest. "I've been thinking about Becca lately. Apparently, she was colicky like Ava. It's hard to believe with as bubbly as that woman is now."

"We should have her out for a visit."

She turned in his arms. "Are you sure? I mean, we don't really know her."

Ferris looked away.

"You didn't."

No response.

"Wow. You ran a check on her." The feeling this gave her wasn't offense, but comfort and warmth—her husband had taken steps to keep them safe, not that there were any signs of danger from Becca.

He kissed her forehead, answering her without words.

"Thank you. I really think I'd like to meet her."

"So would I." He stepped back. "What do you say to a movie in bed after I get a shower?"

"Sounds great. That will give me time to message Becca."

Nora stepped into the bedroom, easing down onto the mattress, the weight of her fatigue making it clear she'd barely see the opening scene.

She opened Instagram.

Nora's photo of the screaming Ava had launched her into Instagram fame. Apparently, what people wanted more than anything was truth. Next to Ava, this was Nora's biggest challenge yet.

With Becca's permission, over time, she planned to open up to her followers about growing up with her dad and never knowing her mom. She could talk about how that had changed her perspective on so many things, and how learning she had three sisters was stretching her even further.

Message from @nora.milford to @beccaboundforglory

I've given it a lot of thought and prayer, and after a discussion with Ferris, we think you should come out to visit. I'm excited to see the photographs you take here on our coast.

Message from @beccaboundforglory to @nora.milford

I'll be there as soon as I get Maddie to take care of my cat! Can't wait to see you all and love on my nieces.

Nora might regret this invitation, but she left the door open to loving it too.

With the end of summer came Terri and Jack's wedding on the beach, an occasion Cassie had been both dreading and looking forward to. It was hard to step into a full celebration when the cloak of death was still covering one's life. Shasta had left a hole that couldn't be filled by anyone or anything else. Cassie thought about how much her aunt had loved weddings, the celebration and significance of the ceremony and reception, not to mention the cake.

Terri stayed with her the week before the ceremony, Cassie doing all she could to keep the conversation on light topics—Terri's honeymoon and Jack's and her happy future—but she was caught more than once staring out the window, remembering.

"Was this something Shasta was painting?" Terri touched the edge of the last canvas, still on the easel.

Cassie nodded. "She and Lark would paint here together. I haven't been able to move it yet."

"I assume you haven't been able to go through her room either, since I'm sleeping in your bed and you're on the couch again." Her words were free of condemnation, but Cassie assigned it to herself anyway.

"I've been meaning to get in there, but it's so lonely without her. And I feel like I'm invading her privacy when I go through her things." She turned to Terri. "I know that's crazy, but I can't do it."

"There's no rush. If you want, I could help."

Cassie forced her lips into a smile, though it had to be obvious that little joy came with it. "It means a lot to me that you offered. But this is your wedding week, and we will not be sidetracked by grief." The words sounded more convincing when she spoke them aloud than they did in the mantra Cassie repeated in her mind.

Lark burst through the door, banging the knob farther into the wall. "Sorry." She twirled and bowed.

Aubrey came in behind her. "We found it." She pulled a tiara from a sack. "Is this what you had in mind?"

Terri clapped. "It's the perfect topper, but what do you think, Larkie-bird?"

"It's perfect for a flower girl." She stood in front of Aubrey, stretching her neck.

Aubrey positioned it on Lark's head, and Lark's movement slowed. She walked around the living room, all grace and poise. Cassie would need to remember this trick.

A storm came through the day of the wedding, blowing hard against the windows as they prepared for the ceremony. Jack was at the lodge with his parents. He must have texted Cassie twenty times asking if this was okay, did he need to arrange another place for the wedding, but Terri remained calm. She'd always been the voice of reason, but Cassie had assumed this would be her turn to take the wheel and keep them away from the edge.

Mr. Watkins and Marshall, along with Jack's family, had given the trail a good trim, leaving plenty of room to make the walk down to the beach without snagging Terri's dress on salal.

As they reached the last curve, music began, guitars played by two of Jack's brothers. A wooden bridge had been laid over the outcropping of stones, creating a smooth path.

While the wind picked up power, the rain held back, and they were sheltered sufficiently in the shadow of the cliff to be able to hear Terri's childhood pastor as he spoke about the meaning of love, commitment, and the vow they were making to God.

Maybe Cassie was still weakened by grief, because as the pastor pronounced them man and wife, she had to dab away tears.

Marshall's hand held hers as they climbed the path to the reception, Lark in front of them, wider than she was tall with all the layers of tulle that made up her flower-girl dress.

At the top of the hill where the trail opened up, he pulled Cassie to the side and kissed the top of her hand. "I was thinking about something down there."

"What?"

"So, I've been meaning to tell you this. It's not an easy thing to say."

Her heart braced for pain.

"I mean, it should be, but the first time . . . I mean, you may not feel the same way. I love you."

She'd known for weeks that she loved him but hadn't wanted to be the first to say the words. "I love you too."

He let out a long breath.

The wind whipped Cassie's hair around her face. She held it back with one hand. "Did you think I didn't?"

"Well, you never said anything."

"Neither did you."

Taking both of her hands, he brought Cassie in and kissed her gently.

They didn't take too much time, but it was theirs—those little moments with the ocean at their sides, the feelings they had for each other out in the open and known. These were the times Cassie would want to remember her entire life.

Catching up to the group, Marshall swung Lark in the air, landing her on his shoulders, where she waved at everyone they passed as if this were her very own princess procession.

In the shop, Cassie hugged Terri again. "Congratulations."

"I couldn't have done it without you." They posed for the photographer. "Did you know that even with all the pins I had on Pinterest, this was exactly the wedding I wanted in my heart? It couldn't have been more perfect. If you hadn't come back to Oregon, I might have missed this."

Terri and Jack could have gotten married at a sewer-treatment facility and Terri would have been glowing just as she did now, but the way it had worked out did feel meant to be. "Gull's Bay is a special place."

"I can't believe I'm married." She held out her ringed finger. "I graduate at the end of fall term. I have big news, but I was waiting to tell you until it was a real thing. Jack and I both have been talking to places in Oregon. Jack has an offer in McMinnville. If I can get something too, we'll be just a two-hour drive away from here and about that far from my parents."

Cassie clapped her hands together. "That's amazing. I admit I've been sad thinking about you two starting a family so far away. I owe you some serious baby-sitting hours."

"I couldn't do that. Children need aunts, and you will be one of the best aunties ever."

Cassie hugged her again. Yes, children did need aunts. Cassie had needed Shasta, and she'd been there for her, protecting, loving, and encouraging her to grow.

"Mom." Lark tugged on her leg.

Cassie bent down. "What is it?"

"Do you know what we need?"

"What?"

"A dog."

Cassie kissed her forehead. "Let's put that on the list of maybes. How about we settle for cake today?"

"Okay, but I want you to know that I'm not forgetting. I've talked to Marshall, and not about the being-my-dad thing. He says he loves dogs. Like"—she held out her arms—"really, really loves them." She ran off to share the maybe status of their possible pet with anyone who would listen.

A feeling of deep contentment filled Cassie. Shasta would have loved that little conversation. She would have taken Lark's side, rallying for a puppy. Somehow, saying no seemed harder with the image of Shasta and Lark in Cassie's head.

It took a team of lawyers to straighten out the logistics of coming back to life after having been dead for well over twenty years.

Cassie was surprised that the biggest challenge was keeping her identity secret from the world. As it turned out, children who showed up alive after that many years presumed dead were the kinds of stories that made for great television. Her attorney brought her a very generous offer to have the story made into a movie, but Cassie turned it down. They had a beautiful thing going here. Only a handful of neighbors knew she'd ever been Ainsley Reynolds.

She would continue to borrow Cassie's last name until she got married herself. At that point, she'd gladly change both hers and Lark's over to her husband's name. She had a pretty good feeling they would all be Baylors, but they weren't rushing.

In the fall, Cassie started teaching at the high school with her temporary license. She taught three classes of biology and two of history. To her surprise, she loved both subjects equally.

She revealed the story to Lark, little pieces at a time, and to her surprise, her daughter never did seem confused, or question how any of it could have happened. The one detail Cassie held back was about Topher. He had given Cassie half of her DNA, but he would never hold the title of father or grandfather. Marshall was showing them each day what a dad was supposed to be like. It wasn't a biological function; it was love, sacrifice, and loyalty. Topher hadn't possessed any of those traits.

Cassie had left Gull's Bay as a young woman, certain there was a life out there, something bigger than what she'd seen growing up in such a small town. Yet she'd been shaped by the waves, honed by their power, until she understood there was life anywhere there was love, and love makes family.

# Author's Note and Acknowledgments

Thank you, reader, for choosing this book. It is such an honor to have you read one of my stories. I hope you are left refreshed and inspired.

Community is such an important piece of life. I believe God designed us to thrive when we surround ourselves with people who encourage, challenge, and inspire us. My hope is that even if you haven't found your people yet, you will soon.

Bethany House, thank you for letting me write this novel. I'm not sure how one company can have so many wonderful people, but it's happened here. From acquisition to editing, marketing, and design, you've created a place where I always feel welcome and heard.

This novel was written during the COVID shutdown, with my house full of a husband and kids all back from closed workplaces and schools. Though life was often chaotic, I'm so grateful for a family who valued my time to work, even when that meant taking up extra tasks around the house. Thank you to my husband, Jason, who even ventured from his only-cooking-breakfast philosophy and learned how to prepare a few other items . . . even if he often tried to serve meat-only meals.

Thank you to Jodie Bailey for continuing to keep me going;

you are a dear sister. Thank you to my critique partners and friends Marilyn Rhoads, Heidi Gaul, and Karen Barnett. You three are a great source of support and encouragement. Thank you to my sister, Kaity, for reading advance copies and still liking me.

My agent, Cynthia Ruchti, made it possible for me to write books for a growing audience. It's a humbling honor to be her client and, I hope, her friend.

But the biggest thank-you goes to my Lord and Savior. There are no words to express the depth of my gratitude.

# About the Author

**Christina Suzann Nelson** is an inspirational speaker and the award-winning author of *If We Make It Home*, *Swimming in the Deep End*, *More Than We Remember*, and *The Way It Should Be*. She writes and speaks about hope after dysfunction. Christina is over-the-top about her passions, including the stories created somewhere in the twists and turns of her less-than-focused brain. When she's not writing, she's working with the Every Child Initiative, chasing escaped steers, reading, breathing in the sweet smell of her horse, hiking with her dog, or enjoying her just-as-crazy family. Visit her website at www .christinasuzannnelson.com for more information.

# Sign Up for Christina's Newsletter

Keep up to date with Christina's news on book releases and events by signing up for her email list at christinasuzannnelson.com.

# More from Christina Suzann Nelson

Zara Mahoney was enjoying newlywed bliss until her estranged sister, Eve, upends her plans, moving Zara to take custody of her children. Eve's struggles lead her to Tiff Bradley, who's determined to help despite the past hurts the relationship triggers. Can these women find the hope they—and those they love—desperately need?

*The Way It Should Be*

# You May Also Like . . .

A life-altering car accident changes everything for three women. As their lives intersect, they can no longer dwell in the memory of who they've been. Can they rise from the wreck of the worst moments of their lives to become who they were meant to be?

*More Than We Remember* by Christina Suzann Nelson
christinasuzannnelson.com

After moving cross-country with her son and accepting a filmmaker's mentorship, Val Locklier is caught between her insecurities and new possibilities. Miles McKenzie returns home to find a new tenant is living upstairs and he's been banished to a ministry on life support. As sparks fly, they discover that authentic love and sacrifice must go hand in hand.

*All That It Takes* by Nicole Deese
nicoledeese.com

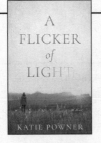

Widower Mitch Jensen is at a loss with how to handle his mother's odd, forgetful behaviors, as well as his daughter's sudden return home and unexpected life choices. Little does he know Grandma June has long been keeping a secret about her past—but if she doesn't tell the truth about it, someone she loves will suffer, and the lives of three generations will never be the same.

*A Flicker of Light* by Katie Powner
katiepowner.com

⬥BETHANYHOUSE

# More from Bethany House

More than a century apart, two women search for the lost. Despite her family's Confederate leanings, Clara is determined to help an enslaved woman reunite with her daughter; Alice can't stop wondering what happened to her mother in the aftermath of Hurricane Katrina. Faced with the unknown, both women will have to dig deep to let their courage bloom.

*Where the Last Rose Blooms* by Ashley Clark
HEIRLOOM SECRETS
ashleyclarkbooks.com

Wren Blythe enjoys life in the Northwoods, but when a girl goes missing, her search leads to a shocking discovery shrouded in the lore of the murderess Eva Coons. Decades earlier, the real Eva struggles with the mystery of her past—all clues point to murder. Both will find that, to save the innocent, they must face an insidious evil.

*The Souls of Lost Lake* by Jaime Jo Wright
jaimewrightbooks.com

Desperate to mend her marriage and herself, Abbie Jowett joins her son in walking the famed Camino pilgrimage. During their journey, they encounter an Iranian working in secret to help refugees and a journalist searching for answers from her broken past—and everyone is called into a deep soul-searching that threatens all their best laid plans.

*The Promised Land* by Elizabeth Musser
elizabethmusser.com

◆ BETHANY HOUSE